Reader's Acclaim for

RJ Blizzard's Incarnate

"A Wild Ride"

RJ Blizzard has crafted an exceptional story that contemplates the best mysteries of the universe, where faith and truth find their way into the human heart. It's a wild ride with engaging characters through conflict, discovery and unforeseen twists that will have you scratching your head until the end. If you're looking for a compelling read of human transformation where religion is not always the best friend of faith, you'll find it here.

Wayne Jacobsen - Author of He Loves Me, Finding Church, and co-author of **The Shack**

All Aboard...

It's not often that we open a book and find something of ourselves in nearly every character. RJ Blizzard reaches in and grabs us by our souls from the very first page. Pack your bags for this journey; you'll love the ride.

Angie Cramer - Oncology Department Johns Hopkins

5 Stars!

It grabs you from the get-go and holds your attention in such a rich and intriguing way. It is this reader's belief your book will takes its place of honor on the bestseller list along with such other noble writing as The Shack, and The Alchemist. Truly an inspiration. Incarnate is a life changing read for some to move past religion to the heart of God.

Deborah Mikell - Artist, New Jersey

INCARNATE
The Incredible Journey of Edward Mayus

RJ Blizzard

Copyright © 2017 by RJB Media

All rights reserved. This book or any portion thereof may not be reproduced or used in any manner whatsoever without the express written permission of the publisher except for the use of brief quotations in a book review.

Printed in the United States of America

First Printing, 2017

ISBN 978-0-9991253-0-4

To Rennay
my wife, best friend,
and first touch,
of Incarnation

STEPHEN

I do believe that everything we see,

everything that is in front of us

is just the visible part of reality.

We have the invisible part of reality,

like emotions for example, like feelings.

This is our perception of the world,

but God is in a grain of sand and in a flower.

-Paul Coelho

Night had darkened Rome. An opened but unpacked suitcase lies at the foot of my bed at the Columbus Hotel, a quick walk from the Vatican. The dogs in the alley were losing their bark, as the musical aroma of Miles Davis' Generique drifts from the Jazz cafe behind the old dark cobblestone path. An open bottle of wine rest on the night table breathing in the damp, dark air that will mature the nuanced flavor for the cup my dear brother Edward and I will share at the other end of my journey. The flesh-colored crimson stained cork rolls off the nightstand.

Sitting on the side of the bed, I reach down to retrieve the fallen cork, while the other hand grips tightly onto a gold-leafed frame holding a photo that marks the shortened sands of time that were my life's gift. I could not taste life's cup that gave to me what has become my agony. I place the sacred photo-image of a love reluctantly released, on the scarred wooden nightstand. My eyes penetrated her portrait; my mind recalled the memory of my beautiful Caterina.

Thoughts drift toward her, not enough cups of coffee shared, but a lifetime of love. My clenched fist press against my nose and mouth yearning to stop this corkscrew to my heart. I recline backward on the bed looking upward. So many sojourners like me have laid in this bed staring up at the stained brown stuccoed-cracked ceiling hoping the next day to touch transcendence as they take their prayers into Michelangelo's Sistine Chapel. Tonight, my plastered dome is empty. God's hand is not reaching down to me; I can hear Caterina's memory gently whispering to me, "God is not there."

I need Him to be. Why has he forsaken me?

Arising, I stand up from my agony. I pull out of the suitcase the small glass tube container with the lavender top, cradling it gently with both hands. This vial holds the source code of life, the code of my spiritual life. Marked with an X Lanciano. I am looking out the window at the night illuminated Basilica that beacons God is here. I hold the small glass vessel tightly in my hand putting it to my mouth with a gentle kiss hoping that maybe God is here. This is my "Great Wanting." The yearning to ease the pain of my lack of faith because I could not bear to taste the cup before me.

Moving toward the nightstand, I set back down on the bed and slid the opened bottle of wine closer to me. Taking my last look at the lavender capped tube, I held it in my fingers above the neck of the bottle. I said a prayer that Edward would take this journey so that my spirit could be redeemed from this cloud of regret and shame. I released the long thin capsule to gently plunge into the bottle. The wine in the bottle overflowed as Edward's gift gently sank to the bottom with the sound of a light clink. The wine was dripping down the label and seeped onto the floor like tears of blood. Taking the cork, I gently forced the bottle closed again. Not to be enjoyed until Edward and I commune together. Wine sprayed into my hands dripping between my fingers. The re-corking of the bottle sprayed droplets of displaced wine onto the nightstand. My head fell to rest on the pillow, praying, hoping to ease the pain into the deep darkness of my new friend, sleep. I glanced over at the picture of Caterina. Droplets of wine were dripping down over her face like tears. Grabbing the framed icon of my love, I tenderly kissed her image and tasted the wine as if I had just kissed her during a quiet dinner. For a brief time, I could feel and smell her presence. The sweet remembrance of her brought momentary peace until the wine dried bringing me back to the reality that my weakness caused me to lose so many grains of sand through my life's hour glass. Anxiety and anticipation of Edward's future journey rescued me temporarily as night overtook me. My journey home would be my redemption: Edward would be my redeemer.

***

The dogs started barking before the first rays warmed the stained glass of St Peters. I knew I had to get an early start so that I could see my dear trusted friend, Father Francesco Paulo Martelli, before catching my flight home. We had made plans to meet, at Anticco Cafe San Pietro, for an espresso and drop my package off at the Vatican Post Office. I learned a day earlier that I could not take the precious tube on the plane and needed a particular license to ship human biological material. I could not risk U.S. Customs discovering and confiscating my secret redemption. Paulo was the only one I could turn to; he agreed to ship my secret vial in a wine bottle from the Vatican.

Seated at an outside table at the cafe, Paulo and I would meet after the first Mass. Paulo was running late, and I was getting antsy about missing my flight. Instantly these massive hands grabbed my shoulder with a loud shout, "Buon giorno mio foretello." I nearly spilled the last of my espresso all over myself. After some conversation, he asked me about Caterina. My look away told him that my emotions were still raw. Before leaving, he asked, "Are you sure Edward will continue this journey for you?"

"Paulo, Edward is the most honest, and wisest man I know. He will do it not only for my redemption but his own seeking as well. He has been searching for the God that we know his whole life."

"Then how come he has not found God?" Paulo in a soft, slow cadence direct voice inquired.

After a quick pondering, I shot back, "I don't know," Grabbing my suitcase and bag containing the bottle and handed it to my friend.

"Asino muto," he laughed out loud with his hand lifting over his head, indicating how was he going to get a bottle of wine in a bag shipped from the Post Office of the Vatican. He informed me that we would stop at a shop and get a wooden box to send the bottle.

Several people with concerns stopped by to talk with my friend. Paulo could tell I was getting aggravated. Finally leaving, he asked, "What are you anxious about Stephen? This is how life happens. You want the universe to bow down to you?" Paulo challenged me. "Things happen, they always happen, casualità creativo in scatola della libertà di Dio." Paulo taught me this long ago. It means creative randomness in God's box of freedom. Paulo always thought that anxiousness and impatience were a sign that one was not living his life.

We walked two blocks toward a small gift store outside the Vatican walls where Paulo knew the shop owner. I grew increasingly agitated that the shop owner could not find a box to transport the gift of all gifts for Edward and myself. She is causing me to lose minutes and interfering with what needs to be accomplished. Then slowly she brought from the back a wooden box with an artisan carved wooden top that had Latin words elaborately etched. Paulo quickly indicated it was okay. Placing the bottle into the box surrounded by shredded paper for protection; it became apparent that we needed more things to prevent the bottle from moving around. I reluctantly unzipped my luggage and pulled out my journals and papers and used them as buffers. Time was ticking. Nothing was more valuable than the safeguarding of my redemption. We sealed the box and placed it in a cardboard box for shipping and went straight to the Post Office of the Vatican. The clerk asked what the box contained.

"My whole life," I replied.

"A gift of a bottle of wine from me, and some papers," Paulo interjected. The clerk smiled at my dear trusted friend and automatically stamped the approval on the paperwork.

Leaving the Vatican gate, we walked out onto the cobblestone sidewalk toward the Largo deli Alicorni where a car was waiting to drive me to the airport, compliments of my friend Paulo.

"Are you sure that package will make it to Edward, my whole life is in that box?"

"God finest creation is on this small blue planet with all its random dangers, why you worry?" he shouted at me as we embraced one last time.

"Arrivederci il mio Broter il mio amico," Paulo said to me as he kissed me goodbye.

Turning and walking briskly toward the car parked at the crossing where the digital sign overhead warned walkers; only forty-four seconds were safe to travel. I nearly bumped into an old black man who was feeding the birds casting his seeds in a spray-like pixie dust that caused the flock to flutter in unison up and down as they caught their morning brunch. His deep dark eyes, shaded under a blue pin-striped tattered bill of a railroad hat, met mine as if he knew me. He smiled holding a cigarette loosely on the side of his mouth. He was like a symphony conductor orchestrating the birds to move at will in any direction he desired. He reached deep into his bag and slung a spray of seeds high into the air causing me to look up, spotting a white dove-like bird hovering in front of me, hypnotizing me for a brief interval of time. Then it flew straight over my head disappearing as I turned to see it vanish above the Vatican gate; a flash of metal reflected off the high morning sun caught my eye as a bearded man ran toward my friend Paulo shouting "Allahu Akbar!"

I screamed, "No Pauuu........!"

Before I could finish my warning, I had dashed the few yards, leaping between my unsuspecting friend and the blade of death approaching his unsuspecting soul. Thrusting forward, through the screams of horrified witnesses to man's evil, I propelled by brother Paulo forward as the blade severed my hand below the knuckles, but missing my comrade. I stumbled face forward to the ground.

Stunned. My cheek lying on cold cobblestones, while my eyes saw people running away in a slow motion hearing their muffled screams to God. The sign warned thirty-eight blinking seconds. Lifting my head, I gaze into the eyes of my friend Paulo now running toward me reaching with horror filled eyes. Raising myself to my knees, I feel the first electric shock of pain race through my arm to my feet; as my severed appendage pushes me into a crawling position. Where is he? Did he run away? Then I hear the scream again of approaching death, "Allahu Akbar!"

I can hear the swooshing sound as the blade cuts through the air, piercing the muted screams. Then instantly I am falling and tumbling through the air in slow motion. I can see the revolving blue sky of an upside-down world, as I'm descending through the air; then mentally bracing myself as I see the hard-cobblestoned ground approaching fast expecting great pain upon impact. Squinting my eyes tightly; only to feel a small thud as my head hits the stone paver. Suddenly deadened sounds of scuffling and wrestling washes over me and I see my attacker pushed to the ground by the Vatican guards. They are driving his neck into the stones as his face looks with grimace upon me. He is obviously in deep anguishing pain. My thoughts are with him. I want to tell him I forgive him, but I feel paralyzed. I move my lips, but I cannot hear. Glancing above at the entangled men the sign ticks off to twenty-nine seconds.

Paulo, bloodied face, hands raised to the heavens, is standing over me crying out to God. He drops to his knees. I want so much for him to embrace me; tell me everything will be alright; that they will be able to repair my hand. He is caressing someone on the ground rocking back and forth crying to God, "Why . . . Why!"

Then the arm of the victim flops to the ground with its hand tightly fisted. I can see the ring briefly. My mind screams in silence! It is the ring Caterina had given me. Then in terror, I realized; he is holding me. The sign read twenty-one seconds. Just then a piece of plastic is thrown over me casting darkness on my last seconds on this earth. I am shocked that I have little pain except for the end of the many dreams I still desired. The smell of blood surrounds me like when you get a bloody nose. I can feel the senses draining from my mind replaced by a sense of calm and anxious anticipation. I cannot make out any noise now, but I can still feel the vibrations of chaos from the ground. Everything is becoming silently slow, but memories are pouring forth over my soul. They are coming to me as if welcoming me. I don't feel that life is draining out. I feel like life is pouring into me. Some memories are from loved ones who have died; others are greeting me from those I am leaving behind. These memories of the past are present this moment; as if there is no time. The last sound I hear is the rapid staccato beeps from the warning sign signaling that the time has passed. It is now darker than darkness. It is quieter than silence.

I am waiting.

I'm still waiting.

I'm afraid to think a thought, because if I can't, maybe this is the end.

I am still conscious.

I still am.

I am here . . . somewhere.

Waiting until it comes to me. Finally, my first thought is to Edward. Take the journey, my beloved brother. Lightness enters my being in consciousness. I am seeing. For the first time, I'm seeing.

Oh, wow! I'm still….

I'm laughing inside for joy.

EDWARD

There are two great days in a person's life,
the day we are born,
and the day we discover why.
-William Barclay

It's night time in Upper-Manhattan. From my room at the Sherry Netherlands Hotel overlooking Central Park, I take in the city that I love. The sights and sounds of life, the stories of the masses marching in unison to the light signals below. Is this what God sees as He looks down on us? Colonies of ants marching in lines of streaming red and white lights all going in different directions. Everyone is heading somewhere, yet nowhere, only to do it all again tomorrow. The last of the autumn leaves from the trees below are falling; signaling the page is turning to the oncoming winter. I'm tired. Where is the bellman with my dinner?

Finally, a knock on the door as the bellman delivers room service. After arriving, I ordered a light meal consisting of a glass of wine and bread. I wanted to get to bed early for a busy day tomorrow. As he set the table in front of the window, he asked, "Looks like the weather is changing. You know what they say, the only constant in life is change."

Looking at his name tag, I replied, "Thanks, Gabriel," thinking about his name. You don't meet many Gabriel's in life.

"You're welcome Mr. Mayus," he replied as I signed the receipt.

"You can call me Edward. Have a nice day."

"Safety and blessings along your journeys Sir," he said leaving.

After a long day's journey, fighting through several train delays, I savored the wine and bread dipped in seasoned virgin olive oil. The warm bread and the quietness of the room settled me down as I unwound mentally preparing for tomorrow.

"The only constant in life is change," I murmured under my breath recalling what Gabriel spoke while leaving the room. I hate that cliché. Not much in my life of fifty-five years has changed. I want to change. I need something to change. Sometimes the changes can be subtle. Other times, it comes as a landslide.

As the night closed another day, I caught myself thinking about Grandma Abba. She was my life's confidant. Other than Hayleigh, my wife, she is the only person I have shared everything. For some reason; maybe it was the bellman's name, but I recalled what she shared with me the day I went off to college. Maybe it was because I had this life-long nagging thought in the back of my mind; something was missing, something that I once knew was no longer there. I can still hear her.

"The angel Gabriel gives every new born child,

everything they need to know about God and life,

then we spend the rest of our lives forgetting."

I need to remember, but somehow I lost my bearings along the path. God knows I've searched everywhere as a researcher specializing on the source of life, DNA. I've spent my years viewing life from the outside, from a microscope and stacks of written journals in the name of advancing human society and discovering the secrets to life. Life does not make much sense to me anymore. I'm fifty-five years old, and I don't feel like I have figured out anything. Matter of fact, I don't know what being human is. I feel like those ant-like creatures below, marching through life, controlled by someone or something outside. I am not sure. I'm trapped inside, with a feeling that there was supposed to be something more. This something more, some deity, some force, was outside of me. I never could see it, or trust it.

Friends say I need to change; I feel I need to remember. I say people always become more and more of what they already are. As a child, I had a glimmering hopeful memory deep in my soul that tells me one can experience a metamorphosis. The glimmer was lost in the process of my forgetting. As years passed, Grandma Abba tried pointing me to the practice of letting go all that I had become, while consigning to oblivion my innocent sight, heart, and freedom. Remembering is redemption.

It is never far from you. You breathe a sparkling shimmer occasionally during a sunset, a song, movie, or look on your child's face. But like the air you exhale, it vanishes. I still hope that I may see it once again. These are the buds on your tree of life. However, that gnawing piercing feeling that you are eating the fruit of the wrong tree gives you hope that what you have forgotten, your tree of life, is the only real thing out there and you can find it once again. This search is my pearl of great price hidden in the field, and if we knew it was there, we would sell everything owned; digging until we find it. I've forgotten so much I cannot even see the field.

One last swig of the wine, I am tired, ready for bed and my mind to stop. Sitting down at the foot of the bed, I glance at my still unpacked leather duffel bag resting on the luggage rack. That luggage has journeyed many places yet in a sense, nowhere. I fall back onto the bed still in my clothes looking at the ceiling. My eyes slowly darken. Something is not right. There is . . .

***

The wheels of the train were clanging loudly like the sounds of chains. I could hear just under the muffled "metal on metal" shackled sounds, the muddled voices of the people, who were wearing dark sunglasses, some barely whispering, some shouting, but all at the same volume. The sunglasses were the type that blind people wear. Amongst the muted babel I could hear the whimpering of slow tears sliding down the cheeks of the sunglass covered eyes of some of the travelers. I could barely make out the sounds, because of the slow rolling thunder of the wheels that would often slow to a stop, only to start again with a loud clang as the heavy couplings that bound all the cars together would pound straining to pull forward. Sometimes it appeared that the train stopped and even reversed for a little bit, only to start lunging aimlessly forward again picking up speed. The people in the caravan of endless cars seemed to be communicating, but their lips did not form the words that I was hearing. It was as if I was watching their lives; while simultaneously hearing their inner thoughts. People were sobbing over their laughter while holding hands with a person that did not even appeal to them.

I raced effortlessly through the cars, the doors open automatically, allowing escape. No one exited toward the doors. The passengers appear to see me. Some say "Hi Edward," and mysteriously, I can see their eyes. They are haunting, they see without looking to see. I have seen these eyes before. I cannot place them, but I recognize the look of fear and loneliness, the heartbroken eyes; are yearning for something. They are like the elephants at the circus; held by a rope tied to a small spike. They could be free in an instant. Instead, they remain following some unexplained instruction outside the sounds of silence.

Every seat occupied, I feel lost. My heart is pounding. The air is too thick to breathe; I can feel the walls closing in on me. I must get off this train. Where are, we heading?

Frantically exiting through the door, I pause between cars to gather my breath; looking out at the dull beige sepia-landscape. It's undefined; lacking clarity and detail. There is a hill, and at the top I see a figure beckoning me to come. There is what appears to be a ray of sunlight beaming over the peak distorting the shadowy figure dancing, and casting a shadow of wild color on the slope of this large mound. The silhouetted figure takes a few steps down the hill. I see her close. I gasp, "Mom!"

She says nothing, but her warm smile and loving eyes communicate simultaneously; sadness, love, happiness, and hope that everything will be alright in the end. I can tell without words; she yearns to take my place. I remember that look; every time my task-driven father would punish us, or stamp out the fun of his kids; calling it idleness and foolishness of the devil. Slowly, she faded as the train rounded another bend. Looking in the direction where we are heading; it's rocky, and I can tell that we are heading into rough terrain. Mom is no longer in sight.

Moving further back, the door opens. There standing in the aisle speaking to all the people seated in rows wearing their dark glasses is my father, the Reverend Edward W. Mayus. He is holding his Bible in one hand, and a magnifying glass is tightly gripped by the other. A man I love, loathe, and pity at the same time. It's not my Dad I loathe, but the God that he is yoked with that denies his humanity. I am crying like a child reaching out to touch the hand of his father, who judges him not worthy.

He is the only one standing on the train. He turns and looks at me, and says, "Glad you can be here son, take a seat if you can find one, we are busy here building the Kingdom of God." Like always I listened and took the only seat I see available right in front of him.

"Not that one son, you know that's your mother's place, she is always with me," looking upward as he praises the Lord. My father is speaking to his listeners, but they cannot hear and are pleading for more, but I can listen to what he hears; and it is distorted, much like the sound that comes from a deaf-mute person. You must work hard at understanding them. "Amen," periodically is shouted on cue toward this circus master.

Directly behind the open seat is my step-mom Martha clutching her ever-present Day-Timer keeping Dad's life organized. She married my father shortly after my Mom's death. Mom died during the birth of my brother Stephen, of an undetected heart defect. My dad, a former world-renowned heart surgeon, never forgave himself and thought God was punishing him because of his neglect of my mother's heart. That's what caused his tectonic conversion shift into full-time ministry. I believe he viewed it as fixing spiritual hearts; a debt he had to pay; his way of painting blood over the doorpost, his man-made redemption. She was the woman my Mom could never be but was perfect for my father's new profession.

Across the aisle was my younger sister Johanna, who seldom smiled around the family. Johanna and I were dad's biggest disappointments, she was a lesbian, and I was worse; an agnostic; I just simply did not know. I'm frantically looking around for Stephen; he was my best friend; besides being the most spiritual person I ever met. He gives me hope that I could maybe one day have a belief. He can be found nowhere. Whenever he was around, my soul breathed freely; today the walls are closing in like a vice.

Moving onward, I stop again to catch my breath in between cars. My heart is pounding. I look immediately to my left, and there is another train on another set of tracks. It's keeping pace with us. The passengers also are wearing the same sunglasses. I wiped my eyes to clear away the dust; I noticed that I was not wearing glasses. In the windows of the companion train, traveling this strange pilgrimage, are the John Kandy family, the funniest and craziest people I have ever met. It is a brief respite from my angst. Their two children were named Cotton and Penny; need I say any more? I envied them because of how happy they always seemed. They are laughing and pointing at me, while John is giving his wife the bunny ears behind her head. But, I am hearing crying instead of laughter. John's wife, Candy, need I say more. She felt it was a hoot when they met and it was destiny when they married. Candy was making the heart sign and pulling it apart every few seconds like a sad clown.

Immediately behind them was the Beaman family, Giles, and Julie, they were a mixed marriage. Giles, a black man, was my best friend and the most stable man I knew. He always seemed to have it together, and I could talk about anything with him.

The tracks were starting to spread apart and get further away, but I caught a glimpse at my dear trusted colleague, Dr. Ayazz Imwas, a world-renowned heart specialist from Syria, who came over to this country during the first Gulf War. As he was drifting further away I saw that he stopped waving and mouthed the words, "I'm sorry dear friend."

I stood there staring as I watched the train disappear around the bend trying to understand this feeling of heaviness that was now pressing on my shoulders until my emotions could no longer be tolerated, I had to find Hayleigh.

Moving frantically through the train hoping that somewhere the dread ends. The door opens many cars back. Sitting right in front of me is Buford Pearl, my father-in-law, eating ribs with his usual bib hanging around his neck like an infant, and sauce in the corners of his mouth. He says to me, "Where is Hayleigh?" as he continues sloppily chewing loudly. He was a good man, I just never liked him, because of how he affected everyone around him. He was the warden of the local county jail and everyone, like his prisoners, towed the line. I never could understand why; but even Hayleigh, his daughter, my wife, never crossed the line. Seated by his side was May, his wife and college sweetheart, busy wiping his chin. Always with her was her purse, chain-linked handles strapped around her neck like she was holding onto the world's top secrets. Glancing down, I saw the tops of a pair of ballerina slippers hanging out of her satchel of valuables. They looked hardly worn. Directly behind was their pride and joy son, Deacon, a by-the-book success story who founded the top real estate company outside of Richmond Virginia. Next to him is his exact opposite brother, Cash, the spontaneous failure, who had tried many times to measure up to his brother. He was my favorite of the family. Even though he was the middle child, he was the big brother to down-syndrome Buddy, the youngest, and the only one without sunglasses on the train.

Buddy looked up and spoke clearly to me, "We are not supposed to be on this train." It rang so clear that I panicked and started to cry out where is Hayleigh and the rest of my family. No one answered.

I ran through the cars; my heart continued to pound. Car after car I raced. What is going on here? I must get off this train. The wheels are moving faster and faster; then the door opens. There are Maggie and Tommy, my children, sitting in the car. A sense of relief fills me. Maggie has her kids Aidan and Eden clutched tightly to her chest, surrounded by snacks, toys, and her ever-present iPhone, posting away about her life to friends that I have never met. Tommy, my son, sitting by a window playing his guitar; boringly strumming the strings that are slightly out of tune. I recognize that melody. It was the first song he ever wrote. My God, he played it over and over for us. He was so proud and happy then.

I should do something.

"Get those damn glasses off!" I screamed. I don't want my children and grandchildren staying on this train. I turned to look outside to find a place to get off. Suddenly there she was.

Hayleigh, my wife, sitting next to a man also wearing the glasses. I did not recognize him, but he had a lab coat on with a stethoscope dangling underneath his head with the ear tips still in his ears. The stranger was looking out the window watching with wondering anticipation as a child tethered to the back seat of the car window.

"Hayleigh," I pleaded, "We have to get off this train!" I could tell she understood me and desperately wanted to leave, but she gently leaned into the man next to her and wrapped her arm under his, as he just sat there gazing out the window. Who in the hell is this guy? I cocked my arm back to hit this son of a bitch when Hayleigh looked at me, lifted her hand between me and his heart, pleading that she loved this man. My heart was crushed. I don't know what made me stop. Somehow, I felt she deserved to be loved. I wanted the best for her and never felt I could give it to her. I looked over at Maggie and Tommy, and they had tears dripping down behind their glasses as if they were waiting for me to do something.

They stared. Tired of waiting; Tommy and Maggie lowered their heads and turned away. Distraught filled me. Then I heard Hayleigh say something that I could not quite understand. She looked up at me and uttered these direful words of hope, "We all could be happy again, . . . remember?" She looked at the man next to her and repeated it to him. There was a pause. He turned to me, this stranger; he took out his ear buds and lifted his glasses to look up at me.

"Oh no, nooo!" The stranger was me. He sat there with nothing to say but stared at me with contempt. The next ten seconds felt like an eternity. Swish!

In an instant, I found myself at the end of the train. There was only one person there and thank God it was my Grandma Abba, Ruth Mayus, the rock of my life, the only one, besides Stephen and Hayleigh, whoever brought sense to my life and feelings. She understood me.

Looking forward through binoculars, she asked me to lean over and whispered over the shackled clanging sounds of the wheels, "I am not supposed to be on this train, but I had to come for you." She pointed toward the tracks we were leaving behind.

"Oh my god," I thought to myself. I could see in a vision-like state; the ghost-like lives and dreams that never happened of all who were on this train. The art, songs, words not spoken, deeds never done, lives not lived, works never completed, and people never loved, were all being trampled under the weight of this train and left behind. It was too much to take in.

"Grandma Abba, we have to do something."

Grandma Abba asked me to bend near, "There are many trains to perdition."

The sudden sadness of the sense of loss was torturing me. This feeling must be like Hell. A minute went by, I asked her, "Where is Stephen?"

She unwrapped the binoculars from around her neck and handed them to me pointing. I started to look through them, and they were not focused. I looked around, and she was gone.

I turned in the direction she pointed and viewed a kaleidoscope of blurred colors that became focused. I saw high on the full colored hillside, my brother Stephen. He was having fun climbing to the top with the biggest smile on his face. The feeling was the happiest I had been on this wild nightmare journey I thought. Then I noticed higher up. The rocks are starting to tumble. I screamed to Stephen, and though he was far from me, he seemed to hear me. He turned and waved to me; waving for me to join him as the lens instantly filled with a roaring gray, beige cloud of dust. BEEEEEEP! BEEEEEEP! BEEEEEEP!

"Oh crap!" was my first thought as I leaped up from my pillow and smashed the heck out of the alarm clock to put an end to this unrest. My clothes are drenched in perspiration. The same dream that I have had for years. Only this time it was more vivid and real. It was a nightmare. No one had ever died in these dreams before, much less Stephen. I sighed and wiped the sleep from my eyes.

I reach for the remote to turn on the news before planting my feet on the floor to start my last day on this research project. I was glad this grant was over, and we were meeting to go over the final draft. I was to meet Giles Beamon for an 11:00 AM coffee at the Starbucks to go over the presentation. I look out the window over Central Park. It's mostly a dreary day that looks like it could storm any minute.

I stretch and stroll slowly to the bathroom. I was never a morning person. Another thing my father hated. By this time in the morning, he had already read his Bible and prayed for about an hour, and was planning his days of staff meetings at the Hillside Community Church, a large church of just under 3,000 members, located just outside Baltimore where we grew up, and I still lived. Some days he would wake us up by blasting open the door and ripping the sheets off the bed and pulling me by my feet until I dropped on the floor.

Splashing water on my face to jump start my brain I observed how beautiful this hotel was. I was staying at the Sherry-Netherlands Hotel, overlooking Central Park. I decided that I would splurge on the last day; and my good Muslim friend Dr. Ayazz Imwas, the Research Director, allowed me this one indulgence.

I wished I could have brought Hayleigh; she loves places like this. She is an interior decorator and loves classical architecture and design.

Looking at the mirror, I was taken aback by the reflection of myself. It's the same look I had when I saw the stranger, myself, in the dream. It brought back that same sense of a loathing heaviness to my heart that I felt during my nightmare. I had always had problems seeing the good in myself, but this was different. Thankfully my research work had given me the sense of self-worth that could get me through the years. It's maybe the gift, or curse, my father passed on to me. The sense of performance and success as defined by others outside was never enough. I could never figure out what it was, but I had that gnawing feeling that something was missing. I wanted to be as self-assured as Dad and to have a sense of faith that I could believe in something as strongly as my father. I just could not accept his beliefs as real, and I could not understand why. Stephen seemingly navigated his way to spiritual peace.

I heard the gurgling sound of the coffee pot signaling that the coffee was ready. As I was pouring my much-needed cup before my shower, the newscaster broke into the weather report to announce that an American in Rome has been beheaded by an Islamic extremist while leaving the Vatican Post Office outside the Vatican. Details to follow, but confirmation is that the victim is an American, and his identity is being withheld until next of kin are notified. My God when are we just going to blow these guys up and be done with it?

Sipping my coffee looking out the window at the storm clouds approaching, I can only wonder what the family will feel like that gets this news today with the Holidays only weeks away. I look out the window to my right, and there is an eerie patina Gargoyle staring at me as if it has some danger to present to me. The Sherry-Netherlands is famous for its castle-like architecture, and the gargoyles ominous presence are everywhere.

Beedy Beep... Beedy Beep... Beedy beep ... Stepping out of the shower I could hear the ringing of my cell phone, but I could not quite get to it before it stopped. Crap! It's from my father. I can't handle a call today with all I need to do. I also spot a calendar reminder that I have an early breakfast with my sister and her significant other. I can't bring myself to say, girlfriend. Her significant other has just landed a gig in an off-Broadway play, and I am supposed to see it tonight. Johanna is doing set design, and it is the break that both have been looking for since she arrived in New York. She is excited that I am in town.

I've got to step on it to make it. Beedy Beep ... Beedy Beep.

"Hello honey," I answer to Hayleigh.

"Are you ready for your final meeting? It's going to be wonderful to have you home for a change", she says hopefully.

"Yea honey I'm looking forward to the holidays. How have your headaches been?"

Hayleigh had been suffering from what we thought were migraines the last few months. We chalked it up to stress because things have not been great between us lately. There was nothing earth shattering, but merely a dulled thought in the back of our minds that we were drifting apart and somehow we did not even know the other person.

Hayleigh, ignoring my question, stressfully asked me, "Look I hate to bother you, but I have to plan for the holiday dinners."

My reply is my usual, "Can't you just handle this yourself. Hayleigh, I have to go, but I will go with whatever you decide."

"It's not that easy Edward, you know your father and his demands along with balancing out the expectations of my family. We have Thanksgiving in less than a week and Christmas right around the corner. It's hard as hell to keep everyone happy."

"Look Hayleigh, we will figure this all out when I get back. Don't you have to get some decorations out for the house. We can talk when I get back, I am meeting Johanna and her . . . whatever. I'll see you tomorrow, and we can figure it out then."

"No, I will figure it out then, like usual," she utters in contempt hanging up.

Beedy beep! Beedy beep! Beedy beep! Oh, god now it's Martha, she probably wants to know about the holidays. I push the decline call button, as I run out the room to get the concierge to hail me a cab.

This day cannot get any worse.

The Call

The battle line between good and evil

runs through the heart of every man

-Alexander Solzhenitsyn

Racing out the lobby door, "Your cab is ready sir" the bellman barks. Ducking into the cab, I greet the driver with a hello. His I.D. badge is hanging from his visor displaying his name as Abdul Wadud Fariq.

"Abdul," I shout, as I lean forward to tell him where I need to go; but he only stares at me through the rear-view mirror. He says nothing as the cab pulls away. I try again to give him the name of the Sault Saint Marie, a coffee shop on Park Avenue. His silence indicates the bellman told him my destination.

My thoughts go to the news report I heard about the poor American who was beheaded in Rome. I want to ask Abdul what he thinks about this. How can a religion believe this way? Hell, as far I know he could be part of a sleeper cell.

Heading up 59th St., we stop at a light to make a left onto Park Avenue. As we make the left, two people are crossing the street with canes and those same dark glasses. My mind is thrust back to the pit-in-my-gut feeling of last night's dream. Shaking my shoulders quickly, trying to shed this nightmare from my mind.

"Seven dolla and feefty cents," Abdul utters his first words to me. I hand him a ten and slam the door. There standing in the window of the coffee shop waving is my sister, Johanna. I look down as my phone vibrates. It's my wife, Hayleigh. I decline the call and head in toward Johanna as the wind picks up signaling the approaching storm.

Johanna picked this place because she worked there as a server and barista when she first arrived in New York. It's where she met her friend and lover, Emilee Brett, an aspiring actress who lived three floors above. They have lived together ever since. Through the years, I had never met her. I can't remember anything about my sister's past relationships, but only vaguely know Emilee as her longtime companion and partner through conversations. They were enjoying their first professional break. Emilee was the leading lady in a new off-Broadway play Sins of My Father, while Johanna was the set designer.

My recollections of my sister were that she was always a loner and loved to read. She seldom was included, nor sought to be active in any of the Mayus' pastimes. I was looking forward to seeing her. She always expressed a deep love and caring for me. I was the older big brother to Johanna, her only branch to the Mayus family tree since her younger brother, Stephen, was traveling the world.

"Jo! you are looking good" as we exchange an initial awkward hug on my part.

She grabs me a second time and embraces me with, "Eddie, Eddie, am I so glad to see you. I have missed you so much." She backs away looking me over with her hands still clutching mine. I can tell how much I mean to her as her eyes fill with happy tears. It feels good to connect with someone this way. Both of us continue holding both hands, savoring the moment. Johanna and I had not been together since last summer when she visited Hayleigh and me at Bethany Beach.

"Well, congratulations on your play, I can't wait to see it tonight," I broke the warm silence.

"I'm excited too," she responds with the giddiness of a schoolgirl modeling an adult size dress from an attic trunk. Johanna radiates a beautiful smile as large as her blue eyes when she is happy. I don't think I can ever remember any time where she was this full of outward joy.

"Emilee is coming right down; she is running a little late; you know how it is with two women sharing one small bathroom" she embarrassingly states. "She is looking forward to finally meeting you," Johanna says with intention.

I awkwardly ask, "Before Emilee comes down, I have to ask you about the holidays Johanna. Hayleigh would love to have you join us. It's been a long time since my grandkids Eden and Aidan have seen their aunt. What do you say? Can you make either Thanksgiving or Christmas?"

"Will Dad be there?" she disgustingly asked, turning her eyes away from me. She knows the answer and how the holidays are run around my father's wishes.

"Dad does not want his 'abomination' to ruin his holiday," she sorrowfully speaks, her eyes welling up.

"He never called you an abomination," I counter and briefly pause, "He blames Emilee."

"Oh, so she is the abomination...this is supposed to make me feel better," she responds in anger, but not at me. My father's dominance on the Mayus family had caused Johanna to feel shunned. This loneliness was a terminal cancer in my sister's soul.

"Why did you even to bring this up? I am an outsider Edward. Can't you see it's been that way my whole life," her voice quivering.

Staring into her sad eyes, I plead in a soft whisper, "Look, Jo, I understand. Believe me. I feel like an outsider too. You may very well be an abomination to Dad, but I chose to doubt his faith, his religion in his mind I'm agnostic. That makes me more of an outsider!"

"Oh, more great logic, you're losing your touch Edward," her voice rises slightly to a loud whisper.

We both just sit there staring at each other. I break the awkward silence with a smile. We both start softly laughing until Jo let's out a snort, and we both realize that the holidays are a hopeless cause for the Mayus clan.

"I just can't stand the thought of you not being with the family and those that love you during the holidays."

"Eddie, I am with my loving abomination," more laughter ensues. "I have other close friends, and some of them love God also." After a momentary pause, "Eddie, I love God; and I hope God loves me."

I reply, "Well, you are ahead of me, I am not sure about God at all."

Ping! Johanna gets a text, "It's from Hayleigh, she says for you to accept her call, it's important." I ignore what Jo said.

Just then the door opens with a ringing of the bell and its Emilee. She is stunning, slightly older than Johanna, and more sophisticated. Whenever I have seen these two together in a Facebook post, my mind wanders on who could be the male in this relationship. They both are beautiful women, and I certainly could not entertain the thought long. It was puzzling. I recalled a conversation.

One night at The Vineyard, our favorite restaurant in a little town called Havre de Grace, Hayleigh grew angry with me. We were discussing Johanna and Emilee over a bottle of wine. She pointed out to me how hypocritical and sexist I was in my thoughts that only a male figure could initiate love in a sexual context. Hayleigh then proceeded to outline our love-life history. She shut me up for good that night when she finished our night with these words, "If I waited for you, we still would not have kissed yet, and there would not be a Maggie or Tommy." Touché, I thought.

Gracefully she walked through the café tables; I started to stand and reach my hand out to greet her when she took it and pulled me close. Kissing me on my cheek and whispering, "It's so wonderful to meet you finally. You make Hanna so happy, which makes me happy."

We order our coffee and pastry when Johanna's phone rings. She looks like she has seen a ghost. "It's our father," she surprisingly states.

I respond, "Maybe he wishes you well on the play"? Johanna rolls her eyes, then lets me know that she never told him. She pushes the decline call button making doubly sure that she did not press the answer button. We talk for another hour about the play, which is about a young woman and her mother breaking free of an overbearing father. I thought to myself that Johanna should be the actress in this play. Time was beginning to press on, and I had to get to my meeting with Giles to go over the presentation. I stood up and walked behind both Johanna and Emilee; bent down to give them both a kiss, which even surprised me; the surprise on Johanna's face indicated her pleasure. She appeared excited about me coming to her show tonight. I was just as excited.

As I walked away, Johanna said, "I have a surprise for you tonight."

It added a little mystery to my anticipation of the night.

***

Leaving the coffeehouse, I noticed that the sky looked more ominous. The approaching storm would not hold off much longer as the wind blew briskly. I made a quick dash to meet Giles at the Starbucks near the Mt. Sinai Hospital. A quick review of our presentation and I would be free the rest of the year.

Huffing and puffing I walked into the noisy establishment, "I'll have a Venti Caramel Macchiato," I barked to the barista while looking around for Giles.

"First initial and last name," she smiles at me all bubbly.

"Uh . . . Edward. . .uh . . . E . . . E . . . Mayus," I answered.

"Eeeee Maaayuuus", she slowly sounds it out while writing it on the cup. I spot Giles in the corner as he acknowledges me with a wave. I impatiently wait for my beverage. I can hear the music playing in the background. It's Nowhere Man" by the Beatles. I hum inside my mind while waiting . . . "He's as blind. "

Waiting for the person in front of me to pick up their drink, I notice the white cane in her hand. My humming continues . . . "What he wants to see." The graying woman gently pats the counter looking to grasp her vanilla latte. I move in front to help her reach for her cup when we both grab it together; my hand is on top of hers.

"Sorry, I was just trying to help, it must be tough not being able to see," I regretfully whispered toward her.

She turned around as if looking at me, "It isn't exactly hard to see if you want to see, there are all kinds of ways to see life, but thank you for your kindness," as she gently poked her white cane touching the center of my chest as she walked away.

My thoughts hummed inside my head, . . . "Can you see me at all."

"E MAY US," the barista barks out, "E May Us." I grab the cup and head over to where Giles already has some papers laid out on the table.

"Well, friend, are you ready?", Giles asked.

Giles and I had worked the last five years to try and prove that behavior could change by altering the genome sequence of DNA in animals with the hopes of changing human behavior. Giles was my best friend and colleague over the years, a man of deep faith. While he was positive that DNA alteration could only influence the physical life, I was more hopeful of the emotional behavior change.

Giles was excited and thought that we had opened frontiers for others. "Well, Edward, I must say in reviewing our research findings, I am encouraged that there is a possibility to change behavior by altering the genome sequencing of DNA in living animals, but I am still not as hopeful as you about modifying human behavior. I will concede that the possibility is there, however remote. Ayazz will be pleased."

Ayazz was our boss. Dr. Ayazz Imwas, a Muslim, is a world renown heart specialist from Syria. I was introduced to him by my father, who was then the Chief of Johns Hopkins Division of Cardiac Surgery. They were friends. My dad was a famous surgeon, developing cutting edge techniques that could repair damaged hearts of people most would see as hopeless. People would come from all over the world to study his gifted techniques. Dr. Ayazz Imwas, who grew fond of me over the years, had a hand in funding most of my research during my career. We became close friends and colleagues.

He and my father grew apart after my mother's untimely death from heart failure. My dad blamed himself. He soon turned to religion. As a Pastor, there was no reason to commune with the infidels.

"Giles, I'm glad my academic expertise can please Ayazz because the Mayus clan has not been able to master the real-life heart at home."

"Eddie, what's going on?" he asked closing his laptop.

"Giles, look it's nothing, just more of the same; it's just life, and I'm just a guy like everyone else that has not figured it out. Look we have to get our ducks in a row for the presentation, let's get to work," I said opening my laptop.

"Edward!" He whispers loudly as he firmly with one hand turns my shoulders to face him directly, "We've known each other for a long time. You and I were best men at our weddings. Our lives and families have been blessed. You are one of the most intelligent people I have met, but lately, you always seem on the edge of discontent. I worry about you. What's wrong? Don't you see it? You can't be that ungrateful."

"Look, Giles, you don't have to be such a judgmental jerk about it," I snapped back.

Giles barks right back, "I'm not a jerk, I'm concerned, Edward. What's going on? Look, if you think I'm judging you; you are dead wrong. I'm concerned. You have not seemed happy for a while now."

I wiped my face with both hands, stopping a while at my forehead, before going straight back over my head through my hair, my fingers are massaging my tense neck. I rocked back on my chair with a long exasperated sigh, "What are we doing here? I mean Giles, really. What are we here for?" Does marriage, families, homes, money and careers do it for you? Well, it's not enough for me. It's not enough," as my voice trails off to a whisper before rocking back in disgust.

Giles rests his chin on his tense fist staring at me in disbelief. "Eddie, you don't love Hayleigh anymore?" He pleads the question; fearing the answer.

He probably thinks I'm going through a mid-life crisis. Hell, I've been going through a life crisis for the last ten years, and my best friend doesn't know it. How could he, it's happening inside me.

I angrily lash out, "Don't be stupid Giles, of course, I love Hayleigh. It's us I hate. It's me; it's my life. It's every damn thing that should be meaningful and relevant, and it's not there. Where did it go? I'm fifty-five years old, and I'm supposed to be passed this by now!"

"God, Edward, I had no idea," Giles' shoulders drop, and his eyes bleed confusion and concern as he lets out a sigh, leaning forward with his chin resting on his fist as he always does before he says something incredibly relevant. Not this time. "It will all make sense someday. How does Hayleigh feel about this?"

"That's just it Giles; she doesn't even know me anymore. I have nothing to give her, and I hate myself for it. It has destroyed her and my family. It's destroyed me. I feel like a man going through life blind, chained to a life that is crushing my heart and those around me. Hayleigh wonders if I am present to her. We are left to meander through our dangling conversations. She feels we are drifting apart; she fears she does not make me happy. Hell, I can't make myself happy! The other day, during one of our arguments I shouted, 'My life is not one of your rooms that you have to decorate!' Giles, that is what she does. She makes things beautiful, warm; and I was rejecting her," I spoke, as my eyes look down in contempt of myself.

"The look on her face was emptiness. I've seen that look many times lately. It's getting worse because now I want to bring her happiness, but, I am afraid of not being able to deliver. If there is one thing that is not an option for a Mayus, it is failing," I announce. "So I do nothing," as my voice trails off.

Then as if ridiculing myself with a monologue, I state with my fingers pointing towards the heavens, "The great Edward Mayus, Hopkins scholar, and part of the long line of accomplished heart surgeons and researchers; and he can't find happiness much less make someone happy. How pathetic. I watch my kids grow and see the same dullness in their lives, I want to be there for them and Hayleigh." I ask my friend, "Doctor Giles, give me some of your wisdom."

"God Edward, I don't know what to say, but that I will be praying and I know you will get through this. After all, you are a Mayus," he grins at me. We both laugh a little.

Mmmmmph! Mummmmph! Two quick muffled sounds emanate from my phone displays a text that Giles immediately spies. "Aren't you going to answer that?" Giles asks, "It's from Hayleigh, and she says it's an emergency, please call."

Responding to Giles, "I know she has been trying to get hold of me all morning. It's probably about Thanksgiving dinner and family issues. I will get back with her later."

Giles picks up my phone and hands it to me with an astonished look on his face, "I thought you wanted to be present?"

"We have to finish reviewing the presentation."

"I'm not looking at another slide until you call Hayleigh."

"If it will make you happy," I reluctantly snap the phone from his hands.

"At least you will make someone happy," he retorts with a grin on his face.

"You can be a real ass sometimes," I replied.

I pushed the speed dial and saw Hayleigh's face appear on my phone as it always did; that youthful look that used to be her when we first started out. It always made me feel happy to remember her that way. Every once-in-a-while, spontaneously I saw that look in her eye that told me she was still there. The phone did not even get a half a ring before Hayleigh picked up and I could tell something was wrong. I stood up to walk away. All I could hear was a muffled sobbing sound and Hayleigh calling my name. I walked outside of the Starbucks so that I could talk louder and get her attention. Immediately I thought something happened to Maggie or Tommy.

"Hayleigh, Hayleigh!" I pleaded, "Are the kids alright? Calm down." Hayleigh relaxes and takes a breath; I softly spoke, "What happened, what's wrong?" I could hear her breathing while she remained silent.

"I want to be there for you but I can't," she stutters out softly.

"Hayleigh! What happened?"

"Stephen!" she yells.

As I walk across the street in front of a park bench for a little privacy, I can see Giles through the window asking with a gesture if everything is okay. I shut him down with a raised hand as I ask Hayleigh, "What is wrong with Stephen?"

A long silence and then she cries out, "Stephen is dead!"

I collapse on the bench whispering, "Oh God, not Stephen, please God, don't take him," as I scream louder looking to the sky as the rain starts and the sky explodes. "Where is he, what happened, are you sure, who told you?" I screamed into the phone for answers. She is now sobbing out of control saying something to me that I cannot make out, but I know she is angry at somebody. "Hayleigh! What happened?" I loudly plead.

She stops weeping, catching her breath, she moans, "They killed him, they killed him, those animals killed your little brother, Stephen is gone!"

I am drenched in sorrow as I sink back into the park bench.

Giles is running toward me with an umbrella. He knows something is wrong. I am frozen on a bench, the only person in the park, in the middle of a storm. He opens the umbrella to ease the rain, but nothing can stop the internal raging storm.

"What's wrong Edward?" He huffs out after running across the street, "What is going on?" I have my other hand to my ear to hear what Hayleigh is saying. I am drenched so Giles cannot see my tears.

I am loudly pleading with Hayleigh, "Who are they? Who killed Stephen?" The look of shock on Giles face looks like he is about to be hit by a bus.

There is now silence. The only sound is the rain pelting the umbrella. I am not sure how much time passed, but the first sound I hear is Hayleigh sniffling softly, before speaking plainly and deliberately into the phone, "Stephen was in Rome visiting his priest friend at the Vatican when he was attacked by a terrorist."

Oh, my God, my thoughts went right to the newscast this morning.

"It's all over the news Edward."

"Hayleigh, how did they kill him?" I ask her knowing how it happened, but desperately hoping to hear something else.

"Edward, please don't ask that question."

"Did they behead him"? She moans out an inaudible yes as I bellow out crying to God, "How can you, How can you"! I pushed the button to end this pain.

Giles and I stayed on the bench for a while in the storm. It seemed like an eternity. His arm draped over my shoulder embracing me with all he could give. It was enough for the moment. I was not feeling anything. I gathered myself.

As we headed back over to Starbucks, I looked over to my friend, "I'm starting to doubt that we can change human behavior."

Our table was the way we left it before the call. "I'll call Dr. Ayazz and tell him we need to postpone the presentation," Giles said to me.

Immediately I shot back, "No way! I can do this."

"Edward?" Giles looked at me. I told him I would be alright to get through some simple academic presentation.

As we were gathering our laptops and papers, the gray-haired blind lady appeared on my left smiling at me. "Young man, I hope that life will teach you to see from the inside, it's quite remarkable; it's one of my favorite ways to see," she calmly voiced to me as she walked away.

SCENES

All the world's a stage,

And all the men and women merely players;

They have their exits and their entrances;

And one man in his time plays many parts,

-William Shakespeare

Giles and I walked into the room; I was met by my trusted and indispensable assistant Jacklyn Trades. She had our slide deck already loaded, and I could see the title slide already displayed. Jacklyn let me know that Hayleigh had called several times this morning needing to speak with me. She also said that she was meeting Hayleigh at Penn Station at 3:20 and bringing her to my hotel. She apparently did not know why Hayleigh was coming.

I turned to my right, and a graduate assistant was placing a lavaliere microphone on my lapel. Just then Dr. Ayazz appeared to my left reaching out his hand to me, "Salaam" he softly spoke which was his style.

This Muslim greeting of peace filled my heart with anger. It was his religion that killed my brother. Immediately, unrecognizable feelings boiled up inside of me as I recalled my dream from last night. I could still see his somber face in my dream mouthing the apology through the window of the train. Vile thoughts filled my heart toward a man who has been nothing but kind to me my entire adult life. I shook his hand without making eye contact. I could not bear the thought of seeing the man whose religion murdered my little brother Stephen. I wanted to grab him by the throat, shake him and scream what the hell is wrong with you people!

"Is something wrong Edward"? Ayazz whispered to me grasping my arm with both hands. I walked away without acknowledging the inquiry, angrily stepping up on the speaker's platform ready to get this over. Dr. Ayazz looked to Jacklyn with a surprised and quizzical look on his face.

Giles made one last attempt asking, "Are you sure you want to do this; I think I can muddle my way through your slides?"

"Where is Jacklyn, I need some aspirin." My head was pounding. I could feel my blood streaming through my brain. Giles got Jacklyn to bring me water, and I took the pills right as Dr. Ayazz was introducing Giles and myself.

"Good afternoon; distinguished colleagues, graduate assistants, researchers, and educators, he slowly and deliberately with his thick Syrian accent pronounced the words. Philip Zimbardo has said that human behavior is incredibly pliable, plastic and the line between good and evil is permeable, and almost anyone can be induced to cross it when pressured by situational forces. That is the question we all have been trying to understand; and maybe one day, shape human behavior."

The pressure inside my head was mounting as my thoughts raced toward Stephen's memories of growing up and all our chats squeezed into flashes of time. I could hear the clanging of the train inside my head of my nightmare from last night all racing and then the sepia image of Ayazz's pleading, 'I'm sorry.'

I looked up startled from my internal raging when I heard the click of his next slide.

Reading the slide, which was his boring academic style, "Physiological Psychology is a method or approach to the understanding of behavior . . . genomic structure to the phenomena of behavior."

Ayazz adlibbed, "In other words, can we change human behavior by changing the physical genomic structure? If this is possible then we may be able to manage human behavior to produce a better species and as such, a better world."

The next click sounded like a hammer on a spike. Thoughts are bubbling like hot molten lava ready to erupt. My head feels like an ice pick driven through my skull. How can a man of Islamic faith talk about human behavior and making a better world?

"Next slide," he motions. Thud! It is the last thing I saw that afternoon.

Despite everything, I believe that people are really good at heart.
-Anne Frank

All I remember is reading that slide, and my guts are exploding inside me at the audacity to say that people are good. The very next face I saw was Jacklyn wiping my head with a damp cloth. Giles and Dr. Ayazz hovering over me. "You collapsed Edward," Giles stated.

Dr. Ayazz leans over to whisper in my ear, "Dr. Beamon told me what happened; you must rest and allow God to give you peace. It may happen that you dislike a thing which is good for you and it may happen that you love a thing that is not good for you. And God knows, and you do not know; states the Quran."

I stared him down, and he had to look away and move back. I did not want to hear anything religious. I wanted to grab him by his shirt and tell him it was his bullshit ancient religion that killed my brother in the first place. I needed answers, and my hate sufficed for the moment.

As I stood up with the help of Jacklyn, I motioned that I was okay and we went out the back-side door toward the hallway that led to the lobby of the hospital. Jacklyn called for a cab to pick us up and take me back to the hotel.

"Why didn't Hayleigh tell me what happened," she said in the cab.

"Hayleigh wanted to break the news herself, she tried all morning, and I was ignoring her call," was my reply.

Jacklyn gave me that look that I always got from her when she felt I was ignoring people. Jacklyn had countless times saved me from human relation blunders. "I don't want to be a nosy body, but what happened? Why was he in Rome? Why did they choose him; of all people?" she sought answers from me that I did not have. "Are you going to be okay while I go to Penn Station to meet Hayleigh. She is supposed to arrive in about an hour and a half."

"Yea, I need just to get my bearings."

"Edward," as she patted my arm, "You will get through this; you are a good man."

My thought was yea, and Stephen was a hundred times better and look what it got him; nothing makes sense anymore. I walked up to my room in a daze. I collapsed in the chair in my suite. I don't even remember pouring the drink I had in my hand.

Then it hit me. Stephen is gone. I will never pick up the phone and call him again. I use to talk at least once a week and every time I hung up, I was a better person. I used to call him my Younger Big Brother because he was my spiritual rock in this world. He was the one person, other than Grandma Abba, who gave me hope that there was a reason for this existence. He saw something that was in me that I could not find myself. It was so clear to him; yet foggy to me. Stephen could break free of the restraining religion of our father, while still finding something that was real and pure.

Me, my journey went from doubt to throwing up my hands and choosing to believe nothing. The beliefs of my father's religion did not match the reality of my life experience. Oh, I wanted to believe, in a bad way. I needed to understand. It would have made my life much easier. But I could not honestly make the connection. Years of modeling the perfect family in youth groups and marriage retreats for the sheep, so that they would not lose hope that they could see their way to the other end of Glory. But now Stephen is dead and so is my path to redemption.

"God Dammit God! How could you allow this to happen!" I screamed as I slammed my drink on the coffee table cracking the glass top over the wood. Wiping my face, with both hands I started to well up, but as usual, I could stop by deflecting. I picked up the remote and flicked on the television. Can you imagine, I just lost my brother, and I am turning on the tv. What is wrong with me?

I can't believe it, was my first thought when there on the news was my father interviewed. The Reverend Edward W. Mayus of Hillside Community Church read the caption below his stoic face. He did not look like a man who had just lost his youngest child. After the reporter, had asked the obligatory stupid question of how he was feeling, he went into his stock answer during times of tragedy.

"First I'd like to thank the Lord Jesus Christ for the strength he has given my family and our church to get through this awful time," was his reply to the question. "Without my faith and the faith of my brothers and sisters in the Lord, we could not get through this; it is times of suffering that God makes us stronger, Amen and praise the Lord!"

"What do you have to say to the alleged perpetrator of this crime?" asked the reporter.

"First-of-all there is no alleged murderer, my son is dead, and it was captured on video for all the world to see. The Bible says that we are to forgive our enemies, and I do forgive him. However, I do want to see justice enacted and I want him, whoever he is, to pay the price for the death of my son."

The reporter ends the interview understandably with wishes of prayers and sympathy to my father and our family. "To God be the glory," my dad abruptly states as he gets cut off.

My god, still performing the role of professional pastor. The poor man can't even be a human being at the worst time a father can experience.

The phone rings, and its Dad. I don't feel like answering it. I am not in the mood for how strong we all must be and that we are witnesses to the faith.

"Hello Dad."

"How are you holding up son?" was his first response; never even giving me time to respond. "I'm just thankful that your Mom was not alive to go through this, bless her soul. To think she died giving birth to Stephen to have his life end like this."

I thought that was a strange thought at a time like this.

"I guess you talked with Hayleigh," I got in a word.

"Yes, she told me that she spoke to you about his ...death," as his voice trailed off at the sound of the word. "What in God's name was he doing in Rome of all places," he demanded to know searching for clues as to why this happened. "God had his hand on him for the ministry, how can this be happening?" he moaned.

Dad always looked to Stephen to come back and lead his church after he had given up on me years ago.

Then the conversation turned. "They killed my baby boy Edward, those heathens killed my little boy," he wailed into the phone. "I told him he belonged in God's church, not trouncing all over the world into that evil cesspool Muslim infidel countries. I told him, they wanted nothing to do with God," he shouted emotionally nearly breaking into tears into the phone. I could hear my step-mom Martha whispering to him that they had visitors in the parlor that he had to remain strong. Clearing his throat, he told me he would call me later to go over plans for the funeral, but he had to tend to God's flock now.

I said to Dad, "Hey Dad . . . I love you," as I heard him walk into the room triumphantly.

He shouted to the sheep, "He will change my sorrow into joy."

Just then Martha was on the phone saying, "He knows you love him, Edward. I hope that you can be strong for him, he needs you now more than ever. You're all he has now Edward; it's time that you stand up for God and be counted." She promptly left to be at his side. Click.

Poor Martha was trying to keep all the pieces moving and organized. I wonder if she had some organizational structure outlined for my Dad's grieving in her little book that she kept by her side. She was still a lovely lady, and I did respect her growing up.

She only knew this part of my Dad after the death of my mother. Dad always had a spiritual side, but after my Mother had died, he turned to religion to serve his penance. Earlier, we never saw a lot of my Dad due to his being a world-famous heart surgeon: when he was around, he was full of life and a happy, playful father to Johanna and myself. He loved music, books, and plays. It was from him that I grew to like jazz. He would play the piano while I was growing up. If Martha only knew that Dad met my mom, Mary Elizabeth, at the Woodstock festival. He has never talked about my Mom in her presence, but Mom one day showed me pictures of my Dad carrying a topless girl on his shoulders while my mother sits on the side. That night they slept together and fell in love.

Now I am left with a father who cannot even have a normal human emotion because of his religion. I guess that's why I just can't believe in his God. How could God allow this to happen to Stephen? I buried my face in my hands and remained quietly emotionally silenced.

Walking over to the window with the sun going down over the city, picking up my drink, I looked out over a city of ten million people busy going about their lives never thinking that the person next to them could snuff their life out in a flash. The ominous gargoyle to my right is seemingly looking directly at me, and then I see an image to the left against the cloudy sky of Stephen that startles me. It is the reflection of the TV on the window. They already have his picture; this astounds me. It's the photo of him on the hill waving after climbing the summit in his beloved rusty Jeep TJ. I loved that picture. Last night's earlier nightmare comes rushing back to my mind. Stephen has the same look he had before the landslide. Was Stephen trying to communicate with me? He had probably already been dead a few hours before I feel asleep. There he was triumphantly waving me to join him; and then the landslide. I cocked my head back swallowing the last of my drink dissolving these thoughts into the New York skyline. Looking down, I spot Hayleigh getting out of a cab and hugging Jacklyn. It's the first sense of relief I have had all day. Hayleigh has always been my anchor when needed.

Waiting for her to get up to my room seemed like an eternity; looking through the peep hole I see the elevator doors opening as Hayleigh steps out carrying an overnight bag. She gazes into the hallway mirror primping quickly as she has always been one to care how she looks for me. I am glad she is here. Even though, as the years have moved forward, we have struggled to connect; I need her now more than ever.

I open the door shocking her. We embrace tightly. Hayleigh bursts into tears and murmurs something indecipherable into my chest. It does not matter; I connect to the most basic real thing in my life. I can breathe. I remember how much I love her.

Hayleigh looks up as we shut the door and asks, "Edward, oh honey, how are you doing? I wanted to tell you after your father called with the news, but you never answered the phone after our early morning call. I hated to break the news to you over the phone, but it was all over the tv. Then I just decided to catch a train to be with you."

"I know, I had to prepare for the presentation," I told her. "I'm sorry I did not pick up. I was a little disheveled over another dream. You know the train nightmares I have ever so often. Only this one was different. Stephen died in a landslide," I pondered quizzically staring straight ahead into nothing. Just then the news continued with the never-ending news feed loop with Stephen's picture. "That's the dream I mean that's the picture that was in the dream right before he died, he looked just like that! Then he was gone. Just like that, he's gone, and I was awake not knowing the reality that he had died. Hayleigh, it's been that way my whole life. I don't know what is real whether I am awake or sleeping? There is no difference."

Hayleigh looked seriously at me, placing her soft hands over my temples, leaning toward me, "Now is not the time to tackle your existential bent Baby. Just grieve. It's not the time for you to be my brave knight in shining armor. You don't have to understand it today. You don't have to make anything better," as she left the room to unpack her luggage and for me to unpack my thoughts.

She always had a way of grounding me so that I never fell off the precipice of my existential demise. Most of the time it was by pointing out in a humorous way the chinks in my armor. There were many, and I was always surprised how easily she saw them. She loved me anyway.

One day Hayleigh said that my chinks were what revealed the surprises in our relationship that made her love me more. They represented the hope that it could get even better. They revealed parts of me that she wanted and enjoyed to know. As the years went by, I showed less, and that caused her to search me out more to discover newness in our relationship. I regret that this came across as nagging to me. I treated it so and killed off some of her natural, innocent inquisitiveness. The very thing she loved about me, I withheld. I guess somehow I thought I was strong, after all; a knight's armor must shine. I was wrong.

Hayleigh was organizing my room when I recalled her look in my dream. It was a look I had seen in recent years of hope and disappointment combined. Then I recalled what she said in my dream, 'we all could be happy again' as if asking a question. I wanted to rush in and grab her and let her know how I feel, but as usual, I do not. I am beginning to wonder if I feel at all. Another word goes unspoken, a moment lost. I am losing my life.

Just then Haleigh re-enters the living room of the suite where I am staring at the TV without watching. "When was the last time you ate?" she asked. When I told her that, "I only had a bagel with Johanna early this morning . . . Oh damn! Johanna! Hayleigh, what are we going to do about telling Johanna?"

"She might already know," Hayleigh thought.

"No, there is no way, tonight is her big night with the premier of her play. She has been at the theater all day. She is expecting me to be there. She is excited. I have never seen her this joyful. I can't drop this on her until the night is over.

We must go to the theater tonight. I have to tell her in person," I decided.

Hayleigh went into action, "I will order room service, you have to get something on your stomach. I will call the concierge and order cab service." I left the room to get a shower and gather myself and figure out how I will break the news to Johanna.

***

I stayed in the shower for what seemed like a long time, as if the falling water would act as my personal baptism and wash away my stress and sorrows. I heard the bell boy deliver the food and I put my robe on and headed out.

Hayleigh and I sat down and started to eat; even though I had no appetite, I at least decided on forcing down the soup. "I just saw your father interviewed on Fox; he is going to be on tv tonight."

"Is that sick or what," I lashed out. "My brother is dead! Now he is a hero when all he was doing was living his life out as he loved. Before this happened, only a few people in this country; and hundreds in the world even knew of him. All the work and the wonderful life he led was worthless to everyone. He is now a hero to millions because he is dead. The act of a crazed religious lunatic zealot has made my brother Stephen a hero. They don't even know half of how great he was," I choke back the tears.

"And now my father is on every damn newscast performing his religious duties for the sake of keeping the sheep strong. The poor man can't even grieve like a normal human being. He always must be performing. He still must work for the sake of being a witness to the faith. It's not human; it's not normal!"

Hayleigh sits there intently letting me vent. "Dear, why did you then feel compelled to deliver the presentation this afternoon?" she inquires nonchalantly in her Hayleigh way. I immediately drop my spoon into the soup along with my napkin signaling that this conversation is over.

I'm not mad at Hayleigh, but she always had a gift of a laser-focused ability to strike with clarity. I'm just like my father I thought, always performance driven. I moved across the room to look out the window. Hayleigh looked up toward me, with a deliberate, intentional thought to diffuse the situation, "Maybe you shouldn't be so hard on your father; you know honey, the abyss between you and your Dad is frightful only when you look down. When you look across the divide at the person, he is closer than you think."

***

After such a traumatic event, time becomes surreal. The minutes last an eternity and the hours pass quickly. I was dreading going to the play because of having to tell Johanna. I have never seen her so happy; and now I must tell her that Stephen, our rock in this world, is dead. She will be shattered. Like me, Stephen was the person that gave us hope that this world had meaning and God was loving.

As the cab was pulling up, the crowd was meandering away and lingering at the door since the theater had a smaller lobby. They seemed genuinely pleased judging by their smiles and discussions. The play must have been a hit. We made our way into the theater where I immediately spotted Johanna down by the stage talking with some of her friends.

She came running up the aisle with the joy of a child on Christmas morning. "I was worried you didn't make it, where's Stephen?" she said scouring the room. I just sat there frozen in time saying nothing while tears welled up in my eyes. "Eddie where's Stephen?"

"Is there a place we can go to talk?"

"No! I want to know where Stephen is!" As her voice raised and others turned to see what was happening, Hayleigh reached out an arm and wrapped it around Johanna's shoulder, leading her backstage, she whispered to her that something has happened to Stephen and Johanna quietly went with her both hands covering her face.

Immediately after spying the conversation from afar, Emilee came racing over, as if I had said something hurtful. "Edward, what the hell is going on?" she asked.

"Emilee, it's not what you think, but you better come back with us, Stephen is dead; and I have to tell Johanna." She covered her mouth and started to weep.

"Her and Stephen were going to surprise you!" Emilee whispered through her hands covering her face.

Grabbing my hand and gazing into my eyes as if she was feeling the same hurt that was stabbing me, she walked back with me continuing to squeeze my hand harder with every step to talk with Johanna. It was comforting to know that someone was experiencing the same sadness; I was surprised it was Emilee.

Stepping behind the stage curtain into the very world that my little sister had designed, I was taken back by how much it reminded me of our house as children growing up. The family pictures were arranged the same way I remembered as a child. Hayleigh still had her arm around Johanna on the sofa near the center of the stage. Johanna looked up spotting Emilee and me approaching her. Emilee stayed with me still holding my hand. I slid the coffee table aside and moved an ottoman over directly in front of her. I reached over to touch her hand, and she grabbed both mine and Emilee's as I apologetically spoke the words, "Stephen has been killed."

"God nooo nooo!" she whimpered softly. She tried to speak, her lips moving while nothing audibly could be heard, she bellowed a gasp trying to breathe, but she could not. Hayleigh jumped up asking some of the crew for a glass of water. Emilee immediately went to her side, and Johanna buried her face into her shoulder; sobbing and gasping to breathe. The only words I could detect were Stephen, God, and how. I just sat there alone on the ottoman, longing to express these same feelings that were cutting inside of me, but my thoughts to remain strong for everyone as usual allowed me to appear stoic.

Hayleigh came back with bottled water, and Johanna lifted her head out of the chest of Emilee to look toward me taking a swallow of water. After a deep breath, she asked, "How did it happen, was it a car accident?"

"It doesn't matter," does it, Johanna? Don't ask; it's not worth knowing."

Hayleigh, interrupted, "Edward, she is going to find out." Turning to Johanna and Emilee, she blurted out, "Stephen was murdered by an Islamic terrorist in Rome."

"Murdered?" cried Emilee as Johanna sat there stunned, "I just talked to him a few days ago; he called when Johanna was out and needed the address to ship some packages to our apartment. He wanted to surprise you. The boxes arrived this morning. That's why Johanna did not tell you she was coming home for the Holidays. You know, she would only come home if Stephen was coming back. She did not want to ruin the surprise. He was taking an earlier flight once he found out you were coming to the theater."

"Hayleigh, how was he murdered?

"Johanna it doesn't matter." I said.

Johanna interrupted, "What do you mean; it does not matter Edward; how did he die? Please don't tell me . . . Oh God . . . was he. . . Was he torrr . . .?" I nodded my head. She burst into tears again falling to her knees in front of the sofa hitting repeatedly the cushion. Emilee sat there staring at me with an empty look until she spoke up, "Was he beheaded?"

I nodded again. Emilee rushed away to a corner as Johanna howled in agony. I could hear Emilee gagging in the back-dressing room.

I leaned forward and reached my arms around my little sister hugging her, bringing her close to me. Hayleigh stood above us both leaning down and kissing the top of my head. "It's going to be alright Jo," I whispered as we rocked back and forth, sitting in a make-believe living room; that looked like our childhood home. The memories of me holding her the night our mother died giving birth to Stephen came rushing back.

I repeated just like that night, "Everything's going to be alright." I looked up at Hayleigh as if asking her a question. Her look was the same look she had on her face on the train in my dream when she said, 'we all could be happy again.' I could tell she was worried about me; about us.

Time passed, and her friends were gracious to give us the privacy and space to gather ourselves. Johanna clung to me and asked that I not leave her just yet. We decided to take a cab to her apartment. As we are driving up Broadway, Johanna's phone rings. She sighs and says it's probably Dad again. As she looks at the phone, she can tell it's from overseas. It's probably from Italy, so she asked me to take the call.

"Hello . . . This is her brother Edward. And you are?"

The caller identifies himself as Francesco Paulo Martelli. "Call me Paul, first, Edward, I want to tell you how deeply sorry I am at this unspeakable tragedy. Stephen was a dear friend of mine, and we spent countless hours working together. I feel like I know you and your family. My reason for calling was to express my sympathies and to get your address. Right before the incident, Stephen dropped off a package for you. He was so excited for you to get it. He found out that he could not take it on the plane. It was a gift of all gifts to you. That is why he stopped by to see me on his way to the airport. After this tragedy happened, I feel that I need to get the remainder of his belongings to you quickly. Where should I send them?

After I had given him my address, we arrived at Johanna's apartment where I had started my day. I motioned to the girls to go on into the coffeehouse. Hayleigh was still inquisitive about the conversation, but I waved her to go ahead and that I will be there shortly. Before the call ended I asked him one question, "Were you there when my brother died? I could hear him choke back and clear his throat, "Yes..." He then told me the story.

***

As I walked into to the Sault Saint Marie, Hayleigh called out and motioned me to come into the cafe. Emilee had determined that their apartment above was too small; they had a relationship with the owner that they could use the cafe any time after hours. I plopped down on the chair without saying a word.

Hayleigh could tell by the look on my face that I was in a state of shock. "Honey, how did the call go?" she asked.

"Oh, fine, he expressed his sympathies," I mumbled.

"Edward, that's all you talked about for the last 15 minutes. Who called?"

"Stephen's friend, Father Paulo," I shot back staring into the distant neon flashing light. All I could see flashing was the word Saint pulsating as if to a heartbeat. Lights do that shortly before they burn out.

From the look on Hayleigh's face, I could see she understood that I did not want to talk. It was a look she had seen many times.

That did not stop Johanna. "Did he know how it happened?" she prodded. "Edward! You know something . . . Tell us! I need to know. I am trying to come to grips with this whole thing, and now you are acting like Dad and holding out. I deserve a chance to sort this out too."

I just continued to watch the flashing Saint beating like a heart.

Hayleigh and Emilee, in unison demanded that I share the conversation. Emilee pleaded for her beloved Johanna, "Edward, Jo needs and deserves to know what happened."

"I guess you're right," I said as I looked to Hayleigh for confirmation. I then recounted what miracle of a story he told me.

"His name is Francesco Paulo Martelli, a good friend of Stephens. They had done many missionary and research projects over the last ten years in several countries. They had developed quite a friendship. Stephen called him his Paul. Paulo says that he was the intended victim. Stephen had just dropped a package off to Paul. It was to be my Christmas present, but Stephen had learned that he would not be allowed to carry it on the plane so he asked if Paulo would send it. They joked about my present being the Gift of the Magi. Stephen said his goodbyes. As the cab started to pull away, a stranger wielding a machete from the crowd charged Paulo from behind screaming. Stephen jumped out of the cab and blocked the blade with his hand as it descended towards Paulo's neck."

Continuing, on, "Paulo was still shaken but managed to squirm away. Stephen's hand was nearly severed and bleeding profusely. The animal then turned to Stephen and beheaded our brother before the Gendarmerie could subdue him. I gulped and swallowed my moment of silence."

Hayleigh looked at me intently. She knew me so well; I sometimes felt she could see inside my heart. "There is more Edward, isn't it? Finish the story," she prodded.

"I can't."

"You have to get it out, Edward."

"Paul told me crying, that as the bastard was captured, and his head . . . I can't even say it. As the terrorist was being pressed down on the ground by the Vatican policeman, Stephens' head was in front of the killer, and he could see that Stephen was mouthing the words 'I forgive you.' There was no sound, but Paul says that he could read his lips as Stephen mouthed it the second and last time. He said it happened in slow motion." I started to cry inside me. The sign burned out.

I looked at Hayleigh. "The reason Stephen is dead is that he wanted to get me a stupid Christmas gift," I thought out loud. "The greatest person I have ever known is dead because of me. Where in the hell is God!"

I broke down, ramming my fist and swiping the coffee and spoon from the table in anger. I then buried my head in my arms on the table and wept. Hayleigh, Johanna, and Emilee; all stunned but holding on to each other.

The night ended where it started that morning, but there was now a horizon of pain to sail through; I had no idea how to navigate without my brother. One call changed everything.

Bird Catcher

We can easily forgive a child who is afraid of the dark;

the real tragedy of life

is when men are afraid of the light.

-Plato

We left the Sault Saint Marie late that night. I took the two packages that had arrived earlier, that Stephen had sent ahead. By the time we arrived back at the Sherry-Netherlands Hotel, we were drained. We decided that we would catch a late morning train and have the large box sent by FedEx back to the house. I looked over at Hayleigh, thankful she was here; she was grabbing her forehead tightly. She noticed me staring at her and immediately dropped her hands down.

"You alright?"

"It's nothing, probably just stress; don't you worry Baby," she softly whispered as she walked behind me rubbing my shoulders and neck.

We talked a little about what had happened that day. I was glad I was the one to break the news to Johanna. I would have hated if she was to find out from the news. I was angry that it interrupted what should have been one of her happiest days. Where is God's plan in all of this? The fragile ironic reality of life is that at a time of one's great ecstatic pleasure, great sadness is the other side of the flipped coin. How does a person make their way through life? When on the very same ascent up the mountain, a great joy and a great sadness awaits. At least she could enjoy the moment, but there would be no basking in the afterglow.

Hayleigh bent over and kissed me on the top of my head and announced that she was going to bed. I told her I would be in shortly. I just wanted to be alone a little while.

Hayleigh came around the chair and knelt in front of me as if begging me not to fall further into the abyss of my discontent. She knew how far I had already fallen; and that I was barely hanging on to her lifeline.

"Edward, promise me you will not climb this mountain alone, I can't bear to lose any more of you."

"Honey, I don't even know what I've lost; I don't even know who I am. Stephen was the one person I could maybe someday become; he was the light that somehow flickered deep inside of me. God, I miss him already; and it has not been twenty-four hours." Looking in Hayleigh's eyes, I could see her disappointment.

"Hayleigh, this has nothing to do with us, with you. My God, I love you more than anything, but you can't give me what I must find. Stephen had it and always told me that he sees it in me. But it's gone. He is gone. Does that mean it's lost? Maybe I lost my chance at true happiness and redemption?"

Hayleigh, stood up cupping my cheeks with both her hands, "Maybe you can find happiness if you can let go of what was supposed to make you happy," as she gently kissed me. She could always bring me a glimmer, a shimmering that gave me hope. I was truly blessed.

"Hayleigh, how in the world do you love me?" I asked.

"I liked your butt," she said with a wry smile taking my hand and leading me into the bedroom. As we laid together on the bed, Hayleigh said, "Eddie, you are going to get through this, your journey is starting; I don't know why I feel this way, but Stephen's death will help guide you." We both fell asleep in each other's arms.

***

My eyes caught the light penetrating the dark drapes in the bedroom. The rumbling storm had lifted, and I could feel the dull vibrations. Suddenly I realized it was not the distant thunder, but my phone in the other room. The sound stopped. The groggy fog of my soul lifted. Dragging myself out to see who was calling; I saw three missed calls from Johanna.

I called her back, and it did not even get through the first ring before she shouted, "There are reporters and TV cameras everywhere!"

"What are you talking about Johanna."

"Edward, there are cameras everywhere. I have to get into the theater to get the stage ready."

"Well just ignore them and get into the cab and go," I replied. "How in the hell did they find you? I questioned. "Just ignore them, Johanna."

"Edward, it's a little bit more complicated than that," she indignantly responded.

"Johanna, don't you think you are over-reacting?"

I could hear Johanna was getting irritated. "Have you seen the news? Our father is all over the television telling everyone about his faith, church, and how strong he remains because of it. How do you think it's going to look while I'm interviewed as I leave with my lesbian lover? Dad will be so furious he won't even allow me near Stephen's funeral."

"Do you have a fire escape?"

"Don't be an ass Edward."

"I'm not kidding Johanna; call a cab and have them meet you in the back alley and you and Emilee are off to the theater." I heard a click, and the call went dead.

Hayleigh came out of the room looking out the window and asked who I was talking to, then exclaimed, "What in the hell?"

I rushed over to the window and below were cameras and reporters. I called down to the concierge, and they were apologetic, and they assured me they had not revealed that I was staying there. I asked them to secure car service to Penn Station and to have them meet me in the back-kitchen entrance of the restaurant. They were very helpful and agreed to send a staff person to escort us to the kitchen using the freight elevator. I told them we would be ready to go in about an hour.

I turned on the television, and of course, Stephen's death was still the breaking news story for all the networks. We quickly packed as I grabbed Stephens small package. The concierge was on time waiting to escort us through the kitchen. We donned our sunglasses and were whisked away like we were some famous celebrities.

A nondescript black car was waiting in the alley. Making a quick right turn, I could see the crowd of cameras with their backs to us waiting to pounce on their victims with stupid questions.

***

Penn Station was a zoo. Rushing down the steps toward the train platform, we barely made it on time. Making our way toward the back as the train started to leave; we looked for two seats together. The clanging metal chained sounds brought back the haunting nightmare of my dream. I could feel my heart racing, and I was sweating as I struggled with my baggage dragging behind me. Finally, Hayleigh spotted two seats in the back, and I was relieved to sit down and calm my heavy breathing. We sat in front of the door, and it was broken leaving it slightly ajar. Allowing the constant sounds to ring in my head.

After taking a deep breath, I turned toward Hayleigh; she still had her sunglasses on. I asked her to take them off. She inquired why. I gave her some romantic, silly answer that I loved how her eyes looked and I wanted to see them. She gave me a doubting quirky smile and removed them. I could not let her know that it reminded me of her in my dream when she was so unhappy. The memory of the look on her face when she asked 'we could be happy again,' I could not bear. I thought could we be happy again? Could I be happy? I just stared blankly forward.

Click, click, click, the sound startled me as the Amtrak conductor asked, "Where are you going?"

My mind had been drifting in and out of the events that had happened, my dream, and the dreading of going through the funeral process with my father. The question had not clearly registered with me as I blurted out, "Home . . . I'm going home."

"Sir, where is your destination?" As he clicked, clicked, to try and snap me out of my foggy haze.

"Oh . . . Ah Baltimore," I embarrassingly answered as if I was a complete idiot while Hayleigh laughed silently into her hand. I gave him my ticket, and he clicked it and moved on. Stopping to triple-click again in my ear as if to wake me up.

"Are you okay Edward?"

"Yea I was just in a daze thinking. He caught me off guard," I explained. "I was thinking about Stephen when he asked me where I was going; the first thought was I was going home. Then it threw me; he said he needed my destination. That's a troubling question at a time like this. Where am, I heading Hayleigh? I love our home, but is that where we are heading? Stephen found his home, but it was not a place. Stephen never had a destination, and he was the happiest person I have ever known."

"You think too much Edward," Hayleigh spoke, "You think way too much."

Not much was said as we processed the last twenty-four hours and the future anguish that awaited the next few days. Hayleigh was worrying about the arrangements that I am sure would fall on her, along with whether I could recover out of this malaise I was teetering on for the last several years.

Then about the time we were passing Trenton New Jersey, I decided to open Stephen's package. I had been staring at it the entire trip running my fingers over his name. I wondered what went through his mind, not knowing that this package would be one of the last things he did on this earth. Running my keys through the packing tape, Hayleigh put her hand on my hand as if to stop me; asking if I was sure I wanted to do this now. Ignoring her, I continued ripping the sides of the box and saw that the box contained mostly letters, and photos. I spotted a full journal. It was his journal. Stephen always kept two journals; one was personal the other was his work. This was his personal journal. He always said that a person could convince himself of anything when it was speech or thoughts, but when you wrote it down in front of your eyes and soul, there was no lying to yourself. Your words and thoughts were staring right back at you. I never started a journal, but it was always one of the things I wanted to do. It's how most people live their lives as an accumulation of things not done.

There I was holding the thoughts of my beautiful brother in my hand. I opened the first page. It had one entry.

April 18

Just discovered the music of Dylan.

For an old guy, he speaks to my heart.

One song shreds me - It's Alright Ma, I'm Only Bleeding.

My first thought was that Dylan is Stephen's kind of songwriter. Always busy changing, always living. Thumbing through some other pages of writings and photos along with sketches; about three quarters through the journal I saw his last entry written on the day he died.

November 22

I can't wait to surprise Edward with my news and be with him during the Holidays

I am about to give him a gift of what he was looking for his whole life.

I pray that he takes this journey with me.

After this time of my Great Wanting I turn to Edward.

My eyes started welling up as I thought about this gift that cost my brother his life. My mind was racing with thoughts pouring in about this gift. The gift I was looking for my entire life; what could it be? I noticed a photo sticking out behind the page of his last journal entry. I pulled it out. I gasped and grabbed my reading glasses that were on my nose putting them tighter to my eyes to make sure I was seeing what I thought I was seeing. I had a hard time breathing. I dropped my hand down so that I could not see the photo any longer. The intensity of the feeling was too much to take.

Hayleigh looked over at me, "Edward, you look like you have seen a ghost?" she inquired. I simply handed her the photo without saying anything. "Aww ... that's a good picture; that's how I want to remember Stephen," she continued, "He is happily waving hi to us."

"He's not waving hi to us; Stephen is waving goodbye."

"What do you mean Edward."

I then proceeded to tell Hayleigh about the dream. She knew I had this recurring dream before, but never did anyone die.

"This photo is the exact place where Stephen dies in the landslide of my dream," I exclaimed, "It's the same look on his face and the same clothes. I thought he was waving me to come, but he was saying goodbye. Hayleigh, when I was dreaming the other night, Stephen was already dead. Was he reaching out to me?" I started thinking; what did he mean? What was he trying to communicate? What is this gift of all gifts he had for me? Maybe, I thought, this life has a purpose.

I was confused, yet I could breathe for the first time in the last 24 hours. Maybe Hayleigh was right; Stephen's death may help guide me on my journey. It certainly appears that he is trying to teach me something.

***

Driving from the train station to home takes about an hour, but like many times you drive almost in your sleep, and when you've arrived, you can't remember how you got there. I was startled when I turned onto Hep Road which leads to our home located in a little village called Woodstock. We had a family farm that my father bought when he was a famous surgeon. Stephen was not yet born, but my Mom, Mary Elizabeth, fell in love with the place and needed the serene peace and beauty that the farm brought while my father was globe-trotting around the world as the medical celebrity. It was a fun place to grow up. Most of the land was leased out, but we still had nearly 100 acres of forest and streams to play while growing up. After Mom died giving birth to Stephen, my father never returned to the place my Mom loved.

Immediately after Mom's death, we moved into a villa and lived there alone with my father, along with various Au Pairs from foreign countries whom my father always sought to convert, and the periodic monthly visit from my favorite lady, Grandma Abba. She was a wise woman, a philosophy professor, who had traveled and experienced more of life than most people. I think she visited us often because she did not trust how my father would raise us. She felt compelled to round out our performance-driven father with a spiritual awareness and an emotionally enriched life.

Grandma Abba was close with my mother and took on that role for me. She became my Mom; and while I missed my mother, I could not have asked for a better, more loving confidant in my life.

She did not connect with Johanna in the same way; I guess losing a mom is harder on a girl. Johanna wanted to connect with her father; she could never quite get what she was looking for from him. He could not give her what she needed.

Stephen benefited from Grandma Abba the most. Since he never knew Mom, he was influenced greatly by her. He was the male version of her.

Later we returned to the farm, but the haunting memory and spirit of my mother, Mary Elizabeth, was too much for my father, and grossly unfair to his new wife Martha to overcome. My dad wanted to keep the farm in the family. I was finishing up my studies and had decided that I wanted no part of my father's world, so I went into DNA research of the heart as my specialty. He knew I would not make a lot of money, so he offered to let me live there and pay him over time. I took him up on the offer so I could hold onto the memory of my Mom and a life that I thought I was going to live.

Hayleigh and I married and moved in and started our life in Eden. Eden is what my Mom named the farm. I did not get the connection, but Grandma Abba says it was because of the Bible and a Joni Mitchell song. She wanted to get back to her personal garden.

Turning into the long driveway toward the house, passing the Eden sign, which badly needed painting and the letter E was upside down, barely hanging on, I could spot Martha walking down the porch stairs toward the car with her planning book in hand. Instead of stopping in front of the house where I usually park, I pulled around to the back of the rear building we use as a garage. She came high-stepping around the corner chasing me. Hayleigh following close behind in the other car nearly ran her down.

As I exited the car, she was right there with her checklist. She started right in with the coming day's logistics which made we wish that we stayed in New York with the reporters, but I knew she meant well.

"Edward, I have some things we need to go over to help things run smoothly," she barked out like a school teacher talking to children.

"Martha, I just spent 3 hours on a train, one hour in a car coming back after hearing my brother was murdered; can I have a little space to gather myself?" I shot back.

"We all are recovering from hearing about the death of Stephen; I'm just trying to help your father; he is taking this hard."

"Stephen was murdered, killed by a savage animal Martha! He just didn't die. . . Look I'm sorry; I know you are trying to help, I just need a little space," I blasted out at her. Immediately Hayleigh came to my rescue and took over the conversation leading her away toward the house while I retrieved the luggage.

As I was bringing the luggage through the back door, Martha was leaving and yelling some last-minute instructions back at Hayleigh. In the twinkling of an eye, she was gone, and the silence was golden. Hayleigh started to inform me when I motioned for her to wait a bit so I could find Grandma Abba.

She always required that you address her as Grandma Abba, not Grandma, not Granny, and never, never Abba. She felt that she had a position in the family, and her status required a formal name that was respectful of that role. Just as I had motioned, there she was smiling, but with tears in her eyes, right in front of me.

She lifted her hands upward as usual, and I gave her a big hug as she whispered, "Stephen is dead, but not gone, Eddie; not gone."

"I know Grandma Abba, I know," I said back to her. Her eyes looked surprised, and she smiled. Let me get this luggage upstairs, and then we need to take one of our love-walks. Over the years we developed a habit of taking hikes and walks when I needed to sort things out. Love-walks happened a lot after Mom passed away. The years poured out, and I got older. Our love-walks happened less because I got lost in life. Hayleigh and I did this practice early on in our marriage; but kids, career, and time ate away at our intimacy. I could tell Hayleigh wanted to go by the yearning look in her eyes, but she intuitively knew I needed the insight of Grandma Abba.

I dropped the luggage on the bed and changed into a sweater and jeans grabbing my tan beat up jacket with the leather trim that Hayleigh hated, and I loved. I walked out and spotted Grandma Abba waiting on the front porch dressed in a southwestern hooded poncho that made her timeless. She had an eclectic style that denied her age.

"Have a good love-walk, you owe me one," she quipped, as she sipped her coffee. "We need to talk about the logistics. Martha gave me the instructions; you have a major part," she futilely tried to explain as I was walking out toward the porch. I stopped and stared back. She shrugged her shoulders as if it was the norm. It was. My father was behind the scenes orchestrating everything.

I let the door slam and grabbed Grandma Abba's hand and said, "Let's go; what path do you want to take?" She answered, "I want to take the path you choose."

"I want to go down to the lake," which was my favorite place and I had fond memories of talking, but mainly listening to my Grandma Abba reveal truths about life, God, and mainly how to navigate my father.

It was a windy but clear day. The kind of day I loved to go for walks. Grandma Abba knew where to go before starting out on our love-walk. We had to stop at the oak tree that she called The Mary Tree, about 50 yards away from the house. It was a beautiful old oak that was split about twenty feet up. It happened the day my mother died. We are not sure how it happened, but since my father never returned for a few years, it was never cut down. My Grandma Abba would always stay here at Eden when she visited. She was sure it was dead, but the next spring it bloomed. From that day on she named it The Mary Tree. She said it was her sign that Mary Elizabeth was living. I guess that's why I feel compelled to stop off periodically and just think. I feel a spirit there. What I like most are the acorns. Don't ask me why, but I love holding them in my hand on walks. I usually have them in a coat pocket and have been known to roll them in my hand during meetings, or whenever I am thinking. Maybe I feel close to my mom. Hayleigh one Christmas, bought me a gift of sterling silver acorns for me to roll in my hands. It was never the same, and they ended up at the bottom of my sock drawer before New Year's Eve.

After selecting my acorns, we started our love-walk. "Has anyone told you the plans yet?" She asked me.

"No, Hayleigh intercepted Martha for me, so I was spared the details, we are going to talk when I get back," I answered over the crunching leaves on the path. "So tell me, how he is controlling the event."

Martha had filled Grandma Abba in while she awaited our arrival; my father had decided that there would be a small intimate funeral for family and close friends only because Thanksgiving was right around the corner. The body would arrive in two days. So, the small funeral will be held Wednesday the day before Thanksgiving.

Grandma Abba then surprises me as she balances her way through the worn path, "You know your father wants you to do the eulogy."

"I can't do the eulogy!" I exclaimed, "Hell I don't even believe what he believes . . . I don't even know what I believe . . . Has he lost his mind?"

She turns and stops me softly saying, "He does not know what you believe, but he has a tremendous amount of faith in you Edward."

"Well, he sure has a funny way of showing it."

Grandma Abba mused continuing our trek, "You were my first grandchild. You had a beautiful soul, much like my son James. James had a hard time with his father also. He could never cope with the legalistic lifestyle of a respected judge. My husband, your grandfather, was a good man but quite narrow in his view of life. Your father fit in very well. He was not the creative type like his brother James. Your uncle died of an overdose, due to his inability to live the life that would be validated by the man he admired and loved. Joshua was emotionally devastated. Your granddad, after much agony and reflection, would not allow your father to go into the practice of law. He told him it stymies personal growth because one is trained to live in a narrowly defined box. In his later years, he became more disenchanted with the practice of law, because the narrow box produced lawyers, who to be creative, were forced find loopholes to evade the common good. That became the practice of law, finding loopholes. He died of a heart attack, which I believe was caused by a broken heart after losing James. Your father decided to go into cardiology. Your father was much like his father and made huge demands on his children. After the death of to your Mom, it was my calling to make sure the same thing would not happen to my grandchildren."

Taking another breather while she caught her breath.

"What does that have to do with my father controlling everything and asking me to do a eulogy, about something I have my doubts about," I asked. "I can't talk about something that I don't know for sure is true."

"Of course you can Eddie, people do it every day, at least the people who are happy," she chuckled. "What are you sure of Edward?" she softly asked me.

I was not sure of anything, and the question left me puzzled. I just continued walking in silence, trudging through the leaves crunching beneath my feet. After about a hundred steps, I volunteered, "Hayleigh, I'm sure of Hayleigh . . . Grandma Abba, yea, . . . I'm sure about Hayleigh."

"Are you positive Edward?" as she stopped and looked up at me; "That's not a good thing," she shook her head while cupping her chin with her wrinkled hand.

"Why do you say that? I questioned with a look of surprise.

"Edward, we take for granted the things that we are certain. The things we are certain, start to die the minute we cement them in our minds and heart. Take for example an artist who paints a sunset. Every stroke the brush takes brings a feeling of ecstasy as the artist creates his masterpiece. The true artist will never think it the best sunset ever because upon that simple declaration; he will no longer be able to experience the painting of another sunset, or worse; the artist lives in agony, futilely trying to repeat or better the experience. As a painter of sunsets, he starts to die. For a short while, the artist can bask in the glow of his masterpiece, but eventually, the afterglow flickers out and dies like the paint that was formerly alive with different possibilities of colors. Human beings are God's creations made in the very image of the creator. They are His canvas and likewise the creators of their own canvas, their life. It's a beautiful precious gift, Edward. God never stops creating. He makes all things new. Why would you stop creating? It's what you were made to do."

Relationships are much the same Edward, the second you decide that Hayleigh is the one thing that is true, you have frozen her in time, you have killed what she could become to you. You will eventually take her for granted, and one day, if you are lucky, you may be able to start it all over again."

"Grandma Abba, I think I'm already there," I uttered remembering Hayleigh's plea in my dream. "Can I start over?"

"Edward, you can always start over. You start over every day of your journey. That's what is meant by being present. Jesus said it this way; 'give us this day.' However, there is a way of starting over that is better than hitting a reset button. That's what most people do. They will have babies, get new houses, cars, and jobs attempting a lesser new reset journey. Ignoring everything that has happened and revealed along their path; they opt for their controlled orchestrated trail that is wide and trampled by many before them. They repeat this time and time again. It works for a short while. The journey seems exciting and new again. The couple declares it true and good; then it starts to die."

I look puzzled, and she responds, "It dies because they have cemented the relationship and their lives on the terms they have negotiated and understand at a single point in time. Later, when the journey reveals something new and unexpected along the path, they respond in a manner that fits their frozen version of the truth that they created. They refuse to change, to grow. They are not courageous enough to live presently in faith but have relied on the things they have negotiated as truth. Life's journey is being created new every day. Your unwillingness to accept what it must reveal is a lack of faith."

"You see Edward; it takes faith to love someone. The minute you think you know the person truly, there is no need for faith. Loving a person deeply requires each one to work at building their love along an uncharted path. Each turn has the chance to reveal something new about each other as you both grow, creating a freshness. It takes faith because when challenges along the path are uncovered, the other mate grows and becomes a new person. Faith requires the other to grow also. Sometimes the newness revealed is positive and sometimes negative. That is why it will demand trust to continue. How can you cement the truth about a person when the journey always presents something new, something neither has ever faced? How can you be so sure? But if you love one another, you will accept life, your journey, as a mystery and embrace it. Having faith in a person does not mean you know them thoroughly, it means you trust them. You trust where they are going and who they are. You don't know exactly how they will turn out. But your love tells you to trust. A relationship with God is the same way."

"Tell me then the better way to start over."

Grandma Abba continued walking ahead and waited for a while as if letting what she had just said ferment. "Eddie, Eddie, my beautiful mind Eddie, always looking for the way, having to know everything. Even as a child you would not attempt new things unless you knew everything about it."

She stopped and asked me looking directly at me, "Do you remember when I gave you your first keyboard for Christmas one year. I loved the excited gleefulness in your laughter when you opened it. You were giddy. You would not even take it out of the box until you took lessons. You never turned it on until you understood everything. I can't tell you the way Edward, but I can tell you something about taking a journey and understanding the way."

"Tell me Grandma Abba, tell me."

"The better way to start one's journey over; is to accept the original journey you were once on from the time of your childhood. When you were young, and your heart was pure. You had visions of how your life would be. A person who has journeyed well continues to dream and follow those visions. The dreams change but remain true to the visions. The child has visions of being a hero or a princess worth rescuing. The dreams of the adult hopefully play out true to their vision."

I earnestly countered, "Grandma Abba," sighing, "It seems rather childish to continue to follow visions; after life comes along, grades have to be achieved, marriage, children, bills, and jobs." Pausing, then shaking my head, "God and death," I questioned throwing up my hands. Toss in God, His will, His rules, and His burdens; your vision does not stand a chance."

"Now we are getting somewhere Edward," she mused. You speak with disdain of education, love, children, money, and vocations. Let's take my artist analogy further. You talk as if they are merely the paint. Grandson, they are the colors that will make your canvas a work of art. These things are more than the paint you see them as. Everyone gets the primary colors on their palette Edward; it's the combination of seeing the colors and how we see the world that creates the beauty on the canvas of our lives. The artist first places the color on the canvas and decides that it is not right; so, he adds a little more umber, and a dollop of burnt sienna and then the path is just the right color. The artist vision decides that the sky needs a hint more of cyan and magenta and the beauty leaps off the canvas. Being true to his vision he sees what is truly there. Edward, these mundane things of life are not paint, they are the colors that will reveal your journey and place your life in the proper context.

Just then we came upon the path that I forgot. It was a rocky path down toward the river. Grandma Abba would never be able to navigate her way down the rocks; it was way too steep for her frail body to traverse. She looked down at the water then looked up at me. "I use to carry you when you were a young boy; now you must carry me along the path," she said.

"You trust me?" I replied.

"Always have," she said as we stepped and stretched from boulder to rock to boulder on the way down. It was like an amusement ride to her.

I was slightly out of breath but marveled at her willingness to trust me down the rocky path. We sat on the edge of a rock that we had sat many times while visiting the river.

"Let's get back to the journey Edward," she continued. "You mentioned God and death in the same breath; as if they were an impediment along the journey. Edward, you could not be further from the truth.

God is like the brush in the painter's hands as if they are one. The brush can create infinite forms of beauty, by mixing the colors, strokes, and techniques. The brush, like God, does not violate the artist vision of creation. However, if the artist opens his eyes, and is present, he will be astonished at the periodic intrusions of a natural brush stroke that astounds the artist with something new to his vision. That is the miracle Edward!" she laughed like a little girl. "God appears as a twinkling of an eye ever so often."

"Death, Edward," she continued like Gandalf. "Death allows us to see the importance of every color of the journey because the colors indeed fade over time in this world. Cherish them. Every color Edward is a step along every good journey," she folded her hands as if to say I am now finished.

I sat there taking it in; as if hearing the truth, but not quite knowing what to do with it. "So you think I'm not allowing God, the brush, to help me paint my journey?" I asked.

"You really try my patience Edward!" she stated loudly and emphatically. "What am I going to do with you? You're not even on the journey. You're studying the paint!"

I just sat there in shock at what she just said looking at her; I could see the hurt in her eyes; she probably saw the puzzlement and frustration in mine.

"Jeez Grandma Abba, I had no idea you thought so highly of me," I satirically stated with a sideway glancing grin. But I knew she was right.

She then asked me to follow her over to a log that had fallen across a small pool of water; when she spoke, "This is the spot where I last saw your mother alive. She would give birth to Stephen within the week. She lamented that your dad, a good man, was killing your vision. She told me that Eddie must be free to think, create, and explore and your father shunned this for a life of accomplishments and performance. She felt this burden could be too much for a young heart to overcome. What your father never understood, is that what he loved most about her was her unbridled love and freedom to live her own life. He loved her colors and viewed her like paint."

She motioned me to follow her as she proceeded to slide and shuffle her feet across the fallen tree to the other side. "Don't do that Grandma Abba!" I quietly gasped as I tilted my head back and forth as if balancing her body. I was afraid she would slip and fall. I didn't want to do it, but she beckoned me to follow. I stepped onto the fallen tree.

At the other side, she quipped, "See Edward, you would have never done that on your own, but the journey revealed the opportunity." We sat on the log on the other side and had one last chat.

"After Mary's death, you, like your father; wanted answers. He found them in a religious palette with very little colors. You, who had so many visionary colors inside you, could not see the canvas your father painted for you. You doubted his God because you only looked at your father's limited colors. His canvas did not answer why your mother died, and today still cannot answer your Stephen question. But that does not negate his faith, Edward. He has more faith than you, because he sees less on his journey, his painting, and still, loves God. You see more and are patiently waiting to study the paint; never fully taking the journey. You can't quite believe in God because you will not take the journey to discover him. God is the journey. Edward, when are you going to pick up the brush?"

I cleared my throat like I always do when I'm uncomfortable, "This God thing has stymied me for most of my life. You use to tell me a story once that has haunted me. Stephen loved it. It was his favorite story you told; the one about the Bird Catcher. I feel like that bird, and my father is the Bird Catcher. I have never quite shaken it.

"Yes, I remember," she bemoaned, "I had no idea it troubled you. I never actually finished the fable, Edward, because I was not sure how it should end. I think I know how it ends now."

"Can you tell it one more time?" I asked, "Maybe a fifty-five-year-old can get it."

She started the story as usual:

"There once was a good man named Papam that loved birds so much, that to protect them; he took the beautiful winged creatures from the time of their hatching and placed them in a large protective square cage away from danger. He was known as the Bird Catcher. Papam draped a large black sackcloth over the three sides so that the birds were only facing one direction toward the wall because everything else was dark. Their only source of light came from a fireplace behind them that reflected off the wall and dimly into the cage. Papam would sit for warmth in front of the fire and speak to the birds about how much he loved and protected them. Papam could hear the birds flying aimlessly around inside the cage. He would tell them to stop so that they do not hurt their little wings and get frustrated. The birds listened and heard Papam and thought that the flat, dull lit surface of the wall was the light of the world. The little winged creatures were never allowed to fly from the cage. Their lives consisted of continuously gazing at the wall in front of them and periodically hearing the words of Papam. It was so dark inside that they could not see clearly each other, or themselves. Papam assured them that they should be grateful for his protection and love. There were many rows of birds."

"Sometimes, Papam's friends and the objects they carried walked between the fireplace and the tiny fowl; shadows were cast on the wall much like a shadow puppet show that a child would enjoy. The little winged animals could not see any of this behind them and are only able to see the shadows cast upon the wall in front of them. This was the world they lived and watched. The sounds of the world echo off the shadowed wall, and the tiny captive birds falsely believe these sounds come from the shadows."

"The shadows become a reality for the tiny feathered flock because they have never seen anything else. The creatures do not realize that what they see are shadows of objects in front of a fire. The shadows are merely a substitute for the real living things outside the cage. Some birds think that there is more. Some feel that they were meant to fly free. One of those birds was named Cleopas."

One day Papam accidentally left the cage door slightly ajar. Cleopas, the caged bird, is freed from the metal bars that hold him captive. The others heed the warnings of Papam and remain in captivity. After flying out from the open cage door, Cleopas sees the fire roaring in the fireplace. The light hurts his eyes and makes it hard for him to see the people and objects that are casting the shadows. All he can see is the roaring light of the fire. His eyes have not adjusted; it is frightening to him. If he sees that the figures on the wall are not reality, but that the people and objects are the real world, his truth would be shattered."

In Cleopas' distress, the freed bird desires to turn away and fly back to what he can see and is accustomed; his life of shadows. He has a decision to make. He can return to the cage where the light never showed brightly, but it was the world he knew. Or he could fly free into the new unknown reality and be free."

This is when Grandma Abba would ask us kids how the story would end. It was always some version of a happy ending. Today she told me how the story ends.

Grandma Abba continued, "Or suppose...that something should pull him...by force from within, out into the light of the sun. The freed Cleopas would be distressed and in pain, and this would only worsen when the radiant light of the sun overwhelms his eyes and blinds him. The sunlight reveals the new reality and knowledge that the freed bird is experiencing. Slowly, the eyes of Cleopas adjust to the light of the sun. First, he can only see shadows.

Gradually he can see the reflections of the world and the reality that has always been. Eventually, he can look at the stars and the moon at night until finally he can look upon the sun itself and is he able to see and reason about reality and what it is. What he felt in his heart was real."

Grandma Abba continues saying, "Cleopas would think that the real world was superior to the world he experienced in the cage; he would bless himself for the change, and pity the other imprisoned winged fowl and would want to bring his fellow cage dwellers out of bondage and into the light."

"One day, Cleopas returns. The returning winged creature, whose eyes have become acclimated to the light of the sun, would be blind because of the darkness when he re-enters the cage; just as he was when he was first exposed to the sun. The captive flock would infer from the returning freed Cleopas' blindness that the journey out of the cage had harmed him. They would never undertake a similar journey. The captive birds decided that they would silence anyone who spoke of another reality. Cleopas, brokenhearted, still could no longer see in his old world. He was given a choice to remain in their known world of shadow reality created by the loved Papam, or fly free into the unknown. Cleopas remembered what he had seen in the new reality and burst out the cage in joyous flight never to return. Papam discovered the open door and closed it. The remaining birds took their place, gazing at the wall, comfortably numb in their world.

I just sat there in thought. I've never decided on my reality, my journey. I have been gazing at a wall of my personal knowledge my whole life. I've been stumbling through life in the darkness like a blind man.

Just then Hayleigh appeared on the other side of the fallen tree. She shouted, "I knew I'd find you two here; dinner is almost ready. Edward, Martha called for your Dad, he wants to know if you will perform the Eulogy. I told her that I did not think you would but that I would ask you."

I looked over at Grandma Abba and stared into her eyes chuckling, "Tell Martha I will do it," I shouted as we both smiled.

"What did you say?" she exclaimed cupping both her hands around her ears. Grandma Abba smiled. "You heard me," I shouted back. Hayleigh walked away shaking her head. She had no idea I was about to start my journey.

REVEALED

I am no longer afraid of becoming lost,
because the journey back always reveals something new,
and that is ultimately good for the artist.

-Billy Joel

Grieving has a rhythm. It is like breathing. At the time of loss, you battle for air and fight the suffocating, claustrophobic pain. Each gasp taken in rushes in the memories needed for your soul's letting loose. The large gasp of air breathed in is released with a little slow soothing exhale. The precious past moments stored in the hearts embrace. The embracing brings life to the departed and you as well. Time passes, the rhythm becomes balanced, and the memories are a salve to your soul. They come to you like oxygen. It sustains your inner life. You inhale and then exhale. Breathing in the memories and moments are what is needed to sustain the part of you that is dying. Another person's life continues a part of you. It's a beautiful thing.

Dinner was good tonight despite my lack of appetite; my mind quieted. I decided to get away by retreating to my office, a sanctuary located in the corner of the house with large windows giving me a panoramic view of the property and the long driveway. There were spaces of time that passed when I felt as if nothing had ever happened to Stephen, then the long still silent moments that lasted for minutes that seemed like hours swung back and forth like a pendulum between joy and devastation; as fond memories fought for space with the helpless visions of his tragic death.

I had placed a call to Tommy after my walk with Grandma Abba, and he responded with a text saying he would be arriving at Eden later that night. I was glad to hear that Maggie was stopping by with the grandkids, Aidan and Eden. I needed the diversion.

Maggie was a single mom working as a music teacher and part-time voice coach who stopped singing long ago. Maggie's real name was Margaret, born on the Fourth of July. The hit song that year was Willie Nelson's Always on My Mind; little did I know that would be the theme of my relationship with my first born beautiful daughter Margaret Marybeth Mayus. The lyrics haunt me to this day; the little things I could have said and done.

Maggie was a beautiful girl growing up, always battling with being a little plump; she was full of life. She had a beautiful voice beyond her years. My fondest memories are of her singing Oh Holy Night on Christmas Eve every year for the family. It was as if we were on the hillsides of Bethlehem listening to the angels. These times always gave me a glimpse that God was with us. By Christmas night, after the shredding of wrapped presents was over; so was that feeling. My Dad was boastful of her when she sang during church services. Everyone was mesmerized by her voice and her eyes; they pierced inside your soul welcoming you into her gift. Dad used to call her my little Christian Star.

Then the music stopped. It was the Christmas season in 1994. Margaret was twelve years old and had always been one of the lead vocalists in the children's cantata. The final song was to be sung by Mary, the mother of Jesus. Everyone assumed the part of Mary would be played as usual by Margaret, but they changed the arrangement so that another girl could sing the part. She did an excellent job, and Margaret seemed fine with the idea.

Margaret was given the encore solo to close the night. It was a new song that year called I Hope It Finds You Too. She sang it beautifully, but at the very end, her voice trailed off into a whisper of softly spoken tears.

"My soul told me once before, to search my dreams and look no more, and then my heart will find Christmas," the last verse was barely audible and slow "I hope it finds," an unintentional long pause, "you too," as she ran off the stage sobbing.

Hayleigh and I both left our seat quickly to find her backstage, but she was nowhere in sight. We searched every room, and I only found her coat. We were concerned that she was trying to walk home, which was too far and too cold for her to even try. I was starting to worry now. I stepped outside, and I spotted a shadowy figure in our car. I walked over, and I heard the doors lock.

Margaret, "Let me in, I asked. I then pushed the key fob opening the door and slid in the back seat. She was still whimpering as she sniffed back her emotions. I immediately went into my inherited dad-fix-it mode.

I remember saying to her, "Margaret, you need to look at this as a life learning lesson; you can't always get what you want. Sometimes life is not fair, but this will make you stronger in the long run," as I reached out to pull her closer as if like Solomon, I solved her personal crisis. Feeling good about myself; she pulled away.

"Let's go home Dad," she said.

About that time my Dad appeared tapping on the window, "You did great Margaret," he said praisingly to her. She turned away, and I got out of the car moving him away. He assured me that she would outgrow this and go on to be an inspiration to the world. I remember thinking what an odd thought. His granddaughter is crying in humiliation, and he is worried about her inspiring the world.

That night as we pulled into the driveway, Margaret bolted out of the car and ran into the house. Hayleigh knew something else was wrong, but we gave her space. Later she came down to have a few Christmas cookies to take back upstairs. Hayleigh asked her what was going on and why did she get so upset. Her answer shocked us.

"God does not like fat people!" she calmly stated then started to cry.

Hayleigh inquired calmly, "How did you arrive at this preposterous idea?"

She then recounted an earlier conversation at the beginning of Advent that she overheard between Timothy Sludge, the Executive Pastor; Caine Banks, Ruling Elder, and my Dad. They were discussing the Christmas Pageant. The Music Director had requested that Margaret not play the part of Mary because she did not fit the mold. People had grown to expect Mary to look a certain way. Timothy Sludge told my father, "Margaret was not the person to play the part of Mary."

The Music Director conceded that Margaret had the stronger voice, but not the look when he conveyed, "The people are not expecting to see Mama Cass as Mary!" My Dad chuckled along with Sludge. Margaret did not even know who Mama Cass was until she googled her that night and was mortified with humiliation.

Hayleigh ran over to hug her as Margaret broke down and sobbed, slouched down sitting on the kitchen floor. Hayleigh smothered her with love and tears as she sat and leaned into her wounded soul, not being able to stop the bleeding of the dreams and identity pouring out of a twelve-year-old girl. Hayleigh looked up at me to hear me say something. I was so furious with my father that I felt paralyzed. Margaret gazed up peeking from behind the shoulder of Hayleigh, her eyes reaching through the tears, pleading for me to rescue her from this dying.

"Grandpa is an asshole; he didn't mean what he said," I blurted as I stormed out.

The little things I could have said and done, I just never had the time.

Margaret did not sing that Christmas Eve; it was the worse holiday of my life. The Christmas season has never been the same since. I regret that night. My little girl was hurting, and I am so consumed with my anger over a father, a God, and religion; that I could not be there in her greatest time of need. The crisis was a watershed moment for Margaret that I, nor Hayleigh saw. Margaret started high school and refused to be in anything musically, starved herself, lost weight, became popular, and she became Maggie to all her friends and eventually her family. I miss Margaret.

***

Maggie had been a big help contacting all the friends and relatives and was working with Martha ironing out the details of the next few days. She came rolling through the door like a whirlwind with kids trailing right behind. Her eyes are obviously swollen due to crying.

She dropped her bag and phone on the foyer table and directly marched toward me, "Oh Daddy, why? Why?" as she pleaded for an answer that long ago, resignedly, she knew was never going to come. I just stood there with my Maggie, hugging her and sharing a cry I knew should have been with Margaret years ago. "Dad, God's going to see us through this, I just know he is." I knew by the look in her eyes that she was fearful of losing me into a deeper abyss as was Hayleigh back in New York. Maggie and her mother talked often, and I know my angst had been topics for the last several years as I looked for answers that never came. Hayleigh walked over and embraced us both until Maggie turned to her releasing me of the burden to produce strength and direction into a situation that I was rudderless.

Maggie and Hayleigh went into the kitchen where Grandma Abba was waiting. I sat back down in my chair with my glass of wine and started looking over Stephen's journal. Aidan was still in my office. He loved looking at the books and marveled at my telescope I always had focused on something in the universe.

I was holding the picture of Stephen in my hand when he said, "That's the picture they are showing on television of Uncle Stephen. It was God's plan to take him."

"Who told you that?" I loudly and abruptly asked in a stern voice as he raced out of my office toward the kitchen. "Who told you that?"

I could hear in the kitchen Hayleigh challenging me, "Edward!"

I sank back into my chair. Was it God's plan? If this is God's plan, then I'm beyond anger. It was something religions say whenever anything goes wrong, and nothing makes sense. When something goes well suddenly, it's a blessing that somehow you earned for being a certain way or reaching an arbitrary standard of whoever was the 'grand interpreter' of God. For me and others, it was always my father and his take on Christianity and the theologians that have gone before. I likened it to the parent that always answers every child's questioning with, 'because I told you so.' Just like every inquisitive child, that answer did not cut the mustard. As time goes on most people, stop asking and live quietly and desperately trying to tag some relevancy score to their existence. Not me. That would have been death for me as I sit here barely spiritually breathing. My father and his church barely had a handful of fruitful formative notions hanging on their tree of life to offer. The fruit somehow always benefited the church. I just wanted to know something that would make this life meaningful. Now, my grandson, Aidan runs around already giving up asking the questions; willing to go through life being tossed around like a pinball and the paddles are directed by God. What a disheartening way to grow up, and I have nothing to offer him.

My thoughts drifted to Stephen's life and his death. He should have been here in this room with me. Stephen understood purpose in life. It was because of his faith in his God that I could hang on to hope. He questioned and found answers that transcended words expressed in life that breathed love and hope with every breath. He found a tree of life that had many fruits. What was his faith?

Images continued to surface like lava forming below the dome of a volcano. I was not there to hold him! He died alone! What were Stephens last thoughts, his head . . . laying on the cobblestone walk? Was he angry? Did he feel betrayed for living such a life?

I slammed my wine glass down on my desk with a loud smash; wine was raining down everywhere. Both my hands covering my face and mouth muffling the inner rage and grief of the tears I needed to release. A silent internal pause waved over my soul until the vision of Stephen lying there mouthing "I forgive you" came upon me. It was if I was there, but I heard only the word "forgive" whispered. The other words were not audible. I then began to wail a cry that came from a place that was new to me. It was a place of deep sadness and joy. A soulful space I had never discovered. I can't explain it, but it was a place I knew I had to explore, and Stephen was leading me there.

Hayleigh and Maggie and the others came running in, and I embarrassingly bent over in my chair covering my face. Grandma Abba immediately ushered the kids out to the great room, Maggie started to clean up the wine spill, while Hayleigh knelt beside me enveloping me with her tenderness without saying a word as I slowly gathered myself over the next few minutes. She stood up as I straightened myself in the chair. She continued to touch my head as she stroked my hair easing the stress. I took Hayleigh's hand and kissed it ever so gently to thank her for being her.

I whispered, "Stephen is still with us," as Maggie brought in a cup of hot chocolate and a few cookies. Looking at Maggie, knowing she heard my comment, I spoke sarcastically, "I hope that does not ruin God's plan."

She put her hands on her hips, cocked her head to one side and left murmuring, "Daddy, what are we going to do with you."

For the first time in a few days, I was breathing life. The release of tears was good for me. Hayleigh went back out to continue cleaning up and preparing for the onslaught of visitors that would be descending on Eden. I turned around sipping my drink looking through the porch at the many bluish hues of the fields and trees from the light of the moon. I turned back to grab a cookie and was startled to find Grandma Abba sitting in the chair in front of my desk sipping her hot cocoa.

"So you have discovered that Stephen is still with you?" she grinned.

"Grandma Abba it was weird, I heard his voice, not in the room, but inside my mind," I explained, "But I could only hear the word 'forgive,' nothing-else."

I was not ready to go back there yet, so I quickly changed the subject. "Maggie thinks it's part of God's plan like God has people murdered and tortured for some inexplicable reason that we will all have to trust. We will understand one day when we get to see the re-runs up in heaven, and we will all applaud at what a wonderful plan it was. Does God then take a bow and accept a cosmic Oscar?" I ranted.

She almost snorted her hot cocoa out her nose laughing.

"What is wrong with people?" I exclaimed.

She took another slurp of her cocoa and quietly agreed, "I think you are right, Stephen has not left us, Stephen would have described it precisely the way you did," she said still with amusement.

We both enjoyed our short break of laughter when I interrupted, "What do I do with that? My daughter believes that she is a cosmic piñata that God sometimes fills with prizes and other times whacks you with a stick, worst of all she hands this crap down to my grandkids!"

"What do you believe Edward?" she inquired, "What did you hand down"?

Pausing for a while letting out a sigh shaking my head, "I have no idea what I believe, I just know what I can't accept, and I won't believe. My life is upside down. I guess I don't know how to believe."

Grandma Abba softly spoke, "Edward, maybe you're seeking the wrong answer? You are asking the wrong question. It's not what you believe, but how you choose to believe. Everyone believes something. Even nothing is something," smiling a devilish grin as her eyes peaked over her bifocals.

"When I asked you on our walk earlier to share with me one thing you were sure of, you mentioned Hayleigh, but you could have said my marriage. You didn't. You said Hayleigh. Why? Because it's Hayleigh, you trust not the institution of marriage. You have developed some beliefs about your marriage because of the trust and experiences that you have lived with Hayleigh together. It's the same with beliefs. Beliefs are not the thing. They are the results of your journey. Your relationship with . . . Who?"

"You see Edward; you don't need beliefs to take the journey. You need faith. Faith in someone, even if it's simply you. Your father came to me years after your mother's death and asked me to pray for clarity in deciding to start his church. I told him I would not be praying for clarity; however, I will pray for trust. He never asked me to pray again."

She continued, "You have rejected your father's religion based on a set of beliefs handed down to you. These beliefs were passed on to him. However, they are not real beliefs. They are what I call 'adherences.' Let me give you an example. When I first started my women's group, Rahab's Ragamuffins, your father hated that name. I asked every woman to write down what they KNOW about God. The caveat was that they could not offer up anything that they read in a book, or heard from a friend, teacher, or preacher. Well, there was a sudden quietness that enveloped the meeting with most nervously fidgeting, crossing their legs, sipping their tea, or looking down at the floor intently searching for something to say. Well after several uncomfortable minutes I let them off the hook. My dear friend Rebecca asked, 'What are you getting at Ruth? I feel dumb.' I explained to Rebecca, 'All I am trying to point out is the difference between beliefs and adherences.' Take for instance the resurrection. You were not there, and you only know about it from a secondary source. I am aware that you hold this to be true, but it is only an adherence to a tenet that others have come to know. It can only become a belief if you can experience it yourself firsthand. The disciples did not even believe it; despite the witnesses telling them. Only when they experienced Him did they believe. They could only believe what they experienced themselves. Much like you believed in your marriage, because of what you experienced in Hayleigh." Grandma Abba rocked back in her chair studying me to see if I comprehended.

"Grandma Abba, I'm fifty-five years old, and you would think I would be passed this, you'd think I would have solid beliefs," I spoke staring into my cup.

"Edward, what are fifty-five years? It's just a measurement of time for human beings to measure some accomplishments, most of them inflicted by others and few of them coming from within. You think an eternal God would reduce our journey to a few years? Of course, not! God has no time. Your journey is endless, and it's a beautiful thing," as she smiled gazing at me with her eyes watered.

"I hope so Grandma Abba; I hope so," I sighed.

Just then I spotted a cab coming up the driveway. I thought it might be Tommy so we made our way out to the porch and the gang was all there to greet Tommy. I stayed on the porch while the others gathered around the car and to everyone's surprise out popped Emilee sprinting to the other side to open the door. I thought that odd, but figured it was like me opening the door for Hayleigh. First thing visible that came out of the car was crutches followed by Johanna helped by Emilee and the cab driver. I quickly moved to help Johanna, but Emilee had her.

"My God, what happened Johanna?" Hayleigh inquired.

"Ask Eddie; it was his brilliant idea," she squawked back.

I looked at Emilee, and she smiled, "The fire escape was not such a good idea; it was a little higher than she anticipated. She hung on the final rung for nearly five minutes before dropping down to the concrete alley."

As she passed me, I put my fist over my mouth as if feigning a cough and looked away to hide my smile as I imagined her hanging there cursing me out loud. "The idea worked!" I shouted out as she hobbled up the stairs into the house, "You got away from the media."

Johanna lifted her crutch in the air as if it were an extension of her middle finger, "Funny Edward, funny."

The cab driver handed me the luggage and I made my way into the house. Hayleigh was propping Johanna's foot onto the coffee table, and Emilee was applying ice. Johanna asked me to come over and look at it to make sure it was just a sprain. As I was manipulating the ankle, I could see tears dropping from Johanna's face. "Does that hurt?" I questioned. She nodded no, but she looked up into my eyes with deep pain.

"It's just you and me Eddie, Stephen is gone, it's just now hitting me," she whimpered before erupting as I leaned into her, while she sobbed into my shoulder. The interlude of a brief interruption of respite had passed; the corkscrew of suffering resumed its twist into the heart. As I held Johanna and gazed around the room at the sullen faces staring down at me, I could not help but recall these same countenances on the train in my dream. It was a feeling of Deja vu. Maggie is clutching Aidan and Eden with tears dripping from her eyes. She knew better than others the loss of everything that she ever loved starting with my Mom, her grand-mom, whom she worshiped more than me. The look was the same as the night Maggie stopped singing. Her life was a series of events where she loses everything she always loved; her loser husband Frank, who left her shortly after Eden was born and now her uncle Stephen. Hell, sometimes I get the feeling Maggie believes she has already lost me. Hayleigh is embracing Emilee who is distraught that her beloved Johanna is drowning in the hurt and fear that she is losing the hope of her place in a family.

Hayleigh's water soaked eyes are yearning for me to resurrect from the dead. Her dark eyes were pleading and hoping that 'we could be happy again.' Grandma Abba, wiping the drops of sadness off her glasses, looked at me with a look of suffering, hopeful, peace. Only she and I knew that this was the beginning of my journey and that all things would come together. It's ironic that we are all gathered around mourning Stephen, while I felt that I was the one who had died.

Time lingered, while the last sobs whimpered out awkwardly, like a group prayer, when no one knows when to say Amen. What just happened was a sacred for me. Life is coming to me while I am living. My story to this point had been merely the longest prologue ever written. I did not know where it would take me, but I was no longer going to be an observer of life.

Maggie broke the ice with a slap on the kids' shoulders, "Let's get some cookies and hot chocolate!"

Everyone slowly peeled away. I lifted away from Johanna and backed into my chair near the fireplace. Emilee gracefully came toward Johanna sitting next to her. Johanna looked up wiping her tears of grief; she embraced Emilee, encircling their arms and emotions as if one. Johanna softly whispered, "I am so blessed." They clutched each other in a gentle sway that I did not want to see end. They indeed were blessed. I could have never felt that word 'blessed' with them before tonight. I was so happy for Johanna that Emilee was in her life. It was a sacred moment that I will never forget.

As they unwrapped their arms, Emilee looked over at me and asked, "Edward? Are you crying?

I immediately declared a deliberate, "No." I turned toward the light of the fireplace.

Johanna chimed in, "Yes he is! Edward, you are tearing up! I did not think you were that sensitive. I like this side of you." Emilee did not say a word as she rose out of the chair toward me beckoning me to stand. She gently took my arms lifting me emotionally from my chair; cupped my face with her warm hands and whispered, "Thank you . . . Thank you so much."

"No, thank you," I barely audibly got out, clenching her hands to my heart, "Thank you." We hugged as I looked over at Johanna's face that was beaming. Emilee knew that she was seen that night. She was not merely Johanna's lover, and Johanna was not an abomination; not tonight.

The tender moment was fractured by some commotion coming from the kitchen. Eden came running into the room yelling that Great Grandpa was here. Immediately a tension filled the room for everyone, but Grandma Abba. I felt that was strange him coming in through the back door.

"Look what I found wandering outside," came Hayleigh's voice. Little did I know that she was talking about Tommy.

"Tommy!" screamed Johanna, "Oh my God, you are getting so handsome."

Tommy, holding Hayleigh's hand, made his way over to me and I gave him a bear hug and told him how glad I was to see him. Tommy had quit school and headed to Nashville to become a recording artist. He always loved music. Tommy never committed to music as a profession until after years of barely getting by in college. He started out in pre-med like all the other Mayus males. Tommy majored in girls, music, and drinking. He used to come into my office and play my jazz records. I think he wore out my Miles Davis albums. He could play virtually any instrument by just picking it up. As a teenager, my Dad talked him into joining the worship team as keyboardist and lead guitar player. That lasted only a short time. The music director said he was too creative and talented. His playing was taking the focus off the worship. No wonder I grew to hate organized religion; my daughter was not slender enough, and my son was too creative for God. Tommy came to me one day and said he was dropping out of the music ministry. He said 'Dad, music is not a ministry, it is art! I feel like I'm playing in a marching band.' Unlike Maggie, Tommy continued playing and writing music, however, it was only heard within the four walls of his bedroom.

"Where is my dear Mama," boomed a voice from the kitchen as the swinging door opened wide. It was my Dad. Just then my Grandma Abba quickly moved to comfort him, and they collapsed into each other's arms swinging back and forth like a pendulum while gently moaning a muffled weep. They had talked on the phone, but this was the first time they had seen each other since the tragedy. I was touched by the warmth and sight of a powerful man being consoled by his frail old mother. I never got to see much of this human side of my Dad. There he stood inconsolably crying like a child reaching out for his Mommy. Martha, his wife, could barely look at what was unfolding before her eyes. It was her duty to make life easier for my Dad, and there was nothing she could do at this interval in time. I felt sorry for her because she had a look as if this was the first time she had seen this human side of Dad. In front of me, was the Dad I yearned to see.

The only words Dad shared to his Mom were, "He died a hero . . . He died doing the work of the Lord . . . And the animals killed him! They killed him!"

The rest was murmuring that I could not understand, but Grandma Abba could, but she did not say a word but was merely present with her little boy.

Their grasp slowly ended, and Martha was there with a tissue for Dad. He quickly gathered himself and apologized, "I am sorry you all had to see that, he will take our weakness and turn it into strength . . . All things work for good for the righteous. We all will get through this and God will be glorified!"

I could feel the disappointment and anger building underneath. My Dad just exited stage right. It's as if he dashed into the telephone booth to put on his trusty spiritual cape. The mega star of religion enters the stage. The Dr. Reverend Edward Mayus Sr. has now reappeared.

"Dad, why are you sorry? You're with family, you're hurting, we all are hurting, and it's okay."

"Son, we have to be strong, we have to demonstrate faith, we have to deny ourselves and pick up the cross. We must have beliefs to live out as a witness. Maybe you should examine your beliefs. We will take this up at another time."

Dad did not like being questioned. He then made his way around the room gently grabbing everyone's hand with a cursory glad-to-see-you gesture. He deliberately overlooked Emilee, and she immediately left to go into the kitchen.

I followed her to find her drying some dishes. "I'm sorry Emilee," I said. She turned around; her eyes were filling up.

I reached out, but she said, "I'm okay, I'm not mad at your father, these are tears of sadness for him. He is caged. He lives life as a circus animal doing tricks for a treat and performing for others. His God is the Ring Master."

"Wow, I never quite heard it put that succinctly," I thought out loud.

"Besides I was expecting a Jezebel, abomination, or an exorcism; I think it was a good start," as she winked at me and threw the dish towel in my face.

As she walked away, I said, "Emilee, we are lucky that you are part of the family." She winked again and joined the family in the great room. I retired back to the sanctuary of my office.

The solace did not last long when I heard a knock on the door. It was Martha who wanted to let me know that Dad wanted to talk with me about the eulogy. "Can't he come in himself?" I asked. Just then he appeared along with Tommy, as Martha exited.

"Dad, could you have been more obvious?" I interrogated.

"What are you talking about?"

"You know what I mean Dad, you completely ignored Emilee."

"Who's Emilee? He said playing dumb. I ignored his little games with no reply.

Tommy interjected rolling his eyes, "It's good to see some things never change around here."

"Oh you mean that girl," Dad responded looking away from me.

"The girl; she has a name, and she is important to Johanna if that matters to you."

"She's not family, and this is a family matter. Let's get back to what's important; we are here to grieve and celebrate Stephen."

I just shook my head thinking that Stephen would have no part of this.

Dad jumped right into ministry mode, "I've already talked this over with Tommy, and he has agreed to sing Amazing Grace at the service as the last part before the benediction. He will sing right after you deliver the eulogy." I looked over at Tommy, and he weakly acknowledged this as fact.

He continued, "Edward I have taken the liberty to have Martha type out a few verses for you to cover in your talk. Martha!" he barked out, "Bring those verses to Edward." Martha came scurrying into the office and handing the sheet over to Dad who promptly pushed them in front of me. "Now I want you . . ."

I looked down and to the right raising my hand like a traffic cop. "Dad, I will look at the verses later; you wanted me to do this, and I agreed, and I will," I abruptly stated ending the conversation.

Dad just sat there frozen staring at me as his eyes watered up. I was pleading inside my soul that he would just burst into tears and that the fortress walls would come tumbling down and I might get another glimpse of my Dad. I felt like a little boy pleading with his father to just play catch.

"Okay Eddie, just remember, we have to be strong people of faith."

"I know Dad," I said as I reached onto his shoulder. He placed his hand onto my hand that was resting on him thanking me for doing this. As we stared into each other's eyes, I could see a man who was tired and weary. Emilee was right. It is sad.

"Martha, let's get home, Edward has a lot of work to do," he weakly ordered. He walked out much quieter than he rolled in. Maggie came in asking if we wanted some cookies and hot chocolate. We politely replied no. Tommy, an extremely health conscious handsome boy, amusingly asked if she knew that stuff was killing her.

"Probably no more than this stuff," I sarcastically said as I pulled out of my credenza, a half empty bottle of Balvenie Port Wood 21 Year Scotch and two glasses. I reserved this for special occasions and times when I needed to get a good night's sleep. The special occasion was I was about to start a journey and the first leg I would be sharing with my son. I also would need much help sleeping through the unresolved pain of Stephens death and what I had to say at the funeral.

Tommy went over to the usual shelf and pulled out his favorite Miles Davis LP, Kind of Blue, and placed it on the turn table. I was old school, and I preferred the vinyl over the digital compact disks. The last time we did this was when Tommy set off for Nashville. Now I am setting off for God knows what or where.

Just as the base line snapped on the song So What, I asked Tommy why he agreed with my Dad to play at the service. He told me that he was not doing it for my father. He was playing for Stephen, whom he thought was a cool cat that was real.

I have a song I wanted to play for him and I will sometime soon. "It's Blackbird, a Beatles cover, but I think it is meaningful to Stephen," he reasoned. "It speaks of a bird that was created to arise, to be free. That's how I see Uncle Stephen."

He was right about Stephen. I enjoyed his speaking of singing for Stephen as if he is present; it made me feel less of a loss and that Stephen was somehow still with us.

"When did Dad ask you to play Amazing Grace?"

Tommy recounted this, "As the cab turned into the driveway I spotted the sign still needing repair and asked him to stop and let me out. I wanted to take a walk up the long driveway like when I was a kid coming home from school. I walked over to the sign and picked up a rock nearby and proceeded to tap the loose nail of the large E in Eden."

"Yea I've meant to fix that sign for years," I mused.

"I stood back admiring my handy work when another car pulled in; it was Grand-Dad."

"The passenger window rolled down, and Grand-Dad shouted out, 'Hey stranger, it's going to take a lot more to fix then nails. Hop in.' As we pulled away, the E fell again hanging below the bushes so that all that could you could see were the three letters d-e-n."

I thought that's apropos.

"It gets better, Dad," Tommy continues barely sipping his scotch, "I did notice that there were a lot of tissues in the trash bag next to the passenger seat and that Grand-Dad sounded like he had been crying. I felt compassion for him; I had never seen this side of him. Then, Grand-Dad tells me that Stephen would want me to sing Amazing Grace during the service, so I reluctantly agreed without the option of saying no. Just as we are pulling up to the house, Grand-Dad orders Martha to turn off the headlights as we drift up slowly to the porch. We stopped and got out of the car. I watch in amazement as he and Martha tip-toe up the steps and instead of going to the front door; they spot everyone through the large window. They just stand there watching Emilee and Johanna embrace. Grand-Dad murmurs, 'Forgive them Lord for their abomination' Martha is just shocked with her hand over her mouth and nose as if she just saw someone vomit. Then after you and Emilee hug, Grand-dad starts to walk back to the car, but Martha pleads that we must take care of Stephen's arrangements. Grand-Dad relents and disgustingly looks at me and says, 'Lord forgive me for failing to raise up righteous children.' That's when he decided to go around to the back-kitchen door."

"That lying hypocrite, he knew the whole time; I knew he deliberately shunned Emilee!"

Tommy rose out of his chair saying, "I am tired, it's been a long day; do I still have a room here?"

"Smart-ass," I retorted, "You're right next to the heathens."

"My room is right next to you and Mom?" Tommy shot back humorously.

"This is a house of heathens," I laughed.

Tommy as he was leaving bumped into his Mom, turned and asked, "I'm going to do a twist on Amazing Grace?" I encouraged him saying flipping the back of my hand up, "Go ahead, to hell with him, I might read from the Quran."

Hayleigh, chimed in, "Boys! Behave now. Maggie, and the kids left, Johanna and Emilee are hitting the sack, as well as me. I'm still battling this headache." I was concerned because this had been going on for a few weeks. I suggested that we should check this out soon. But, Hayleigh, as usual, brushed it off. She kissed me and headed out knowing I would be following right behind after finishing my drink. It had been a full day of emotions, and I was drained but glad that we were one day closer to moving past the death of Stephen and on to my journey. I did not realize yet that my journey had already begun. I wondered what path my journey would take. Pushing myself away from my desk, I noticed that Tommy had barely wet his lips with my Balvenie. I certainly was not going to waste any drops of an expensive bottle of scotch. I threw that back and was now ready for bed.

Another Dream

It is by no means an irrational fancy that,

in a future existence, we shall look upon

what we think our present existence, as a dream.

-Edgar Allan Poe

The wheels were clanging like chains as the train moved from darkness to light intermittently through a series of tunnels. I could tell we were going through tunnels because of the roar of a wall of noise clamoring off the dark echoes was unbearably loud; only to be eased by the silent, peaceful feeling when entering the light. This light would be too short before we would start to hear the thunder of another approaching tunnel of darkness. The thundering sound built to a roar that drowned out the chains. It was the sound of many crying, moaning, and wailing with every tunnel passage, the dreams and hopes of the living pouring out of their souls. The hemorrhaging would subside briefly during the interludes of light which were getting shorter in duration as the journey continued. Then the train abruptly stopped. I could see the back of my Dad in front talking with the passengers. A few in the back were getting off smiling and high-fiving each other. But the ones that mattered most to me were still in this car. Then I heard the chains start to rattle and clang again as the train was starting to move. I looked up and the last persons leaving were Stephen and a stranger. "Don't leave!" I screamed. Stephen gave me the thumbs up sign like a NASA engineer would give to the astronauts as they closed the hatch door. He was gone.

The train was rolling again, and I did not know what to do so I started shouting at my Dad, but he did not turn around. I was getting angrier as the train began to speed up and I did not know where I was going, or where this train would take my family and friends. I shouted to my Dad again, but he did not turn around. How much more loss can we take before there is nothing left. I moved more quickly toward Dad, and he was walking away. I wanted to grab and choke him for not hearing me. I got closer and closer as the train gathered speed. It was hard to keep my balance as the train moved faster and faster, rocking side to side. Just then the thundering swoosh into darkness filled the car, and the sounds of loss filled the car again, the wall of sound was more intense than ever; crushing in on us as if the rail car was getting smaller. It was getting hard to breathe, and I stumbled to the floor unable to keep my balance; then another quick swoosh of light came upon us, and I found myself at the feet of my father, with my family looking down at me; their eyes pleading for relief. My father finally reached his hand down to lift me up, and I started to cry. As I began to stand, my family and friends, helped me up and spoke words of encouragement that warmed my heart and brought joy. I could feel the strength of my father's hand lifting me the final ascent to stand upright. I turned toward my Dad.

Oh, God!

It's me!

***

"One, two, three, and four" Blaaaang! I am awakened to the electric guitar chord of 'B flat' strumming from Tommy's room. Sitting upright in my bed in a cold sweat, I caught my breath and recovered from my nightmare. Tommy was singing Mary Chapin Carter's Soul Companion. I sat there listening to him; he was getting good. Tommy sounds out the words about the courage to confront the unknown ahead.

I made my way over to the bathroom to splash some water on my face, to wash this troubling dream from myself when the music stopped. I screamed to Tommy, "Is that the way to wake somebody up?"

"Sorry."

If I had a dollar for every time my kids said sorry I would be a friggin millionaire.

"I didn't know you were still sleeping," Tommy yelled.

Just then Hayleigh came in speaking, "Glad you could join us; I'm glad you got a good rest. I'm sure the two scotches had something to do with it," she said while reaching around me for an Aleve. "I can't get rid of this headache."

I was still hand wiping my face when I told her the dream returned. She expressed that I should be used to it by now. "This time it was different Honey. Stephen was on the train and left giving me the thumbs up as if saying goodbye," I recalled.

I continued to explain how the train was moving faster and faster into light and dark and everyone was hurting in the darkness and barely hanging on in the shorter intervals of light. I was whispering as if hiding something.

"Hayleigh, I could hear the life roaring out of everyone, so much life, it was very painful to listen. Dad was there leading the passengers, everyone we know and love, including you. I was in the front, and I could see what was occurring but Dad could not. I tried to make my way to Dad to tell him what was happening but he kept moving away from me. The speed and pain were too much, and I collapsed crying out like a little child for him to help me. His hand reached down and finally lifted me along with help from you and our friends, only it was not Dad. It was me. That's when I was jarred awake by Tommy's music. What do you make of that?"

She just stared at the reflection of me in the mirror looking tenderly into the image of my eyes. "Edward, I hurt for the man that is the image I see in the mirror and would do anything to make him happy." She then turned me around gazing directly into my eyes, "But, I am desperately fearful of losing you, the real Edward," as she pressed her hand gently to my heart, "That I will never get him back and that he will never find me again."

Hayleigh continued, "I was up early because I could not sleep and Grandma Abba came to me and said it was my turn for a love-walk. We grabbed some coffee, she grabbed my arm, and we walked for about an hour while you slept. She could tell that I was fearful and asked me what I was certain. It took me fifteen minutes before I could answer. I was sure about the man I first met, who saw me complete in my youth but fearful that he can only see portions of me now. The fear has imprisoned us because we cannot grow. I can't grow, and it is claustrophobic. I am left to love a man who is standing still. I so want to love him more . . . in much more ways; I want to love myself. I am fearful that if I love myself more, I will end up on a different path; he will never find me. Grandma Abba left me with hope. She said you are starting to see. She stated that you are being called to another path and you are about to paint a masterpiece."

"As far as your dream Edward," she turned me back around to face the mirror, "That is between you and him, pointing to the man in the mirror and me. I love both men, but I need the man that is looking in the mirror," as she squeezed my shoulders and wrapped her arms around me. I told you back in New York; I feel that you are setting out on a new journey. You will figure it out."

She walked away with a kiss from her finger to my nose. As I brushed my teeth, I doubted whether Hayleigh trusted in my ability to navigate this new journey or simply welcomed any change. Any change of path had to be welcomed and encouraged considering the last few years. I then put my jeans and worn out sweatshirt on and headed downstairs for some coffee.

Grandma Abba was in the kitchen drinking her tea, and I glimpsed a rushing Hayleigh as she was leaving to head to the store to prepare for Wednesday's burial and the onslaught of visitors along with Thanksgiving the next day.

"So I heard you and Hayleigh had a nice little walk. I'm about to paint a masterpiece. That's a lot of pressure." She just sat there grinning like she already knew something.

"Hayleigh's a good woman, the perfect one for you," she judged between her sips of tea.

"I agree, Grandma Abba, I agree," I affirmed, "She says she trust and believes in me, but I am concerned that she has no other options, considering the trajectory of my life up until now."

Grandma Abba added, "Why are you concerned with how she feels about the prospects of your journey?"

I replied, "How can she possibly have faith in me?"

Grandma Abba started to get irritated, "You test me, Edward. If Hayleigh and I already saw the end of the journey, it would not be faith; but we trust you! Why is that a problem?"

I questioned myself out loud, "Maybe I don't believe in myself?"

"That's the first thing you've said that makes sense in the last few days," she amusingly stated, "Edward, trusting in beliefs does not produce faith, it just regurgitates spiritual pooh-pooh." I immediately snorted my coffee through my nose, and we both enjoyed the laugh.

Just then a delivery truck was pulling away and heading down the driveway. A few moments later, Tommy came in with a package with a strange stunned look on his face.

"You look like you've seen a ghost, Tommy."

"This package came for Stephen," he stammered laying it on the table and pushed it toward me as if it was contaminated by the plague, "It's weird."

I gazed over at the package and in bold print was Stephen Peter Mayus with my address. He had planned to spend Thanksgiving here at Eden. The box just sat there on the table. No one is reaching out to touch it. It was a silent quiet. It was one of the last things Stephen did while on this Earth. He packaged up my present and shipped it from the Vatican post office. It was the greatest of gifts he told Francesco Paulo Martelli. I could not bring myself to reach for it. Somehow it felt like it was the reason he was not here. I was afraid that if the gift was a trinket or an old artifact of some sort, which Stephen was fond of finding and giving; I would be furious to know that he lost his life for something so trivial. We stared at it for what seemed to be an eternity but was probably a minute or two. Then I quietly stood up and grabbed the box, walking away without a word.

After all, it was just a box with a gift inside.

No big deal.

So, I thought.

MASTERPIECE

Existence is a series of footnotes to a vast,

obscure, unfinished masterpiece.

-Vladimir Nabokov

The breeze was blowing warm on that November morning. I finished my coffee at my desk staring at Stephen's package; in the background on my computer was playing Dylan's When I Paint My Masterpiece. The irony does not escape me that the words are about a person in Rome who runs up a hill following the wild geese, but everything is going to be different when he paints his masterpiece.

I needed to devote time to Stephen's eulogy, but the package was drawing me in, like a siren's call to a lost ship at sea. There was consolation and respite while thinking what I may say about Stephen's life lived for others. I needed to convey his example of a rich story lived out in complete abandonment to his God. Trepidation overflowed my soul. I could explain the what and how of Stephen's life. But the why of his life is what I feared and desired. How can I speak to the why I have never known? Everyone wants to know the why. Time and Stephen had stopped, but for a box that contained a gift. I wanted answers. Everyone wanted and needed answers. Perhaps they were in this package. I grabbed the box and headed to the basement.

I felt like Neo in The Matrix. I could hide this box, this haunting time capsule barely three days old, in this basement of old musty artifacts of the Mayus past and march proudly into my new journey of ignorance and illusion. Or, I could explore this new journey in the truth of reality.

I immediately grabbed a box cutter; opened the side door out of the basement and made a beeline to the one place I sought when I needed to think. After reaching the old oak tree, I stood there with the package in one hand and the box cutter in the other leaning with my clenched hand on the rough bark, looking up the trunk of this majestic oak. I pleaded with God to help me understand. I heard and felt nothing. The grieving moment brought me painfully back to when I lost Mom. I died inside that day also. I am dying today. Slamming the tightly-gripped cutter against the hard, rough bark until it shattered and I slid down to the ground crying, with my back leaning against the tree. The place I could always go and at least feel the presence of Mom is now forsaken. I closed my eyes hoping to see or feel something. The memory of my dream, Stephen leaving, giving me the thumbs up sign played inside my mind as if I was watching a re-run of an old family movie. Only the projector was stuck and repeated the same scene over and over of Stephen, and his thumbs up sign getting closer and closer. I spotted the blade of the shattered box cutter to my right, and I started to slice open the box straight down the middle in a surgeon-like manner.

Just then the wind picked up, and the leaves were swirling around me as I opened the box to reveal an old wooden box with a carving of a chalice and engraving that read;

Hic est sanguis meus, qui pro vobis funditur.

Non bibam amodo de hoc genimine vitis,

donec regnum Dei veniat.

What did this mean? It appeared to be in Latin, and the box was obviously old. I recognized the word sanguis which is blood in Latin from my pre-med days. My heart briefly sank; an Italian artisan carved wooden container.

There are hundreds of artisans selling outside the Vatican. Surely there had to be more. I was buoyed by the constant remembrance of Stephen's thumbs up. Dare I open it now? I spoke softly out loud, "Come on Stephen, give me something to work with."

Breathing in deeply, I opened the wooden box, and a few onion-skinned papers flew out and were caught in the wind that gusted. Stephen who was an avid hiker always traveled lightly and was conscious of the weight he carried in his backpack.

The box was filled with shredded brown paper that immediately started to blow everywhere as the balmy breeze picked up leaving some soaked crimson-tinged paper and a brown large stuffed envelope. Something must have leaked during the flight. There was red liquid all over the envelope. I opened the envelope which had lots of papers. It appeared like old research papers with handwritten notes paper-clipped together. There was also a small brown moleskin journal with the word Lanciano hand-written on the cover. I could tell that this was Stephen's handwriting by the way he wrote the letter L. The journal's left corner was soaked with the red liquid as if blood stained. I set the envelope and journal beside me to my right. Moving the wet shred aside revealing two wine glasses with initials etched into them. They were an S and an E. The shred was getting wetter toward the bottom of the box where I discovered a bottle of wine. I guess the bottle must have pressurized during the flight and started to leak which seemed unusual. I had shipped many a bottle of wine from Europe in my life. I guess it was not secured enough during shipping.

It was Stephens favorite wine, a bottle of Ravello Monache Reserva from the Amalfi coast in Italy. Stephen always spent much time in Italy after returning from his many Mideast mission trips, and this was his favorite wine. I examined the bottle to detect the leak and was surprised that I could see that the bottle had appeared to have already been opened and re-corked. I thought that peculiar. I sat under the tree pondering; this was the last task that Stephen did before he died. He deliberately boxed this up for me. Stephen left these items, one old antique box, an envelope of random research papers, a journal, two wine glasses, and an open bottle of wine. Why was Stephen so eager to give me these? Then I recalled the dream. Thumbs up!

I headed back to the house with my gift in hand to discern the mystery of what was before me and what was coming, but first I needed to prepare for the eulogy and the service. I could not let the church and God forbid, my father down. But more importantly, I could not let myself down. I needed to unearth some meaning in my life. Somehow this box would lead me to it.

***

Time ticked away that afternoon with me holed up in my office sanctuary combing through Stephens personal journals that he shipped over in the earlier package. I wanted this eulogy to be centered around the celebration of Stephen's life, his thoughts, and what he believed. The mystery of the gift box had to wait as it hovered in the background on my credenza and in my mind.

Thumbing through Stephen's journal writings revealed a man living life to the fullest in every way imaginable. In my mind Stephen was not a missionary; he was Indiana Jones searching the world for the hidden treasures in life. While he did unearth various artifacts, the treasures he explored were the countless people he met along his paths way. These people were the gems that he discovered and wrote about in his journal. The stories, photos, and notations jotted down on these tattered pages could fill ten thousand lifetimes. I was moved to tears by some of Stephen's stories. The sorrow was joyful and disturbing at the same time; I can't quite explain.

There was an insert in the journal clipped to a page from two years ago. Stephen did not write every day like many. He appeared to write as a cathartic exercise. His word glimmerings were like prayer. The insert was titled 'Chidike' (pronounced 'Che Dee Kay'). The one-page insert recounted the tragic story told to him by the nurse. Here is my recollection of the event.

Chidike, a young nine-year-old boy who lost his legs from just above the knee in a terrorist incident by Boko Haram. A group of these monsters were hanging around the village which they had taken control. A skinny six-year-old Chidike was enamored with these soldiers, wanting to be just like them. They let him play with their guns. The commander patted Chidike's head calling him a soldier for Allah. He wrapped a belt around him and sent him to his mother in the market square telling him to shout 'Darul Tawheed,' the name of the leader of Boko Haram. As Chidike made his way across the street to the market, he was met by his frightened mother who was observing from afar in fear. The skinny little boy proudly made his way toward the bustling market barely audibly shouting, 'Darul Tawheed,' above the busy noise as the soldiers laughed with amusement at their newest recruit.

Chidike was too skinny. His small hips couldn't hold the belt up. The belt fell to his feet. Boom! The commander detonated an explosive device killing many in the square along with Chidike's mother. Chidike was spared, as the explosive shrapnel remained low, but it cost him his lower legs.

I was horrified at this savage story. I continued to read Stephens notes that told the story of his encounter. Stephen came along a while later and met Chidike as a boy, no longer valued and looking at life as a beggar. He no longer had the ability to have a healthy productive life in such a hard country. Stephen was working at the hospital in Nigeria where Chidike was recuperating. They connected, and Chidike became more than another patient. The young boy's name meant 'the strength of God' in his native language, and Stephen recognized this in the little boy. Stephen's time was coming to an end as his visa was set to expire. He could not let his new friend suffer without legs. He went into action and secured prosthetic legs with the help of Dad's church and connections my Dad had in the medical community. Stephen was indeed like Jesus in the life of one Chidike. He helped a young man walk. I merely produce paper reports and lectures. No wonder I yearned for what Stephen lived. Grandma Abba was right; I only studied the paint, while Stephen created masterpieces.

The pages easily turned many revealing relationships, lives encountered, and experiences lived. Some on the surface appeared mundane but next to my life; these were epic adventures. What was more important was that they changed and molded Stephen. He was the sum of his relationships and journey; I was the sum of the ideas inside my mind. I encountered my books, music, and studies. I was trapped inside the mind of my thoughts, while Stephen lived free in the lives of others as if everyone was a gift of another door opening to life.

After catching my emotional breath and quenching my soulful yearning for significance with each tattered turned page, I encountered the periodic pangs of suffering and doubt that Stephen often felt. I must admit I was confounded by this finding in Stephens jottings. The very life I ached for and desired to believe in; produced such suffering and doubt. I already knew about doubt and did not want any part of suffering.

Sometimes the words were drenched in anguish as if Stephen was suffering as much as the people he was helping. There was a brief notation about eighteen months ago concerning a fourteen-year-old girl named Afet, who was sold into slavery to Tali-ban soldiers who ravaged her body over several years. She was brought to Stephen's tent barely hanging onto life; discarded like an asset that wear and tear had rendered useless. Stephen scribed into his journal this encounter:

Her haunting eyes were void of life as if they were blank. I had never seen marbleized hardened eyes like this. They were frozen as if in a state of the constant anguish of seeing horror, but not seeing at all. I approached her frail corpse-like body to examine her. She weakly spread her legs awaiting another savage assault. I collapsed to my knees in front of the cot where she vulnerably laid. I cried tears of deep sorrow and rage, holding onto only her feet; afraid to touch any other part of her body, for what seemed like an eternity. She just simply laid there dead to life, trapped in an eternal hell with no escape. I wrapped her in the sheets and pulled her into my lap laying her head against my chest and rocked her while I quietly cried a soulful soft howl for 11 hours. I could tell she was crying even with the absence of her tears that had dried up long ago.

Stephen wrote questioning;

Who were her parents, I wanted to let them know that she was safe? I wanted to end their suffering. The physician in me wanted to do more and examine what I perceived would be a myriad of health and medical issues for young Afet, but intuitively I knew she needed love and human touch. She did not need a doctor. As the hours slowly passed, I rocked a gentle sway like a pendulum of the heart. Cursing God with the angry agony of my thoughts of what this tender child had endured; while experiencing the connection that poured out of my soul for this lost pearl. This was my grace.

I was shocked to see those words written from the pen of Stephen. Stephen and Afet eventually fell asleep.

I embraced the empty hardened wineskin that was the body of young Afet, I made sure not to slide down from this sitting position, less she awakes in the morning and feels that I was just like every other man. As the sands of sorrow poured out the night; dawn was approaching, my cries had slowed to brief whimpering intervals. I could feel the hardness leaving her body, and the coldness of her extremities began to warm; finally, her eyes shut, and I could hear her breathe. Her fist that laid upon my chest began to open and gently press warmly against my skin and heart. I quietly drifted off to a calm rest.

Stephens last entry into his journal concerning Afet was when he recounted how he awoke, feeling a gentle tap of the finger of young Afet on his chest.

It was rhythmic, and I eventually determined it was to the beat of my heart. I looked down, and Afet was looking up, watching me. She was not smiling, but I could tell that she was seeing. Her eyes were not marbleized and absent; there was a track of a tear running down and across her nose. I gave her a gentle hug and smiled, and she moved her head to my bosom. The tent flap opened and in came Caterina with another woman. They came to take Afet away and wash her. As she was being pulled from my arms, she hugged my neck and softly whispered something to me in Dari, which was her native language. The other woman lifted her up and left. As Caterina was leaving, I asked her what Afet said. Caterina translated, "Afet said 'your sweet breath filled me, and I heard a heart for the first time."

My thoughts were that a beautiful young woman had lost her humanity, her soul taken and killed by evil. With all the countless men, she was with; she never had a human interaction. She was, for the first time since taken from her mother's arms, touched by a human being. I was overcome with joy and awe. I wept in quiet, joyous, uncontrollable laughter. I stood up to splash water on my face and thought that I had just witnessed a miracle. I saw a person reborn.

After reading Stephen's journal, sitting stunned in my chair at this recounting, I heard in the background, *Amazing Grace* coming from upstairs. Tommy was rehearsing for the service on Wednesday. I felt a piece of me missing, and that grace had not entered my world; at least not the grace that Stephen had found.

Just then Hayleigh knocked on the open the door to not startle me softly asking me how my eulogy was coming along.

"I finally felt like I know what I will say that will capture the memory of Stephen." A few seconds passed. "Have you ever cried for another person Hayleigh? I know that sounds stupid, but I mean really cried tears of sorrow as if you were hurting as bad as them?"

"Edward, I am a mother and a wife. Of course, I cry, but most of the time, I am too busy to cry. I am simply plowing through life. You think too much Edward."

Hayleigh did not quite get what I meant by the question, and I was too confused to explain it myself, but somehow, I knew that I have never suffered nor loved the way that Stephen was capable. I knew that on this journey I was about to embark, I was not prepared, but it was now a path I had no options but to travel. The dream, Stephen's death, and now the gift lurking behind me on my credenza; all calling me to a road never traveled, but the road sparkles with hope. I closed the journal. I had all I could handle for now.

***

Monday night was a restful and uneventful night. Tommy and Maggie went to see some friends. Grandma Abba had her Rahab's Ragamuffins meeting. I still laugh at the irony of a Bible study being named after a whore. I enjoyed that it must have torqued my Dad.

Hayleigh and I sent out for Chinese food and had a reflective time together discussing getting through the next few days. Hayleigh had been fantastic and had the Thanksgiving meal catered so that the family could enjoy a good meal. She would have limited time because of Wednesday's service.

I was personally dreading Thanksgiving, which was normally my favorite holiday. While I enjoy holidays, I viewed this one as an interruption. I needed time and space to go through this darkness and move forward, hopefully to a space of peace. All the friends and family would be around making demands and offering concerns and insights. I did not want to be fake and nod my head in agreement in idle chit chat.

The night was brisk with a full moon. It was a night where the silence was only broken by the small periodic breaking branches from the wind whistling through the trees. Hayleigh and I had decided to go for a walk down the driveway to the end of the road. I put on my usual beat-up jacket with a scarf but no gloves. I hated gloves because I could not feel my trusty acorns. Hayleigh, only wearing a sweater, bundled up with a scarf, gloves, and a winter headband to cover her ears. Hayleigh always underdressed on our walks. She knew that I would do my best to keep her warm and draw her close to me. She was an artist at the little subtle dances that would send the messages to me she needed. She needed me close.

Walking along the gravel dirt road, the sound of my feet kicking a rock occasionally was the only thing to break the verbal silence until Hayleigh asked, "Edward, what did you mean earlier today when you asked me if I had ever cried?"

"Honey, I did not mean 'have you ever cried.' But, have you ever cried as if you were one with that person, feeling the pain when the other person was hurting."

"Well, of course, Edward," Hayleigh indignantly replied as if I was questioning her, "I had cried for you and the children many a night when I thought you were hurting. What are you getting at; what is the point, Edward?"

"The point is," a sigh; a long pause ensues before I stumble over my thoughts, "The point is I don't know, but I know that Stephen knew." I shared with Hayleigh the story of Afet in his journal.

"Hayleigh, Stephen loved Afet so much that he felt her suffering and did not even know her. He suffered the agony alongside her. That is what healed her. I'm not talking about crying because you feel sorry that the person had to go through so much pain, or that you may miss them, but that you are with them and living the suffering alongside at that very moment. I'm not talking about physical pain. Medicine can almost always stop that. But they cannot stop the suffering. Hell, Hayleigh, I can cry at a movie, a song, play, and when I see you hurting. When I see, you suffering I don't want to cry or suffer with you; I want to fix it because I want to end this feeling for myself. There is something fundamentally wrong with that. Ah, what the hell do I know? Sometime during my life, I stopped growing."

Hayleigh grabbed my arm and with a tight tug cheerfully said, "Maybe you are just starting to grow. I have a lot of faith in you Doctor Mayus, as does Grandma Abba, and your brother Stephen. That's a great fan club."

We had made it to the end of the long driveway, and we stopped and shared a long embrace. It was a tender moment that gave me hope that there was more to be revealed. Turning back and heading home there was the sign EDEN with its broken E hanging by a thread. My thought was that the E was symbolic for me. I went up to it and tried to set it straight. "There we go, it's fixed!" I proudly proclaimed.

As we walked away gingerly quiet as if sneaking behind enemy lines, Hayleigh whispered, "Why are we so quiet?" Then we both heard the squeak as the letter fell and both burst into laughter.

"I'm going to fix that one day," I snorted.

"I think you will, I think you will," Hayleigh answered with a smile. "Give me those acorns!" she demanded. I willingly handed over to her my precious acorns worn smooth from hours of philosophical pondering about life. She then threw them far into the dark abyss of the tall timbers. "Acorns are useless if you don't plant them," she explained.

I was in shock staring into the darkness. Hayleigh motioned to head home. I shook my head in disbelief. We giggled like two teenagers who just figured out that they loved each other. I asked her if she was getting cold and she affirmed with a wink. I took off my coat and draped it over her shoulders. I froze my butt off all the way home, but we both felt warm inside.

We trudged our way back up the long driveway running the last 30 yards in a race to see who would have to make the hot tea. Of course, I showed no mercy; since she threw away my acorns. Besides, the tea tasted better when Hayleigh made it because she would serve it with a foo-foo honey stick and maybe even a light snack. I would have thrown two tea bags in two paper cups as if it was to go. She asked me to start a fire and bring Stephen's journal into the great room.

Hayleigh read the parts of the journal I had told her about and could hardly bare to read about Afet. The journal is hard to read sometimes because things got out of order. His random writings would get scattered out of sequence in the tattered memoir and clipped sheets of paper. We were both amazed at this quiet but rich life that Stephen led.

By the second cup of tea and another log on the fire, Hayleigh shockingly exclaimed, "Oh my God," holding the back of her hand against her forehead.

"What's wrong? . . . What?"

"Stephen was coming home to take over your father's church! He has a girlfriend named Caterina," she shouted in disbelief. I reached for the journal and Hayleigh released it after reading the last few words flopping back on the sofa. Ripping the journal from her, I was not going to believe it until I read it with my own eyes. There it was dated one week before his death.

Dad seemed relieved and excited that I was finally coming home to take over his position as Senior Pastor. I do not think that Dad knows that my ministry could become akin to throwing a few spiritual tables around, but with what God has revealed in my life over the last few years, I finally feel that I have something to share as a human being to other human beings. That became my calling. My life in the wilderness is ending. I never saw myself as a 'B' team theologian, chosen only to espouse the teachings of the 'A' squad.

Over the last two years, Caterina taught me so much about life. I never thought I could love a woman as much as I grew to love her. Love is no longer a proper word. Nineteen months of pure blessing. I have seen both happiness and much suffering in my lifetime, but nothing could have prepared me for the brilliant joy that she brought into my life. Now she is gone, and the pain sometimes is unbearable, because I know that her sweet breath is still filling a room somewhere on Capri, and I am not there. My agony will continue until the day I hear that my beautiful bird is set free. I am wrapping up my research project that I cannot wait to share with Eddie; I will not return to my old life again. What a surprise it will be for Eddie. I can't wait to see him and give him my gift this Christmas. SM

I sank back into the sofa along with Hayleigh. We just looked at each other stunned. Who was this Caterina? Was she the same woman in Afet's story? Why was Stephen coming home to take over Dad's church? Why is a bottle of opened wine, two glasses, in a wooden box such a great gift?

It was getting late, but Hayleigh and I could not stop reading until we found out about Caterina. As Hayleigh flipped through the pages, I went through the loose thin parchments of Stephen's life as if they were ancient hieroglyphics on an archaeological dig. Then I noticed a different coloration of two pieces of papyrus that were noticeably higher quality paper. However, it was at one time crumpled up and eventually flattened out again. It was a letter to Stephen, and the second page was signed uncompromising love, 'C'. The 'C' had to be Caterina. Who else could it be? I read the letter out loud.

My Wonderful Anchor,

Our talk last night was long and hard and your words desirously persuasive. How I have desired that this cup passes my lips for another time, even if but a brief few more months, or just a few more sunsets. Another dawn with you would make it an eternity of love. Love had passed my heart long ago, and rich contentment took its place without a whimper, and many days of joyful rest and peace followed. God had become my lover and his creatures, my children. I was hiding from my great suffering, helping orphans in Nushki. Then you came along. The intimate love embers that never burned with another were ignited into a rapturously unexpected fire. There was never a morning in our short soul embrace that I regretted our meeting. There was never a sunset where I was not blessed and grateful to know that I would share another morning of loving you. You loved people like no one I have ever seen, but I watched the suffering you endured loving them. Your love quieted the doubts in my soul that were hidden for years over my illness. I now know that my Father has been suffering with me and I trust Him.

Now I call on your love for me to make me a promise. I have a dilemma. My great suffering is marching toward me far more rapidly than I feared. I anguish at the thought that your love for me will now be a source of even greater agony for you. I cannot watch your pain when there is no hope. If there was only one thread, I could hold onto you forever. You have given me a lifetime of love, and I want to die in the sweet memory of that. I cannot bear to live out my life watching you suffer.

By the time you are reading this, you will be at the public dock in Positano, where we agreed we would meet. I am sorry that a messenger had to deliver this note, but I am sure you understand why. I am on the morning ferry to Capri to live out my short days. I will not be saying goodbye today because I need to hold on to the hope you always gave me. I picked Anemone flowers from our favorite picnic field. As I sail pass Positano, I will throw them over the starboard side. If you see the purple Anemone's floating toward you; you may follow me to Capri. If you do not, then you will go and live your life. I am asking you to promise me this if you love me. You have never lied to me. My prayer will be that the purple flowers will pass Gibraltar saving you from the suffering. Fondly remembering our song, humming Boots of Spanish Leather.

Uncompromising love, C

I guess the flowers never made it to shore I thought. Hayleigh believed she never tossed the flowers overboard. That is how she knew Stephen would honor her wishes and protect the memory of their love. I wondered if Catarina even knew Stephen had been killed.

Hayleigh was wiping away her tears, and I could hardly get through it without feigning a light cough to mask my choking up. Hayleigh noticed that there was a photograph taped to the back of the second page. As she takes the photo in her hand, she remarks, "She is beautiful." I snatched it away quickly, and my heart stopped, then raced, until I was overcome with emotions of sorrow, and confusion.

Hayleigh could tell I was taken back. "Hayleigh, this is the stranger with Stephen in the back of the train car waving to me."

***

The next day my head was reeling with this new knowledge of Stephen's life. It changed a lot of what I would cover to celebrate Stephen. I took calls most of the day from people expressing their sympathies and letting me know they will be praying for the family. I do not think that I ever said that to a family that lost someone. Maybe it was because I was a preacher's kid; it was automatically assumed. Truth be told, I would not have any idea what to pray. I certainly had to brace myself for the barrage of misguided beliefs and traditions that come with the awkwardness and fear of humans dealing with death. More importantly, I had to speak something to the people that my brother would want. I was not going to trivialize a life lived with religious clichés and theological baubles that Stephen despised. The hardest part was I feared that the audience was expecting just that.

As the day was moving forward, I was getting a little edgy. Earlier in the day, I got a call from the Senior Executive Pastor Timothy Sludge. After a few minutes of him describing the plans, logistics for the burial service, and going over his plans to name the east wing of the building Stephens Hall; he started asking questions on what my message would be. He was investigating if my message talked of strength and if it would focus on Stephen being a martyr for the faith. He explained to me how Stephen is enjoying his reward for persevering for his faith and pointing out that people need to hear this message. He went on to ask me if he could have an advance copy of my talk?

I responded with a pointed question, "What do you need that for?"

"Edward, everything at Hillside Community Church is recorded for posterity's sake, but we respect the privacy during funeral services to not record the family. But we like to have a written documentation of what transpired."

An awkward silence occurred, and Sludge nervously cleared his throat when I responded sternly, "You don't own my brother or his memory, and you are not going to control this as if it's just another one of your programs. No, I do not have anything written, I am going to speak from my heart."

"Look, Edward, I know that this is a difficult time and I apologize if I am offending you. Stephen's death is tough on all of us, we all loved him."

"When was the last time you talked to my brother?" I countered. More awkward silence and I could hear his hand cover the phone. "Uh-mm, Edward, do you have any notes we can use then?"

"No, I have no notes."

"At the end of your talk, we were planning to start lightly playing some music to intensify their spiritual emotions. It helps them appreciate the message and enhance their feelings."

"No notes! No music Sludge! Tommy is playing the last song per my father. That will be the end of MY BROTHER's service. Got it! And by the way, you don't have to worry about Tommy's physical appearance while singing. He's a health nut and in great shape!"

I then hung up before he barely got out his "What?" I am sure that he had no clue about his soul-killing of Maggie years ago for the sake of the kingdom.

***

Later that night, I was visited by the 'consigliere' of my father. That was what Stephen called Caine Banks, Ruling Elder, and proprietor of Banks Funeral Establishment. Sludge handled all the services when you were alive. However, Banks managed your last service you attended, if you were a member of my father's church. It was always at Banks Funeral Establishment. It was here that you got the last shakedown. Your last chance to donate to Hillside Community Church. It was an offer very few families refused.

Caine met with me in my office. He was not a very personable guy, coming off as cold and calculating. Banks was comfortable operating behind closed doors; almost never did he do anything in public. He never taught a class, spoke at a service, or lead any ministries, yet he wielded much power. If you did anything out of step with the church, you got a call from Caine.

Elder Banks commenced with idle chatter as he inquisitively walked around my office with his finger over his lips pointed toward his nose as if he was about to ask for quiet. He stood staring at the carved box with the bottle of wine standing up and the wet shred that was still in the box. Picking up some of the shreds he put it to his nose to smell. Stephens papers were scattered around my desk and guest chair. Caine opened the conversation, "Looks like we had a little accident," motioning toward the wine bottle.

"Yea, I think we have had an accident around here," I responded. I cleared Stephen's papers from the guest chair so Caine could sit.

"Cluttered desk, cluttered mind, my father use to tell me," he condescendingly spoke.

I turned; paused, looking directly at him until he could not maintain eye contact. He bent over to re-tie his shoe. "Well sometimes, that's what happens in life Caine. Life gets scattered, and you must deal with the clutter. But you don't have that in your business, do you? I mean there is not much life happening in your firm?" I pointedly shot back.

Caine, emotionless, ignored my poke and replied, "I'm just here to help facilitate, Edward. Pastor Sludge said you were not in agreement with his approach to the service. Is there any problem with handing over your transcript? You know he is only doing his job at the bequest of your father."

I got up and reached over to shake his hand signaling that this meeting was about to end, "No, I don't have a problem. I also don't have a transcript or notes. If I did, I probably wouldn't hand them over."

Shaking my hand with that fake power grab handshake by placing the other hand on top; with ominous concern conveyed to me, "I'm sure you will not let everyone down. Your father is counting on you."

***

The day before Thanksgiving was overcast but started off well considering this was the day my brother would be cremated. I was thankful to experience a dream free night and felt rested. Giles had just pulled up to take me to the service. I could tell something was wrong. Giles and his wife Julie were coming toward me in a distressed manner. I spotted another car behind them with Dr. Ayazz, my friend, mentor, and colleague standing next to the dark sedan. Giles met me at the bottom of the steps while Julie passed and gently squeezed my arm moving toward Hayleigh who had just come onto the porch.

Giles moved toward me saying, "He wanted to be the person to tell you."

I pushed him away and started to walk toward Ayazz reaching out my hand saying, "Thank you, friend, for coming, I did not expect you to make it here from New York." Shaking his hand and hugging awkwardly, he pulled back and became emotional as tears ran down his cheeks. I could hear his wife Beenish crying inside the car. "What's the matter Ayazz?"

"It's my son, my son, my son," he cried.

"Did something happen to Abisali? Ayazz dropped to his knees wailing. I lifted him up continuing my interrogation, "What happened to your son?"

Ayazz gathered himself and finally spoke calmly, "Abisali, he murdered your brother, it was my son who killed him, I just got the news this morning when he called, and I did not want you to hear it from the news."

I just froze. My chest is pounding. My God, it was if Stephen had been murdered again. My friend and mentor's son killed Stephen. I stood there looking down at the ground, and I could hear Hayleigh crying in the background.

This whimpering old man I called friend started to say something, "Ah ahh I ….".

"Ayazz! Get the hell off my property!" I screamed.

He started again, "Edwar…." Turning away, I threw my fist down on the hood of his car, and Beenish screamed inside.

"Shut up and get the hell off my property! And take your savage religion with you!"

Ayazz sheepishly got back into his car. I motioned to Giles to get in the car and pointed for us to leave.

As we sped past Ayazz, he mouthed the words through the window, "I am sorry."

***

The ten-minute ride to Banks Funeral Establishment allowed me time and space to breath. Giles told me that he tried to stop Ayazz from telling me, but he had to catch a plane to Italy this morning. He had come into town to be there for me before he got the call. He felt he owed it to me; to tell me in person.

I wondered how many people know and most importantly does Dad know? If people knew, then the day would be about the story and the beheading, instead of about Stephen.

As we arrived there were a few people already there, and the staff were courteous and appeared as normal; as much as a funeral can be. As I passed Caine and Sludge, they came up to me and gave me an obligatory hug. Everything appeared calm. Then as I turned to walk down the hall, I glanced to my left, and there was the coffin. Immediately my legs got weak, and I burst into a cold sweat but no tears. Giles grabbed my arm, and I motioned toward the men's room where I vomited. Giles cleaned the mess up as I stood in front of the mirror staring at myself, not knowing if I could do this. Tommy walked into the bathroom, as I was throwing water onto my face trying to gather myself.

"You ready for this Dad," he asked as he gave me the thumbs up sign. I looked at him and gave him the thumbs up. I now knew I was not alone. We headed into the room.

My father arrived right on time and was seated to my left and in front of Tommy who was sitting on a stool with his guitar. I gained strength and love from Hayleigh who was sitting with Maggie and the grandkids in front of me. Her family, the Pearls, were there behind her along with many family friends and church members. Sludge had arranged the first two hymns and scripture readings. They were part and parcel of millions of funeral services across the world. Scripture was read as if you were reading the ingredients of a cake mix. The hymns were sung like a school song at graduation. I was waiting for the old staple. Que. Dad's wife, Margaret gets up and recites the Twenty-Third Psalm. Then Sludge rises from Dad's right side and kindly and graciously introduces me to bring forth the Eulogy for Stephen Peter Mayus.

I rose from my chair and could tell that my mouth was dry and wondered if I could get a sound to come out of my lips. A small sip of water and I started to talk about the greatest friend and man I ever knew. The twenty minutes flew by as I recounted the stories I found in my brother's journal. I could see in the eyes of the people that Stephen was becoming more than their martyr or hero he had previously been defined. He became a human being living life with his God with doubts and faults. There were not many dry eyes in the room after the stories of Chidike and Afet.

I closed with what I had learned from Stephen's journal.

Stephen's sojourn revealed the secret to life. The secret was not to lose your soul! Your true self. Your human self. Stephen's path points to a human being that embraced life so much that he could not lose his soul. He accepted and embraced that he was human and made in the image of his creator. This was Stephen's why. Stephen was made to live life. Stephen's Jesus was a human being who lived life and revealed Stephen's why. The why is the reason for his journey. Stephen loved and suffered. He discovered that you cannot do only one. A life fully lived involves both. That is your cross to bear. Your cross you must pick up, or you will leave your life behind. You will not know love if you do not know suffering, and you will never suffer if you have never loved. Follow Stephen's example and live!

I motioned to Tommy to start to play. Tommy did a soulful jazz arrangement of Amazing Grace that was poignant and isolated that stopped time for all that heard it. Even Dad was focused on the words. As the song came to the traditional end, Tommy continued to play as you could only hear the slight sniffling of tears from the room. Then he added one more verse that he wrote for Stephen.

Living of the world, has left me blind

Wounded heart left I to live

Unchained, my heart, to be set free

My act of grace to forgive

The last verse grabbed me as my vision of Ayazz standing before me pleading for compassion, but I could not offer it then, I am not ready now. Where do I go from here? On what page, have I found my new story beginning? How will I paint my masterpiece?

MASKS

We wear the mask that grins and lies,
It hides our cheeks and shades our eyes,
This debt we pay to human guile;
With torn and bleeding hearts we smile,
And mouth with myriad subtleties.

Why should the world be over wise,
In counting all our tears and sighs?
Nay, let them only see us, while
We wear the mask.

We smile, but, O great Christ, our cries
To thee from tortured souls arise.
We sing, but oh the clay is vile
Beneath our feet, and long the mile;
But let the world dream otherwise,
We wear the mask!

-Paul Lawrence Dunbar

Many handshakes later I stood staring at the polished austere coffin that contained the body of Stephen, but I knew without a doubt, he was not there. He was here. The real question was; where am I? I had no idea, but I knew that wherever I am, I would not be there much longer. My life and space were about to change. The room had emptied and was quiet; my father was looming in the background waiting for his turn to come and say his final goodbyes. Grandma Abba is holding onto his right arm, while Martha's hands gripped his left tightly as if holding him upright.

Hayleigh came up behind me with her hand resting on my shoulder, holding my other hand. "Your words were comforting to everyone Dear," she whispered encouragingly. "People are waiting outside to tell you how much it meant to them."

"They're not my words, they were Stephen's words," I replied. "Words are meaningless without a human being behind them."

"Thanks, Hayleigh, it means a lot," as I squeezed her hand. Tommy and Maggie came up to pay their respects. Maggie gave me a hug and teared up knowing that she would miss him dearly. Two fingers touched her lips and reached the top of the wooden container. Maggie melted into Hayleigh, and they walked away. Tommy placed his guitar pick onto the casket, which I learned is what musicians do. Tommy just simply stated, "Thanks." He turned to me saying, "Uncle Stephen is the reason I quit school and started my music career," he said as he walked away. I never knew that about Tommy. He just came home one day and announced he was quitting college and moving to Nashville.

I stood before the lifeless wooden box alone, my mind wandering through the empty rooms of my soul, seeking answers where there are only more questions. Where was God in this?

One more cup of coffee in the morning and perhaps Stephen takes another cab ten minutes later to see his friend at the Vatican. A flat tire to protect my brother? Why not one more traffic delay? For a God that is supposedly controlling the billions of stars and countless universes; is it too much to ask? I can feel the sorrow gurgling below the surface, fighting with the anger and frustration that is choking my mind. Stephen, why did you have to send me this gift that I do not even understand? I am not worth it! This whole situation is not worth it! What did you know Stephen? What makes this suffering worth it? I leaned slightly forward as if to touch the casket to say a goodbye, but my hand instinctively knew; he was not there and went directly to cover my mouth to hold back my swallowing of tears. I just stood there with my head bowed staring at the floor. Then I felt a hand take my hand weakly.

It was my father's hand. He weakly held my hand and said, "You did good Edward. I knew I could count on you." My Dad's grip was so much weaker than I remembered. I could not recall the last time he held my hand. I remembered at the graveside of my mother; I reached out as a little boy, and he did not take my hand. Now again, I wanted him to hold it tight with that strong surgeon's grip he had when I was a little boy. Instead, he reaches out for me to hold his hand.

"I don't know if I can get through this. I'm going to need you, Edward."

"Dad, I'm here."

The emotions swirling around in my head continued creating a surreal moment that time forgot. This moment was what I yearned for my whole life. I wanted the tender human part of my father. His humanity was reserved for the saving of lives of his heart patients, only replaced by his salvation he brought to his flock. This was the man I wanted so desperately to love, but could not reach because of my doubts about his God.

It was getting time for us to leave. The funeral attendants were gathering in front to take the body for cremation. Dad took one last walk around the casket. His hands, never leaving the surface, he wiped away all the smudges left by the previous hands that had said their goodbyes to make perfect the last vessel of his beloved son before he would return to dust.

The halls now quiet, as the people had decided to respect this sacred period for the family. We moved slowly away. The saddest part about this time was that Johanna felt she needed to wait until the family finished. As I glanced back, I could see Emilee and her crying before the casket saying their goodbyes in front of the funeral staff as if they were second-class members of the family. My father was clueless to what was transpiring.

Lurking in the background were Banks and Sludge ready to be at the beckon call of my Father. It was then I knew that I should be the one to tell him about who killed Stephen. "Dad, we need to talk about something," I asked directing him and Martha toward another room.

"Can it wait till later?"

"No, I think you need to know this now. Let's go into this room."

Both Banks and Sludge started to make their way into the room when I asked them to step out. "This was a family meeting," I said sternly looking Banks straight in the eye. You could never look Banks into both eyes; his head was always cocked to the side as if suspiciously examining you. Grandma Abba ushered them out of the room.

"You heard what Edward said."

"Where's Johanna?" I asked. Grandma Abba motioned to Johanna to come in, and she obliged. Emilee remained in the hallway with Banks and Sludge.

"You too," she barked, pointing to Emilee. I can only imagine how this perturbed the religious 'Consigliere and Capo Bastone' waiting outside. No wonder Grandma Abba had a slight grin on her face as she sat down.

"Dad, there's something I need to tell you about Stephens death. We know who murdered Stephen. This morning Dr. Imwas stopped by the house."

"What does that have to do with the animal who murdered Stephen?"

"Dad, we identified the person; it was Ayazz's son who killed Stephen."

"What!" he shouted angrily burying his face into his clenched fist. "Ohhhhhh my God, I have had that kid in my house, how could he?" wailing on and on, "How could he? I pray that animal rots in Hell!" Dad firmly tapped his fist to his face and sobbed. "Oh, God this test is too much!" he mumbled into his clenched fist.

I cannot believe he thinks God is testing him. For what? There before me, was this man of God, with rock solid beliefs that I yearned for and wanted to be true; juxtaposed against the frailty of the human condition of a broken man that I hardly knew. I wanted to embrace this broken man, but could not approach the father of my past.

Martha asked Dad where his medicine was and started to search his pockets and then she asked for some water. Emilee left to get water as Martha found his pills.

I asked, "What medicine, what's wrong?"

Martha proceeded to tell me that my father had been suffering heart problems for the last year and he has been keeping it quiet. Things began to make sense why Stephen was coming home to take over the church. Dad was breathing heavy and asked to lay down. Martha gave him his pills, and Grandma Abba was left standing fragile off to the side looking worried. It was troubling to see her like this, but this iron man was still her little boy. I went over to comfort her, and she informed me that these episodes have been going on for over a year, but my father had sworn everyone to secrecy.

Banks, Sludge, and Martha, loaded him into the car and took him home. As my dad left he rolled down the window, "Stephen would have been proud today son, and so would your mother, I'm going to be counting on you."

***

The ride home with Hayleigh driving was a welcome relief. Wiping my face with both hands; I thought tomorrow is Thanksgiving. Hopefully, I can see something to be grateful. For now, I remained a prisoner of my thoughts driving home.

Maybe Maggie was right, and it is part of a grand cosmic plan. It is my turn to get beat like a piñata. Is God the Grand Chess Master? Is life a game of strategy that I should wonder what His next move will be? Some call this strategy . . . 'God's will.' Where does the Devil come into this? I never could figure this game of life out. Am I playing against the Devil or God . . . or both? The deck is stacked. Poor Adam never had a chance. Neither do I. Startled as Hayleigh made the left turn into Eden, I knew I was back to reality.

"There's my Daddy waiting at the door to greet us," Hayleigh attentively observed, "I'm going to drop you off here then take the car around back."

"Gee thanks," I countered.

I never cared much for Buford, her Dad; and I am not sure he cared much for me. Maybe I have a problem with father figures I thought. Our relationship got off to a rocky start when I first met him. Hayleigh had taken me to her home during college. Her mother May and she carried her stuff up to her room and left me alone with him in the parlor as they called it. The parlor was for company, and it was the room all strangers were ushered into at the Pearl household. We sat there uncomfortably staring at each other. He leaned forward toward the coffee table in front of me and straightened the large book with a ballet dancer on it. He broke the silence with a question, "How do you feel about capital punishment?"

"What?" I stammered. He repeated the question as I strived for an answer, "Well, Buford."

"Mister Pearl," he corrected me.

"Mister Pearl, I'm against it; I do not think we should give the government the right to kill anyone."

"The book of Leviticus says an eye for and eye."

"Jesus hated that verse," I responded. He got up and immediately left the room leaving me alone for an eternity that lasted about twenty minutes. He never spoke to me the rest of the weekend. Hayleigh said that I should count my blessings. He had just executed one of his prisoners the day before.

Buford Pearl was a decent man who meant well. He just saw the world simply and in a certain order. In Grandma Abba's vernacular, he had no palette, just a large black Sharpie. Buford ran his household like he did his prison. Everything was neat, controlled, and in order. Hayleigh was the only escapee having traveled far away to college to find her freedom, but her father's emotional tentacles always were there and reared up in Hayleigh's lack of confidence and unsurpassed willingness to meet everyone's expectations.

Buford reached his hand toward me as I climbed the steps to the porch, "I'm sorry for your loss Edward. The boys will be up tomorrow for Thanksgiving."

"I appreciate that Buford." I made my way into the house and spotted Annamae Buford, Hayleigh's mom who we called May, teaching Maggie's kids Aidan and Eden how to dance. The laughter was a nice respite from the gravity of the last six days. Hayleigh's mom was a beautiful woman; she was studying to be a dancer when she fell in love with Buford. May Pearl had already been in some regional dance companies and had a promising career. She left dancing. Buford could not see past the pragmatic need for a mother to be at home raising a family. Hayleigh believed that her Daddy, who was just a guard at the time, could not take the chance that May Pearl would eclipse his meager career in criminal justice. So, he found a way to blow out the candle before the light shone too bright.

Hayleigh remembers how her father smiled when she and her Mom danced together when she was a child. He was noticing May's joy. After a few years of dance lessons, Hayleigh was made to quit because the spark inside her mother produced a depression that affected their marriage. Hayleigh took up art instead, and the family strung a life together that from the outside, was indeed a strand of fine pearls.

The remainder of the day was filled with laughter and intermittent tears, eating, and reminiscing about stories concerning Stephen. What a mixture of people? Somehow this started to feel normal; it was a good normal. Why do we have to wait until death to share intimate thoughts and feelings? The departed hardly ever knew how we thought. Are our moments living only valuable during this time of grieving? Does our life only have meaning in the afterlife? God, I hope not. It might be a little late for me, but it can't be for my children and grandchildren. I called my father to check on him as the night ticked down. Martha answered the phone and informed me that he had been sleeping most of the day. I thanked her, and she left me with this cryptic message, "Edward, please don't let your father down."

"Martha, I'm not going to let him down," I responded thinking she knew something.

"I hope not, I hope not," Martha whispered as she hung up.

***

I was watching the fire burn down in the great room when Hayleigh stopped off before going to bed and asked me not to be too long. I could hear Grandma Abba finishing up in the kitchen humming Amazing Grace which brought me back to Tommy's last verse that he wrote for Stephen. I was singing his verses lightly to myself when at the very end, I horrifically recalled Stephen's last attempt at a word was . . . I forgive you.

Living of the world, has left me blind

Wounded heart left I to live

Unchained, my heart, to be set free

My act of grace to forgive

As the last words of the song spilled gently from my lips, Grandma Abba's edifying presence entered the room with her nightly tea. "What a beautiful way to end the night hearing those words," she lightly proclaimed.

"Well, I'm not ready to choose forgiveness quite yet Grandma Abba."

"You don't choose forgiveness Edward, you live it." I was not ready for a spiritual tête-à-tête with my mentor tonight, but her words rang genuine and rich.

"Grandma Abba, when I called to check on my father, Martha sounded peculiar. She was trying to convince me of something that she was not at liberty to talk about, but none the less was troubling her. Do you have any idea what's it about?" Grandma Abba leaned her lips into the warm drink, sipping her tea with an all-knowing Cheshire grin that touched both edges of the cup.

"You know something, don't you?"

"I don't know anything about your journey, Edward, but let's say, I have seen a few signposts," rising rose slowly from the chair. I gave her a hug good night. As she floated out of my office I could hear her talking to herself down the hall, "It's going to be quite an adventure for you." She shuffled off humming Amazing Grace.

***

As I turned back toward my desk, there was the presence of the gift staring back. A wooden box with Latin markings carved on the top, an envelope with a small moleskin journal, research papers, and a re-corked bottle of Ravello wine with two initialed glasses; was beckoning me to explore what Stephen died wanting me to have. I went over and laid my hands on the old box rubbing it like Dad touched Stephen's coffin. I simply stared at it for a time. Memories whirled around my mind like a funnel where my thoughts disappeared into a vortex of life and confusion. The whirlwind calmed as I opened the wooden box. Earlier that day I was staring at a box that contained the remains of Stephen; now I gaze into a box that contains the last thoughts of Stephen. I set the bottle of wine on my desk along with the two glasses to my right. I then moved the envelope and journal behind the wine. I closed the box to move it to my credenza when I spotted the Latin inscription. Using Google Translator to decipher the meaning that pixeled quickly across my screen.

This is my blood, that for you is being poured forth.

I will not drink from henceforth of this fruit of the vine,

until the kingdom of God comes.

I obviously recognized that as the scripture verse quoting Christ in the Upper Room before he was crucified. It was the first communion that the people would repeat to this day. The Eucharist was the only time on Sundays that I felt a real presence or connection to God. In its simplicity, I could appreciate this act. Regardless of your lot in life, this one act I can meaningfully participate.

I deduced that Stephen had planned on enjoying a communion with his lost souled brother upon his return to take over our father's church. Stephen must have quite a speech prepared that would turn his poor doubting brother around. I must admit, I started to get a little angry at Stephen because I could not get my head around what could be so spectacular that would be the gift of all gifts for me. It certainly could not be in old research papers, or a small Moleskin journal titled Lanciano.

I retrieved a corkscrew and proceeded to open the previously opened bottle of Ravello. Putting the bottle to my nose to make sure that the wine had not gone bad I was pleasantly surprised to smell the usual nose of the fine Ravello blend Stephen was fond of partaking. I poured a glass for me and a glass for Stephen with a smile on my face. I was just glad that no one was here to view this crazy idea, but somehow, I felt I was honoring my brother. I bowed my head and said nothing to God. The quiet peace that came over me said all that needed to be said. I took it that Stephen was pleased.

I reached for the second glass etched with the S and sipped the first taste before emptying the remaining red liquid in a few quick swallows. I put the glass on my bookcase behind the credenza, vowing that no one would ever drink from this glass again. I then took up my glass marked with an E, gave a toast-like gesture toward the emptied glass resting on the bookcase. This communion of wine and thoughts is the last brotherly act I will do with my beloved brother.

"Thank you, Stephen," I uttered quietly and with slight embarrassment, placing the glass down next to the envelope and journal. I picked up the journal titled Lanciano like Bilbo solving Gollum's riddle in the Hobbit. I was not going to bed before understanding the greatness of this gift. This was going to take a while, so I started to pour myself another drink when I heard a 'clink-chink' of glass.

I stopped pouring. I was curious about the sound. Puzzled, I re-started the pour and heard it again. This time I felt a tiny vibration from the bottle. Holding the bottle up to the light I could see there was something dark, but I could not make out this mysterious object. I had a wine decanter in which I emptied the remaining wine that exposed a test tube with markings on it. I lightly shook the bottle trying to retrieve the glass tube without breaking open the contents. This was going to take some doing, and I did not have the patience. I walked outside and down the steps of the front porch. Spotting the rocks lining the mulch and bushes I laid the neck of the bottle on top; picking up a smaller rock I began to tap the bottle trying to break off the top. After several taps, each one delivered with more force, I decided that this was not working. My curiosity was driving me crazy to discover what were the contents of this vial that Stephen had purposely placed into this bottle of wine.

After two quick glasses of wine, one's logic is blurry. Picking up a large rock and with one whack the bottle shattered into pieces. "Damn!" I yelled in a whisper as a sliver cut my hand slightly, but I was more worried about the tube inside as I lightly pushed each chard of glass aside. There it was; completely intact. I was relieved as I held it in my hand and stood up.

Just then the window upstairs opened and Hayleigh hollered out the window, "Are you alright? What are you doing Edward?"

"Uhhhh, I'm okay, I'm searching for something."

"Did you find it?"

"I don't know, I'm not sure," as I examined this glass tube looking at the long road leading out from Eden.

"Are you drinking?"

"Just a little."

She slammed the window and went back to bed. I had a long night ahead of me.

It was nearing midnight, so I went to the kitchen to start a pot of coffee. I could not take my eyes off the test tube. There was a dark substance inside, and I could hear what appeared to be another solid object tinkling inside when I vigorously shook it.

Returning to my office, I placed the tube in the empty wine glass and picked up the journal marked Lanciano and started to read. The pages told a tale I could not fathom. It started out like this as the words leaped off the pages.

My friend Fr. Paulo Francisco Martelli told me of a miracle recognized by the Catholic Church. That has been scientifically studied and researched over a long period.

It became known as The Miracle of Lanciano. The miracle occurred in the 700s in the town of Lanciano, an ancient city of Rome. The original name for this city was Anxanum. Monks of Saint Basil founded a monastery as patrons of Saint Longinus, who was the Roman Centurion at the foot of the cross who proclaimed that Jesus was indeed the Son of God as he pierced his side with a spear.

Looking over the old manuscripts in the Vatican library I found a wealth of information. The different accounts all had the same narrative. Below is the summary.

A monk, that to this day has never been identified, offered the Eucharist at a Mass. He was well versed in the sciences but had his doubts on the teachings of the church that the bread and wine became the body and blood of the Christ when the Priest consecrated the elements. His doubts were like mine, and he doubted that the Lord was even present at the Eucharist.

This day as he pronounced the words of consecration, the bread changed into flesh and wine into blood. The monk was moved in such a manner that he began to weep uncontrollably. He called the parishioners to gather around the altar and displayed the miraculous wonder before their eyes and said, "O fortunate witnesses, to whom the Blessed God, to confound my unbelief, has wished to reveal Himself visible to our eyes! Come, brethren, and marvel at our God, so close to us. Behold the Flesh and Blood of our Most Beloved Christ." The news of the miracle spread.

Shortly after the occurrence, the Blood coagulated into five globules of different sizes, but the Flesh remained the same. The archbishop ordered an investigation. The testimony of witnesses was recorded.

Flesh and blood appeared to be human flesh and blood. The archbishop sent a scale for the weighing of the globules: each globule weighed the same as the other individual ones (although different in size) or as all five together or as any other combination. Eventually, the Flesh and the globules of Blood were placed in a special ivory reliquary, but not hermetically sealed.

The Church did certify this miracle

The relics to this day remain in the church on display under the care of the Franciscans.

The relics have been investigated over the last 1300 years, and the real miracle is that there is no visible sign of deterioration. Wow is that unbelievable? When I went to the actual church, I was amazed at the physical appearance of the relic.

The most thorough study occurred in a two-year research study in 1970-71. Pope Paul VI permitted a series of scientific studies on the precious relics to verify their nature. Dr. Odoardo Linoli, professor of anatomy and pathological histology, chemistry, and clinical microscopy, and head physician of the hospital D'Arezzo, conducted the study. He was assisted by Dr. Ruggero Bertelli, professor emeritus of human anatomy at the University of Siena. The analysis was performed in accord with scientific standards and documented, and Dr. Bertelli independently corroborated Dr. Linoli's findings. In the second study in 1981, using more technically advanced medical technology, Dr. Linoli conducted a second histological study; he not only confirmed the findings but also gathered new information.

I was astounded at reading Linoli's actual findings from his own words below that I have recorded.

The flesh is real flesh. The blood is real blood.

The flesh and the blood belong to the human species.

The flesh consists of the muscular tissue of the heart.

In the Flesh, we see present in section: the myocardium, the endocardium, the vagus nerve and the left ventricle of the heart for the large thickness of the myocardium.

The Flesh is a "HEART" complete in its essential structure.

Flesh and the Blood have the same blood-type: AB.

In the Blood, there were found proteins in the same normal proportions (percentage-wise) as are found in the sero-proteic make-up of the fresh normal blood.

In the Blood, there were also found these minerals: chlorides, phosphorus, magnesium, potassium, sodium and calcium.

The preservation of the Flesh and of the Blood, which were left in their natural state for twelve centuries and exposed to the action of atmospheric and biological agents, remains an extraordinary phenomenon.

I must say that besides my doubts, it is hard to arrive at any conclusion but to say a miracle has taken place. My faith that is revealed to me now is that it is the body and blood of Christ.

Stephens findings were accumulated over several weeks of studying the original Latin and Italian writings. But I must admit I was impressed by the last work of Linoli. I was trying to assess if I could be ready to take the same leap of faith that Stephen did, but I kept coming back to Stephen's gift. Why? While this is a great story, connecting this to me was still perplexing.

Dated two weeks later was a note jotted down from Fr. Francesco Paulo Martelli who I talked with on the phone in the cab in New York.

My friend Fr. Paulo told me during my studies: The beauty of the miracle of Lanciano reflects the words our Lord spoke, I am the Bread of Life. He who feeds on my Flesh and drinks my Blood has life eternal and I will raise him up on the last day. For my Flesh is real food and my Blood real drink. The man who feeds on my Flesh and drinks my Blood remains in Me, and I in him. We must, therefore, never forget that when we participate at Mass, we witness a miracle.

***

While this was interesting, I still needed to dig deeper into his journal. There were more jottings about his feelings toward this miracle. Stephen and Caterina even traveled to Lanciano to explore this miracle. Stephen held out great hope that maybe they could touch a piece of God that could bring healing to Caterina. Stephen wrote a prayer in his journal.

My Father, I do not know how to pray,
I am a beggar at the gate,
Looking for the water to move,
My Lover is failing and her soul is waning,
I reach even for any thread of hope,
while her loss of life approaches.
I confess my weakness to not accept this cup,
But hold onto your strength,
that will see me bitterly through.

Continuing to turn the pages of his journal, I discovered Stephen was buoyant over the anticipated meeting of Paulo's dear friend, Father John D'Amellio. D'Amellio was the lead scientist at the Vatican. D'Amellio was involved in continuing research of the blood from the Miracle of Lanciano.

Pouring another cup of coffee, I read what intrigued D'Amellio was that Stephen had explained what research I was doing. He too was interested in the potential of changing human behavior through epigenetic alteration, which was changing genetic structure. Obviously, we are light years away from understanding this process, but it theoretically is possible. The problem lies not in the many different combinations of DNA strands but in a million combinations of unknown triggers that turn-on the various parts of DNA that are expressed which could alter behavior, which makes all human beings unique even when family members share the same DNA. Most of our DNA are not used because they are not activated. How and why they are not activated; no one has figured that out. But the clues are buried in the triggers and complex proteins in the blood that affect what strands are activated.

I lifted my head out of his journal and was getting weary. Speaking out loud as if Stephen was in the room, I talked to myself, "Okay Stephen, what are you trying to tell me. This is a great intriguing story but what does it have to do with me? Why do I need to know this? What were you going to tell me if we were together?"

Stephen was searching for the miracle for Caterina. It never happened. Then how and why do I become the focus? Surely it cannot be because of my limited research project. Wiping my glasses and face, I decided that I needed to plow through. I was not going to be able to sleep until I found my answer. The clock in the great room struck midnight and I dove straight back into the journal like a miner searching for gold.

It was not like Stephen to chase supernatural phenomena. His faith did not need any validation from the outside. The miracle never happened for Caterina, but all through the pages, his love for Caterina bled through the paper. There were stains on some journal pages that I would bet were tears. I turned the next page and the only words spotted, written boldly with a marker.

YES! YES! John agreed!

What did John agree to do? As I was reading, I was as excited as Stephen. What was his excitement about within two weeks of his death? How does it have a bearing on me? It was only two more page turns until the dots were connected and the story came to a shocking halt. The jubilation of Stephen was shattered in a few days. Stephen received a telegram from Caterina that was clipped to the page. She had gone back to her Capri to retrieve medical records. The telegram said:

Bad news-(STOP)-I was confused-(STOP)-My blood type is A-(STOP)-I am sorry for causing you such pain-(STOP)-I will meet you as planned in Positano to discuss future-(STOP)-Love C

The next notation of Stephen was one single word of an unfinished sentence.

God?

Stephen had spent the last several months of his life trying to save his beloved Caterina. I was weeping and my tears joined his stained tears onto the pages of his journal. He wanted and pleaded with God for more time with his lover. Little did he know they would never be together again because a flower did not float to the shores of Positano. It now became quite clear that Stephen had been talking with Father John about the possibility of using the blood from Lanciano to somehow help Caterina, but the blood from Lanciano was Type AB. A person with Type A is not compatible with AB. Stephen was looking for a miracle in the blood of the Christ. I turned the final page that had notations. It had one scribbled entry... *Edward!*

Why my name? I still had more questions than answers. I felt I am starting over. I don't know any more than when I started. Why am I part of this heart-wrenching episode in Stephen's life? The answer would hit me like a sledgehammer to the chest in mere minutes. Folded behind the next unwritten page was a small envelope stamped and addressed to me. Stephen never mailed it. Did I want to read this letter? I had no choice; I quickly ripped it opened and began to read.

Edward,

I will be returning home shortly. I will be taking over Dad's church because of his illness. That is another story we will talk about upon my return. I am crushed and hollow as a man. I have lost something so precious to me. Her name is Caterina, and God gave me nineteen months of a glimpse of eternity. I wasted three months trying to hold on. Three months I would give anything to have back. Those months would be another lifetime. There is a cavern in my heart that I cannot explore due to the pain. I lost so much time that was given to me and now it was for naught. That anguish is what kills me every night before sleep rescues my soul. When presented with such a pearl of great price and you waste away this gift because you selfishly cannot deal with its mortality and your weakness is exposed. I confess that my desire to enjoy the gift was greater than my need to love the gift, but I loved her greatly.

That brings me to you, Edward. The only one I can turn to in hopes of finding relief of my torment. I will explain more when I see you and we are once again together. Our correspondence over the years has allowed me to follow your work and your life. Our talks when I have been home, have been some of my favorite times in life. You have taught me much and I will forever be grateful. Now I need you. I need your professional expertise and for you to trust me. I do not know where this journey will take us, but I need you to help me know that I did not waste this last long fight for Caterina on a childlike hope for a silly miracle.

I cannot explain everything in a letter and we will have hours to talk about this when I arrive. But we must move fast and complete this task before Thanksgiving. I need you to be ready with equipment to perform a blood and stem cell injection.

Edward, you will be the recipient. Your blood type is AB. You are the only one I can trust. I will be bringing back with me the stem cells of our Lord. I have the DNA of Jesus Christ and His blood type is AB. Jesus was fully a man, a human being. My friend John has been studying His DNA for years, and it appears like a normal human being, but we don't know about what the complex triggers that are in His cells that turned-on parts of the DNA that made him the second Adam. If your bone marrow adapts and starts producing blood with these triggers, then we may understand more about God. John has assured me; if it does not take then everything will be normal. If the stem cells start to produce more blood cells and stem cells, then you will have the Lord's trigger mechanisms that He had. This could potentially turn on strands that were turned on in Him. This is what I was hoping for with Caterina. I was hoping that a strand in her DNA would be turned on and heal her. I hope you agree with this journey Edward. If I could take it myself, I would.

Brother to brother,

In life and death,

Stephen

The letter just slipped out of my hand and fell to the floor. I rocked back into my chair. My eyes bore down in a glare, focusing on the glass tube that my brother just revealed contained the blood and stem cells of the man called Jesus the Christ. Before me was the DNA of God. I already knew I was going to do this; I just needed to know a reason and how. I picked up the letter and put everything back into the envelope. I now knew what the murky substance was in the test tube. It was liquid gas that helps in the vitrification process to preserve cells. The gas turns to a liquid when nearing the end of its efficacy. That is why

Stephen instructed that the process needed to be completed by Thanksgiving.

I picked up my cell phone and called Giles Beamon, my doctor and best friend. After several rings, Giles picked up, "Um mm Edward . . . what's wrong?" he stammered.

"Nothing is wrong Giles; I need your help."

"Edward do you know what time it is?"

"Oh crap. I'm sorry Giles, but this can't wait, I need your help."

"Go on," he whispers.

"I need you to meet me at the lab."

"What!" he exclaims and I can hear him telling Julie his wife that nothing's wrong and Edward is just acting crazy.

"Giles, I have never asked you for much, but I need you now. I will be there in thirty-five minutes. Don't let me down. Stephen lost his life for this and I can't let him down."

I then hung up, not giving Giles the chance to talk me out of this. I knew he would be there. I grabbed the tube and envelope, put on a jacket and quietly closed the kitchen door behind. I could never explain this to Hayleigh and she would be dead set against this; much less the professional consequences for performing such an experiment. I turned the car on and drifted away keeping the lights off until I was far from the house.

My drive over to the laboratory was a brief time of reflection of my feelings for what Stephen had gone through in his last months of life. Feeling a sense of fulfillment that I was doing something in honor of Stephen that he asked of me. I have never done anything this crazy and spontaneous since I was a child. It was a good feeling. I had no idea that the journey I find myself on could be this exhilarating. I'm coming alive with fear and anticipation. It is certainly a welcome respite from the grief of Stephens death and my banal existence over the last years. This act I feel I am doing; it is for someone who is alive. Stephen's death has somehow brought me back to life. As I pulled into the parking lot, Giles car is nowhere around. I wonder what Grandma Abba would make of this?

"Well I am sure not studying the paint," I laughed to myself.

Bright headlights came up from behind blinding my vision. A dark shadowy figure came walking up behind me knocking on the car window with a key. It was Giles.

"This better be good Eddie."

I followed him to the office building door as he unlocked it and disabled the alarm. We took the elevator down to the lab. Giles never said a word to me in the elevator; he just stood there glaring at me.

Unlocking the laboratory door, we made a beeline to his office, turning on the light, he sat down, threw his keys on the desk and demanded, "Alright Edward, what the hell is going on? What's this all about?"

There was a long sigh before I asked, "Giles, I need you to give me a blood and stem cell injection."

A long pause as Giles' mouth froze open ready for his next word, "Edward, you're joking with me, aren't you?" I shook my head no. "Well, I'm not finding any humor in this. You get me up in the middle of the night and ask for a stem cell injection. Have you been drinking?"

"No Giles, I have not been drinking."

"That's not a good answer Edward because that means you have lost your mind. I can deal with a drunk Edward, but a crazy Eddie is above my pay grade. Tell me the truth; we've been through a lot Edward; you need to level with me."

"It's better off that you not know Giles, trust me on this."

"Not good enough, buddy."

I could tell Giles was not going to move from his position. I then proceeded to tell him the story about the gift, Stephens letters, and journals. I handed the research papers over to him and he glanced at them as I continued. He listened intently with not a hint of emotion. He asked for the tube and I handed it to him. He laid it on his desk next to his keys and stared at it intently.

"Stephen was a good man, I admired him greatly and knew how much he meant to you, my friend. You are a brilliant man; one of the best thinkers I have ever encountered. I am a lesser man than either one of you, but, I am a great friend."

I nodded starting to interrupt, but he motioned with his hand as if his mind was made up on his intentions. There was nothing for me to say. He picked up a life-sized pewter paperweight of an apple from his desk and rolled it gently in his hands.

"I could be a good guy, and grant your crazy request, or I could be a good friend, and crush this fragile piece of glass and save you from your predicament, hoping you will thank me later."

My eyes began to water and I could feel the blood pounding through my veins in my temples, but I made no move to stop him. I just stared into his eyes. He slightly raised his arm and slammed the apple down with a loud smashing sound; my eyes never left the window of his soul.

"But I am a great friend."

A few seconds went by before my eyes left his glare and dropped to discover that the apple smashed into his keys. The tube was intact. He picked up the tube and motioned me to follow him.

We went into a procedure room down the hall. As Giles was opening the container and removing the smaller specimen tube containing the Lanciano miracle he commented how small the amount that was inside. He examined the blood and stem cell amount and determined that it had previously been through the centrifuge. As he was further prepping for the procedure, he looked over at me and thanked me.

"Giles, why are you thanking me? I am the one who is grateful. You are doing this for me. I know what you are risking."

"No brother, I still am thanking you. I did not know what I was going to do right up until the time I dropped my hand. The fact that you never flinched or made a move to stop me showed me that you trusted me. That means everything. If you trusted me then how can I not trust you now? Isn't that what relationships are about?"

After discussing the procedure, Giles handed me some sanitary underwear and told me to go to the bathroom and remove my jeans and disinfect the right cheek and hip of my butt. "I may be a great friend, but I am not cleaning your ass."

I walked out of the bathroom with embarrassment. I had dripped the orange/yellow liquid down my leg and had tried to wipe it off but it turned my whole leg yellow. Giles just grinned. The small amount dictated that we place it directly into the bone marrow, the source of human blood production, so that there was a better chance of the stem cells reproducing along with the combination of triggers that turn on the various strands of DNA. The only risk was that there was an outside possibility that some of the disease-fighting DNA strands could be altered that fight modern day diseases. But hey, this was the DNA of the Lord. I'll take my chances.

Giles came out with the longest needle I have ever seen. This will help reduce the pain of the injection. Lay down on your side. "Don't worry this will hurt me more than it will hurt you," he said with a smart-ass smile. "Besides it's the next needle that I am using that will pay you back for tonight."

After about fifteen minutes had gone by, Giles felt like the pain inhibitor was working; and he brought out a large thick syringe-like device that would place the stem cells in the bone marrow.

"You have to be kidding."

"Stop whining the last person who had these stem cells was crucified on a cross." Giles explained that the pressure was only going to last a short time because of the small amount being injected. In a matter of minutes, it was over.

I had a difficult time walking so Giles drove me back to Eden. It was about 3:30 AM in the morning. Pulling into the driveway Giles pointed that I needed to fix that E on the sign.

"I know Giles."

"Maybe by tomorrow you can just lay your hands on it," he chuckled, "Weren't you a carpenter in an earlier life?"

"Funny Giles, you are a riot. Turn your lights off and leave me off here, I don't want to wake anyone." I turned to Giles and thanked him for everything. I soon knew I would see him and his family for Thanksgiving dinner in about ten hours.

I went in the back-kitchen entrance hoping to remain quiet opening the door and tip-toeing lightly I was startled. "I was worried about you Edward," inquired Grandma Abba looking out the window above the sink.

"Oh, don't worry about me, I was out changing my palette."

"Looks like you were drinking and breaking bottles."

"Good night Grandma Abba."

"Why are you limping"?

"Let's just say I took a leap of faith Grandma Abba."

She smiled.

I moved toward the great room and found the remains of the embers of the fire barely glowing. The poor old lady was up all night worried about me. I did not want to wake Hayleigh, so I just collapsed on the couch. The last thing I remember was Grandma Abba's hand patting my head as she shuffled to bed and I dropped into a deep, peaceful sleep.

***

I could hear the clanging, banging, sounds of metal rattling in my ears. The train was slowly, aimlessly drifting forward, barely moving. The others were sleeping. Their dark glasses were removed, which made it easier for me to recognize them. Many were friends and church members I had known for years, but there were others that were new. I could briefly make out Hayleigh up front with her head leaning on the guy I hated; who was me. This was the last car. I got up and walked toward the end and opened the door hoping to find Grandma Abba. There was no Grandma Abba.

However, there was a little old skinny black gentleman, with tired, droopy eyes smoking a cigarette, sitting on a small stool leaning against the railing. He had an old beat up train hat that rested back on his receding gray-haired head, exposing layers of time-worn wrinkles.

"We have been expecting you," he said in a slight southern aristocratic accent, "Care for one?" as he reached his hand forward holding out a pack of cigarettes.

"I don't smoke cigarettes, I am an occasional partaker of fine cigars," but I reached for one saying, "What the hell." He handed over his cigarette to light mine and I mentioned, "These things will kill you."

"Not here, out there," the man pointed with a nod to the dark countryside that was just becoming visible with dawn approaching.

"What do you do? Are you like the conductor or something?"

"No need for a conductor on this train, these people ain't going anywhere." Perplexed at his troubling answer, we just sat in silence for a time. I noticed that his cigarette never burned down; while mine was slowly disappearing. Since I did not ask again, he volunteered the answer, "I am the Brakemen."

"So, you can stop this train?" I asked.

"I stop the train, that's what I do".

"Is this semantics? The people look miserable on this train. Can't you stop and let them off?"

"I just stop the train when someone tells me."

"Well, I'm telling you. Stop this train!"

"I can't."

"Why!" I demanded to know.

"You ain't on this train anymore, you are not a passenger."

"I just saw myself on the train with my wife Hayleigh," I retorted.

"No, you saw her with the old Edward; he's dead now. She is just clinging on to old dreams of happiness."

"Have you seen my Grandma Abba?"

"No, but she is a frequent visitor who takes people off the train."

Then he said something haunting, "Do you have a brother Stephen?" I nodded yes. "I think I saw your brother Stephen the other day visiting. He was trying to stop the train for you, but you were not ready. He took another person, a beautiful young lady, I believe, a new passenger; I don't remember her name. It's highly unusual for a new passenger to exit the train so early."

"Look! How can I get you to stop this train?"

"You can't, only the passengers and the Engineer. You are a visitor now."

"Where is this Engineer?" He smiled and pointed forward with an opened hand saying, "And you are a doctor?" shaking his head.

I immediately marched forward to meet this Engineer, when I turned to ask the Brakeman his name. He was gone. Racing through all the cars, I was astounded at how many people were on this train and somehow, they were all part of my life. People were waking from their slumber and putting on their dark glasses. As I was approaching the final forward car, a passenger who looked familiar dropped his glasses on the floor. I stopped and picked them up and started to hand them to him as he was trembling. He was expressing his thanks then I pulled them back, he lunged to grab them as if I was a thief. I put the dark glasses on. I could see nothing. I took them off and looked out the window, then put them on again and I saw nothing. I gave them back to the man and said, "You can't see anything."

He gave a voided fearful grin and sighed a whispered, "Yea, I know." He sat back down in his chair and held his wife's hand.

I finally made it to the front, but to get to where the Engineer was I had to climb a coal car. There were welded ladder steps reaching the top. Daylight was breaking and the train was starting to gain speed as the passengers awoke from their trance-like dullness. As I reached the peak of the car I could see a tunnel was fast approaching, I leaped downward crashing into a tuck-and-roll onto little pieces of scattered coal in a virtually empty dusty metal box on wheels. Dusting myself off, I could see the Engineer with his hand on the throttle. As I made my way toward him amongst the noise of the exposed engines and wheels roaring, I noticed that he was a rather short fellow, almost dwarf-like. He stood on a stack of various old academic books so that he could see over the top and reach the throttle. He was wearing the standard Engineer's navy and white pinned stripe hat and overhauls. His clothes were remarkably clean, absent of any coal dust or grease grime. I tapped him on his shoulder and it startled him; he was asleep at the wheel. Embarrassed he held up one finger indicating that he would be right with me. He pulled down on the throttle as the train sped up. He reached his hand out to me and shook my hand. He had a nicely cropped gray beard, a curly white flyaway mane of hair, and little small round spectacle glasses. He had the usual old train operator bandanna around his neck except that it was not your typical red color but was made up of many colors and had tassels hanging from each end dangling in front. Underneath I could detect a white collar tight around his neck with a light blue shirt.

"Well, I can say this is quite a surprise. It is not often I get anyone up here. I heard about you," the Engineer said.

Shaking his hand and pointing to the empty coal car, I volunteered, "Looks like you are running out of coal."

"Oh, pay that no mind, we don't have any need for coal."

"Well, how are they going to get where they're going without coal?"

"Who? Oh, you mean the passengers. There not going anywhere," he proclaimed smugly then continued, "They have a lot of learning to do before they will understand. That's why we Engineers are driving the train."

"But you just said they are going nowhere, so why are you driving the train?"

"We certainly can't let them control it now can we!" he indignantly scolded me. "Now what brings you here?"

"I want you to stop the train," I demanded.

"Why do you want to stop this train?"

"So, my friends, loved ones, and family can get off."

"They can get off anytime they choose."

I shouted back, "But they don't know that!"

"Yes, they do, but they are too fearful."

"I suppose you furnished the dark glasses for them," I countered.

"Yes, that has been a quite nice addition that we are proud of; it makes everyone quite calm on their journey."

"But you said they are not going anywhere."

"Why friend, they are heading to eternity. Isn't that enough," the Engineer countered. "Why should they worry about today? I tell you what, you seem like quite a good fellow. I will stop the train up ahead for a few minutes. If anyone wants to get off, then they can. I will inform the brakeman."

I immediately rushed to the back of the train where Hayleigh and the kids were. As I rushed back, I was screaming at the passengers and my friends to get off the train. Some of them were laughing at me. Some were frightened. I was making their kids cry.

Rushing backward, I spotted Hayleigh as the train was coming to a stop. "Hayleigh, we have to leave, there is a life out there! Trust me! Come on Maggie! Tommy let's go!"

Hayleigh turned and asked old Edward, "What do you believe Edward? Is there a life worth living out there?"

Edward turned to Hayleigh, took off his glasses, looked at her with tears in his eyes, "I don't know what I believe honey."

Hayleigh looked up at me and said, "You go ahead, maybe someday we will join you."

"I'm sorry Hayleigh, I'm so sorry," I cried out. The turbines of the engine started up and the roll forward began with the blast of steam releasing the brakes.

"Go!" she released me. I ran to the back where I met my friend the Brakeman. Standing on the last step down, before jumping to the ground I looked up.

The Brakeman pointed to the top of the hill. "Mom!"

I let go of the safety railing and leaped off the train. I felt as if I was floating down. I am now in a place of reality and dream because I know I am dreaming while sleeping on my couch, but I can't have it end now. As I land on the ground, I can spot Mom up on the horizon. I start running toward her. Her smile and joyful laughter can be heard between my breathing as I race up the incline.

"Eddie, Eddie, my wonderful Eddie."

I stumble in my mad rush to embrace her, walking the last three steps on my knees. My head buries against her stomach as my cries reach directly into her heart. I am crying like a little boy that I was when she died. She is holding me with all the comfort that I remember as a child, even her smell is the same except the warmth it brings me intensifies. She has no tears, just simply pure joy and blissfulness. She pulls me up with her hand and looks at me with a love I cannot fathom. It is speaking to me as if in a language that I can interpret but not understand. Then she exclaims how tall I became. I want to tell her all about my life, but she places her finger over my mouth with a light, delicate shhh sound. "Eddie, I know all about your life, and I am proud. We only have a very short time."

"Mom is Stephen around?"

"Of course, he is and he cannot wait to see you one day."

"I can't see him now?"

"Not now, I need to tell you something," she quickly says as if time is running out.

"One thing Mom. Is it real, is everything truly real?"

"Ohhhhhh, Eddie, it's so real. It's more than real; it's true, it simply just is." She went on hurriedly as if I might be woken up by a telephone call or a knock on the door from my slumber.

"Eddie, I cannot help you in your journey. Your journey is as unique to you as each star and snowflake are different. Every so often, a person gets a glimpse. Edward, hear me, the train that you just came from; understand this, my loved son. Hear the word from him."

I felt a lightness lift me as if I heard something I've never heard before. Like the first time, you heard the Hallelujah chorus.

Just like that; I was on the train again with the Brakeman who spoke to me, "I was wondering where you went to."

He had that same cigarette. He motioned to me with the pack. "No thanks. My Mom said you would reveal something to me."

"It's the favorite part of my job, only happens occasionally. Just over those hills, are many paths that lead to life revealing each unique human journey that never ends. The making of all things new continues into eternity," the Brakeman announced like a sage.

"Why don't they stop the train and get off? Why don't you tell them?"

"That's something they must learn themselves on the journey; it can't be told or taught, it's too unique to each person," he responded sincerely. "I don't know how to tell you about your journey, only God or a person that loves God and yourself can help you. All these people on this train; they're all in some way blind, brokenhearted, and in bondage. It's the human condition. The irony of the human condition is that it is the narrow gate to life. Few find it because they are too fearful to look. Your brother Stephen and Grandma Abba showed you how to journey. You're searching for truth, revealed your blindness, broken heart, and prison. You were once a passenger on this train same as the others. You studied and did your duty, believed and did what you were told with a promise of a life that is already here. Life is just over those hills. You were told you were on a journey; when all along your sorry ass was sitting inside that car analyzing every belief known to man. Your path will reveal the truth about you. Nobody cares what you believe; they care about who you are."

The wise Brakeman continued, "I'm going to show you what you figured out and those poor people don't know." He takes another puff on his cigarette and I notice it is getting smaller which tells me my time of revelation is nearing an end, "Come on over here." He leaned over the railing as we were rolling along. He pointed downward toward the wheels, "What do you see?"

"Train wheels," I replied.

"Are you sure you are a doctor?" shaking his head in dismay, "Look again."

I gasped as I discovered that the wheels are not moving.

"All these people on the train are not going anywhere! Life is just passing them by and they don't even know it."

"How can I help them?" I asked.

"You'll have to learn that on your own journey".

THANKSGIVING

You can become blind
by seeing each day as a similar one.
Each day is a different one,
each day brings a miracle of its own.
It's just a matter of paying attention.
-Paul Coelho

I felt a gentle tug on my shoulder. "Edward, come on, wake up; it's Thanksgiving and people will be coming over soon."

"No!" I moaned wanting to ask more questions to the Brakeman. I did not yet open my eyes. Hayleigh took my moaning to validate her suspicions that I had a little too much to drink last night. As I lifted myself off the couch, I was sore in the hip area and limped up the stairs.

"How much did you drink last night Edward?"

"Not much at all," I shot back without even a glance toward her.

"Yea! the broken wine bottle on the porch did not give anything away," she shouted up the stairs.

"I'll explain later," I yelled back down.

I felt different. I noticed how clear and focused everything appeared as I walked into the bedroom. It was a partly cloudy breezy day, but the rays burned through the window in small beams highlighting a small crystal glass candle that now sparkled like diamonds reflecting on the reading table in front of the window seat. I had not noticed that candle in years, and today it was vibrantly connecting to my mind. That candle held a lot of life to Hayleigh and I. We were young; I was in pre-med school studying for the entrance exams, she was working two jobs and going to school. The stress was getting to us both and had overwhelmed our young love. I had given up, and she had left our relationship. She showed up one night in my college apartment with a glass candle and a picnic basket. She lit the candle, we talked, drank wine, and made love. The candle burned all night and still burns in our love for one another. Hayleigh saved us that night. Raising the candle to my nose, inhaling the aroma of a place in time that happened over thirty-six years earlier, yet just experienced a heartbeat ago, as if my mind had entered a wormhole connecting to that exact moment.

    I sat gazing out at the day, as the breeze bent the branches of the Canadian Hemlock that had grown taller than the window. I opened the window, and the evergreen fragrance drifted in surrounding my head and senses as if everything had just come alive for the first time. Just then I noticed walking up from the wide trail far off, was Maggie. She was with Aidan and Eden. And they were playing tag with a skinny tree branch. I noticed how happy she was; I had not heard that laugh for many years. I felt an emotion of love that blew warmly through me. I was overcome with memories of my daughter long ago. I missed Margaret. I missed her laughing; missed her joy. The love she was experiencing in the presence of her children had been hidden for years as an adult waiting in hibernation to be revealed. I saw it now. Buried by the wounds of failed relationships that stole her beauty and joy, and there was no one to rescue her. I wanted to be her liberator today. Watching her prance and run with a pleasure unbound caused me to gently tear up at the thought that life's whistle would call her aboard the train. My senses were being overwhelmed with love and sadness for these three humans frolicking in the field. It was if they were shining and everything . . . just was. It was true.

It's not as if I did not previously love my daughter and grandkids, but something was different. My eyes were opening. The scales were falling away. I always felt love when I saw them, but it was contained in that moment. If it was a bad day the feeling was less, good days were shared warmly. The fear of loss, let me know that the lost times could never be recovered. A feeling of loss is not love; love is much more. Today I am seeing and loving them outside of time; for who they are, and I love it. How come I can see this now? I lived a lifetime of stacking and measuring moments when all along this was the reality. I heard Maggie yell to the kids, "Come on in. We have to help Grandma; it's Thanksgiving." I did not want this time to end. Everything was quiet except the sound of the wind that changed direction. Changes were about to come; I was indeed thankful.

The beautiful day was beaconing me for a walk, so I quickly got into the shower. I noticed the amber stained skin on my leg reminding me of my leap of faith the night before. Could this peaceful, joyous feeling be attributed to the blood injection? Raising my head, closing my eyes while the warm streams of water were immersing my face, I could only digest that the moments seemed clear and timeless. I could feel the old washing away as the water poured over my head. Hundreds, maybe thousands of drops falling away from me leaving only a sense of newness that was yet to be discovered. It was hard to describe this mundane moment of euphoria, but somehow it was primal like the first breath of a newborn child. I was starting to remember something that was true. I was feeling like a child who had been in the dark liquid murky womb of his mother, who after birth can now start to see things that are now in focus. The baby does not quite understand, but is quite content to enjoy . . . what simply is; without any judgment of good and evil. I feel as if I am pleasing and good.

My mind is lost in these new thoughts until the next thing I knew; I was looking for my hiking shoes ready for my walk when Hayleigh stepped into the room to get out of her jeans and tee shirt to get dressed for the throng of people coming.

"Glad to see you have risen from the dead," she sarcastically spouted off with a smile, "It's odd, but somehow I think this is going to be a good Thanksgiving." She paused with her finger pressing her bottom lip, "I wonder if it has anything to do with your father not coming over for Thanksgiving dinner?"

"He's not?" I inquired. Hayleigh then recounted that Margaret had called and said he was still too tired and needed his rest. However, he would stop by to have a plate made up, and he wanted to have a talk with me.

"That will be good; I would hate not to see him on Thanksgiving."

She turned around in shock. "Now I know you had too much to drink last night."

"Can't a man change honey? I just see things a little better, your eyes, your hair, your beautiful spirit, and I like what I am seeing." I then moved toward her and lifted her up into my arms in a warm embrace, passionately kissing her until her legs wrapped around my waist. A piece of timelessness passed.

"My God I needed that," she barely whispered catching her breath, "I thought I was losing you again Edward, I thought you were gone, I have been so afraid, but now you are here. . . at this very moment, you are still here." Hayleigh's eyes started to fill with joy.

"Ewe! Grandma and Grandpa are kissing in their underwear!" screamed Aidan who had laughingly passed the open bedroom doorway. Hayleigh quickly raced to the bathroom, and I stuck my head out the door shouting to Aidan that he and I were going to take a walk in a few minutes.

Moving back into the bedroom where Hayleigh was getting dressed for the dinner she looked up and said, "Edward, you rescued me today, and that is why this is going to be the best Thanksgiving."

"Baby, I have so much to share, I see things different, feelings are different, I feel free."

"I can't wait to hear about this metamorphosis darling," she said as she turned for me to zip up the back of her dress. "Now go take that little spy Aidan for a walk while I will explain to Daddy why his daughter was kissing Grandpa in her underwear."

"Tell him he should try it himself," I poked.

As I was walking downstairs, I was greeted at the bottom by Maggie with her hands on her hips. "Daddy what are you teaching my boy?" she jokingly scolded me. I picked her up in a bear hug swinging her gently around saying, "Has anyone ever told you what a beautiful woman and great mom you are?"

"No, they haven't. . . where did that come from . . . Daddy, are you feeling well?"

"Is there anything wrong with being thankful for a wonderful daughter?" I replied letting her down and gently squeezing her hands. She looked at me with a wet sparkling in her eyes as if a distant hope had been fulfilled, but she was holding back on an embrace she wanted to return forever in the past.

"No Daddy . . . there's nothing wrong; I'm going to get a chocolate chip muffin for breakfast, do you want one?" She released my hand, heading back toward the kitchen not quite knowing how to take what just occurred. My joy was tempered by my child who mistrusted love and traded it for the comfort of a muffin. I was weeping inside for her.

"Grandpa, are you ready for our walk," Aidan ran into the room screaming with excitement. Other than a few times playing catch I had never engaged much with Aidan in life. I merely imparted my half-baked wisdom of an old guy that made it this far. He was a smart, intelligent boy with reddish brown hair that loved to fantasize about adventure.

"Walk!" questioning his choice of words, "This will be more than a walk, we are going on an expedition," I corrected him as his face beamed. Glancing to my right, I spotted Maggie and Hayleigh observing the two of us putting on our hooded jerseys. I had an old leather hat that I used to wear fishing, and I put it on Aidan's head.

"I can wear this," he exclaimed, "Is it too big?"

"You look like Indiana Jones," I assured him. He stood in front of the foyer mirror proudly grinning. I walked over to Hayleigh and Maggie and swiped the half-eaten muffin to her shock. "This will be our bait. Let's go, Captain, lead the way!" I shouted.

Maggie shouted back, "Take the wide trail, it's safer." Aidan and I made our way to the barn for the fishing rods.

Heading out for our adventure Aidan asked, "The big trail is the other way."

"You're ready for the dangerous trail, right?" I challenged back. He nodded yes. "Follow me."

After about a twenty-minute hike over moss-covered gray boulders, we arrived at the fishing hole. "Mom never lets me come here," Aidan yelled with glee. This was a new world for him.

"It's your time now Aidan." We fished for about forty minutes and Aidan, who had moved across the pond where a group of boulders had divided the waters, was frustrated.

Another ten minutes passed when I yelled to him, "Cast your line into the shallows on your right." Aidan obliged. The rolled-up muffin ball had hardly hit the surface of the water when I heard the slap of the water and the zinging sound of the reeling drag of the taut line that was rushing away. Aidan was excited and full of delight as he nearly was pulled into the water.

"Grandpa help!" he pleaded.

"You've got this," I shouted back. He finally locked the reel and pulled. I watched as he battled with a frightened glee on his face that he would not have what it takes to win this fight with doubt and fear. I found myself in deep meditation interceding for this battle for his soul. I was awestruck with the insight of this fight with a fish and a nine-year-old boy. A few more violent splashes, Aidan climbing rocks backward to make the final pull of a Santiago-like conquest, and there stood the young warrior atop the rocks holding the trophy of victory.

Making my way over to congratulate and validate his valiant fight, I shouted, "You were fantastic!" He radiated pride and assurance that beamed from his grin and liquid filled eyes. The young man stared at his battle worn conquest in deep thought before removing the hook from its mouth. Holding the fish, which stretched from shoulder to shoulder of the little warrior, in front of his chest as if presenting it to the Gods; walked down the rocks and proceeded to release it back to where it belonged.

I asked him as he sat back down next to me, "Why did you release it back into the water?"

He replied, with the wisdom that only a child knows and eventually loses as they grow older, "The fun was the fight. When I stood there looking at it; the fun was gone. So, I put it back where it belongs."

"Well, that's a great way to put it Aidan, come, walk with me, I have something to show you." We walked the path over the hill to the other side until we came to the place where Grandma Abba and I talked a few days earlier. We sat down on a rock.

"Aidan, you said something a few days ago, that was peculiar to me." He looked at me puzzled. "You said that God took Stephen and it was his plan. Do you really believe that?"

"Yea, that is what Mom told me," he replied, "God has a plan for everything."

I pondered his self-assured answer for a bit and responded with a question, "You really battled that fish, didn't you?"

"It was crazy Grandpa, I thought I was going to lose it when it headed for the old fallen tree laying in the water," he valiantly recounted.

"I know, but you saved it by not fighting it and moving with it," I acknowledged. "How did you feel?"

"Grandpa, I was excited and scared I'd lose it. It was the most fun I have ever had," he exclaimed with pride and joy, grinning brightly. Watching him glow happily about his innocent battle with doubt and fear warmed my heart for his ongoing initiation into his journey.

"What were you afraid of Aidan?" He paused and stammered before answering, "I did not want to ruin the day and disappoint you by losing the fish after you told me where to cast the line, it was like you knew the fish was there. But it was the best feeling in the world when I reeled it in, I never felt so happy!" he proudly stated.

"That was quite an experience, Aidan. I am glad I was here to share in it, but I would not have been disappointed if you lost the fish. I am proud and love you for who you are." I could tell in his eyes that he was happy that he was loved and we stayed in that presence where two humans have connected on a deep level. As a boy of nine, he knew that this time was special. This moment would stay with him a lifetime.

"One last question young man, how would you feel if you knew that it was already planned that you were going to catch the fish anyway?"

Aidan just bowed his head in thought, knowing that the joy and adventure would not have been real if it was pre-ordained.

"Aidan, God does not have to plan out everything. God is always there. He was there with your battle for the fish and your joy when you brought it in. That feeling you experienced was God. God would have been there even if you lost the fish."

"It would be boring. It's like it was not real," was his response looking down at the rocks.

Where did that just come from was my first thought? How can this little boy understand what I just said when I was hearing it for the first time myself? Just as quickly as I pondered these rapid conflicting thoughts, Aidan stated assuredly, "I guess Mom was wrong and Uncle Stephen's murder was not part of God's plan."

"One day your Mom will figure that out. We better get cleaned up before dinner. Let's head up this trail," I pointed toward the steep hill which Stephen had named Stephen's Ascent.

"Mom never lets me go this way. She says it's too dangerous."

I emphatically stated that he was just the man for the task. As we approached the steep rocky climb, we had to navigate the large fallen tree; that fell years ago, during a soaking thunderstorm, causing a rapid river to flow through the property. We heard the large tree crack all the way in the house as it dropped and formed a decent size pond on the left and a beautiful running stream on the right. I would come and ponder life while straddling this fallen timber many times during my life at Eden. I led the way going first balancing myself calmly across the wet chasm showing the young apprentice the way. I then turned around and beaconed him to come. Aidan looked back at me with apprehension and excitement as he started to take the step of faith and walk out toward me. As Aidan took the first step, he began to slip on the moss covered damp log, but regained his balance. Aidan decided that his best strategy was to take slide steps instead of walking directly toward me with one step in front of the other. He took another few slide steps looking directly at me as I encouraged him. Then he looked down at the small rippling pond reflecting his distorted image toward his eyes. The fear started to cause doubt, and the steps became shorter and less stable.

Aidan was losing his balance and swaying back and forth until he looked at me when I shouted, "You can do this." He regained his footing and started to shuffle confidently toward me when he again was overcome by angst and looked at his reflection of fear mirrored off the water. It was as if his distorted image of himself was pulling him into the water until finally with one more forward futile sway of the arms he face-planted into the water with a big splash. Aidan rose with a gasp and must have leaped three feet in the air trying to evade the ice-cold water that originated twenty miles away in the snowy Appalachians. He was beating the water to death trying to catch his breath and stay above. I immediately walked toward him bending down with an outstretched hand I lifted him to the safety of my arms.

As we walked to the shore, I asked him, "Why did you lose faith, Aidan?" He started to cry in a hesitating choppy whimper, "I should have beli...bel...believed you."

"Aidan, I'm not talking about believing me, I'm talking about believing in yourself. Of course, you believe me, or you would not have attempted the walk. You lost faith in yourself."

"I was afraid," he said as he still sought to catch his breath.

"What were you afraid of?" I inquired. "I didn't want to disappoint you; I was afraid you wouldn't like me if I failed."

"That's nonsense Aidan; I love you." I instinctively knew that he felt this way because of the old Edward that he grew to know. I was absent along with all the other males in his life, but now I had this burning love for this little boy trying to make his way through life. This new Edward I did not recognize. The eruption of feelings that churned to the surface since I woke up this morning was overwhelming. What is happening to me? I am becoming a different person.

As we started back to our climb up the hill, Aidan stated, "Boy am I going to pay the price for this with Mom," looking sad, wet, and afraid at what awaits him.

"She's going to punish you?"

"Oh yea, I'm going to have to pay the price for this big time."

"Hold the rods, wait here," as I made my way back down the hill. I walked directly out to the log and leaped, making the biggest cannon-ball dive into the pond known to mankind. The water was so cold that it hurt. What is going on with me? I just did something so crazy and so spontaneous. It felt so good. I lifted myself up onto the log and started walking back up the hill where I was met with a young lad with his mouth wide open with surprise, wonderment, and confusion.

"Come on, let's get home, she can't punish both of us." Aidan beamed with a look of free joy, maybe for the first time in his life. He climbed those boulders up the hill with a confidence he had never experienced. Somewhere deep down I knew this time would be a watershed for him and he was aware that I paid the price for him. He was unconditionally loved. I was exhilarated at his new-found courage and freedom, and surprised at the clarity of the moment that had just happened and felt like a lifetime of learning had just been compressed into mere minutes. What is happening to me, I laughed to myself?

Ascending Aidan's valley of the shadow of death, we could see the house with my father's car parked in front and Aidan's mom waiting on the porch with Grandma Abba. There we were, two muddy, dripping, soaked, adventurers returning home.

"Aidan Andrew, look at you. You are a mess. You are going to pay for this young man! What am I going to do with you?" she righteously and sternly scolded him, grabbing him by the collar.

I grabbed Maggie's hand gently, quickly interrupting his trip to the emotional gallows. "Maggie, that's not a way to treat a courageous young man that just conquered Stephen's Ascent. Besides, he was just following me. You can't fault the boy for that," I interceded, "I'm proud of him, and his mother should be too."

She just momentarily stood there speechless gradually releasing the vice grip on his collar and pulling his neck and head into her in a bear hug.

"Oh Aidan, I am proud of you. Grandpa is right, you are becoming a brave young man," she lightly and happily said as she gave him a kiss on top of his wet hat. "Take your shoes off before you go in to clean up and get ready for

Thanksgiving dinner." Aidan just stood there proudly as a young man, for the first time in the eyes of the adult world. More importantly in the eyes of his mother, he was no longer a child. Maggie released her little warrior who started to race into the house to tell the stories of his adventure to everyone who would listen. "Thanks, Daddy, I never saw Aidan with those eyes. I needed that."

"Aidan needed it too," I answered, "We all need eyes to see, especially to see ourselves." Maggie stayed outside to ponder her thoughts as I left to go inside.

Just then Haleigh met me at the door, "Sounds like you and Aidan had quite an adventure," she whispered while informing me that my father along with Sludge and Banks were waiting in my office to talk with me. As I hugged her, she pulled back, "You're all wet."

"Aidan and I had kind of a baptism."

Walking toward my office, I was surprised at the calmness I was experiencing knowing that I was meeting my father and two men I despised. What is with this assurance in my soul? I must admit it was perplexing as if something had been re-birthed inside of me. Walking in, I noticed a troubling look on Sludge and Banks' faces. This seemed ominous.

Coming up behind my Dad, I grabbed his shoulders in a gentle embrace. "Happy Thanksgiving everyone," I nodded to the three as I made my way to my desk, sloshing in my wet boots, as Sludge stood to shake my hand, Banks remained silent and somber looking at me with his eye suspiciously investigating my thoughts. My father seemed concerned and weak, slumping in the chair in front of my desk. "I expect to see my dad on Thanksgiving, but what do I owe the pleasure of you two gentlemen?" Banks annoyingly answered, "The Lord's work does not stop on holiday's."

"I'm here to support and serve your father," the young Sludge stammered as if not quite sure.

Just then my father spoke weakly clearing his throat, "Edward, I need your help. You know I'm getting old, and my health has not been as good as I would like it to be. My heart is not where it should be. I get tired, and I need to take a sabbatical to sort things out. I've poured my life into my church. I need some time to find a successor. Stephen had agreed to do this before he died. He told me that you would be the best choice. He said that you were the deepest spiritual man he knew. I never saw that in you until your eulogy for Stephen yesterday. I need to count on you Edward, God needs to depend on you," his words pleaded weakly from his lips as if fearful of the response.

"What exactly are you asking me, Dad?"

Sludge then spoke up on my father's behalf. "Edward, your Dad needs you to become the interim pastor until he finds a successor. He will remain the Senior Pastor Emeritus. However, you will become the interim pastor until he finds his replacement."

"Let me get this straight; you want me to run my father's church?" My father's head remained looking downward. "How long?"

His head then lifted with a slight hope, "Just until I find the right man to take the job, Edward," he uttered. Then he hinted, "Maybe you are the right man."

Sludge chimed in supporting my father's ridiculous hypothesis, "Edward, the people loved your message yesterday, they will love that the son of Reverend Edward Mayus is taking the helm of the ship."

I rebutted to Sludge, "Why don't you step up?"

"Edward, I'm the Executive Pastor; I know my role,"

I then turned to Banks who was quietly taking this in, "What say you, Cain"? He silently spoke nothing as he rolled his eyes gently, turning his one-eyed gaze toward my father as if desperately hoping for a change of mind.

I knew at that moment, while I had no desire to become the leader of an institution, I would do this; not for my father, but for the Aidan's, and Maggie's of the world. I felt a yearning that came from a room in my soul I had never opened the door. Sludge let me know that the salary would be handsome and the church would take care of the grounds of Eden as if that had any effect on my decision.

The longest pause of silence weighed on the room as the wet squirming of restlessness in the seat along with heavy breathing was the only sounds that could be heard except the drops of water landing on the oak hardwood floors below my chair.

Looking out at the three men staring, awaiting my decision, I broke the stillness, "I'll do it."

My father clapped his hands gently upward with a, "Praise Jesus," while Sludge was genuinely pleased for my dad. Cain Banks' head just dropped downward into his cupped hands letting out the last gasp of hopeful air through his fingers. He got up and left the room calmly. I looked over at my father, and he had tears streaming down his cheeks; he was genuinely happy and felt like a man whose life had amounted to something and had somehow paid back something he owed. I was glad for him, but at the same time sad; for an old man who at the end of his life still needed someone else to validate him.

I want to take the next three weeks to meet with the staff and get to know the people before I speak my first sermon. They agreed. I inquired to both whether Banks was fully aligned with this plan; Sludge never said a word, but my father assured me he would come around. I let them know a few ground rules. I would only preach two Sundays a month, I would accept no money, and this arrangement would only be in place for no longer than a year. Timothy Sludge rose to his feet and thanked me and said he looked forward to serving with me, and I felt that he genuinely meant it. My father was helped off the chair by Sludge as he came over, we embraced.

He said, "I knew I could count on you, Stephen would be proud." I enjoyed the embrace and the feeling of making him happy, but it was troubling that a man nearing the end of his life teeters between the past and future for his self-worth with no regard for the present. From where do these insights and empathy come? I am seeing my father in a different light. My Dad hobbled out of my office with Sludge at his side.

Just as I was placing Stephen's box up on the shelf, I heard Caine Banks clearing his throat as he quietly slithered, re-entering the room. "Did you forget something Banks?" I inquired.

"Please, I would prefer you call me Cain, that's what my friends call me. Look I want to clear the air since we will be working close together for a brief time. I wasn't for this, nor was I much of a fan of bringing on your brother, but it is what your father wanted. I am here to serve the Lord and your father".

"Doesn't it say somewhere in scripture that you cannot serve two masters?" I retorted. He just one-eyed me up and down silently, his penetrating gaze spotted my mostly empty wine glass sitting on my desk negating this new chapter of my story in his duplicitous soul. He offered nothing.

"Are you a servant for the Lord, or are you a servant for my father? It's not a hard question," I inquired.

"Why did you accept your father's request?"

"That's not an answer . . . Cain,"

I was not going to let him hide behind a question.

After a brief uncomfortable pause, "In your father's world they are both the same," he resignedly spoke knowing he was backing into a corner of his creation.

"Well let's say whoever you think I am serving; I am serving to make sure you don't screw up what the Lord has made," he smugly and guardedly snorted out.

"I'll take any real help I can get Banks," I said with a wry smile.

"Oh, you asked why I said yes to my father; to set them free, to see only one master." He just looked at me puzzled, shook my hand, and wished me a Happy Thanksgiving. I let him know that I would be at the staff meeting on Tuesday morning. He told me that I did not need to arrive until 10:00 AM because he always handled the first hour of business. I told him I'd see him at nine. He quietly left the room to take my father home.

***

After showering and getting cleaned up from my adventure with Aidan and washing the spiritual whitewashed stone dust from my meeting with Cain, I stepped out on the porch for a little quiet reflection before the grand meal. Everyone had arrived with fanfare and chaos, while the peaceful rest deep in my soul felt good. My thoughts drifted to moments of conversation with God as if He was one who loves me. This must be how prayer feels. It was if I was talking to the father I wish my Dad to be. It was nothing profound; simply a rich, warm feeling of thankfulness in being able to experience my time with Aidan. I had so many questions about the calling brought forth to me by Stephen. I had never done anything this crazy in my life, and I was anxious, yet the silence of answers that momentarily were absent brought a beautiful confidence that things were right.

Hayleigh came out on the porch, "There you are, I'm holding dinner only for a few more minutes, everyone is hungry, and we are just waiting for the Beamans to arrive. Giles will be late for his funeral."

"Go easy on Giles, he had a long night," I shot back in defense of my friend.

"How do you know?"

Just then, speeding up the gravel road came the Beamans.

"Hayleigh," after a pause, "We have a lot to talk about?" Hayleigh stared a smile at me with wonder, knowing something good was happening, then quickly disappeared to serve the feast for a family that little did she know; was about to be changed.

"Good afternoon Julie," I greeted Giles wife. "It's morning for us, after your little escapade last night with my husband," she moaned. Giles followed with a pie in hand.

"She seems a little miffed, did you tell her anything?"

In Giles-like humor, "Yea, right after I brushed my teeth, I happened to mention that I placed the blood and DNA of the only begotten Son of God in my best friend's ass. Of course, I didn't say anything," he sarcastically quipped, "that's why she is doubly mad. I disappear for a few hours in the middle of the night, she worries and can't get back to sleep. Gee Edward, it does not take a prophet to figure that out."

We both just looked at each other after what Giles had said and burst out into laughter as we made our way to the table.

***

Everyone was gathering and taking their place at the table while the children sat isolated at another table off the dining room as if their presence had nothing to do with Thanksgiving. This was a tradition my father started years ago. My kids hated it as well as me, but I allowed it to happen. What's worse, is that they place Hayleigh's twenty-three-year-old Downs-Syndrome brother, Buddy, with the children. Here was a beautiful young man who saw life through the lens of joy and innocence that set his spirit free to soar, only to be tethered by a Father, Buford Pearl, and a world that refused to see him as human. It was obvious that we did not even see our children as human. They were not visible, they could not be seen, and like all people, we desire to be seen.

Hayleigh always had name cards to assign seats and had placed an empty chair attached to Stephen's memory. My father always held the head position. This year I was placed uncomfortably at the head of the table. As I looked over the twelve chattering faces that were seated, I knew instinctively that my life up until the start of this journey had no real effect on the people gathered around this table. No matter how much I thought I loved them, I never connected in a way that was meaningful like today with Aidan; and they never connected with me in the way of my desires. I was too busy achieving performance levels that masked my spiritual chasm of blindness, heartache, and bondage. It was my elevation in their eyes; that bestowed on me the disguise I needed to hide the uncomfortable void deep in my soul starved heart. I willingly took part in this unspoken transaction, which allowed everyone to escape the freedom of vulnerability that makes it possible to be human. But, now was different. I was seeing things differently as if for the first time. I wanted to see them.

Ting, ting, ting sounded the wine glass as Hayleigh lightly tapped out a proclamation proudly that I was going to do the annual Thanksgiving blessing. The group slowly quieted until all we could hear the laughter of the children in the other room. I cleared my throat and overheard Aidan describing how cool it was to be on the journey with Grandpa. "I am going to do something new. Excuse me for one minute," I announced leaving the room.

I made my way to the children's table. "Are you guys part of the family?" I exclaimed.

"Yes," they screamed with Buddy being the loudest.

"Then get in here with the people who love you and enjoy Thanksgiving. Buddy, can you and Aidan help me move this table into the dining room?"

We moved that table so quick only spilling a few splashes of milk and soda on the floor. No one paid it much mind. They were just all staring in shock at the rapid destruction of tradition. As Buddy, Aidan and I were banging the chairs and walls navigating the table through the dining room. Cash Pearl, Hayleigh's black sheep brother, stood to help us the rest of the way. We butted one end of the table at the other end where Grandma Abba was seated. I instructed her to take my place. I remained seated about four inches below with the children right in between Aidan and where Buddy will be seated.

Buddy is making his rounds high fiving everyone around the table shouting, "It's a miracle, it's a miracle, I never believe I would ever become an adult. I'm finally sitting at the adult table! I am a man" he gleefully shouts. "This is the best Thanksgiving." His brother Deacon Pearl merely smiles condescendingly at his brother Buddy.

"Buddy, you have always been a man; It takes some people longer to see. Right, Aidan." I commended Buddy with one last high five and a wink to Aidan who understood Buddy's jubilation. "Well I guess everyone's hungry so I will say the blessing. We are thankful for all the food prepared at this table, but may we be more thankful that we are and were loved."

"Amen," shouted Buddy.

Johanna, then abruptly raised her glass before we all started our devouring feast and softly turned to the empty chair that was next to her, "I'd like to also make one last toast to our Stephen, my brother, and friend. It comes from a song in Les Miz, she talked-sang these words, my friend, my friend, forgive me, why I'm alive, and you are gone. There's a grief that goes unspoken; the pain goes on and on."

Tommy then chimed in, "My Aunt Johanna speaking at Thanksgiving dinner, now that's a miracle."

As everyone chuckled, I had one last thing to add, "Since today is full of miracles," as I glanced at Buddy who is still beaming, "I have one more to add. I am taking over my father's church."

Hayleigh was in mid swallow of her glass of wine when it ran down both sides of her mouth onto her dress as she choked on the thought grenade I had just dropped. She grabbed her napkin drying herself as Grandma Abba just started to giggle like a school girl looking directly into my eyes, lightly saying to me across the table, "I did not see that one coming, God has a funny sense of humor."

Maggie piped in, "Daddy; you don't even like church? Johanna just stared at me with tears in her eyes and asked to be excused and ran into the kitchen. Emilee eventually followed her. "What? What is the big deal?" I pleaded looking at Hayleigh.

"Edward, this is a big surprise to just drop on everyone, we never even talked," she reasoned.

"I know, we will talk tonight," I stupidly replied.

Julie Beaman deduced, "That explains last night's disappearance with Giles."

Hayleigh just looked at Julie and then turned to me and sat back in her chair wondering what is going on. Hayleigh hates surprises and wants always to have control of situations.

Giles, knowing more than any person at the table felt that wisdom dictated that he remains quiet.

John Kandy, my life-long joker friend from high school, chimed in with a mouthful of food, "When will the crucifixion take place?" John was always the class clown but deep down behind his facade was a deeply sensitive person.

"Go ahead, you can laugh and doubt all you want, but I know I am supposed to do this. I'm doing it for my father."

The other Pearls did not have much to say until Buford shoveling in food at his normal rapid rate piped up, "I don't see what the big deal is, you all are over-reacting, Edward is a smart guy. He knows how to run an organization. All he must do is keep the prisoners, catching his Freudian slip, I mean people, in control. The Church has been around for years and if the people toe the line; it will be around longer."

Now I started to get irritated. "Well, Buford, I plan on doing just the opposite, I want to set the prisoners free."

Buford without missing a beat and not looking at me said, "That is not how organizations work."

"What if the Church was never supposed to be an organization, Buford?" Buford just continued eating waving me off, his hand dismissively ignoring the question while his fork and knife clinked the plate in his usual irritating way. I started to fire back a retort, but I found myself choking back a slight sadness and hurt. My eyes watered slightly, and my lower lip quivered like when you see a sad ending to a movie. Hayleigh stared at an Edward she had never observed.

Holding back my thoughts, I found myself wishing as if I was praying for this decent man to see the treasure that had been given him. His beloved order and regulations, kept him and his family from the freedom and life he believes he is protecting. Hayleigh had escaped the iron-like clamps of her father by leaving Richmond for college.

Buddy had survived by playing the role of the runt of the litter that everyone pitifully falls in love. He's cute and lovable but never seen. Buddy gives them another opportunity of the challenge to demonstrate to themselves and the outside, the love and strength of their beliefs, sort of a ministry. Buddy never had the driven performance expectations of his father, yet had more to offer than most. The other two brothers, Deacon, and Cash were opposites. Deacon was the All-American College standout from Richmond who made it big in real estate. If truth be told, he would have been a musician if he ever had the choice. Deacon could have been a top drummer in any of today's bands. Instead, like his mother, May, was forced to hear a different beat of the old man. There was no free will in the Pearl clan, except for Cash, who chose non-engagement, instead of the pressure to perform. I liked Cash for his resolve not to be conformed to his father's manipulative grip on the humanity of his family.

"Like I said, when will the crucifixion take place," John asked trying to diffuse the tension. The remainder of the fabulous dinner went off normally with talk about Christmas plans and football games. Grandma Abba occasionally would shoot me a grin that let me know everything was going to be fine. Giles just kept periodically looking at me as if pleading 'what story have we gotten ourselves into.' Eventually, Hayleigh glanced over with her usual 'I'm mad, but I trust you, everything will be fine' look. I reached over and squeezed her hand thanking her. It was a great Thanksgiving.

***

As the men slowly stepped out on the porch after taking their obligatory dish to the kitchen, insinuating that they had done their share, we started our yearly season of solving the world's problems in politics and sports. It always started with a cocktail and cigar, but this time things took a different turn.

Cash, Tommy, John, Giles and I, were already outside sipping on our scotch and smoking a cigar when Deacon and Buford emerged after talking briefly behind the front door.

Deacon thanked me, saying, "Look . . . Edward, my father and I appreciate what you did for Buddy at dinner tonight, but we try our best to manage Buddy's expectations about what he is."

I interrogated him on this point, "Just what is he Deacon?" turning toward Buford, "Mister Pearl, what is Deacon saying?"

Buford, clearing his throat, stammered out, "Edward, what Deacon is trying to say is that Buddy is not like you and the rest of us, he cannot experience life as we do. If he is led to believe that he can experience life like the rest of us, then we are setting him up to be unhappy; to fail. Surely you understand our predicament."

I took a sip, and a long puff on the cigar in a long measure of stillness with only the wind chimes heard as a gust of wind blew through in a different direction.

"No I don't understand your predicament, but I know Buddy's. He wants to be seen; to be a human person. Because he has not accumulated a certain amount of real-estate deals," staring into Deacon's eyes, "Or controlled hundreds of men in cages, you both think Buddy is failing. Maybe you both lack the courage to see Buddy and see his conquest and failures because they make your achievements small. There is nothing wrong with struggle and suffering; it is not something to fear. You can't bear to see Buddy fight because of your fears. Your eyes are blinded at this wonderful human being who is free, fearless and has love in his heart. He sees life more clear than you both," I quivered out choking back my emotions looking sternly at Buford and Deacon.

"Buddy saw and experienced a miracle; you saw a loss of control."

My thoughts were rolling across my mind as I wondered where did this insight come from? I felt I was arising out of a cocoon and could see the present as clear as the past. Time was becoming one. I could see it now.

An eternity of seconds passed as the wind chimes violently blew when Cash raised his glass with a smile, "Here's to Buddy and his miracle of becoming a man today! Maybe someday the winds of a miracle can brush across my face." Cash left the porch with a satisfied grin on his face knowing he had heard the words he searched to find his whole life in his struggle to measure up.

He left with one thing to say to his Dad, "You never even let him participate in the Special Olympics."

Deacon had a look of disgust on his face, but Buford stood staring out at the cool brisk night winds. He was looking out at the sirens song of wild freedom he kept away from all who fell under his control. His eyes were wet, but his face was stern.

A few uncomfortable moments passed by as Giles observed in the background what had just transpired; wondering who was this new Edward who had just arisen from the grave. John Kandy broke the silence with one of his patented jokes. As the chuckles died down, Cash emerged followed close behind by Buddy who to everyone's amazement was holding a glass in his left hand and a small cigar in his right; with a crooked grin, as wide as the crescent moon.

Cash lightly whispered, "I hope you did not mind me taking one of your small cigars out of your humidor."

Looking over at Buford, "Don't worry Dad, its only coke." Deacon just left in disgust shaking his head.

Buddy is looking around; taking in this day of grand initiation, piped up to Buford, "Another miracle Dad! You and me hanging out like men."

Buddy is grinning, taking in small breaths of the little cigar, blowing out even smaller puffs of smoke like a goldfish looking out at the world through the bowl. Buddy re-started high fiving everyone; even blowing up a few with Cash, roaring with laughter, until finally coming to Buford. Buddy's hand held high in the air, begging for the desired response that had never come. Buford turned toward his little man-child sternly staring through into his expecting heart until finally, Buford's hand rose to lightly meet Buddy's while breaking into a slight small grin of enjoyment. A shriek of glee from Buddy pierced the night causing Hayleigh and the others to come running out to the porch to investigate the commotion. May Pearl stood there with her mouth frozen open with her clenched fist pointing toward her mouth and nose. She took one look at Buddy smoking with a glass in hand, and fearfully glancing at Buford until he smiled and gave a gentle hug to May, letting her know that all was good.

"This is the best Thanksgiving ever! I am hanging out with my Dad!"

"You are right Buddy, nothing beats hanging around with your father," I confirmed while Hayleigh just looked at me with amazement on how things were unfolding this day.

As the events that had just unfolded died down, Emilee and Johanna called from the side steps near the kitchen to let me know they were catching an earlier train back to New York. They originally were leaving in the morning, but I assumed that based on her surprising reaction to me taking over my father's church; she decided to leave earlier. The taxi arrived near the kitchen entrance, away from the others. I expected to talk with her during the night but now was the time.

"Is everything alright Johanna?" I asked as she was handing the luggage to the cab driver.

"Sure, every thing's fine," she curtly replied. She gave me a faint hug and peck on my cheek; while walking to enter the other side of the cab.

Emilee broke in with a demand. "Jo, tell him how you are feeling!"

Johanna stood there glaring at the door handle, "Nothing's wrong, it's just me," she dismissively spoke.

Just then Emilee blurts out, "She is afraid she will lose her relationship with you."

As Johanna opened the car door, she immediately started to cry as she leaned onto the door and roof of the cab. I quickly sprinted around to her and hugged her pleading, "Why would you think that you will lose me? That doesn't make any sense Johanna."

"Edward, I've lived this my whole life. I know how this ends. Every person in church either acts like I am invisible, not human or an evil abomination because I am a lesbian. I don't even have a family anymore. My only claim to a family was you and Stephen. Stephen's gone, and now you will abandon me because of religion. I can't be part of your life Edward because of the church. You see how our father treats me. Edward, I'm a lesbian, there is no place for me, I am invisible, I'm not a person, I'm a sinner of the highest order."

I turned her around to look in her eyes. I saw the pain experienced in her soul that was far more real than I could bear. "Stop, Johanna; they are wrong, they are only labels. They are blind, and that's why they can't see you. They only see the shadow of you, and they think that's the real you. They are in bondage to their blindness and broken hearts."

"You, my dear sister, like them also, need to see who you really are in your brokenness so that you can be free. You are not a label. You are a human being. I see a wonderfully beautiful woman looking to be loved like every other person. My dear Johanna, you are loved, and I will never leave you."

She completely turned to me and embraced me like it was the first time she was loved. The cab door closed and she opened the window and said, "Thanks, Edward; I believe in you."

As the cab rode off leaving the scattering gravel dust behind, I walked up the stairs, and Hayleigh was looking at me in wonder. Who is this person?

SCARS

Children show scars like medals.

Lovers use them as secrets to reveal.

A scar is what happened when the word is made flesh.

-Leonard Cohen

The night breeze had calmed by late evening, but I still felt the headwinds of change howling in my head. Johanna was heading back to the norm of New York city where the millions fight to be seen every day. Tommy would leave to continue his Nashville journey in the morning bumming a ride with a fellow musician coming back from a gig in Philly. The Pearls had already retired to their bedrooms looking to get an early start back to Richmond the next morning. Deacon had already departed in disgust looking for the next deal. The kids along with Buddy, Cash, and Maggie were watching the traditional Frank Capra film, *It's A Wonderful Life* in the great room. The irony did not escape my clear mind; they watched this story every year with the hope that their pretend life, may one day be measured in wonderment. Tonight, I feel like George Bailey, for the first time since the death of my mother, I may be hearing the ringing of the bells, but not for the childish dream that an angel has earned their wings, but because all things are becoming new. I'm beginning to see.

John Kandy and his family left earlier in the same Kandy-like manner. He knocked the Holiday Santa hat off the head of Penny, his wife, as they were walking down the porch steps while hugs and well-wishes are shared by friends and family. Penny cannot even have the dignity of saying goodbyes to those she loves and walking as the mom of two beautiful children without becoming the uncomfortable punchline of a joke or prank. Her life with John was a socially awkward life-long punking by the man she married and who loved her dearly, but could not understand. I walked down the stairs to retrieve the hat as Penny was embarrassingly bending down. We both grabbed it at the same time rising together; her eyes dripped with sadness without the tears. She exchanged happiness for jokes, laughter for peace; and the hopeful expectations for the life she once dreamed which had evaporated long ago. I handed her the hat and grabbed her hand tightly expressing sorrow, her look back, showed a distant fading memory of a life never lived. I grieved her hollow sadness and only stared at John as he opened the car door, staring back expecting me to say something.

"What?" as he shrugged his shoulders, "It was just a joke; she's used to it." I could see the dark silhouettes as their car drove off; the chasm of separation of their shadows was as large as the Grand Canyon.

I had known John since a little kid in grade school; always the class clown. Johnny came from a broken family; his father was a nasty, abusive drunk who made John and his sister's life a living hell. John spent many a night at my house recovering from the emotional abuse, hiding his embarrassment and hurt by making everyone laugh, sending the pretending message that he was okay.

I'll never forget his tenth birthday party. After a whining-moaning version of Happy Birthday ground out by sixteen kids and adults, Johnny was about to blow out the candles. His Dad came from behind with his beer in hand and smashed Johnny's head into the cake laughing. We all have seen these childish pranks before, but this was different. His sausage-fingered hands kept pushing Johnny's face into the cake without a let-up. Only half his head could be seen. Everyone stood in aghast at what we were viewing. Johnny's arms started to flap around because he could not breathe as everyone stood appalled at what was transpiring before our eyes until finally his Mom who was snapping pictures with her Polaroid ran over and blasted her camera alongside his Dad's head freeing her chubby little boy. His father then backhanded his mother sending her across the room.

"Mom, it's alright! Dad was only joking with me, he was just joking with me," Johnny pleaded with icing and cake packed into his eyes and nose looking up as everyone was leaving as fast as they could get out. My Mom was tending to Johnny's mother's bleeding nose as everyone left. Johnny just sat there amongst his gifts and splattered cake, not even crying, as he wiped the cake from his face.

"Why is your Dad such a jerk?" I asked.

"He's not a jerk, he was just trying to be funny," he yelled trying to convince me as he had convinced himself. That night Johnny's father hung himself in the garage.

John Kandy, my funny childhood friend, then spent the remainder of his young years making his mom laugh to hide the pain. No one went around the Kandy family for years, because no one knew what to say to a family that experienced this kind of tragedy. John Kandy traded happiness for laughter and acceptance. He made everyone laugh as a painted happy clown in life so that no one could see.

I'm choking up right now at this new revelation about my friend John. My heart is aching, as I step toward the taillights vanishing into the night. I used Johns humor to laugh; while he was crying inside all the time. I never gave a damn about seeing the human person. Now I want to chase his car down the driveway and tell him to wake up. He is loved, I want to see you, and I want you to see me. I want you to be free!

I stared into the night as my friend drove off. Turning around after a few moments of silent meditation which felt like a prayer, I headed back to the house. Giles was the lone person left waiting. He was seated on the steps and had already had a drink poured for me.

"That was some performance you put on today my friend, I've never seen that side of you. How long have we known each other?" Giles inquired. Continuing his assessment, "It's like you have re-invented yourself; like you have become a new person."

"Performance? Performance is not quite the right word Giles. Performance would indicate that I had something to do with this. I don't even know where this is coming from; I have thoughts and ideas that I cannot even describe. Giles, I see with clarity. It's like everything is in focus. My ideas come to me not bound by time. I can see and feel a lifetime of emotions in the twinkling of an eye. I'm one with time, yet outside of time. There is constant communication with someone that is me, but greater than me. I hear things, but it is me that I am hearing. I'm not going crazy Giles, I do not hear voices, but I hear things in my head that my heart has always known to be true and they are in my voice. I recognize the sound of my soul. It's more than my mind. Giles. What is happening to me?"

"Edward, I'm not sure, but maybe, just maybe, it's another miracle," Giles quizzically asked the question. "You think the same thing I'm thinking?

I nodded my head with a questioning shrug of affirmation.

"Edward, what have we spent the last four years of our life studying?" I did not answer, but just continued meditatively exploring what had been rolling in my mind since I leaped into the cold water with Aidan.

"Edward, we have been researching if human behavior could be changed by genetically altering the genome sequence, or could human behavior by itself change the genetic sequence of DNA."

"Your crazy Giles, now I think you hear voices," I retorted dismissively.

Giles even admitted that he thought it was lunacy, but my thoughts drifted back to Stephen and the gift he gave to me along with his hope for saving his lover Caterina. This gift cost him his life. Surely if there is a God than some of this must matter. Maybe it is a miracle. Could I have in me the transplanted DNA of Jesus the Christ, the Son of God? Giles and I looked at each other and knew instinctively we were thinking the same thing. But our scientific training held us back from expressing the possibility. We were trained to wait for the data. This journey had taken an unexpected turn, which I knew would forever alter my existence.

Just then Hayleigh and Julie Beaman came out the front door.

"Giles, I want to get to the Black Friday sales early so let's get going."

Giles and I just looked at each other smiling in irony, knowing that there was a possibility of a miracle that the world has not seen in over two thousand years; and the people closest to us are worried about shopping for bargains. We are all walking a thin line between the sacred and the ordinary. The two are never far from each other, and sometimes they are the same.

Julie was already in the car when Giles and I slowly walked toward it. As we approached the door, Giles reached out and gave me a hug saying, "We will talk tomorrow."

Just then Julie shouted, "And no mid-night calls please unless you hear a message from God."

Giles and I just busted out laughing as Julie asked, "What's so damn funny?"

As the car rolled away, I looked down at a shiny object that was lit by the moon; reaching down I recognized it as Ayazz's 'Tasbih,' his prayer beads. Yesterday he must have dropped it during our bitter encounter. Periodically during today, my mind would drift to yesterday as I ravaged the top hood of his car in anger. This man had the courage to confront me with this burden asking for grace, and yesterday it was not there for the giving, but today my soul is weeping for his pain. We will talk when he returns to the states. I turned and was walking toward the porch where Hayleigh awaited when my cell phone rang. It was Giles.

"Yea," I answered.

"When did you find time to fix the sign?"

"What do you mean?"

"Edward, the E is attached, and the light is on." I can't remember the last time I saw it fixed."

"Well it wasn't me; I did not have any time to do that. You sure it's repaired, and the light is on?"

"Yes Edward, I am looking at it with my own eyes."

"That's strange because it wasn't me."

"Or maybe it was you," quipped Giles.

My eyes met Hayleigh's as I walked up the steps; she stood looking in wonderment at me asking, "Who called at this late hour?"

"It was just Giles." A slight pause had ensued before I asked, "Did you fix the sign out there?"

"Edward, how did I have time to repair a sign on Thanksgiving Day?" she replied rolling her eyes and head back as if I'm an idiot.

"Someone fixed the sign; it's strange".

"Are you sure it was not you during your little adventure last night?"

A few moments passed. "Maybe it was me?" I thought and spoke in a whisper to myself.

I took Hayleigh's hand, and we walked back into our home where all was quiet; absent was all the bustle of the beautiful, surprising time of Thanksgiving. I told Hayleigh that I would straighten up a little in the great room as she went into the kitchen to get us the last two pieces of pecan pie, my favorite, before bed. I spotted a glow coming from my office lamp. I made my way down the hall toward the light when I was startled by Grandma Abba sitting at my desk with Stephens box opened reading his journals that she had spread out over my desk. She embarrassingly and apologetically looked up slowly at me, her piercing blue eyes staring above the spectacles she had resting on the tip of her nose. She needed to know what was in the box.

"It's alright," I assured her, "Well what do you think?"

She spoke softly, "I don't think anything. Usually, when I think, I get answers. That's when I get in trouble. However, I do have many questions. I just have to pick the right questions; the questions that matter." After the clock, had stricken eleven, she continued, "What are you going to do? Are you going to take this journey that Stephen has set before you?"

"I already have Grandma Abba; I already have."

"That explains a few things." Laying her frail, wrinkled hands stretched flat on the desk over the papers bowing her head, she said, "Do you know what you're doing?"

"No Grandma Abba, I don't have a clue, I don't understand," I weakly stated.

"Then this should be a good journey," was her only words as she got up and lightly stepped toward the door as if floating gracefully into the night.

Before she left I stopped her to plead, "Grandma Abba, please pray for clarity."

"I will pray for trust," she echoed through time to me her words to my father years earlier. "No one goes on a journey alone Edward; you will learn trust. On a good journey, trust will produce faith, hope, and love." She grabbed my hands and put them together as if we were praying, "I have to go now, there is a lot of praying I need to do." She headed down the hall into the evening.

"Goodnight Grandma Abba," I uttered. "It has been a good night, hasn't it Edward," she gently answered with assurance.

I met Hayleigh with two pieces of pie in her hands, at the bottom of the steps leading upstairs. "What is Grandma Abba so happy about?" she asked, "She is in the kitchen getting her tea humming like bird set free."

"We will talk about it later," I replied traversing the stairs I noticed how beautiful her eyes sparkled as if tiny pixie dust were emanating from her soul. I stopped her on the steps and lifted her into my arms as she balanced the two slices of pie. I would have made love to her right there on the stairs if Grandma Abba was not in the other room.

"I don't understand what is happening to my Edward, but I like what I see," Hayleigh giggled a whisper in my ear. We headed to our bedroom.

I set her down on the over-sized love seat in front of the window nook that we spent many a night talking before bed. I lifted the plate of pecan pie and for the first time noticed how beautiful it looked. It was just a simple piece of pie, but today I saw the colors of the china pattern which Hayleigh had specially picked out. It was the intricate colors of our wedding flowers that made up the design that she hand-picked, and I could have cared less. Now I noticed them. There was the perfectly placed pie adorned with seven perfectly round small scoops of vanilla ice cream; three on each side with one on the top with a sprig of mint leaf, which I never ate. What struck me for the first time was the love that went into this creation, this work of art she produced for me. This had been created thousands of times for me along with most every meal plated as if she was arranging a bouquet of flowers or creating an original sculpture. I never even said thank you to this artist of my life who loved me and life so much that she cared enough to create this everyday art for us. How blessed I was. How much I loved her, that was never expressed, never spoken in moments that could have been, but never were.

I stood up as she interrupted, "Aren't you going to eat your pie I made for you?" I walked over to my phonograph and placed the Tony Bennett & Bill Evans jazz album on the turntable placing the needle on the track But Beautiful.

"We will eat right after we dance, shall we?" My hand reached for her like I was Fred Astaire and she took mine like Ginger Rogers. She danced while I floated a shuffle around the sofa, but it did not matter, and I could tell by the smile on her face that she did not care. This moment was beyond time and contained a lifetime of love rolled into minutes. The moment slowed as the silky voice of Mr. Bennett was joined by me in a talk-sing duet, "And I'm thinking if you were mine, I'd never let you go, and that would be . . . but beautiful I know."

"Edward Mayus, you are certainly full of surprises; are you sure you are my husband? Well whoever you are, or whoever you are becoming, I love it".

We spontaneously embraced and loved vulnerably that night like never before. For the first time in my life I was more than just Edward Mayus; at the same time, I was less; I was becoming one with another person making me more than when I was alone in myself; I was truly in relationship, so close that we were one. Is this what love is meant to be?

***

The next morning, as I came out of the shower, Hayleigh greeted me with a cup of coffee and a kiss taking my hand and leading me to the love seat where our conversation was supposed to take place the night before.

"Now as you were saying last night before we were interrupted," she coyly said with a smile. "You can disrupt our plans anytime Edward with a night like last night. I have never felt so loved and safe. It started in the morning when you kissed me. I could see in your eyes that you were different. What happened the night before? Where did you go?"

"That's a long story honey, let's go down to my office, I have some things I need to show you."

As we were heading down the stairs, we saw Maggie leave with the kids to go shopping for her Black Friday bargains. The Pearls had got an early start home before we even woke up. There was only Hayleigh, and Grandma Abba left from the family that filled this house yesterday.

I deliberately sat Hayleigh in my chair to start the long process of telling the story of Stephens gift. I briefly gave her an overview, but deliberately withheld the letter with Stephens explanations and request concerning the DNA blood sample from Lanciano. She read and examined the papers and journals for quite a bit of time, before looking up at me with a puzzled look.

"Edward this is all fascinating, but what does this have to do with the change in you?" she inquired.

"Well I have not given you everything," I explained as I handed over the letter after describing the vial in the wine bottle. Hayleigh read Stephens request and then stared at the shattered remains of the wine bottle. I told her about Giles and me, completing the procedure early on Thanksgiving morning.

I pulled the small vial out of my drawer, and she just continued in silence rolling the empty container in her fingers. "Giles did the procedure?" she asked. Her eyes were beginning to well up. She then immediately went and re-read the letter again; periodically sighing with brief huffs of breath signaling some deep discontentment, then returning to stare at the drained Lanciano vessel.

"And you went through with this." Pausing, I nodded yes. "By yourself," she quietly asked in a barely audible whisper. Nodding again, I could see the tears in her eyes were angry and mounting. Hayleigh was getting more upset as time passed until she finally exploded with a tirade of feelings.

"On a decision, as important as this, you did not think to consult your wife? What if something went wrong? What if you are not meant to screw around with things like this? What were you thinking Edward? How did Giles let you go through with this? I figured he was your friend". Moaning into her hands, "I assumed he was our friend. Uhhhh Edward." She continued to sob into her hands clenched over her eyes. "I'm scared, Edward."

"Honey, what are you afraid of?" reaching my hand to touch the tight iron fist covering her eyes. She jerked her hand shoving my touch away. "Hayleigh there is no reason to be afraid honey."

She pushed back saying, "I'm scared of losing you, Edward. I don't want to lose you. You Edward!"

"But I'm changing for the better, I see you, and loving you more, you're not losing me," I reasoned.

"What if it's not you, Edward? What if your DNA is changing and you are not you; what if you are becoming . . . Jesus!" she said in frustration. "You have the DNA of Jesus in you; what do you not understand?" she loudly screamed. "Oh, my God I don't even know how to talk to you now," she wailed in confusion.

"We don't know if this is true yet Hayleigh; besides I'm changing for the better Babe. What if I do become just like Jesus? Is that so bad?"

Hayleigh shouted back in bewildered anger, "I don't want to love Jesus, I fell in love with you Edward! You were what I always wanted, then you lost your bearings, and I lost you, but I could live with the faint periodic glimmers of light that shown from you at times. And now . . . now your behaviors are changing . . . but are your ways changing or are you changing?" she sternly challenged. "All I ever wanted in life, is to love you. . . you," her voice tailed off into a whisper.

"Hayleigh, I don't know that yet, I'm not sure if I am changing into Jesus or not?"

Over the years of our marriage, I learned when to step back and give Hayleigh space. I did not need to become Jesus to figure this out. Hayleigh was physically extremely claustrophobic and hated being physically constrained, but even more so when she felt the emotional walls closing in on her. She reacted much better when given time to free herself from life's maze. I think she developed that skill during her soulful imprisoned world under her father's control. Hayleigh gathered herself, and without saying a word walked from behind the desk stopping beside me; placed her hand on my shoulder with a light squeeze letting me know she loved me.

For the next two days, Hayleigh and I hardly talked. There was not much tension; just a daily, respectful, separate going about our lives. Hayleigh spent much time taking walks and being alone.

I continued to remain seated in the side chair of my desk. I stayed quietly calm in my thoughts and feelings. I was surprised at my calmness and sense of peace. Normally, I would be terribly upset and anxious about Hayleigh's inner turmoil. At times like these in our relationship, I believed in her, but my beliefs were more like longings. There is a fine line between beliefs and longings. But this time I saw her as not just my wife, but as a woman in all her humanness; open, vulnerable, and I trusted her. This time I had faith in her. My mind went back to Grandma Abba's thoughts as I recalled our talk on faith. Looks like she is right. Faith can only grow in a trusting relationship with another person. It's never about what you believe.

Leaving the inner sanctum of my office, I nearly bumped into Grandma Abba just outside in the hall. "You been eaves dropping on me Grandma Abba?" I joked with her.

"No, but I didn't have to; I could hear the whole thing from the kitchen," she smiled back.

"Do you want to go for a walk Grandma Abba?"

"No, I'm too tired, I had a lot of praying to do last night," she shook her head.

"Thanks, I could use your prayers Grandma Abba."

"I was not praying for you, Edward. Let me get my coat; I changed my mind; I will meet you at the Mary Tree." She shuffled to her room down the hall, and I stood wondering why she would not pray for me.

The winds had picked up during the night knocking the last of autumns leaves from above; the cold of winter was not far off. It was too damp and cold to sit on the ground, so I brought two of the canvas sling chairs to sit under the barren big oak tree. Grandma Abba was waiting with two mugs of coffee.

We sat down and sipped until I broke the ice, "Grandma Abba, why will you not pray for me?"

"I did not say I would not pray for you; I just did not pray last night," she answered. I still did not understand, and she knew it. "Edward, did you hear what Hayleigh said to you today?" I tipped my head downward to affirm a yes. "What did she say?" A slight pause ensued.

"She's afraid of losing me."

Agitated and rocking back in her chair, she says, "Edward, she loves you, and you love her, she knows that; she's not losing you. Hayleigh stated she does not want to love Jesus; she is afraid of loving Jesus, of loving God! She's fearful of you becoming Jesus, and she will not know how to love you. Most people don't know how to love Him. That's why we create idols like church services, worship songs, tithing, programs, and doctrines to ease the fear of not knowing how to love the very Creator of our being. It's easier to love the idol than to love Him. The path is narrow, and few find it because they are afraid. We have made God into an idol to fear because we made ourselves to be worthless. The object of God's love has been manipulated to be contemptible. Hayleigh thinks she is worthless in the eyes of Jesus. Why would she want you to become Him? If you become him, she will lose you."

"Grandma Abba am I becoming Jesus?" I asked out loud as if searching inside the cosmos. "If I am, shouldn't I already know this; shouldn't I have figured out Hayleigh's response," I continued.

"Edward, I'm not sure if this DNA thing is transforming you into Jesus, but if it is, do you think you're going to become omniscient? Do you think you are going to know everything?"

As usual, she let me chew on these questions, and I appreciated this, because many times I swallowed the spiritual question without chewing and spit out a ridiculous reply that did not belong to me, but was nonetheless instilled in me since I first saw my first flannel-board-God. I wanted to say yes; that I would be omniscient like Jesus, but intuitively I knew that would be wrong in Grandma Abba's world. I knew I was changing and my eyes were seeing like never before. Somehow on this new journey, I was traveling, I would have to learn what it meant to be like Jesus. I did not reply, but she knew my silence was the answer. A gust of wind blew through signaling that a change was about to happen, but Grandma Abba had not yet finished.

"Edward, tell me, do you think Jesus had faith?"

"Of course," I spit out without chewing; knowing I had fallen into her didactic trap.

The winds were picking up a little more as she continued, "Do you think Jesus was human?" Another trick question my mind felt was conferred to me, as I nodded a hesitant yes. "It's not a trick question Edward," she said as the gust whistled through the branches.

"Yes, he became human."

"Why would you think he had faith if he knew everything? There is no need to have faith if you know everything. Your journey will be over before it ever started if you believe that you will know everything. If you want to be like Jesus, you had better be prepared to be fully human. That's the journey he took. His journey was no cosmic practical joke Edward; it was real; with all the feelings of every person, that was ever born. You think he came to be an actor in a play that was already determined?

Just then an acorn dropped on my head from the tree branch above falling into my lap. Grandma Abba picked it up. "Perfect! Thank you, Lord," as she held it up in the air presenting it as if she had just received a nugget of gold. "You see this acorn Edward?" the interrogation began.

"Yes; and if you make me out to be a squirrel or nut in your illustration, I am going to lock you out of the house," I quipped.

"That would be too easy Edward, too easy," she said with a sarcastic delightful grin.

"This acorn is the fruit of this tree. It is a natural process for this old tree to produce these acorns every year. It does not have to think about it or work hard. It just happens because of what the tree is. We know this tree to be an Oak tree because it produces acorns naturally. You will know if you are becoming Jesus, Edward, by your fruit. This tree has overcome obstacles. It has been ravaged by storms, and split down the middle by a bolt of lightning, but it has stayed true to what it is. Nothing changed what it truly is. It gave you it's gift when it dropped the acorn in your lap with this message, I am still here, I have never changed. If you must work hard to be true to yourself then you are not on an authentic journey. Are you on an authentic journey Edward?"

As usual, Grandma Abba always spoke truth through questions. The chill was getting too much for us as the season's first flurries started to fall signaling the onslaught of a cold winter. In silence, I walked to the house, as my mind drifted to the thoughts shared by Grandma Abba about the natural act of being true to one's self. That had been hard for me my whole life. The last 48 hours had brought an inherent newness that I had never experienced as Edward Mayus. My experience with Aidan, Buddy, Buford, and most importantly Hayleigh, signaled a newness in seeing and feeling. And more importantly, I could communicate these feelings effortlessly with a strength that was natural. The only way I could describe it was that for the first time I was experiencing living from the inside instead of judgmentally observing life from the outside as if I was performing for myself trying to fulfill expectations that were not mine and will never be met. Is this how Jesus lived?

Follow Me

Let yourself be silently drawn by the strange pull of what you really love. It will not lead you astray.
- Rumi

The cold winds blew; the season changed overnight. Winter was here. The remainder of the weekend continued quietly. Time passed with civil, polite conversations about the upcoming holidays. Hayleigh remained cordial and quiet as she worked through her thoughts while starting the process of preparing for the Christmas season. This Sunday was the beginning of Advent, which meant that Hayleigh's gift of transforming the ordinary into beauty was on full display. In a matter of twenty-four hours this old traditional farmhouse would emerge out of its cocoon in all its holiday splendor; with always the expected new touch that she created every year for the family. This was her time to meditate and contemplate the season. I am sure that the story I brought her into has been dominating her thoughts and prayers.

My job was to bring up the boxes from the basement and to take care of the garland and lights surrounding the large porch. My thoughts were to finish this task on Saturday about the time Hayleigh would be putting the final touches on another masterpiece of artistic celebration.

By the time, I came in from the cold, my futzing around had dragged into the evening. My mind meandered through the tangled strands of lights which mirrored my current knotted and twisted journey. I thought about its effect on Hayleigh. I wanted to get into the house to get both her and Grandma Abba to come out and admire my handiwork. As I entered the house blowing warmth on my hands, the smells of the cinnamon pine cones surrounded me like the arms of a friend I had not seen in a long time. Looking around in amazement at this warm living canvas of holiday embrace filled my mind with memories of timeless moments. Hayleigh is truly a Van Gogh of decorating. Every part of the room held a special memory for someone we loved and shared life with as a family. I looked around for the new unique creation she did every year that held a meaning that only we could comprehend. Everything looked in place until I spotted a small gold envelope hanging from the tree with my name handwritten in calligraphic style. I opened the envelope reading out loud in my mind as if it was Hayleigh's soft voice.

My Dearest Edward,

While I am fearful of the latest turn of your journey,

I have always trusted you which has blessed me with a faith in you.

I still trust in you and our love.

Through the years, I have found that we have become one.

Our separate journeys have so intertwined over time that they become almost one.

The gold ribbon that winds through our tree has no beginning and no end as does our love.

I will continue to be by your side and grow in our trust for one another whatever this journey brings.

Love, H

It was always Hayleigh's style to produce an act of love without waiting or needing the immediate response of acclamation and adoration. As I examined further the tree of life created by her love, I could not find an ending or a beginning of the gold ribbon garland. What I found as it turned and twisted through the branches; only to disappear into the dark recesses of the tree, then reappear later, were these small little ornaments that contained pictures of us at different times in our lives. It seemed to go on forever. I knew that night; our journey would continue in a far richer way than I had known before.

Looking for Hayleigh to let her know how much I loved her. I went upstairs and there she had collapsed on the bed after having emptied herself; contemplating our future and creating her gift of love to me. I went over lifting her blue-jean-ed legs, placing them under the covers, warming her for the night. I kissed her gently on her lips as she intuitively smiled in her dreams. I was truly blessed.

I went back downstairs to sit and reflect in front of the fireplace. I'm at the beginning of this pilgrimage yet I feel that the journey has already been years. It is becoming apparent that authentic journeys are not measured by time. The only time is the present, and that is not time at all but, the present just is. This present moment is all we have.

My mind wonders to tomorrow; which is not yet created. For the first time on this journey, I feel like I am praying, because my thoughts are with the people I will affect. I want them to be loved like I am feeling now. I am speaking without words to someone inside of me that knows me as one intimately as a father knows a child. I'm communicating with a Father; my heavenly Father. The human aspiration inside of me begs to put these desires into words that my mind can articulate so that I am not overcome by my senses. This conversation continues more intimate than any communication I have ever experienced. It fills my soul with peace without any reasoning. My heart is leaping inside of me uncontrollably but all the while I am quiet. I then return gently to my thoughts.

Sunday is the first public step in my journey; I will be introduced as the interim pastor of my father's church. How will the people react? I guess that is why Grandma Abba was praying not for me, but for the people I will come across on my journey. Up until this point, I have seen resentment, hate, love, joy, and fear; and this was my family and friends. I guess Grandma Abba was right; people are genuinely fearful and confused about God. If I am on the journey of becoming Christ, I will face these emotions from people. They are captive to these emotions. They will not truly live until they are freed.

I turned out the lights and made my way to the bedroom. The journey before me is filled with uncertainty, but someone inside of me was assuring me that doubt did not exist in the present. I was not quite sure what that meant, but I trusted.

So far only, Giles, Hayleigh, and Grandma Abba know the journey I'm on. It is becoming apparent that the occurrences that happen along the way are merely mirrors reflecting the truth that we are to learn along the path of becoming what we were always meant to be our true self.

***

I awoke that Sunday morning to a beautiful breakfast made by Hayleigh. We talked about the previous few days, and we both are assured that this new journey would bring us both many turns and surprises. We knew the path would be narrow.

Pulling into the church parking lot, we are greeted by the parking attendants, which the church liked to call "Parking Ministers." The idea seemed humorous to me. Did people become stupid on Sunday mornings? No one needed parking assistance for the mall, and everyone appeared to make out fine. Over thirty thousand people never have a problem finding a spot at football games, but the church felt like it was the thing to do. Once they noticed who I was, they radioed ahead, and I was told to head left for preferred designated parking. The attendant kept emphatically pointing to me with the large orange sticks to move left as if bringing a 747 into the gate. I rolled down the window to let him know that I was okay with parking in my usual area. The look on his face was if I had just told him his child was ugly. I made my way through the lot and parked about a hundred yards from the front doors of the church.

As Hayleigh and I were getting out of the car, Timothy Sludge came running toward us frantically telling us to hurry because we needed to be ushered to the back entrance. The announcement about the interim pastor-ship was happening at the beginning of the service, and they wanted me to enter from backstage as my name was announced to a rousing chorus of Onward Christian Soldiers.

I looked at Hayleigh and Grandma Abba in dismay shrugging my hands and shoulders upward; while they were giggling quietly under their breath. "Look Sludge, I mean Timothy, I am going to sit where I always sit."

Timothy frustratingly replied, "But we have a seat designated for you up front, and we planned a grand entrance that your father and Caine suggested. What do I say to Caine?"

"Tell Caine I will be in my seat where I always am," I replied. Sludge marched ahead dejectedly with concern on his face.

As we made our way toward the front doors, there was a small car stopped near the front with a frail older woman with a cane helping her husband out of the car and unfolding his walker. Just then Sludge pointed out as if instructing me, where my new parking spot would be in the future. There was a freshly painted sign screwed onto a wooden post designating me as the Pastor.

He had no sooner finished barking out my orders when I quickly retorted, "I will not need this." I then proceeded to rip out the entire post and to chuck it behind the bushes. About thirty people stood there with their mouths hanging open staring at this scene unfolding in amazement.

"Excuse me, what are your names," I asked the elderly couple as the man slowly made his way to the sidewalk with his wife's assistance.

The man did not answer right away, but the woman replied, "Millie Sanderson and my husband, Sam."

"Millie I'm glad to meet you. Will someone help Mr. Sanderson into the church? Millie, this is your parking spot. Please get in your car and pull right in here." She was startled but quickly obeyed my wishes. I could tell by her walk with her cane that the short walk would be much appreciated. She pulled into the spot with a big smile on her face.

Just then you could hear the music starting, and everyone was rushing into the sanctuary. Sludge was racing to the back entrance to report to Caine Banks who had just observed from afar everything that had taken place. Sludge started to talk when Banks raised his hand holding him off, and they stepped behind closed doors.

The introduction of me as interim Pastor happened quietly with far less fanfare than originally planned which was to my liking. My father read a letter that Stephen had written supporting me to be the one to take over instead of him and felt that God had led the congregation to this point in time. This went a long way in helping the transition. The people were pleased that I was taking over and that my time would start at the Christmas Eve service, on a temporary basis until my father regained his strength. After both services were concluded I was greeted by hundreds of well-wishers with handshakes and hugs, even-though these people hardly knew me. I had not been active in the church for the last twenty years except to attend two or three services a month. It dawned on me that the people had no idea of the person they were getting to become their shepherd. I still was not quite sure what this church was getting.

I was glad the formalities were over. As Hayleigh, and Grandma Abba left the church, Caine Banks, and Timothy Sludge both came up and shook my hand welcoming me on board. I told them I would see them at the staff meeting at nine. Banks reminded me that I did not need to get there until ten like my father always did. I sternly reiterated that I would see him at nine.

***

I told Hayleigh I wanted to walk home and that I would meet her later. She again was suffering from another of her recent headaches and said she was going back home to lay down. There was a path behind the church that cut through the Larkins Farm leading straight to our house. It was a walk that I had jogged many times. Today I felt compelled to walk quietly and be with myself.

The pathway home passed the tree-shrouded fishing pond on the Larkins Farm. Most people never knew this private oasis existed. As I approached, I saw a familiar figure facing away from me with an old tattered orange floppy hat and some lures hooked into the faded drooping brim.

"Is that Abe Larkins?" I shouted out, startling the round-shouldered man knocking his hat off revealing his balding dome.

"Jesus, you scared me," he whispered. loudly as he turned nearly falling forward off the rock where he was standing into the shallow water below.

Abel Andrew Larkins, came from a line of farmers dating back to the early 1800's. His family had been feeding this region for generations. He was named after his father Andrew, who was one of the founding members of the church who died early in the ministry. I always remembered that Abe and his family were leaders and extremely active in the church. Stephen was fond of Abe and were friends until Stephen went off to explore the world. During my years, our paths would periodically cross at various church and family functions. I was impressed by his humbleness and humility. He was genuinely a nice guy. He was a gifted teacher of Scripture. My father felt that he spiritually fed the flock well.

Abe decided long ago that he did not want to be a farmer and leased out most of his four hundred and fifty acres to other local farmers. Abe was smart like his father and took the money and invested into a burger franchise. He now owns seven locations and is still feeding the entire region.

"You playing hooky from church Abe?" I joked with him reaching out to shake his hand.

He looked at me strangely, reaching out his hand as he stammered out, "Yea, uh . . . I guess you could say I'm playing hooky." A few seconds passed, when Abe asked, "You must have been playing hooky also."

I was puzzled and inquired to Abe, "What do you mean?"

"Edward, I've been gone for several years now."

A look of embarrassment came over my face as I thought to myself; here I am the new Pastor of this church, and I don't even know what is happening. I know that I periodically do not attend and have not been active other than to attend on Sunday mornings, but how could I have missed this?

"When did you leave the church?"

Abe could see my concern and embarrassment, and put his hand on my shoulder and assured me, "It's okay Edward, it was a quiet parting of the ways, and there was not much fanfare. Jane and I along with Jenny, left a little more than three years ago," his voice trailed off in dejected shame as he uttered the name of his beautiful daughter Jenny. Jenny was Abe and Jane's only child. She was about five years older than my Maggie, and they frequently sang together in church pageants. Jenny was stunning in appearance and attracted all the boys. She was equally beautiful inside as well.

Abe continued, "I am glad I knew Stephen, he was a great man. I loved hearing his stories when he returned. I miss his fellowship. I was praying before you surprised me that I could find someone I could share."

I could see into his soul. We all can and do; we just usually ignore and adjust our blinders. Abe had just relived the memory of pain as if it had just happened. He continued to speak while his eyes still searched for healing and closure; wanting the pain to be eased that he might be able to see the light of lifting darkness and awaken to a new day. His suffering was the worse pain; long after the initial piercing of the blade of shame, there appears the scar. Abe must gaze upon this covered wound every morning upon daybreak. His days are a mirror reflected unintentionally by those he loves most. Abe's dark lament became his identity; that imprisons him without escape or the ability to see himself no longer. I wanted desperately to release Abe and bring freedom to his tormented gentle soul. I knew instinctively, as if someone else was instructing me; that this type of pain had to be seen before finding the healing and ultimate release from its chains. Time had washed over the pain, dimming the intensity but defined his present moments for eternity. I needed to walk through this pain with him, into the healing and somehow, I felt Abe knew this too.

Abe knew intuitively to continue his story for the hope that somehow his pain would be lifted by his personal confession.

"I guess you're wondering why I left?" he reasoned that this thought was circling my head. But I was more concerned with his suffering then the circumstance. The circumstances are always different, but the pain that we suffer is the same; the degrees of the suffering are a result of how we see our reality.

He laid his fishing rod down and took a seat on the gray boulder placing his hands on his knees looking down toward the ground searching where to start. I squatted down like a baseball catcher in front of him so that I could look directly into his eyes. His eyes watered till the tears were streaming down his cheek and around his mouth as he gently wiped his chin with the back of his hand.

Sniffling back the sorrow, Abe began to whisper in a broken voice, "I don't know why I'm crying like this." He continued wiping the tears away with the palms of his hands. "My little angel Jenny," pausing to gather himself, "Jenny went off to college, Jane and I were both full of anxiety and pride, but we knew we had raised her well, she was a good girl," his voice trailed off pleading his case to be believed. The guilt and shame were laying on his heart, crushing his spirit.

I reached my hand and touched his open empty hand resting on his knee, grabbing it with firmness, squeezing into his body my heartfelt emotion, as if transferring my spirit to this empty vessel.

"She is good Abe, she is magnificent," I whispered to him as his eyes gazed into mine hoping that it was true, but sometimes the carnival mirror of life reflects an untrue distortion of the image in front.

Wiping the tears that were running down the side of his nose with the fingers of his hand he stammered out, "Thanks, Edward, I appreciate that. She is good; she had a lousy father," he whimpered and took one last breath in clearing his head looking up as if wishing he did not have to walk out this moment one more time. But he was still hoping, longing, for the redemption his life needed that is not given to a man emptied out by life and the religion he had sought for comfort.

"Who told you that you were a lousy father?" I angrily inquired, "What happened?"

He raised his hand to calm me down as he began to tell the story.

"Jenny went off to college to study drama. She loved theater. Well, she came home during Thanksgiving of her second year. I knew something was wrong when she arrived Wednesday night; the sparkle was gone from her face, and she barely looked at us. She went straight to her room to go to sleep. The next day she was not feeling well and stayed in her room until it was time for Thanksgiving dinner. After coming back from Thanksgiving dinner with Jane's parents, we walked to the pond. It was right here the three of us sat as the sun was setting over the house. Jenny said she had something to tell us. After an awkward silence; she went on to say that she was not returning to school after Christmas. Jane and I were speechless; we did not know what to say. My God, she was enjoying her life so much. What could have happened to change this? We were so proud of how she was growing."

Then Abe was starting to choke up; he began to lose it as he broke down turning away from me trying to get himself together. I got up and sat down beside him on the rock laying my hand on his shoulder. I knew this was a shock to Jane and Abe, and I briefly remembered my consternation when Tommy told us he was not going back to school.

"Abe, our kids tend to figure these things out; Jenny will decide what she wants to do," I assured him with a gentle grip on his shoulder, but I knew that this was not the source of pain and the aching inside his heart. Abe did not acknowledge my brief assurance instead he looked out over the pond toward his home, longing for the earlier days of respite from the cloud of darkness which his soul could not escape.

After a few splashes of fish jumping in the pond, Abe spoke again, "Jenny was pregnant," dropped out of his mouth like a bomb in the foxhole of his mind. He sat there paralyzed as if it just happened again today.

The life interrupting news, every parent dreads, sucker punched me in the heart as if it was coming from my daughter Maggie. I was surprised at this feeling of suffering hurt that accompanied Abe's revelation. Typically, I could express a sympathy toward the grieving person, but this time I felt as if I was drowning in the emotional dying of Abe and was speechless to utter a word that would apply some salve. I could feel Abe's shameful soul-wounds slicing open; as if he had walked dragging his heart across broken glass during the last years of his journey. I needed to release this father-child from his suffocating bondage of hurt, but the words would not come despite the deep yearning for my breath to form the expression of healing balm.

I clasped his left hand into my two hands as if I was about to pray, he turned to look at me and as he did the geyser of tears flowed down my face as if I was watching my own child die. We embraced in a hug as deep as any two men could muster and broke out in a wail of sobbing in a shared hurt. Muffled apologies are emanating from the buried heads of us both into our shoulders that had become one body. The deep cry of us both brought a short relief. Nothing was said, but something sacred and holy had just taken place. I knew my part was not finished in the life of Abe Larkins and that I was compelled to walk this journey with Abe. Abe sat back on the rock gazing out on the ripples of water as a few more fished jumped before I asked about the pregnancy. "Abe, why do you feel the shame and hurt so deeply concerning Jenny's pregnancy?" I begged to know.

Abe turned looking at me and said, "The pregnancy?" he looked at me and had a slight grin on his face, "The birth of little Jonah turned out to be a blessing for our family. The pregnancy, while quite a shock, was the salvation of our family; it has brought us closer and taught us about forgiveness and suffering."

I was puzzled at the contentment and peace now shining through the very same man that moments before was ravaged with shame and hurt. Looking at the reflection sparkling on the water of Abe and myself, I could see in nature's mirror that parts of Abe were missing, then they'd appear; then go missing as the wind stirred up the water. People do that; they learn the art of hiding parts of themselves when looking inside our soul-mirror. Most people don't look; willing to settle for this spiritual détente within their soul because it is better than their projection of eternal suffering they imagine or think they deserve. Some lower the bar even further with the cliché-like lesson that time heals everything. Time heals nothing; it merely manages the hurt through a lens of unreality. The only salvation is to walk into your reality, but Abe was unable to see, and I was determined to walk with him to discover his truth that he so badly needed to see.

I decided to push inward asking Abe, "I am so glad that Jonah has brought so much to your family, but if not the pregnancy, then what is causing you such great pain? I feel it."

"I know you do Edward, and it means a lot to me; for you to feel my suffering. I felt like maybe, just maybe there was someone else in this world who has been through this and that I might escape out of the hopeless abyss I find myself," Abe reasoned with me. "While Jenny's revelation initially tore us in two, I was not prepared for what was to come next. Not only did we lose the dreams we had for our daughter's life, but we lost the very life we had built over the years. Everything about us was taken away. Being the coward, I am; I stood by and let it happen. That's why I am here, fishing on a Sunday morning."

This was not the Abe I knew. "Abe did you not win combat medals in the first Iraq war? I hardly think they hand out medals to cowards."

"That was different; then I knew who the enemy was. I never saw this enemy coming."

"Who was the enemy, Abe?"

"The church," Abe rocked back placing his hands on his knees than running his hand through his hair while shaking his head pausing, "Hillside Community Church. The church my Daddy helped found along with your father; I poured my life into that church."

"How did the church become the enemy? The church is many things; God knows I've seen a close-up look at their warts, but how could the church hurt you so bad. Abe, you were loved and respected."

"Well, Edward, after we recovered from the first blow from Jenny we circled the wagons and let Jenny know that we would support her through everything. She was relieved and grateful for the love and understanding of her parents. She felt safe; that she could get through this part of her life. Safe, until the church responded."

"What was their response?" I inquired. Abe then told me the story.

"A few days passed when I wanted to let the Elders, who I served with, know what we were going through as a family asking for their prayers and guidance. I called Pastor Sludge since your Dad was on vacation out of the country. I told him what had transpired and he informed me he would let the others know so that they could be praying. I felt relieved and asked that this still is held in confidence until we felt comfortable to share with other friends and family. We were still discerning how we would bring hope and joy in love through this difficult situation. We had high hopes that God would work in us during this difficult situation, that is until we received a call that afternoon. It was from Cain Banks, who said he wanted to stop by to help us walk through this ordeal. I never cared for his style, and never could get close. I felt like I could trust the others."

Abe continued, "That afternoon the black Suburban rolled up the driveway like a government vehicle that was ready to deliver the sad news to the loved ones of a soldier killed in battle. Little did I know; that was what was about to happen. Cain Banks, dressed in his usual dark suit, slammed the front door holding on to his ever-present black attaché, which housed the important papers of the church along with his matching black leather Bible. He stood staring into the passenger seat as if inquiring what was taking the passenger so long. Out reluctantly stepped Reverend Sludge trailing behind Cain's soldier-like march to my front door to accomplish his mission. As the door opened he immediately asked if there was a place to talk; Sludge just looked at me with genuine sadness in his embarrassed eyes. I led them into the parlor, and we sat down. Jane followed us in and sat down by my side anticipating empathy and consolation. Hearing the voices of our visitors Jenny walked in innocently, like a sheep in a den of wolves, thinking that she had already passed the worst hurdle in her journey. The worst was about to come."

The story was unfolded by Abe in precise accuracy as if it happened yesterday.

"Cain asked Pastor Sludge to open with prayer, and he reluctantly stammered through an isolated rote prayer. Cain proceeded to thank our family for meeting with him and expressed his love for our family profusely, while Sludge excused himself to visit the bathroom. Cain continued, while glancing a disgusted stare toward Sludge, to lavish on me praise for my work in the church along with my wife, Jane. The conversation expressed his desire that our service would eventually continue as God's grace, forgiveness and healing worked in our lives. Apprehension and anxiety were closing in as I noticed a shift to a past tense."

"Banks went on describing the leadership's responsibility to follow God's word and guide the flock in the ways of the Lord. He emphasized that we had to be witnesses to the faith. He asked me if I felt that we should follow the teachings of the holy scripture. I nodded yes as if I had a choice. He then pulled from the satchel his crisp, clean black Bible and read from James 5:16 about the need to confess our sins one to another. He again reiterated his love and concern for us as a family and his desire for us to remain part of the body."

Abe took a breath, "I interrupted him to ask, 'What are you getting at Cain?' Cain said sternly, 'You and your family are leaders in the church, and our church is based on the family values of the sacredness of the marriage bond. Jenny; no matter how good a kid she is, has fallen into sin. Your family is a role model for the flock. People will look to the leadership of which you are a part, to handle this in a Godly manner so that full restoration can be accomplished in God's mercy'."

"I asked him what he meant by full restoration. Did this mean we were getting kicked out of the church? He assured me that was not the case; then the but came. He explained that with leadership came a responsibility to live to a higher standard as a witness to the believers. I asked Caine to clarify."

"Sludge, clearing his throat, had quietly reappeared standing behind us witnessing the spiritual lynching, as Caine read the verdict and judgment from his notes.

"Because of the severe nature of this sin, and our leadership position in the church; the Elders feel that a public confession and asking of forgiveness by Jenny will demonstrate the humility and contriteness needed to bring healing to Jenny, your family, and the church. We feel that you should temporarily step down from your position so that you can devote your time to the restoration and healing process of your family. We know that this has been a trying time for your family and how we walk through this as a church will demonstrate God's mercy and love."

After a sterile pause, 'It's in God's Word, we have no choice, I am sure you agree, Abe,' as he stared intently into the eyes of a man soulfully bleeding to death."

"My Jenny, a woman, my little girl, turned toward me. Her pleading eyes, drowning in tears dripping over her quivering lips; looking for her Daddy to pick her up in his arms to rescue her, started to speak but helplessly raced away to the solace of an empty room upstairs. Jane leaped to chase after Jenny only stopping to shout toward Caine, "You disgusting heartless . . ." Then quickly piercing a glance toward me the same message without the words, before running to her lonely little girl as Sludge started to reach out, but sadly looked away."

"I said nothing. Just remained calmly sitting on the sofa staring at the accusers, who I thought were my friends. Caine expressed shock to me at the response of Jane. I remained silent, struggling with the ripping open of my heart. Bleeding out from my soul were the thoughts of my desires to stay faithful to my church, my beliefs, my love for my family, and my selfish love of my identity in this church. As the last drops of spiritual blood poured out of my wound and my spiritual death complete, I told Caine and Sludge to leave."

***

There was a brief pause as I digested what had transpired in a life of a man that loved God by another man that loved God. As Abe unveiled his story of pages not written by him, something inside of me suffered for his family; the surprise was that I felt compassion for Caine and sorrow for the weakness of Timothy Sludge. Love chained becomes bondage. I needed to set them free.

Abe continued, "I never stepped foot in the church again. That's why you found me here fishing, on a Sunday. This is my church now. Sometimes, I even have a little communion with God and myself. I come to worship and give thanks to a wonderful family and admire God's beauty and grace in my life," he kindly whispered out.

"It took time to heal my relationship with Jane and Jenny. When Caine killed me that day, he had killed Jane and Jenny, but it was the start of a rebirth. For months, I could see the heartbreak inside Jane's soul. After a few days, we started to talk again. Now and then I could catch a glance of her looking at me with a yearning for a time in the past, but not trusting the future with a man that left our family so vulnerable. We eventually spoke about what had transpired that afternoon and the fear inside me that prevented me from risking myself for the sake of my family. She described that she was shattered and worried that I would not be there for them. She wanted to believe in me, believe in us again, but eventually, we turned the corner when I met Caine Banks at a funeral."

"What happened at the funeral?" I probed.

He continued, "It was about two years ago; you remember the Griggs daughter who died in the car accident in town. Well, Jenny was friends with her. We were at the graveside service. The small crowd moved to hear the burial words from your father. Jane and I were not aware that we were positioned right behind Caine. Jenny was standing on the other side with the family and her school friends. As your Dad said the final amen; the young friends huddled dropping flowers into a six-foot cavern saying their lost, bewildered goodbyes. Caine leaned over to one of the Elders and whispered pointing a nod toward Jenny, 'What a shame, a beautiful girl, caused so much hurt to a wonderful family.

We lost a good leader because of her sin, and now she is stuck with an illegitimate bastard child that she has reaped. I pray for her every day.'"

"Jane and I heard this, and we could hardly contain our rapid boiling anger over this condemnation. We were delivered, in one moment of time, again to the gallows of our living room that fateful day."

"I do not remember a thing for the next twenty minutes. The next thing I remember was getting into our car when I spotted Caine walking toward his vehicle. I then opened my door as Jane tried to stop me saying it was not worth it. Jenny was befuddled at was transpiring before her eyes."

"Oh Caine, can I have a word with you? Jumping out in front of him; he smiled as if thinking I saw the situation his way. He nodded an eager yes. I asked him to step to the side of the mausoleum building directly to our right. The next thing I must say I am not too proud of, but it sure felt good. I grabbed him by his jacket lapels with both hands hearing the stitches ripping from the seams and proceeded to make a statement to him."

"If I ever hear you, or even feel that you are thinking, that my grandson is an illegitimate bastard, you will be the next person buried! He is not illegitimate; he is loved by God and me! He just stared at me; his eyes were watering with fear. There was a sense of accomplishment watching the cold hard facade of certain control crash down. I walked back slowly to the car glancing back at Caine looking weakly back at me. Jane and Jenny were in shock. From that day, Jane and Jenny knew I would fight for their heart. I suppose you think I should have turned the other cheek."

I searched for the answer to validate a man standing strong, and I was surprised what was spoken from someone, not myself but sounding through my lips, "You have to have a cheek to turn Abe. Most people mistake their weakness as a virtue. They do not have strength, so there is no cheek to turn, they have no strength."

He replied to me, "Oh I turned the other cheek Edward, Caine just does not know it."

I was puzzled, and Abe knew it.

Abe went on, "You never asked me about the father of Jonah. The father is the grandson of Caine Banks. When he and Jenny discovered that she was pregnant, he was so overcome with the fear of the prospect of his family's response that he tried to kill himself. The boy that Jenny gave her beauty and love to was a trembling child. She made a promise to him that she would keep this a secret. So, you see, I did turn the cheek. Jane, Jenny and now you know it."

"God knows it," I assured him, "You are a good man Abel Andrew Larkins, will you walk with me on this journey? Some people need you to fight for them."

"Yes."

SLOUCHING TO BETHLEHEM

Surely some revelation is at hand
Surely, it's the second coming
And the wrath has finally taken form
For what is this rough beast
Its hour come at last
Slouching towards Bethlehem to be born
-W.B. Yeats

While Sunday was a day of surprises for me, Tuesday would bring on a storm of consternation. Winds are howling through the trees sending rain sideways like liquid shrapnel, foreboding a tech-tonic shift for Hillside Community Church. The wind whistled me into the lobby, the door barely hung on its hinges, as I shook off the wet tempest. I was entering my first staff meeting feeling as if this was a spiritual coliseum. It appeared I was late since I could see Caine Banks talking through the glass door of the conference room down the hall. I glanced at my watch to make sure I was not late. I was five minutes early. I'm getting irritated.

Caine peered up at me through the glass door motioning me to enter. Timothy Sludge quickly opened the door and shook my hand nervously.

"Did I miss something, I thought the meeting was at nine o'clock?" I asked looking around at the staff. They looked relieved as if their parent had come rescuing them from the principal's office.

"Welcome aboard Edward, I took the liberty to clarify a few things with the staff to help during this transition period," he motioned me toward the seat at the head of the table. I sat in the open side seat directly in front me. Caine reached toward the seat with his hand pointed in the stop position. "The Pastor's seat is there," Banks instructed me; pointing at the head of the table. I laughed inside briefly thinking that if I was opposite Caine at the head of the table; was he at the ass end?

"I'll be sitting here Caine," I said as Abe Larkins walked through the door. I detected a slightly surprised undertone amongst the staff. "Glad you could make it Abe. Everyone, I want to introduce our latest addition to our team. Abe has a lot of experience with Hillside, and he will be an excellent addition."

Caine Banks looking like he had just seen a ghost asked, "Does your father know about this?"

"Yes, he does, and he is ecstatic that Abe Larkins is back. He never understood why he left," as I stared directly into the eyes of Consigliere Banks.

Banks, pulling out papers from his black satchel and clearing his throat nervously, looked down at the table plotting his next move saying, "Well I will move to make this happen quickly, but you know we are governed by by-laws and budgets. I have to check to see if we have the funding."

"No need to check the funding Caine, Abe has agreed to work for one dollar a year," was my retort as I threw a five-dollar bill on the table toward Abe. "Here's a five-year contract, no overtime," I wagged my finger at him with a smile. The room erupted into a happy welcoming of Abe. Timothy Sludge walked across the room and gave Abe a big embrace, and I heard him whisper a heartfelt apology to Abe under the suspicious glare and ears of Caine. Caine Banks could see the jail locks opening before him as the captives smelled the faint aroma of freedom. I was feeling confident as if I was Bobby Fischer capturing the king of Boris Spassky. Sadness washed over me by the shrinking of Caine into his seat, but looking out at the liberated staff with a confused buoyant hope, who had just had the jail doors unlocked; I was at peace.

Abe gracefully reached out to Caine across the table by offering an olive branch, "Caine I'm looking forward to working as brothers."

Caine then without speaking, motioned to Timothy Sludge to continue the meeting agenda. Sludge reluctantly took control looking around and glancing at the agenda asking the Music Director, Bill Demure, to report on the status of the Christmas Eve service which I had a keen interest in since this would be my first service and Abe and I had already cooked up a surprise. "Well, what do you have planned this year Bill?" inquired Sludge hesitantly clearing his throat.

Bill uncomfortably started to recite the list of songs that he was intending on using during the candlelight Christmas Eve service. The level of excitement barely dripping from his lips made it sound as if he was going to the store for milk and bread. Bill described the logistics of the service and the technical aspects as if it was a Broadway show.

"As the people are entering the sanctuary, the walls and ceilings will be lit with moving snowflakes, stars, and crosses so that we can blend in the secular elements of the Holiday season with the religious symbols to prepare their hearts for worship," he reported.

"Can I step in and ask a question," I interrupted, "Are we preparing hearts for the incarnation or are we performing Jesus on Ice?" The staff smiled with their hands over their mouths. The gathering at the table went darkly and awkwardly silent like when you realize that something is incongruent, yet after a pause, you plow forward because you don't know any other way. They continued to discuss the mundane. They deliberated as if they were consultants for a 'major process engineering corporation' over the distribution of the candles; and whether they should be handed out as the people entered the church or dispersed by ushers before the last song. Onto the next issue; the extra offering for the poor and should it be collected the same time as the normal offering or wait until the end of the service.

The dialog went on and on as if I was listening to Miss Othmar on the Charlie Brown Special I watched with my grandkids the other night, 'Wah wah . . . wah wah wah.' Dropping my head into my hands, wiping the frustration and dismay from my face back through my hair to my neck, I interrupted with a sigh, "What is the Incarnation?" They all just glared at me in puzzlement as the clock struck twelve signaling that lunchtime was approaching. Caine slapped his satchel shut signaling that the meeting was ending. Raising my hand stopping this early scattering I asked, "Why are we doing this service on Christmas Eve? What is the purpose? The crickets of spiritual doubt were screaming inside the minds of the staff.

Caine broke the silence, "The Word was made flesh," he pronounced in righteous indignation. "That's what we believe," he affirmed as others benignly nodded.

"I don't care what you believe; I care about who you are. Who we are is what we believe," I challenged Caine and the staff.

Looking toward Caine, I nodded affirmatively, "Your definition is right Caine, but you're just describing incarnation; you are not telling me what it is, or what is its essence. Incarnation is like describing the wind; you can feel the breeze on your face one moment, but you do not know where it comes from, and just when you think you figured it out, the wind changes direction and sometimes vanishes completely. It's a mystery, and that is the miracle of Christmas. I let this sink into the hearts around the table.

Demure, the music director, excitedly piped up, "I want to bring God into the Christmas season."

Timothy Sludge joined the rally, "Edward, Christmas is a hard time of the year for many, and we want to bring a little joy, a little bit of God, into their lives. What's wrong with that?" Caine sat stoically nodding in agreement.

Leaning encouragingly into Sludge, "You are right Timothy, Christmas can be a difficult time. It highlights everything we want life to be but never is. People are looking for God in the wrong place, and we are helping them. God became flesh, a man, and that's where God is. He is in mankind, even the very least of these. He is not in the music, the program, or the sermon. Kill the lights, snowflakes, and crosses. Keep the songs as is, but they may be sung in a different order depending on how the evening goes."

Before the staff left the meeting, Caine spoke up, shooting a bewildered look toward me as his eyes turned red, isolated, but pleading for validation, "You know Edward, we are working hard to build God's kingdom."

"My kingdom is not of this world," rolled surprisingly off my tongue naturally as if it was breathed out of my lungs from my heart.

"So now your speaking as if you are Jesus," Caine rocked back with his arms folded.

A momentary tension-filled pause left me startled by my answer and his question.

I looked him in the eyes with authority and said, "I'm just quoting scripture, Caine." His eyes bared down on me revealing an underlying steaming anger, isolation, and frustration. "I'm sure you are familiar with the passage."

As the meeting was breaking up, Caine quietly slid away, while the remaining people hugged and greeted me warmly expressing positive anticipation about working together. I could detect that Bill and Timothy were anxious about their new-found freedom and how they would react to the push back from Caine, my father, and the Elders.

Walking out the door with Abe I turned to Bill and asked, "Are you familiar with the song Hallelujah?"

He immediately replied, "We sang that last year, it is on an every-other year schedule because your father loves it so much."

Immediately I knew that he was confused. "Not the Hallelujah chorus. I'm talking about Leonard Cohen's Hallelujah. We are going to use that song in the future; I think you should be the one to sing it."

A radiance came upon his face as he recalled memories of the past, where his heart's desire to create music was not simply a tool.

"It's one of my all-time favorites." He then went on to lightly and softly remember a verse when music was art, and it was life. "I did my best; it wasn't much. I couldn't feel, so I needed to touch, I've spoken the truth, I didn't come to fool you. And even though it all went wrong; my tongue speaks a Hallelujah."

Bill turned to me with a grateful look on his face as his eyes teared up, "How did we lose this? Thank you for re-opening my eyes to the vulnerable humanity of life. We do try our best, don't we? And when we are true to ourselves, when life goes wrong, all we have is our broken Hallelujah."

"And it's perfectly good," I assured him as he smiled back. He grabbed my hand and continued to thank me as if I had just broken the shackles of his chains.

"How did you know that this song would free me and see my passion for music?" he asked.

"Now is not the time," I cryptically answered knowing that his journey would require his passion for being sharpened more.

"One more thing, what do I say when Cain and your father ask if Leonard Cohen is Christian? You know he was Jewish."

"Tell them," a slight pause, "So was Jesus."

***

Abe and I walked out of the room down the hall. We were to meet privately at his house to go over our secret plans for Christmas Eve. Abe asked, "What has happened to you, Edward? You're a different person. I know we have not seen each other the last few years, but you are nothing like I remember. You're like no one I have met in my life. You see things. That is why I said yes to you; to come back to Hillside. You saw deep inside of me when I could not. You saw the hurt and the healing all at the same time. And now I'm free. Who are you?"

"We will discover a lot about each other on this journey Abe. I'm looking forward to it. You can't learn about anyone unless you are willing to walk with them.

Abe continued, "I have to admit I had a little trepidation coming into that meeting with you this morning. I had no idea what I would feel when I saw Caine. I was surprised. I felt sorry for him."

"That's why I chose you, Abe. You can see Caine has just never been loved properly. He shadowboxes with grace; wearing gloves of performance." Abe grinned as we left. The driving gale of change had ceased as we made our way to our cars. The sun's rays were peeking over the hillside through the breaking clouds. But the cold, damp winds of uncertainty were still swirling.

***

Driving home that evening from Abe's, I was brooding over today's developments. While I am accustomed to the familiar mental images of my father and Caine as despised spiritual control masters, I was amazed at seeing Caine in a sympathetic light. Caine's eyes are the eyes of a child begging to be released from a burden. His burden was a battle to maintain a personal faith that validated his existential beliefs about himself. The tear of fear in his eye that needed the release was his precious co-dependent relationship with his church and his religion which required preservation at all cost. This co-dependent relationship was welcomed by most as their experiential answer to their anxieties of their existence. It was an arranged marriage, and my father and Caine were the fiddlers on the roof. Playing the programmed notes as a siren perched high atop the steeple, while balancing delicately as not to fall. I saw so clearly; they needed to tumble. Their fall would be into love, a love for each other, and relational love in the God of the Tree of Life. But their fear hid this from their eyes, compelling them to eat from the Tree of the Knowledge of Good and Evil that the religion's siren call had beaconed them to taste. I had spent my life wandering between these two trees, partaking of neither fruit, just fearfully observing.

What is happening? My heart is lifting every day, every moment. Every minute seems like a lifetime. The terminal angst of bondage is quietly erasing the constant rumbling soulful tremors of fear. The sorrow and suffering I feel are soothed by the assurance of love deep inside. Who am I? I don't recognize myself. I am someone new. Could it be true? Am I becoming Jesus?

Wrap! Wrap! Came a knocking at the window of my idling car. It startled me, and I wondered how I ended up in front of my house. It was Grandma Abba gently tapping her ring on the window. Turning the car off and getting out she said, "I did not want to interrupt you, I thought you might be praying.

"I was just listening Grandma Abba, just listening," I answered.

"That's the best kind of praying," she smiled and quickly informed me, "But, you need to tend to Hayleigh. She had another episode. I took her to see Giles, and he says she is okay, but he wants to run a few tests on her. The headaches are coming too frequently. She says she will do it after the holidays. She is fixing dinner now."

Quietly walking up behind Hayleigh, without her noticing; she is chopping some vegetables, I could hear her humming the old hymn sweetly, *He Touched Me*. I reached out my arms and hands around her waist pressing from behind my body closer to hers in an embrace. She stopped chopping, grabbing my hands and lifting them higher across her breast cradling her as she warmly sighed as she swayed like a pendulum. My lips were touching her ear as I whispered, "What is going on with my beautiful bride?"

"Nothing now," she purred out like a kitten, "Everything is perfect at this moment. I am loved."

"Yes, you are Baby, more than you will ever know. Now, what's going on with you?" I waited to hear her reply as she went back to cutting vegetables teetering on the fulcrum between the present moment of joy and the future path of uncertainty.

Breaking her still silence of wavering fear, she turned toward me, "Giles says it's probably nothing, most likely stress related; he wants to run some test to make sure. I told him not until after the holidays. I did not want anything to ruin Christmas. I'm not worried."

Her eyes told me differently, but her belief in some faith tenet will not allow her to think any other way. "Honey, don't you think you should listen to Giles and get the test done sooner than later?"

"No I don't and where is your faith?" she replied, "It's nothing Edward, nothing. Besides, do you forget who I am married to?"

"Hayleigh, sometimes common sense is the road to faith; faith will be required when common sense has nothing to say."

The next few weeks leading up to Christmas were enlightening. I discovered a whole new side of people that I had overlooked. The same people I had benignly looked past for years in the pews; I now saw the real person inside, instead of the carefully constructed impostor. The people were walking like blind people crossing paths with the white canes tapping out their message of independence keeping the proper distance between them. I wanted to help them see that closing the distance was their only path to redemption.

A lifetime of eating at the foot of the Tree of Knowledge of Good and Evil had produced a vision of saints and sinners. My heart ached to embark on a journey of liberation and taste of the Tree of Life where saint and sinner are one in love. Every saint has a story, and all sinners have glorious pages yet to be written.

CHRISTMAS EVE

Now to the Lord sing praises,
all you within this place.
And with true love and brotherhood,
each other now embrace.
This holy tide of Christmas,
all other doth deface.

God Rest Ye Merry Gentlemen - 1833 Unknown

The large snowflakes had fallen overnight as if Eden was enclosed by a crystal glass sphere and shook by the hand of God. Christmas Eve is tomorrow. The change in the weather was extreme, as a quick nor'easter blew a warm wet breeze from the Atlantic across the Chesapeake Bay and collided with the first cold spell of the season. I went for a walk that morning, up to the top of the hill where Maggie and Tommy played as children swinging on a swing hanging from a towering Beech tree. Hayleigh was quite ecstatic about having a white Christmas. The comforting blanket of a Currier and Ives palette of winter colors took her mind off the upcoming medical test with Giles the following week. Hayleigh and Grandma Abba were baking cookies in the kitchen, and I could hear them both singing carols as they were busy generating the sugary holiday aroma of cinnamon calories that would soon be devoured. I walked in, and the song stopped as I stole a cookie from the pan and biting the head of Frosty not knowing it had just come out of the oven.

"Ha! Haa! Haaaa!" I muffled a whispered scream grabbing my chin, "Hot!" I ran to the sink to rapidly shovel water into my mouth.

Hayleigh and Grandma Abba giggling like two schoolgirls, "Jesus must have flunked physics," Grandma Abba barks out as we all respond with rolling laughter.

Hayleigh resumes her singing and baking after the laughter slowly quieted. She always had an underappreciated voice, not the dynamic booming sound of our Maggie, but like her daughter could sing with her eyes as much as her delicate voice. "Glad tidings of comfort and joy, comfort, and joy, Oh, Oh, tidings of comfort and joy," peacefully breathed off her lips and through the aroma filled kitchen.

Grandma Abba continued her busy shuffling of pans in and out the racks of the two ovens while humming just underneath Hayleigh's beautiful notes. She was separating the cookies because some had cracked or broken.

"Want another one?" she wryly asked me motioning the still hot cookie under my nose. Looking over my glasses to shoot her a stern look, a smile with my head tilted; I acknowledged her humor. "So, tell me, Edward, what do you see during the early start of your journey?"

"I'm seeing a lot of people with not much comfort and joy," I answered. "Of course," I shrugged, "They are given few tidings to start. They're a lot like these cookies. I notice that you are throwing the broken ones in a pile. That's how people are made to feel. If you are broken, then you go over there. If you are beautiful, then you are adored. The broken ones feel unworthy while the perfect ones have comfort assured. In the end, their essence is the same.

I went over and grabbed a cookie off the good pile and took three pieces from the canister of broken cookies. I cracked the good one into three pieces. Putting them behind my back, I brought two pieces forward and gave them both to Hayleigh. "Which cookie is the broken one?" She took the cookies as if taking a wafer from a Priest. Chewing them both individually, Hayleigh shook her head as if not knowing. Turning to Grandma Abba and giving her two pieces. Waiting and eventually looking directly at her, expecting an answer, I opened my hands toward her. She looked equally perplexed.

"Hayleigh, you looked baffled. You could not tell them apart". Turning toward Grandma Abba, smiling at her proud face, "Did you enjoy the taste?" nodding her head affirmative, "Your pieces were both from the broken pile."

I continued, "Grandma Abba you asked what I have seen so far? I see people of the same essence; broken people thinking they are not blessed, and something is wrong with them, while the others feel blessed and righteous needing nothing to validate them, except the smug, righteous difference between the two."

Grandma Abba was listening with extreme pleasure. I continued, "People, like the cookies; they are the same, but see themselves different. The real tragedy is; they rely on each other for the very existence of their identity, which they confuse with their reality. They both need each other. The broken need the 'perceived perfect' to validate a hope and a future trust to substitute in their heart that one day, maybe one day, God will bless them. The beautifully blessed need the broken to validate that God has shown His favor on their worth. Both views rest on a cornerstone from the Father of Lies who keeps them blind, brokenhearted, and in bondage. That's what I have seen on my journey."

Hayleigh, interjected with a question, "Are you going to change the recipe, so there are no more broken cookies? People? That'd be great."

I picked up one of the good cookies shaped like a Christmas tree, which had some green sprinkles layered on top with small little colorful pearls simulating ornaments. Gently tossing it on the counter; it cracked.

"Edward!" Hayleigh gasped, "That was an absolutely perfect cookie."

"No, it wasn't Hayleigh, the crack was always there. It just had not revealed itself," I spoke.

***

Maggie and the children came barging in the kitchen door yelling that it was snowing. School dismissed early, and they were full of energy and joy of the anticipation of Christmas. My heart instantly buoyed up. "Daddy, Aidan wants you to take him sledding out back." She said with confidence, "I told him that I doubt that Grand pop will; he is probably busy with preparations for his first sermon."

"Well, you told him wrong!" I shouted back and lifted Aidan up in the air. "There is only one condition; everyone has to come."

Aidan looked toward his Mom who had a slight sadness in her eyes. She frowned back and issued a polite no, while her head tilted staring at me. Aidan, like any young boy his age, decided that jumping up and down and badgering Maggie would be the best strategy. She finally said "Not this time guys." He gave up and left the room after a pleading stare was directed toward him and his sister Eden. She reached for them as they slid off to watch television begging for understanding, "Mommy's tired and getting too old for sledding guys."

My heart sank. Not for my grandkids. The melancholy eyes of memories revealed there was more than a tired single mom. I looked toward her asking, "Really Maggie, too old?" She looked away and went to her Mom like she always did, asking if she needed help with the baking. I moved in between placing my hand on the side of her cheek. She refused to let her tear-filled eyes meet mine. Hayleigh continued quietly mixing batter. "Maggie?"

She gently pulled my hand away from her face whispering, "It's nothing Dad, really, it's nothing."

"Well, it's something to me," I sternly replied as I started to experience the pain of her wounds. There was something inside of me that in a fractional moment of time I felt her anguish twisting in her soul. It was turning in mine.

"When Aidan said, he wanted to come over to go sledding with you, I was torn, because I did not think you would go. I did not want him to be disappointed." She stammered, "You never went with me? You always had to study some important research about life."

I felt her twisting piercing pain deep inside my mind. Her pain was also my pain because she was right. I had indeed reaped what I sowed. I stood there paralyzed by the truth. Any type of sorry could not bring what was needed for her heart, nor mine. But I had more to offer her. I had this present moment, which I was not experienced in living, but now could plainly see; it was all I could see.

Maggie's words continued searching for balm to ease her distress, "I was stunned when you immediately said yes. All the years of sitting at your feet, listening to your knowledge, when all I wanted was to be with you. I felt ashamed of myself for feeling this way. I was jealous of my son! You wanted to be with him. Was I never good enough?" she cried out.

"You're different. Who are you?"

Hayleigh's mixer stopped. She froze and awaited my answer. Grandma Abba dropped a cookie on the floor but just stared with an empty spatula in her hand. Time stood still as if the last grain of sand had dropped from the hourglass. My vision was murky as my eyes stared at the broken cookie on the floor. Gazing down into the darkness of memories pouring from a past void in her soul; I heard the heartbreaking crying sounds bellowing from another time. The fractured cookie on the floor was my beautiful little Margaret broken on the kitchen floor, her spirit hemorrhaging her love of music and life until the precious little vessel was empty. She was now my adult little girl, still waiting for her father to rescue her. Who am I? Jesus or her father? I am both.

Lifting my head, I see clearly with a laser focused vision that Maggie's eyes are begging to find Margaret again. Maggie learned to cope with Daddy not engaging. Sledding with Aidan opened the wounds scarred over time hiding under the facade of Maggie. Margaret was pleading to be set free from Maggie. The whirlwind of emotions encircling and entangling started to calm. Maggie searched for salvation one more time, "Who are you?"

Her eyes are searching mine for the redemption of a life not lived. Hayleigh in the background, afraid of the answer, hoping her daughter would not be pierced once again. Hayleigh, needed to know for herself repeated, "Who are you?"

"I am," then softly swallowing with quivering lips and soaked eyes, "A man," taking another a deep breath, "Who wants to sled with his daughter Margaret, whom he loves so much."

Maggie placed her hand over her mouth, as her heart gasped a silent cry. Her knees are bending into a partial collapse as her hand held onto the counter. She looked up leaning into me; falling into an embrace that caused us to slide down to the floor. There we both were; cradled together gently rocking back and forth sobbing; words were not needed. Time had stopped. I was where I should have been years earlier. Looking up at Hayleigh, who smiled through tears knew that whoever I was becoming, Edward, whom she loved was still here.

Maggie through her unshackling tears softly spoke, "Margaret, would love to sled with her Daddy."

We stayed there for a few moments more when Maggie, I mean Margaret, shouted into Aidan and Eden, "Get ready! We are going sledding!" Screams could be heard through the house.

Nodding toward Hayleigh, "You are coming too." As she hesitated Grandma Abba told her she would finish the last few trays of cookies.

Everyone was racing around getting dressed, and Aidan was growing impatient. He said that he was going out back to start sledding down our small back hill. I informed him that we were not sledding there. I had called Abe while I was getting dressed. We are going to the big hill over at the Larkins farm. Here is where Tommy and Margaret used to go as kids. Margaret, fear covering her face, questioned the wisdom of going on the big hill.

"Margaret, trust me, everything will be all right," I assured her. "All I have to do is find the old toboggan in the basement." She smiled.

Margaret and I took the first ride down the hill; she held tightly onto my knees like a child as we screamed through the falling snow. Quickly approaching a pine tree, I yanked the sled quickly to the right causing us a quick catapult from our snow missile. We rolled further down the hill giggling like a childhood memory that should have occurred before, but now blooms vibrantly. Back and forth between Hayleigh, the grandkids, and Margaret; we swished through the snow between laughter and joy.

Walking back up the hill with Margaret, she stopped and looked at me and said, "Thanks."

I simply said, "I'm sorry, I missed Margaret."

"I missed her too; I hated Maggie." We embraced and walked up the hill as father and daughter frozen in time as if she was a little girl.

We all had a great time as the two families laughed and enjoyed the spontaneous time together. Margaret and Jenny reconnected. It sparked an idea and some significant changes to the Christmas Eve Candlelight service at Hillside. Abe and I retired to the fire pit to plot out our idea over some hot cider.

***

Christmas Eve

The last snowflake drifted down calmly just after dawn. I awoke slightly sore as the old muscles were not ready for the tumbling my body endured last night. The look of Margaret's liberated eyes still warmed my soul as I laid in gratitude for the sacred moments spent in our conjoined hearts. Stretching to the heavens, my body awoke into a twisting reaching standing position along the side of the bed. I heard the rumbling of tires fighting through the snow pull up to the house. I heard Tommy's voice bellow out greetings to Hayleigh. He had made the long trek from Nashville after his music gig last night. I heard him say he was going to catch a nap before everyone arrived. I knew soon that Hayleigh's family along with Johanna would be coming. We would all gather for the annual Christmas Eve dinner. I could hear Hayleigh, Grandma Abba, and Margaret buzzing around the kitchen in busy preparation for the coming feast.

Grabbing a cup of coffee in the middle of the maelstrom of hustle I kissed Hayleigh on the cheek, and she smiled back with a grin and whispered, "Happy Birthday darling." Then she giggled before realizing that Margaret had overheard her playfulness.

Margaret, chopping parsley, looked up and inquired inquisitively, "Happy birthday?"

"Inside joke Maggie," Grandma Abba replied without interrupting the snapping of her green beans as Hayleigh chuckled.

"I'm not going by Maggie anymore Grandma Abba," pausing to clarify, "I'm Margaret," she explained as she looked at me smiling.

Grandma Abba never looked up, saying assuredly with a smile; as a person who on her journey had seen this many times mused, "It's kind of like being reborn." Margaret smiled in agreement as she looked at me.

A heavy wrapping on the kitchen door interrupted this holy sacred moment. It was Giles with a large box in his hand. He was carrying my favorite gift of the Christmas season. I rushed to open the door and protect this valuable gift that my friend was bestowing on us. This gift was delivered every year. Opening the door, I immediately grabbed the box as if it had just been brought by one of the wise men. Walking it carefully into the kitchen, I took in the culinary aroma of this offering. Giles had been carrying on a recipe from his family that went back generations; Aunt Flavia's Corn Bread Stuffing. I would be counting the hours until this delicacy would dance in my mouth.

Giles greeted Grandma Abba with a hug and Hayleigh with a peck on the cheek. Turning to Margaret, he said, "How is my favorite Mayus, how are you doing Maggie?" Giles always had a soft spot for Margaret and was always concerned for her happiness.

"I'm going by Margaret now," she beamed proudly.

Giles surprised at the announcement replied with a warm smile, "That makes me happy, Margaret was who I loved first; glad she is back."

Giles, with a slight puzzled grin, and I, retreated to my office with coffee in hand. Giles had been traveling, tying up some loose ends of our research project which seemed like such a long time ago, but only forty days had passed since Stephens death. Giles and I had a lot to discuss. I closed the door behind me. Giles was standing behind my desk looking at the wooden box Stephen sent.

"That's the box Stephen sent the blood and wine in; along with his papers." Giles slid his finger lightly across the top Latin inscription like a blind person reading braille. I asked, "Do you know what it says?" Giles shook his head no. "This is my blood, which for you is being poured forth. I will not drink from henceforth of this fruit of the vine until the kingdom of God comes."

"That might be what it says, but what does it mean for you, Edward?" Giles wondered out loud.

"I don't know Giles; I just don't know," I replied. "I'm not sure if Stephen deliberately chose this, or did God have a hand in this vessel?"

"Well, I know that you have caused quite a stir over at Hillside?" Giles stated with emphasis.

"What do you mean? I have not even had my first service," I inquired.

Giles, who was the doctor for many members of Hillside continued, "Abe Larkins came in for his yearly checkup and told me the story of your conversation at the lake. Edward, that man has been hurting for years. He carried a weight that was crushing him. He never told me what it was. I assumed it was because of his daughter's pregnancy. I prescribed drugs that would help him out of his funk, but they never seemed to work. Then out of the blue, he comes bouncing into my office full of life. He tells me that he is back at Hillside and it's all because of you. He said that on that day; you saw inside of him as if he was one in you. You felt his pain, and that was enough to free him. He could not explain it other than to say; only love could understand his suffering, and he saw it in you. In that one moment, you two walked together into the pain. It was then that the tangled web of chains started to loosen until they dropped to his feet. Leaving my office, he shared with me that you bestowed strength in him. Every time he is with you, he becomes a better man, and he would follow you anywhere, even back to Hillside."

Hearing this recounting of Abe's encounter brought me a sense of feeling proud; not in myself but Abe. Pride like a father who watches his son pedal his bike alone for the first time after many bruised knees. A sense of rest that a man is becoming what he was always meant to be.

"Abe has always been a good person; he just needed eyes to see. I just revealed what was always there," I told Giles.

Giles returned to his thoughts, "Bill Demure, brought his daughter in for her flu shot. Bill and I talked a little in the examination room. He was simply buoyant, unlike his usual controlled demeanor. I asked him how are things going, and Bill replied; it could not be better. He said that you rejuvenated his spirit. Bill explained that he had lost his voice in his heart. Music used to come from inside his heart and soul; it meant something to him, it was him. He lost that voice. Playing music from the outside had broken his heart. Then he said something I did not understand. Bill shared that he had spent his last ten years playing victory marches; now he knows that love is a cold and broken hallelujah. It freed him to create and hear music again. He said it was because of you. What is he talking about Edward?

Sipping my coffee and pondering Giles words I smiled and contemplated what I was hearing. "Voice is a jazz term for musicians; it's the unique way a player hears and plays music. It's what makes the note 'C' sound different when John Coltrane plays it versus Sonny Rollins. Even non-musicians have a voice; they just don't see it. You can only see it if you are free. Victory marches and broken hallelujahs come from Leonard Cohen's Hallelujah, which I asked him to prepare to sing one day. I am happy for Bill that he is discovering his voice, his true self again. I will be interested to see where this new journey takes him," I mused.

Giles stared at me with a puzzling countenance, as if I was from another world. I guess he was expecting a different reaction from me. He sat down in the chair in silence, then continued, "You don't get it, Edward, people are responding to you. They never responded to you like this before. Timothy Sludge's assistant Julie confided in me. You saved her marriage.

"Giles, I have never talked to her," I questioned him.

Giles continued as if not hearing me, "I know, but it was something you said in the first meeting. Pastor Timothy and she discussed it when they went back to the office. You said something like; 'I care what you are, and who you are. That's what you believe.' She was ready to leave her husband. She has shared with me over the years their struggles with the marriage. Frank, her husband, was a nominal Christian showing up mainly on holidays and some special occasions. Julie grew up and was at church every time the door opened. This has caused problems in their marriage. Frank was a sports fanatic, and Sundays were his day, especially in football season. After that meeting, she examined herself and determined that she still loved Frank, but never took part in what he loved in his life. He likewise pushed back against her faith which was important to her. This created the gap that held back their marriage."

"You know what she did?" I nodded what, with a shrug. "She surprised him; bought tickets to the next Sunday's game for him and her. She surprised him that night, and he was shocked and ecstatic when he learned she was going with them. He could not believe she was not going to church that Sunday. They had a splendid time to share life together that day. That day was a holy day. The next Sunday, he got up early to fix breakfast for the family and asked what time is church. He has gone the last three weeks. She learned that love is not something to believe. It's something we live. She remarked that you said it without any fear and with authority like it was inside you. Edward, do you know how significant this is? You're changing people. Julie says the entire staff except for maybe Caine is different. Sludge is worried about being caught in between the battle they see coming, or that when you leave after a year things will go back. Sludge does not know where to place his allegiance. He is worried about feeding his family."

I moved over to the open box and pulled out the broken bottle and stared for a few brief moments before asking Giles a question. "Who do you say that Timothy should pledge his allegiance?" Giles peered over his glasses unwilling to state what for him, was obvious. "Timothy is like Peter, who wants Jesus across the water to beg him to step out. Timothy never looks inside himself to see, but instead is fearful. He is fearful of himself. He cannot see the real image of who he is. Timothy will walk into his fear and finally see that the Father has equipped him for his journey. His freedom depends on this."

Giles leaned forward, "That's what I mean Edward, what is going on? Are you changing into. . .?

Peacefully resting back in my chair, my index fingers resting on my lips I answered, "Giles, I don't know." I started to cry inside as if someone close was dying peacefully but somehow was better off. It was a good grieving; a good letting go.

"Giles, I am, still Edward, aren't I?" I pleaded for an answer. "I feel like Edward, but I see differently." I continued slowly deliberately uttering out my thoughts to myself and Giles, "I took a walk yesterday through the falling snow toward the path," pointing toward the window I continued, "That led to the swing that hung from the old Beech tree. A great weight fell on my heart for Maggie, so much that it was hard to trudge up the hill through the snow. I felt sorrow, but it was not me, but Maggie who was being trapped in deep suffering; trying to make it up the hill. It was her pain. The weighted heaviness was crushing me as I continued my climb up that hill. The air was silent; all I could hear was my boots punching footprints into the fluffy white powder. Catching my breath on the windless hillside, I could hear the flakes landing on my face as if a butterfly had just touched a flower. This brief assurance of moving on in Maggie's pain gave me peace. My senses were heightened through the passion for her release. Finally approaching the crest of the hill, I felt a warmth spill over me as if a blanket had just enveloped my soul. I could hear children's laughter amongst the birds singing high up in the tree disregarding it was winter. It momentarily felt like a new Spring. The grinding of the swaying rope, pendulums of gleeful laughter could be heard in my mind. Time was not in my soul, and I was lost in the moment. Touching the bark of the tall tree, I spotted a carving."

I love my Dad is what the etching read.

"I broke down and cried as I heard her laughter in my mind as a little child. Her words pierced the bark of the tree as well as my heart. The words every father wants to hear; are the words every person wants to be able to say with assurance. The laughter of the little girl on this hill is what Maggie has been trying to find her whole life. Maggie never could get up this hill; since that one fateful night. She has been looking for Margaret ever since. The laughter died, and the cold returned."

"Giles, when I turned back toward the house, I discovered the footprints of my past trek had disappeared; washed away by the pure snow. Heading back to the house, I saw clearly that the wounds of the heart could be healed. I knew that I would free Margaret so that she would be re-birthed from the chains of Maggie's life. I had no idea how this would take place but trusted that it would be revealed. It was that night."

Giles sighed softly, "Edward, whatever is happening, whoever you are becoming, I just don't know, maybe you are both Edward and Jeez . . ." Giles did not utter the words that he believed but could not risk saying them out loud.

"Jesus," I finished his thought. "Giles, during the last several weeks I have been trying to understand. I would come to my office to pray. Only the prayers were more of a listening and intimacy that I had never experienced. This intimacy was God. It was like when you have been with a lover, and as you lie there in each other's arms, there is nothing to be said, only experienced. It's like the inside of each other is being shared without words, because words are too shallow for this moment."

"Then the world invades back into your mind; is this God's plan? Was this part of some journey that was destined? Or maybe, I should have never started this journey? I needed to discern what it means to be Jesus desperately. Then an inaudible speaking overwhelmed my mind and spirit; trust. The feeling that overwhelmed me brought peace. If I was becoming Jesus, then Edward could not possibly understand what was happening. If I was still Edward, then I had to trust. The only way I would ever know was to continue the journey and trust that it would reveal the truth."

Giles wiped his face saying, "This is too heavy for me Edward, I wished I was never part of it, but fearful if I was not. But for the sake of science, I captured what was left of the DNA in the tube. We can compare the samples after some time has passed; maybe next September. We can discover how much your DNA has changed. Who knows maybe we will have the DNA of Jesus." Giles, shaken and puzzled, left shortly to go pick up Julie for dinner.

***

The sun was setting, painting the muted cyan sky reddish orange at the horizon as friends and family gathered for the Christmas Eve dinner. It was still daylight. Johanna and Emilee arrived in a taxi as the last of the food was being placed on the table. Greeting them on the porch, I hugged Emilee, and she was as natural present, and approachable as ever. I could see why Johanna needed her in her life. Johanna did her usual jump into my arms and squeezed me with a bear hug.

Swaying back and forth; I whispered to her, "I'm glad you and Emilee are here."

"How could I miss your opening night?" she replied laughingly, "Besides you still owe me, our show was picked up by a larger theater near Broadway; I expect you and Hayleigh to be there in the front row this time."

"That is great news; I am so happy for you."

After Johanna, had arrived, we were all gathering around the table that included everyone; my father was tiredly approaching his chair. Before me was the family and friend landscape that was changing; My thoughts on everyone had changed in the last weeks.

I could not help but feel sympathy for my Dad, the Patriarch of this family. His self-identity once shined brightly till now. The wax is waning as the flame of his candle burns down. I am saddened for a man that I angrily misunderstood, he eluded me, and I eluded him; I loved him for what I wanted him to be but had contempt for what he had become. The sympathy was not directed at who he is, but at what he cannot see. My father had created an identity that appears eternal; as if time, will never run out. He cements his existence in an echo of time, but the journey demands him to change. He cannot see; his identity is a mask. Nothing in this world stays the same. The path unveils our identity. Our identity is not created but revealed. There it goes again. These thoughts, what do they mean?

Leaning in to hear this once booming voice that is now barely a thin whisper, he asked, "What are you speaking on tonight?" The look in his eyes is a desperate plea to continue his existence and validate his struggle. It is a lonely winter of life's final chapters begging for an external validation.

"It's a surprise Dad, you will just have to wait and see," I responded.

"You know I don't like surprises son, what's the subject?"

"Incarnation," I placated, but little did he know that tonight would be much different. I quickly moved onto asking him to say the blessing. He obliged with the usual blessing of the food, fellowship, and season; ending in a pointed plea that God grant me wisdom this night. The wisdom was for him; that I might bring affirmation to his life's work. I could tell that he was concerned. I am sure that Caine had broadcast his dislike of my leadership thus far.

Seconds after the final Amen was repeated by everyone, the passing of dishes commenced with the precision of a fire brigade. Buddy, who I sat at the head of the table was to my left. I noticed that he had a stylish shirt unlike his usual undersized small-child attire consisting of the juvenile horizontal striped polo shirt that always slid up above his belly and baggy jeans that were rolled up around his Jack Purcell's. His hair was not the usual child-like cowlick mess. He had a slight moussed spike in the front reflecting a new-found confidence and strength. His shirt collar was slightly popped. He reached for his wine glass, filled with white grape juice, and tapped the spoon on the side. Tink tink tink! Lifting the glass standing was the newest man of the family. Everyone stopped silently as the last clink of a fork was laid on the plate.

Buddy raised his glass, "I want to make a toast da greatest man who ever lived."

Everyone stood silently expecting their Buddy to name Jesus as this person. Buddy started to choke up before he could finish. The awkward hush that blanketed the room was interrupted by my father who raised his glass coming to aid Buddy's toast, "To Jesus."

Before the clinging of the first drink, Buddy blurted out, "To Eddie! My friend," as he started to cry he leaned over toward me and buried his head into my shoulder, "Because you loved me." Buddy sobbed for a few moments and other eyes filled with tears at this genuine display of emotion. I stood and returned the embrace. Buddy turned away from the table embarrassed by his poignant display that most never have the courage to reveal. Buddy and I stood before his dearest friends knowing we had shared something on that porch that night. While Buddy could not articulate this watershed moment, he knew that he knew. We both knew that night he was loved. Buddy was always loved, but more like a person loves a cute pet. Buddy could not articulate, but he knew the difference. We are all aware the difference when we are loved. He was loved because he was seen for the first time in his twenty-some years as a human being, a man. Buddy Pearl was freed from the prison of his Down Syndrome. I can still see his face proclaiming to all what they never understood. It was a miracle that Buddy and I shared.

Moments later we unraveled the embrace, and I stared into his grateful eyes and thanked him, smiled a big grin and we fist pumped signaling that dinner can be resumed.

The sounds of clinking silverware returned, my father, reminded us that Jesus was the reason for the season in his religious way as people continued eating and briefly acknowledged his proclamation. Looking across the table, I saw Grandma Abba slyly grinning; she knew that maybe Buddy and my father were both right this Christmas Eve. Giles at the end of the table simply stared at me in careful observation looking for any data that he could measure that

I indeed was becoming Jesus. Hayleigh simply reached under the table and gently squeezed my hand.

Hayleigh's father Buford spoke up, "Since we are busy toasting, I'd like to make a toast to the newest working person at this table," raising his glass, "My son Buddy." Everyone around the table clapped, and Buddy beamed with pride.

"That explains the new look," I replied by fist-pumping the new dude look. Looking at Buford, I saw for the first time a genuine happiness and pride at a young man starving for his affection.

Buford nodded toward me with his glass, "You said something to me Thanksgiving night, out on the porch. I've always wanted to protect Buddy, by controlling his world mainly out of my guilt-ridden broken heart. The next day it occurred to me that I was controlling my world. I could not bear disappointment to come to Buddy, but it was me that could not stand the disappointment. Holding him back was my way of holding on; holding onto the world I controlled. Here I was a warden, a father, who had imprisoned my own son. I never let him be seen. I never let him experience life as a human. A young man guilty of nothing except having a millstone-around-the-neck father. Buford's eyes misted over, and his lip quivered until he regained control. "Edward, you not only helped Buddy, but you saved me also; and for that I am grateful; thanks."

"It takes a good man to have the courage to see; you Buford, are a good man," as I tipped my glass toward him.

Immediately Buford's wife, May Pearl, chimed in more good news, "Buford and I just put a contract in on a building in downtown Richmond. I'm opening up a school of dance." Looking over at my grand-daughter Eden, she smiled saying, "After Buford had observed how happy I was teaching you to dance, he suggested that I start up a school. I feel like a young fairytale princess getting rescued from the tower. We are also going to include a unique curriculum for people with Downs Syndrome," she declared as she smiled at Buddy.

"I'm going to get a girlfriend there," Buddy heartily boasted while laughing behind a sheepish grin.

Hayleigh looked at me in astonishment then turned to Buford and May, "Why Daddy, aren't you full of surprises, I can hardly keep up with the changes in our men." Hayleigh was genuinely happy, but it was bittersweet. The father she always loved, had become the man she craved to love.

Giles simply marveled at what was transpiring. He had nothing to say, but I could tell he was wondering what my journey had for him. He was watching others changed and affected. He was looking at me; and now the line between Edward Mayus and Jesus was blurred. I was still Edward because I still had the doubts and fears of any human being, but I had the light of quiet strength shining from somewhere I did not know. I had no sense of time as if there was no beginning or end but was simply just present in which I saw things as if living in another world. But the world I now saw influenced the world I once knew. Giles just intensely stared at me in a searching way, but we both had no answers that our scientific minds demanded. I knew that the mystery would be revealed in the unfolding story of my journey.

***

The gun-metal blue hue of the earlier fallen snow blanketed the two hillsides that surrounded the long driveway to Hillside Community Church. The moon's bright light bounced off each evergreen branch that held the new heavy snow on this calm night as if nature had decorated its own Christmas trees.

Driving up, I spotted Abe organizing a few men with two trucks loaded with wood and large barrels. I lowered the window, and Abe gave me the thumbs up that our surprise insurrection of the Christmas Eve service was going as planned.

Walking in the door, I was met by a frantic Timothy Sludge, who rushed over demanding, "Thank God you got here early, the tech crew does not have your slides. Can you give them to me?"

"I don't have any slides. I will only need one slide. Ask them to look up the definition of incarnation and write it on the slide. It's the only thing we will need. How many songs are we singing to start the service?" He indicated three as he was writing down my instructions. "Good after the first three songs they can delete the remaining slides, we are not using them; we will be doing something a little different tonight. I do need a microphone. I will be starting the message from down on the floor."

Sludge was busy stressfully taking down all the instructions knowing he had to report to Caine what was transpiring. "So, you are not going to be seated up front alongside myself and Caine?" Sludge asked knowing the answer, as he let out a sigh aware of Caine's coming reaction.

I replied as we walked down the aisle toward the side entrance, "That's correct and as far as I'm concerned that big throne-like chair can be used as firewood. I'm not going to be elevated above the people as if I have a seat of importance. Don't you think that is counter to my Father's message?"

Timothy was startled at my direct response and seemed intrigued by my Freudian slipped question, but an answer came from Caine lurking in the shadows behind the door. "Your father picked out that chair, I was with him when he did."

"I'm not talking about that father," I replied moving away. "I don't want anyone sitting up front tonight."

Sludge immediately asked, "Where do you want us to sit?"

Turning incredulously, I answered, "With your family."

Caine was apparently dismayed, "What is Larkins up to outside?"

"It's a surprise," I retorted quickly.

"People don't like surprises," Caine shot back.

"People love surprises Caine; it's change, they hate. Everything that is living is always changing. If it's not changing, it's dying."

I left the two men stunned and sought out the sound crew for my microphone.

***

The service started off well with the singing of the carols that everyone was finally settling down to enjoy. There was a buzz about the night that everyone could feel. It was my first official public arrival as minister, and the exciting murmur from the staff had reached many already. They were filled with anticipation about a man they hardly knew. Their anxious prospect was heightened driving up between the two hillsides glancing and wondering what Abe Larkins and his crew were cooking up. The empty chairs up front signaled that things were not normal. The absence of Caine up front overseeing the ceremonial ritual that had become their life pattern over the years was to some unsettling. The Reverend Timothy Sludge welcomed the congregants as usual and then promptly walked down the steps and took his place with the people, with his family. His wife who had been saving his seat beamed a smile toward him, and his two little kids fought to get near their Daddy whom they had never worshiped with during a Christmas Eve. Before the Music Minister, Bill Demure, had sounded the first note of *I Heard the Bells on Christmas Day*, you could hear one of the Sludge's children exclaim as he held her in his arms,

"Daddy, you get to spend Christmas Eve with us?" as she gleefully shrieked her excitement. The gentle, sad, happy sigh is heard amongst the crowd enjoying that her Daddy will be in the flesh, in her life, for the first time on Christmas Eve.

The last chorus of God Rest Ye Merry Gentlemen was calming down to a hush. The lights had dimmed as they usually do before my father started into his sermon. But no one had yet appeared. An awkward, uncomfortable silence filled the large cavernous room. There was a slight hum coming from the bass player's amp until eventually, you heard it clicked mute. I clicked my lavaliere mic on; it was as loud as a snap on a drum snare. I started to hum the last carol we sang. Everyone was wondering where the slightly off-key humming was coming from, except the few nearby pew sitters who spotted me sneaking in the back and taking a seat about a third of the way up the aisle. I was dressed in jeans and a weathered tan canvas leather coat. I had a nondescript wool ski cap pulled over my head.

Lifting myself up so I could sit on the back of the pew so all could see me. I spoke in song very slowly, deliberately and poignantly like a cantor. "*Now to the Lord sing praises, all you within this place. And with true love and brotherhood, each other now embrace.*" I then allowed the words to float through the air and hopefully into their hearts. I repeated even slower, "*And with true love and brotherhood, each other now embrace.*"

Climbing down from my makeshift perch, I slowly made my way down the aisle still speaking, "This is most likely going to be the least amount of words spoken to you by a minister on Christmas Eve. But if you can open your eyes tonight, and listen to your heart you will receive the gift everyone desires. Tonight, will live inside you forever. That's a long time."

About half way down the aisle, I turned and spotted my friend John Kandy who was still playing the funny guy with his crazy Santa hat. He showed me his open palm just underneath his chin, which he was using his other finger to simulate a spike being turned into my hand as if signifying that I was about to be crucified.

"Not yet John," I smiled acknowledging that I got his joke, "Tell me, John, what is the most important part of the Christmas celebration?"

John stammered slightly, and I knew I would pay the price later with his joking for putting him on the spot. John volunteered, "Spending time with family and loved ones."

No sooner than the last syllable left his lips, his daughter and son, Penny and Cotton, piped up in protest. "We never see you Dad!" Candy, John's wife, immediately hushed the children. John looked surprised at his children's reaction.

Cotton continued despite his mother's effort, "Well he doesn't; he never plays with us!"

John immediately placed his hand on Candy's shoulder and removed his Jolly-Old-Elf hat, "It's okay, they're right," as dejection and failure-filled his eyes. John knew that not only was he not present in their children's lives, but he knew deep down that Candy was not only silencing the children for John's sake but her own heart's sake. The fun-loving facade of the Kandy family was all they had to offer themselves and the world. John only offered, "My life always seems so busy with work and all."

Rescuing John from this moment of vulnerability and embarrassment I offered, "John, you are not alone." And I heard a few gentle 'Amen's' emanating from the room and many affirming nods of the head.

John and his family were like countless other families. The incarnation was a mere theological concept taught to them over the years to be doctrine and held as a foundation for their faith. Incarnation is not something to believe in, but it is meant to experience. The Kandy family had yet to experience love in the flesh. I knew John's, heart. He deeply loved his wife and children, but his heart was broken years ago by a father that was incapable of loving him. John grew to think himself unworthy of love. Tonight, John Kandy will experience incarnation.

I spotted another man to my left swallowing back his emotions that were revealed by the tracks of his tears that followed the wrinkles of his time-worn face, weathered by years of suffering. I did not know his name. I inquired knowing he had something to share, "Friend, what is Christmas to you?"

The frail man rose to a slightly hunched standing. He was a tall, slender man. "Most of you all don't know me; my name is Lawrence, most friends called me Larry. I have not been called Larry in a long time. When I think of Christmas, I try not to. I only have one feeling. Lonely." Motioning toward John, "You are a lucky young man, you have children that want you. Love, you. Loneliness is a long agonizing death before your heart stops beating. My wife and I only had one daughter. She got in trouble, and I could not handle her rebelliousness and what I felt was sin. I drove her away. Eventually, it drove my wife to an early death of a broken heart. So, you good man are blessed. Me, I'm just a lonely old man, who when he goes through the Christmas season; I simply see what could have been, what should have been. I'm tired of being alone, I want to be touched, I want to be loved, by anyone, but especially my daughter. Don't even know if she is around. I hear I may have a grandson. The moment was a silent pause in time. Loneliness. That's what my Christmas is about."

The torment of his soul deeply affected me. I felt as if I had lost Margaret all over again. Wiping my tears, I moved toward him. "Thank you for sharing Larry," I said, gently hugging him. He did not want to leave the embrace for a few moments. People were touched by a man, who was in their midst for years, but hardly knew. As he sat down, he whispered in my ear a thank you. The people started to reach out while still in the pews with hands resting on his shoulders. Larry was reborn that night. It was already starting. The Incarnation was happening.

Looking up, I saw that Abe was in the back listening to Larry's story. He motioned to me that everything was ready. I saw him beckon his wife Julie to come with him.

I looked around at the blank faces where the brutal cancerous honesty was gnawing away their mask. Slowly and rhythmically I spoke the words again, "And with true love and brotherhood, each other now embrace. This is the good tidings. Be truthful. How much true love and brotherhood are you experiencing tonight? Who is embracing you?"

Just then a young man stood and said, "I just got off work and raced over here to be with my family. I still must run out tonight before the stores close to find my wife a gift. I don't even know what gifts my son will get tomorrow."

His wife looking up at him reached her hand to his in support as her head slumped down. The young man looked at his wife as he descended back into the pew, "I think I missed Christmas again," he softly regretfully spoke.

A young tired, sad eyed woman, a single mom widow, with no nearby family, stood and said encouragingly, "This church has helped me a great deal, you have been gracious with your gifts of food and supplies during various times since my husband died in the Gulf."

Looking toward Larry, "Larry, I can identify with you; I too am alone; even with two children. I am invisible as an adult woman. I want to be seen. I am not just the poor single-mom widower who needs help. I need to be someone. Tomorrow, I will open presents with only my two beautiful children. We will have a nice simple Christmas meal. I cannot offer nor receive gratitude for the food, or ask how someone's life is going. Christmas highlights the dark void in my life."

I was struck by the honesty and how much people can see. This assured me that my surprise would work. I asked the tech crew to put up my one and only slide. I simply read it out loud and gave them an invitation.

Incarnation,

-a person who embodies in the flesh

a deity, spirit, or abstract quality

"The beauty of the Christmas story is its simplicity and mystery. It cannot be studied. We don't even know the actual date that the birth took place. What we believe, is that Jesus became flesh and He was Love. Love came to live in us. Tonight, we are going to try something different. Instead of me lecturing you on the Incarnation, you are going to become the Incarnation."

"I'm dismissing the service early," I ordered. "You are free to go home if you wish or you can join your family and friends and share in the good tidings of comfort and joy. I hope that you experience life and love together. Embrace what is embodied in you. Outside those doors in the small valley is a chance to connect with your loved ones, to see your friends, to free yourself from the hustle bustle of time. Go outside, love someone, embrace each other, and have fun." Caine came marching out of the glass booth in the back.

The slight murmur of a roar filled the sanctuary. Kids were racing out the door with parents trailing behind. Caine stopped Sludge and his family who were racing out like children on the last day of school.

I met Hayleigh and the grandkids, and we were making our way out when Caine came upon me asking, "What do you think you are doing?"

"We are going to experience incarnation instead of talking about it," I replied, "I hope you will join us."

"Timothy, gather up the elders for a meeting in the conference room," Caine barked out.

"Timothy, join your family outside," I retorted. Timothy was confused.

Just then my father appeared, "Timothy go on," he motioned; he bolted like a thoroughbred out of a gate. "There will be plenty of time for meetings; it's Christmas Eve, no one wants a meeting." Caine's blood vessels strained his face into a reflection of the surface of Mars. He stormed away.

My Dad just simply looked at me slightly puzzled, "You have faith that this sort of thing is going to work?"

"If I were sure, then it would not be faith, would it?" I wondered out loud. He chuckled, and I could tell he had a speck of amusement as if he was enjoying this tête-a-tête with Caine. "Dad, you regret asking me to take over?"

"Son, if I regretted, then it would not be faith, would it now." he responded with a wink.

After a few brief conversations with some parishioners, Hayleigh and I made our way outside. Hayleigh gasped, covering her mouth, "Oh my God, my eyes have never seen anything quite as beautiful, Edward, look."

Taking it all in, "Unbelievable," I exclaimed.

The sapphire cathedral skies dotted with diamonded stars was the fresco that canopied the two snow covered slopes leading to Hillside Community Church. The towering pines and leafless Beechwood silhouettes reached upward overlooking the mass of people below. The trees were highlighted by the amber glow of many blue drums scattered about roaring with warm fire beaconing all to come closer for the warmth to share. This is what Van Gogh must have seen before he painted Starry Night.

I must admit to myself that when the idea initially came to me, and I discussed it with Abe, I thought that tonight could be my first and last day as interim Pastor.

Strolling further out into the mass of people, I could see families building snowmen together, their laughter roared like the fire that lit the hillsides in which they frolicked. The laughter echoed joy instead of humor. There is a difference. If you listen carefully; you can hear and see the distinction.

There was the Kandy family, enjoying a good old fashion snowball fight. His wife along with his son and daughter were ganging up on poor John. John was rolling around in the snow laughing as he tried to stand, while his kids kept pushing him down. Tumbling down the hill, the family stopped just in front of me. John's head covered in white powder as he belly-laughed with joy holding onto his kids. The scene recalled the haunting memory of him with the white icing caked into his face, only this time John felt no need to make others laugh. They were bringing him joy. He was loved and freed to accept it.

John Kandy rose from the ground and lifted his wife to her feet, embracing in a warm hug and kiss that melted the snow away with the warmth of their love. John's kids both hugged him at his legs and waist. They said some words together as a family that I could not hear but felt the embodiment of love. They walked away to roast marshmallows and get hot cocoa; John looked at me, his eyes said thank you. John Kandy learned how to become the Incarnation.

Continuing my observation walk, I ran into the young couple. "Hey, where are the children?" I asked, "You better get going before the stores close; you need to get something for that beautiful bride."

"Oh, after we played in the snow as a family, I called my parents to come pick them up," he replied.

Eagerly and proudly his wife chimed in, "I told him, the best gift he could give me is to be with me. So, we are planning to close this place. This is such a wonderful, beautiful Christmas Eve. The best, ever."

I spotted the widowed single mom, laughing and talking with a group of adults while her little boys played with other small toddlers. Her eyes were not tired; they were bright as the stars that night. This was her gift from the Incarnation. She was seen tonight. She is a human being created a little lower than the angels but much higher than a widowed single mom.

Just then Julie Beaman came up behind me and said, "Well, Edward, Giles says that this is a miracle and you created this. What has changed in you, Edward? Did it have to do with that middle of the night escapade you and my husband are so tight-lipped about?"

I simply smiled and said, "It is a miracle, isn't it?" We sat there observing.

Julie continued, "I wanted to reach out to her, she reminds me of my sister in California. She is a single mom, with three kids. I tried to approach her to ask her to join us, but she was already invited to spend Christmas day with the Browning's. Look at her, look at how happy and relaxed she is. I've watched her kids in daycare about twenty times and never knew anything about her. How did you know that the people would respond this way?"

"People deep down always want to be human. That's what they were created to be. If they can see, they can be healed and freed to live the life of the Imago Dei. It's in their DNA," I smiled as I walked away.

Walking back, I grabbed Hayleigh and the grandkids and climbed the incline to steal a quick sleigh ride down the slope, in which all the children took opportunity to toss snowballs at my head. I laughed at the idea of them throwing snowballs at my father. Fortunately, none connected. Walking back toward the building I had to stop and look around. It was quite a miracle, and the miracle was surrounding me. Am I a miracle worker?

Just then I saw Abe standing next to my father and his wife Margaret, with Caine at my dad's side bending his ear. Before I made it up the steps, Timothy's Sludge's wife stopped me, "I just want to thank you. This is the first Christmas Eve Timothy, and I have spent together since his second year of seminary. Our children have never spent Christmas Eve with their father. Look at him enjoying his kids. It's a real blessing. I will never forget this night. It's as if God visited our family tonight. That's how I feel; I can't explain it." She hugged and reached over and kissed me on the cheek.

I started to pull away saying, "That's the beauty of the Incarnation. You don't have to explain it. It's simply grace. You just experience it."

Reaching the top step, Caine delivered me a stern accusation, "Well I hope you know what you did to the church budget!"

"No I don't, but I am sure you're going to tell me," I volleyed back as my father grinned.

"Since you decided unilaterally to forgo the offering, we are now behind budget."

"Isn't this the last week Caine?"

"Yes! but I was planning on continuing to grow the surplus." He defended.

"How much do we have in the surplus?"

"One-point-one million," Caine shot back proudly. I just looked at him and shook my head and walked over to Abe.

"Abe, where have you been? I've been looking for you," I asked quietly.

Abe responded to my inquiry, "I have another surprise cooked up."

"You know one more surprise might just put poor Caine over the edge. Can we spend one-point-one million dollars tonight?" We both chuckled under our breath.

"Another surprise? Are you bringing in three wise men? Maybe you arranged for the star of Bethlehem?" I snorted out laughing with my friend.

"It's better than that," he assuredly said. My mind was spinning thinking about what this could be. Before I had any more time to interrogate Abe, a loud swish came from behind along with two thumps of snowballs knocking Caine's hat off onto the ground. Caine, my father, as well as Abe and I, turned expecting to see some playful children. Instead, it was my Margaret along with Abe's Jenny who were the culprits.

"Sorry Mr. Banks," they giggled out and ran away like two school girls prouder than peacocks. Margaret shot me back a look for approval. I gave her a thumbs-up, and they continued to laugh.

Banks tried to dig the snow out from dropping down the back collar of his coat. Picking up his hat that had been blasted off his head by the woman, he murmured something underneath his breath about his hat being worth nearly three hundred dollars. Brushing it off with his gloves he huffed and puffed away leaving us with, "I hope everyone is enjoying school recess instead of a real Christmas Eve Candlelight Service."

My Dad just shook his head, "That guy can frustrate me to no end." He let out a sigh that was barely audible. "Son, I have to tell you, I've never seen the people this joyous. It's a miracle."

As Caine's black SUV made its way out of the parking lot, the kids bombarded it with snowballs causing him to slam the breaks momentarily. I guess after realizing the futility and most imminent danger of getting out of the vehicle; he continued onto the remainder of what I could not fathom as good tidings of comfort and joy as he rolled out into the dark of the night.

I then felt two hands on my shoulder then drop around my waist to give me a big hug. It was Johanna. She whispered in my ear, "This is crazy, you have overturned everything in one single night. The whole night is remarkable. I've spoken with a lot of people who say they have more Christmas spirit than all the years of their life put together."

Johanna looked over toward Dad and uncomfortably said, "Merry Christmas Daddy, how are you feeling?" Emilee was standing slightly behind her remaining quiet.

My father looked over and politely but earnestly said, "Merry Christmas to you little girl." He ignored Emilee as if she was not there. Hayleigh came up behind and placed her hand on Emilee's shoulder.

Just then Abe interrupted, "Here comes the surprise Edward."

Everyone's interest was piqued. Abe explained after hearing Larry's story, he recognized that his daughter worked for him at one of his McDonald's. He made some calls and found out she lived only about fifteen miles from here. My wife and I drove to her house. I explained to her what I heard.

Abe went on, "When she was younger, she got pregnant her senior year of High School. Larry was devastated. Weeks later, she had a miscarriage and Larry didn't believe her. He accused her of having an abortion. Things were said. They have not seen each other or talked in over seven years." She misses him.

I immediately started looking to see if Larry was still around. "Has anyone seen Larry?" I spotted him helping the youngsters with their sleds making sure that they did not slide into the pathway of a car leaving the parking lot. We started walking toward him. When we got about thirty feet from him, Abe put his arm in front of me blocking me from moving any closer.

"See my wife at the top of the hill," he pointed out, "She is with Larry's daughter and grandson. That's the surprise. They are going to sled down to meet him any minute."

Just then Abe's wife waved, signaling that they are coming down next. The saucer started to pick up speed as it descended the hill. She was guiding the saucer toward her father while still holding onto her son. Quickly coming upon her father, she quickly turned causing her and her son to spill out sideways. Larry raced as quickly as his old lanky body would allow to check on their safety. As he approached his pace slowed to a crawl and eventually a frozen stop.

Larry could not believe his eyes but was not sure that his mind could be trusted to guarantee that this miracle was happening. Larry, like Lazarus, was about to be raised from the dead. Larry stuttering and stammering out, "Suzy? Is that you Suzy?

"Merry Christmas Daddy." she answered reaching out her hand toward him.

"It is you, you're Suzy, my Suzy, you are here," he cried out falling to his knees into an embrace of his daughter. They rocked and wailed muffled words of apology into each other's shoulder and chest for what appeared to be five minutes, occasionally breaking to stare into the eyes to make sure this was happening. The outside world stood still and could not see the translation, but the words were spoken directly into their hearts. They stood up helping each other. He turned, a little boy was standing aside quietly, taking it all in, looking up toward this tall gentleman.

"Daddy, say hi to your grandson," she proudly announced.

"I have a grandson; I have a grandson?" he exclaimed as he picked up the unsuspecting boy hugging him in a bear hug grip that was never letting go. "I am your Grandpa; do you know that I'm your Grandpa!" he shouted startling the boy. "What's his name, I don't even know his name?" looking toward Suzy for an answer.

"His name is Lawrence," she said with a measure of pride, "I call him Larry for short."

***

The bright silvery white moon was now high in the sky. The diamond stars shimmered. The fires were beginning to dim. The snow was changing from the amber glow back to the gun-metal blue hue. Other cars stopped by that saw the earlier glow. There was one homeless family that lived in a car that said they could see the glow in the sky from the Seven Eleven where they had stopped for dinner. They were looking for a place to park their four-wheeled home. The light like the star long ago brought them here. They slept that night in the warmth of a home where true love and brotherhood lived in the flesh and embraced in life.

Hayleigh and I were leaving after saying many goodbyes. We started our drive out of the parking lot slowly drifting as we took one last look at the miracle on Christmas Eve. There was a spontaneous gathering of the choir members that remained at the top of the steps. Someone had hooked up a speaker and microphones. The candles that were originally planned for indoors had made their way to everyone. The choir started to sing *Silent Night* as the flames moved through the crowd of people. Our car slowly made its way toward the long driveway. I acknowledged them as we drifted slowly through the pleasant verses. Everyone knew that tonight inside the ordinary they found the sacred and holy. The last people we saw before turning onto the road was the young couple who chose the gift of relationship over a store-bought gift. Huddled together over a fire. All, was calm; all was bright.

***

Hayleigh and I laid in bed that night recounting the wonderful stories that took place this night. Abe said he heard even more. Hayleigh looked at me and whispered, "Edward, God is truly in you, none of this could have happened without you."

"Hayleigh, I'm happy for everyone and the joy that it is bringing people, I still can't help to think what this journey is, for Edward, for me. When I took the DNA, did Edward die? I love you more than ever, but is it Edward or . . ."

"Shhh," Hayleigh whispered placing her finger over my mouth.

As the candle burned down, we embraced each other, and each moment as the day was ending. Margaret was on the porch by herself humming. She then started to sing the first verse of *Oh Holy Night*. I had not heard her sing that song in years. This was my little miracle as I quietly drifted off to sleep.

Hineni

Hineni, the declaration of readiness,

no matter what the outcome,

that's a part of everyone's soul.

-Leonard Cohen

The punishing brisk winds blew icy cold the following days after Christmas. Nothing was as bitterly raw as Giles stinging cutting words, "I'm terribly sorry Hayleigh, I don't know how to tell you, so I will just come right out and say it. You have a brain tumor."

The moment the last syllable was forced from his lips, Giles turned to me and endlessly stared examining my reaction.

Hayleigh's filled eyes peered into the dark abyss of uncertainty where faith struggles to align with reality. It never does. That's why it's faith. Time stops. The hourglass has been turned on its side, a particular type of death. It's the worst kind of death. A dying grounded between time and timelessness. She swallows and chokes on her fear that is lodged deep inside her soul. Hayleigh battles and fumbles inside her mind. The courage needed has yet to be revealed. The courage to live in the present, between time and timelessness. No matter the circumstance, it is where life is found.

For me, time was out of mind, but anxiety was lurking behind a tomb of shadows. The fear I was experiencing was Hayleigh's internal dread. Her vulnerable, lonely fear deep inside was why I was filled with sorrow. I wept. Quietly. I likened it to a parent's cry; when their child is experiencing anguish without them. To know a child is suffering without your comfort is unbearable. Hayleigh is my wife; not my child. But she needs my comforting assurance like a child.

Giles leaned awkwardly forward, feeling compelled to deliver his usual doctor-clinical strategic assessment of Hayleigh's condition, but instinctively knew that his typical physician god-like assurance would fall short of what his friend would offer. Giles continued to study my reaction looking for any data he could confirm divine. His only overture to Hayleigh was whether she had any questions.

Hayleigh, silent, just looked at him; then turned to look at me. I was still conflicted. Her countenance was both adult and child-like at the same time. Hayleigh was simultaneously a child hoping for answers, a lost woman, looking for the questions. Amidst the silence, I looked back honestly into her eyes for a moment. Giles desk clock sounded the ticks that could be heard above the quiet as if it was the metronome of life. I counted off in my mind the ticks. When I got to forty-four, I reached over and touched Hayleigh's hand lightly. Michelangelo was right. A simple touch is all a human being needs.

Hayleigh smiled and broke down into tears. We hugged a while. Giles came over and put his hands on both of our shoulders.

He gave her a tissue, assuring her directly, "I'll be with you every step of the way, we will fight this, and besides, you have each other, you have Ed . . . ward," his last word hesitantly trailing off as if he did not know what to call me.

She sniffed back her tears thanking Giles without words laying her cheek on his hand and smiling. She looked at me for more comfort saying, "Well, they say everything happens for a reason?"

"I guess you are right honey, things do tend to happen," I countered half-heartedly. Hayleigh detected my half evasive reply, but was assured by my next encouragement, "I'm interested in how we move forward."

The three of us went over Giles recommendations for an oncologist and further testing that would be done. Hayleigh seemed more at ease and less fearful, but I was uneasy on how she was shifting her emotions and mindset. In life, there are as many critical stages as there are stars, most of the time we cannot see them. They are hidden by storm clouds or bright light. However, there are certain crucial junctures in life; even the blind can easily witness with a little soulful reflection. These moments, lived and experienced properly, bring beauty and grace into the life of every human willing to see. I could not bear to watch Hayleigh's soul plundered of these treasures in exchange for the benign neglect of her heart so that I could be spared my heartache. Everything does not happen for a reason. Believing this does not ease the pain for anyone. It hides it.

We stood up to leave knowing that the next year would be like no other. Giles would be making the calls to the oncologist at Hopkins. We would wait to hear. I had a meeting back at the church.

Hayleigh, leaving to go to the grocery store, turned to Giles and myself with a touch of irony said, "After the news that we just discussed the last thirty minutes, I'm going to pick up bread and milk. I guess life does go on. Doesn't it?"

I merely grinned and agreed, "Yes it does Baby, life goes on . . . today." She gently closed the door. I admired her resilience.

Giles asked if I could remain awhile. He just continued the puzzling stare as I sighed, wiping my face, resting back in the leather chair.

"Edward, what do you think?"

"What?" I incredulously questioned back at him.

"Edward, you have to be thinking something, I saw your mind working the entire time. I watched it, but you said little. Your eyes toward Hayleigh were distressed in discomfort; you were uneasy about something."

I leaned forward, my arms resting on my knees, hands clasped together I said, "Alright, you want to know what I am thinking?"

I continued agitated, standing up and walking toward the window, "Well you are going to be disappointed. I am conflicted."

Giles was pouring coffee into two cups; handing me one. "I was shocked when you told us the diagnosis. Shouldn't I have seen this coming?"

I start to vent out loud my inner thoughts, "I am looking at this beautiful child of God frightened and feeling isolated. It's what happens during these watershed moments in life. It's not happening to anyone but you. You feel alone. Then the thought erupts inside my heart; this is not a child, this is my wife, my lover. The foggy thoughts finally clear; a Déjà vu-like image comes to my mind of Lazarus. This is how Jesus must have felt. Hayleigh like Lazarus, in her mind, wants to hear the words of life, an invitation back to the living. Jesus still wept and was burdened with sadness. But he raises Lazarus anyway."

"Wait, are you saying that raising Lazarus was not a good thing?" questioned a confused Giles. "What does it have to do with Hayleigh?"

Two more sips of coffee, looking out the window, watching Hayleigh battling the headwinds getting into her car, I continued, "Since I set out on this path, I have only spoken and done what was revealed to me, somewhere deep inside myself. It was drawn from a well in which I never had drunk, but feel as if I have tasted its familiarity all my life. I can't explain it.

Giles interrupted with assurance, "Well I can!"

Another taste of coffee and I continued, "Am I going to heal Hayleigh? I demand this to be revealed to me, but when I heard Hayleigh say 'everything happens for a reason' my heart dropped. I then knew this cup would have to be tasted by Hayleigh and myself. Even if she truly believes these hollow words. However, deep down there is the idea, that gnawing agonizing betrayal, that God somehow has a reason for the agony He has authored. The deck is stacked. God cannot lose the theological chess match. The victim overcomes the challenge and is somehow defined as becoming a better person from lessons learned; or they are crushed under the suffering, living out the lie that they were not good enough to see the reason. You're left alone; somehow you must back into grace from this weak futile position. This is a lie, and nowhere near the truth."

The remaining coffee is slurped down as I continue my pleading with Giles, "Hayleigh just found out ten minutes earlier. How could any whole person believe that the suffering is eased by such a trite cliché that is handed down by people not tasting this cup, not walking into the experience? How could one believe that there is a legitimate reason for cancer, the death of a child, the crushing loss of love, or a brain tumor? It's absurd."

"Why didn't you stop Hayleigh right then and there? What's wrong with Hayleigh looking for some reason or purpose in what's happening to her?" Giles defended Hayleigh, willing to support that there could be some cosmic reason for everything. "I saw your displeasure, but you never corrected her."

Edward replied, "Purpose and reason? Purpose and reason are not the same thing. Reason seeks to understand. Purpose requires faith. Reason is attained. Purpose is revealed. Reason is acquired by works. Purpose is endowed with grace. And wisdom is the combination of both."

I continued, "Giles? Correcting her? There is no right or wrong here. These are her beliefs now. This is all she was given by religion. Taking her beliefs will not give her faith, it will leave her isolated and alone. This journey together will reveal her faith that is already there. That is my faith in the Father.

Giles still looked perplexed, "But will you still heal her like Lazarus?"

I thoughtfully and slowly answered him, "My friend, I don't know, I am still a man. I still pray. I have feelings and longings like you. I desire that Hayleigh is healed, but I trust and wait for it to be revealed. My trust in my Father gives me faith that she will be blessed. I too weep today as Jesus wept for Lazarus. I know why he cried. I don't want Hayleigh to walk the same path."

Giles just flopped back into his chair and sighed, "Brother, I am glad that I am not you, but I am truly blessed to know you. The weight of your words bear down into my heart and produce an inner joy that flows in me that only you know. I know that you know it."

"Giles, I know," as I started to leave.

"Edward, you said you knew why Jesus wept at the tomb of Lazarus. Why if he was aware that he was going to bring him back to life did he still cry?" Giles inquired once more.

As I opened the door leaving, I looked back at Giles and explained, "Lazarus lived thirty years after his resurrection. It is said that he never smiled during that time, because of the effect of seeing the lost souls in his four-day stay in death. There was one exception when he spotted a person stealing a pot. Lazarus smiled and said, 'the clay steals the clay' and laughed. You see Giles, reason is not all it's cracked up to be. Trust is far greater."

The door closed.

THIN LINES

Don't let this throw you. You trust God, don't you?
Trust me. There is plenty of room for you in my Father's home,
I'll come back and get you so you can live where I live.
And you already know the road I'm taking.

-The Message

There is always a narrow path. It is a thin line between the sacred and the ordinary. It is where life is lived and experienced by people who see. All others travel the wide path. I can't any longer.

***

Months after I left Giles' office that day, I was still conflicted. Was I becoming Jesus? Many of my nights were spent in the garden of my soul weeping for the healing of my beautiful Hayleigh. Other times crying for others who were lost and broken. Torn because of my effect on helping others in the redemption from their blindness that leads to the loss of heart and freedom; while my wife and lover suffer. I am not sure where the passage of my story was leading, but I could feel the pathway narrowing. Most people stop at this point. The narrowing, like a microscope starts to bring into focus the reality that surrounds us all. Nothing is what it initially appears. It is so new and manifests itself so dangerous that you want to return to the previous comfortable created known. But if you experience the tipping point of courage to hear the real inner siren's call, the narrow trail now beckons and invites you into something new, something free, that has yet to be revealed.

Whether I am Jesus or not, I still find myself constantly praying for eyes to see the cup of what is being revealed.

A few weeks after Hayleigh's initial diagnosis, we were given the tragic news. Hayleigh's tumor was a stage three cancer but was a series of small tumors concentrated in part of the brain that made it inoperable. My heart collapsed in agony as she looked to me for comfort to evade having to make the decision about radiation treatment. Giles told us to take our time. There was no rush in making this decision.

Riding home in the car was silent, forsaken, and long. I could hear every breathing sigh emanating from her tired body. The stone caught in the tire kept time as it clicked out the remaining revolving's before arriving home. Her head rested back on the seat, looking up to nowhere. We pulled up to Eden and approached the house, turning the engine off we just set there in stillness.

Hayleigh broke the uneasy calm, "What does God want me to do Edward?" she lightly cried out as if it was two questions directed at two people, or maybe one question directed to one person. Who was the object of her interrogation?

Internally struggling, to come to grips I responded uneasily, "Are you asking me what you should do?"

"No, I'm asking what does God want me to do, there is a difference, it matters."

"Hayleigh, why does it matter?" I gently and softly inquired.

"Because I want to do the right thing, I don't want to displease Him," she sighed in confusion.

"What happens if you do the wrong thing? Are you afraid you will not get your miracle?"

"Don't be silly, of course, I believe in miracles. I've never doubted. I think that's the reason for your journey.

Everything happens for a reason, doesn't it Edward?" she pleaded for an answer.

I only acknowledged her proclamation of faith earlier in Giles office. Now she demanded an answer.

"Everything happens for a reason for those gazing into the past. Hayleigh, people desire a spiritual autopsy to confirm their beliefs that they confuse as their faith. Everything happens for a purpose that reveals their beliefs which become their faith. This journey, you and I are on, will reveal the meaning if we have trust. Trust is always in a person."

"I trust you, Edward, I believe that you are going to heal me. For whatever reason, plan, or purpose; I believe that I'm going to be healed."

She looked at me with firm focused misty eyes that were hanging onto a rope with all she had. I did not want her to be hanging onto a rope for survival. I wanted my Hayleigh to live through this journey with eyes wide open for the revealing of the purpose. The silent air between us hid the turbulence inside my mind as thoughts bounced around ricocheting through my heart. I grasped for words like a blind man trying to find the curb before crossing the street of confusion. I moved my lips trusting the syllables would form the salve needed for her soul.

"Do you trust God?" I asked. She surrendered a grateful, relieved nod yes. "So, do I." I smiled assuredly. "Then you are living . . . today."

Hayleigh leaned into me, embracing me through the fear with everything she had. She wanted more but trusted today, the story, the page she was living in this chapter of her life. "I'm going to live today; I am going through with the radiation."

From that moment on, my inner turmoil of being conflicted on how to live if I was indeed becoming like Jesus started to fall away. I was starting to see my journey as an acceptance of a cup that was being offered to me by life. The journey inside this life revealed I was becoming Jesus, while in some way still being Edward. I was awakened and conscious to the author of life in a manner having never experienced. Words of truth were spoken into me, but not from the outside, but from inside. The voice of my thoughts was mine, yet not from me, or at least from a part of me that I had never known. I was still Edward, I still was concerned for Hayleigh's healing, but Edward was dying in a way. He was becoming less so something else could be more. Was this something else Jesus? This new person overtaking me could see the path of uncertainty without fear. The lines of Edward and Jesus were starting to become indistinguishable. It was if we were becoming one.

***

The months following was a journey of growth as I walked the trail of uncertainty. At every turn were new revelations surprising my soul. The journey took me down the path never traveled by myself. I loved Hayleigh like never before. Don't get me wrong; I always loved her for how I saw her. Now I loved her for who she was. I saw parts of her heart that she had never unlocked or was too afraid to reveal. I regret that for all these years I had missed out on who she was. This caused me to love her in a new way. It's as if she was reborn in my eyes which caused me to love her greater. There was an eternal strength and beauty that I had missed all these years. The intimacy in our relationship grew because I needed to be close to her both physically, emotionally, and spiritually. Together we found in the present that there was no time. It was if she did not have cancer of the brain. We were living together, where the past and future did not exist. There was only the undefined moment that lasted an eternity of joy in our minds and hearts. We made love because it was our chance to taste and touch heaven and come back and do it again. One night, during an early March snowfall, Hayleigh had just finished her first round of radiation. We were sitting in front of the fireplace of our empty house, our naked bodies wrapped in a blanket. Hayleigh asked me to come dance out in the snow. It was something she thought stupid but always wanted to do. It was one of those crazy things you say but never feel is going to happen. She gazed out at the pure snow, looked at me with her warm dark eyes, and asked me to come dance naked in the snow. Throughout our life, she had always had this side of her that yearned for this crazy feeling of freedom, to not be under someone's thumb. Me being the less outwardly free person always pushed back on her free spirit. That night I heard her heart yearning to live through all of life's experiences. I stood and lifted her up as the blanket fell to the floor. She was shocked and inquired was this happening? We raced out the front door onto the porch which was covered in about six inches of wet snow where we waltzed as I sung lightly Clapton's *Wonderful Tonight*. After a few verses, we had pirouetted around the entire porch. Hayleigh was exhausted and asked to go in with a beautiful smile. I lifted her legs up, and she kissed me as she thanked me while I carried her across the threshold as if we had just got married. That night we made love like we were just married. She remarked that she was so surprised that I agreed to do such a silly thing. She recognized that I heard her heart.

Is this what it is like to live like Jesus. I felt that night like I rescued my bride and she felt loved and free. That evening, Hayleigh saw me as her first love. The tumor was gone that night as if it never existed. She would wake in the morning knowing it was still there but also knowing that we could connect once again and she could taste freedom in the present. Hayleigh continued to believe that this all was happening for a reason and that I was going to bring healing.

***

Tommy came home early Spring, tired of playing the bar scene in Nashville. My songwriting son wanted to quit. He had been grinding out his existence for over six years and could not get the visibility needed to get the break that could springboard his career. His band, *The Acorns*, had a tumultuous split in a storm of ego clashing leaving Tommy sailing alone. He was the songwriter for the group, but the others wanted to go in a different direction leaving Tommy without a place, and brokenhearted. He could not see a way out. His journey had stopped. In Tommy's mind, he was at a dead end. There are no dead ends in life's journey; there are no crossroads, no forks in the road. People who chose not to see reality, see the world as a tangled maze of intersections, forks in the road, and dead ends. These are illusions of people who follow the well trampled wide path woven out by others. This is not their true path. Life's true sojourn reveals a long winding narrow path that only you can choose. Few have the courage to walk it.

I stepped onto the back porch that one Spring morning, coffee in my hand. There Tommy was on the porch sitting in a chair, looking away, out at the Elizabeth tree. He was lightly picking his guitar to the same tune when he was a kid. Tommy probably sat a thousand times in this rocking chair as a dreaming child. It was the same tune he strummed in my nightmare. All his belongings in a duffel bag were lying behind him. He explained what had transpired in Nashville. He turned and looked at me through aviator sunglasses. I could see the dried tracks of his tears on his cheek.

"Dad, it's over," his voice quivered.

"What's over son?" I asked. He continued describing the same human tale of relationships going bad that has been repeated since the time of Caine and Able. Instead of a physical murder, most people deliver wounds that cause a slow benign dying in one's soul. People are left to bleed out their lives unless you figure out how to stitch up the piercing. But the scar is the constant memory that inflicts the dull fresh pain daily. It's the worst kind of death because you become trapped in time. Humans were meant to be eternal, not frozen in time. The reality is that time does not exist when living in the present. I need to heal his wound before the scarring. "Let's go for a walk."

A gentle breeze was brewing from the south. We took off on the path toward the stream that Tommy had walked many times in his life as child. He used to go there when he was learning to play his guitar. We were headed to what Tommy, as a child, called *the arena,* because it was a natural rock formation hollowed out with a small ledge that held a boulder that looked over a forty-foot wide pool of water. The acoustics were perfect and amplified his voice and guitar to where he thought he was singing at a concert. Many days his friends would gather to hear him. Other days the oscillations from the sounds of his guitar were his fans. Most of the time it was where he went to dream. It was where his heart was. The path now was overgrown since few people had traveled it for years.

"You sat on this rock with me when you came home from college. You told me you wanted to make music your life. Music was what made you come alive. It is what made you excited. So, Tommy, why do you say it's over?" I asked him as we sat on the rock.

"Because it is, Dad!" he barked back. "I'll have to start over. I've spent six years playing music in bars building a name for the band. We were just getting a following, some traction. I guess they lost faith in me."

"Do you love music?" I inquired, "Can you still write and play music?" I was throwing pebbles into the pond making small ripples that would travel the entire circumference of the waters.

Tommy shook his head and replied, "Yes, I can still write and play music." He looked up into the canopy of trees futilely wiping the frustration from his face.

"Oh, I see," I responded as I continued to throw pebbles. "Why are you so distraught? I thought you always wanted to make and play music. Music was going to be your life. You were going to be like a kid at Disney. So, what's changed?"

"But I want to play in front of thousands of people; I want to have people buy my songs. Is that so wrong?"

I threw one last small pebble into the center of the pond before answering. Rubbing the back of my neck, I said, "You see those small ripples?' He nodded yes. "Where do all the ripples end up?"

Thinking a while, "On the shoreline." he whispered.

"Those ripples are your music, your life." I picked up a larger rock sitting at my feet and threw it up in the air toward the middle of the small pool of water. "Is that what you are telling me you want to do, make a big splash? I thought you wanted to make music?"

"Yea, … Yes, that's what I want to do. I want to make a big splash."

"Where do all the ripples end up?"

He stood and started to walk away from me muttering under his breath, "On the shoreline."

A few moments passed when I explained, "The effect is the same for you. Your music reaches and touches people." I let a moment drift by as the last of the ripples reached the shore. "Tommy, you are trying to serve two masters. One is music, your true self; the other is the world's validation, which you can't control. It's the latter that is making you unhappy. By losing sight of your true self, you are blinded by the temptress siren of fame and recognition. Maybe the others are listening to the world's deceptive seductive call for glory?"

"What if they are right, and I'm not that good?" he pleaded for understanding.

Standing and walking over to him, I put my hand on top of his head like a father would with his child and shook his hair. The brief assured touch of a father's validation from the past, brought a slight smile to Tommy's face. I pointed to across the pond, a forty-foot distance and recalled, "Remember when we use to do this. Let's do it!"

I then bolted across the rocks that dotted a path to the other side which was a shortcut to the trail home. Maggie and Tommy were always amazed that their Dad always made it across. If one could time their leaps precisely, it appeared as if you were walking on water to the other side. Huffing and puffing, as I made it to shore, I turned and shouted to Tommy, "Come!"

Tommy was hesitant. Just then a loud crackle and a BOOM! Landed nearby as a typical springtime storm blew in. "I'll just walk around," he reasoned with me from across the water.

"Come, you can make it!" I shouted. "It's the only way you can beat the storm."

Tommy was reluctant, as another crackle could be heard from above. With hesitation, he started slowly, picking up the gazelle-like speed that was necessary for the final leap. SPLASH! Into the water, he fell. Rising out of the knee-high water, Tommy trudged the last ten feet to shore. He looked up at me annoyed saying, "Great idea Dad."

"Why did you lose faith, son?"

"I did not lose faith. I knew you could do it, you always do it," Tommy retorted.

"I'm not talking about faith in me. I'm asking why you lost faith in you," I stated, as we made our way up the shortcut beating the impending storm.

That night, Tommy got a call from an old friend, Angel Stevens. She was always a fan of Tommy. When she heard, *The Acorns* had split, she had been trying to reach Tommy for days. She had covered several of Tommy's songs over the last year. She wanted him to join her on tour. Her band was the opening act for Van Morrison. Tommy's stay would be short. He had to catch a train to New York that night. Tommy would be playing before large crowds.

Dropping him off at the station, he grabbed his guitar and duffel, looked at me and said, "Thanks for helping me see." I grinned and wished him well.

***

The journey continued for many at Hillside Community Church. Cain continued his clandestine meetings waiting for me to falter. The people that were ready to see were healed in their hearts allowing them to be free to see their journey. Everyone feels they are on a journey, but if you cannot see reality, you are merely on a cosmic treadmill, trapped in time. A person can spend a lifetime going nowhere.

I only preached from the pulpit ever so often during the year. I hate even using the word preach. Growing up, I acquired a disdain for the condescending proclamations from professionally educated technicians with a Master's Degree in of all ostentatious things, Divinity. Can you imagine, when one studies a subject such as engineering or business, they become an engineer or a businessperson. How can a person become an expert in Divinity?

I only participated in the service on alternating weeks. My content came from what I experienced during the week, and the people I met. The other weeks were orchestrated by Caine and his religious, political controllers; hand picking dogmatic preachers of fear and inadequacy of humans that kept the people from the narrow path. Caine, felt he was counterbalancing my approach of telling stories about life on the journey. Little did he know that he was shining a light of truth into the people's lives. I was offering a life of freedom and grace, while Caine's religious gospel was about control. People like Caine have an illusion of being in control. When presented with the truth, people will always choose freedom. They are simply wired this way. The people are observing the difference of living in freedom or dying in bondage. Timothy Sludge, who became a valued confidant over the last few months, reported that the numbers of Caine's cadres continued to drop over the summer as the church attendance started to grow.

Instead of standing behind the pulpit, my Sundays consisted of having raw open discussions with people about life. By the end of January, we had moved the pews around and set up a platform with a sectional sofa amongst the people. Those that made themselves available and vulnerable shared as humans on a journey. They were humans struggling with doubt, abuse, divorce, sexual identity, adultery, end of life, relationships, money, and careers. This was balanced out by persons who were happy, prosperous, and healthy. What everyone learned, was that all had struggled with the same identical issues. There was not much difference in the human condition of anyone. Judgment fell at the foot of the cross quite literally as this all took place before the forty-four-foot cross in the front. No one in the congregation had any idea who the person would be on any given Sunday.

When one is on a journey, they cannot be defined in time by those that sit and eat of the *Tree of Knowledge of Good and Evil*. These were people of courage and faith. They bestowed on the listeners the same. The faith was not in a belief system but a person. The person was Jesus or another intimate ally along their trail. The listeners understood that most of the time the thin line between the ordinary and sacred was indistinguishable. The courage was in the trusting to reach out to that person. The church observed how the people regained their proper sight so that their brokenness could be made whole allowing, them to be free. This is what I had to offer; sight, healing, and freedom. I spoke to each and everyone in the pews the grand existential question everyone needs to know; *In my journey, my life, where is God?* The service was renamed *The Never-ending Conversation* because the message did not end as a three-step concept or a program of principles and propositions on how to live. These things most people forget before kick-off on Sunday. Instead, the conversations continued with the very individuals who made themselves available and vulnerable. There were countless dinners and coffees where the dialogue continued. In the end, people were exposed to the *Tree of Life* and partook of its fruit, faith, hope, and love.

***

One of the remarkable Sundays occurred shortly after Mother's Day. It was nothing short of a miracle, and I was surprised. One day, Abe Larkins and I were eating breakfast at one of his burger restaurants.

"Edward, everyone is still talking about Christmas Eve. Do you know how many people were affected by that night?" Abe inquired.

Just as I was getting to speak, a ragged older man came out of the bathroom humming what I believed to be *He Touched Me.* He appeared slightly mentally disabled as he approached us and looked at Abe asking, "Are you, Mr. Larkins?"

Abe replied, "Yes I am, what's your name?" reaching out, Abe shook his hand. "This is my friend Edward; he is the pastor of my church."

"Interim," I correct him shaking the ragged gentleman's hand.

"My name is Charles, but people call me Cholly," he proudly slowly stuttered still shaking my hand with a grip that did not want to let go of the human touch. "I want to thank you, Mr. Larkins, for the food you give every night in the back-parking lot. It's a real blessing. I pray for you and your family every night. I thank Jesus all the time because of you," still holding my hand.

Abe had made it a habit of distributing the leftover food at the end of the night shift. Abe and I invited him to join us. We asked him what his favorite was. He politely responded that he could wait until tonight. We insisted, and he finally relented, "I love it when you have Fish-Fillets Sandwich's. Do you have Fish-Fillets today? They say it's healthy for you. You don't always have Fish-Fillets at night."

"I think we can rustle up a Fish-Fillet sandwich for you Cholly," Abe said with a smile. Cholly laughed and stomped his feet in pure joy over the prospect of eating during the day. We got to know Cholly that day. He was the son of the Pastor of a small Baptist church about five miles from Hillside. He was developmentally disabled, not retarded, as he insisted and reminded us during the complete recounting of his life story. He always worked and had jobs that his parents had secured for him. I remembered when his parents were killed by a drunk driver. It was big local news. Well, Cholly still lived there until the bank foreclosed on the house more than a year later, leaving Cholly with nowhere to go. He lived in the woods behind the home he loved, praying for a miracle that one day he could go back home. He had the faith of a spiritual giant. He told us, on the coldest days he would sneak into his father's church because he still had a key. There he would sleep under the cross with Jesus watching over him. He said his parents always told him that Jesus would take care of him.

As the time was breaking up, Cholly put his fries in his pocket informing us that his friend Oscar loved fries and he wanted to share them. Abe ordered another order of Fish-

Fillet and fries and told him to take them to Oscar. Abe told Charles to return the next day. Abe had a thought in mind that he could find him a job to do in the restaurant. Abe eventually refurbished a shed on his property and turned it into a tiny house. He employed Cholly and Oscar. They turned out to be top employees. Oscar and Cholly also attended church with Abe and his family. What we were more impressed with was the depth of their relationship with themselves and God. There was no difference. To them, loving each other as brothers and family, was the same as loving God.

I had an idea and invited them one Sunday to be part of *The Never-ending Conversation.* The congregation was floored and awestruck by their deep spiritual life that was lived out in the quiet corners of a small forest and now a shed on the Larkins farm. They all remarked that they had seen Cholly and Oscar around the county, and had merely passed them off as lazy common vagrants. Oscar recounted the first time he met Cholly. Oscar was formerly an electrician from Pennsylvania. He was working on an apartment construction site. Several months after the project had ended, there was a fire due to faulty wiring. Oscar knew the contractor had used equipment not up to code. A mother and her child had died of smoke inhalation. Oscar never could forgive himself for not speaking up and descended into depression and eventually homelessness. One cold, snowy night, about two in the morning, Oscar had decided to end his life with a bullet fired into his mouth. He broke into Cholly's deceased father's church to pray one last time for forgiveness. Oscar confessing and praying out loud in the third pew suddenly heard what he thought was a voice from God. The voice said, "I forgive you."

"What?" he shockingly asked in anticipation. "What did you say?"

"I said I forgive you," the voice in the dark said coming from the front, near the cross and the portrait of Jesus.

Oscar began to cry begging to hear those words one more time, "Please say it one more time."

"What are you deaf?" the voice asked, "Do you not understand that you are forgiven." Then Cholly sat up from the first pew. Cholly and Oscar talked the remainder of the night until the sun beamed through the stained glass, lighting the portrait of the Christ. Cholly spoke the words of the Lord that Oscar needed to hear. Incarnation.

There was not a sound could be heard throughout the sanctuary. Two men were gathered one night, and God was there. That day at the end of our time there was an enormous basket along with several boxes delivered to the platform. The boxes and baskets were filled to the brim with Fillet-Fish sandwiches. The congregation was instructed that each person takes at least one sandwich and deliver it to the poor or homeless in under an hour. There were just over three thousand sandwiches. It took about a half hour to disperse them throughout the congregation. Some took one; others took several. I looked at Abe as the sandwiches headed out the door and we just grinned at the level of excitement exhibited by the people. Cholly was simply stamping his feet with joy as he laughed from somewhere deep inside.

I was not sure how many of the people would follow through, but that night Abe stopped by the house. Grandma Abba answered the door, and I could hear Abe's excited voice asking, "Is the miracle worker at home or is he out walking on water," as he laughed his way through the front door. Hayleigh and I were relaxing in front of the fireplace. "Who are you, Edward? I know your name is Edward Mayus but how did you know?"

That day, people flocked to Abe's surrounding fast food stores and purchased over two thousand more Fish-Fillets than a normal sales day.

Eden to Rome

Rome is the city of echoes,

the city of illusions,

and the city of yearning.

-Giotto di Bondone

My time as a pilgrim leader in the lives of the people at Hillside had started in the Winter, the dormant season. I had spiritually existed in this slumbering time most of my life. Winter gave way to Spring, the season where all things are made new. This was the season of my rebirth, which felt more like a rediscovering. Was I uncovering Edward or was I becoming Jesus? The hot, humid Summer months brought countless stories into the lives of many whose eyes were opened to see the thin line between the ordinary and sacred, where reality comes into focus, and the way made clear that leads to life. This narrow path leads to the Tree of Life. There were still some not courageous enough to see their true self; they settled for the wide path that led to the Tree of the Knowledge of Good and Evil. There is no reality along this road, only illusions. The Fall signaled my time of shepherding was coming to an end as the chilly night winds breezed through the trees. The harvest moon reflected brightly on the fruit in many lives. The illuminated stories were too many pages to recall. But I knew deep inside, the last chapters of my time at Hillside were coming to an end.

The respite for my father had done him wonders. We started to reconnect. Monday morning breakfast at Abe's fast food establishment began to become a regular staple of our lives. Our conversations centered around the operations of the church and my Dad would offer his opinions periodically. As time, marched on our conversations turned to the lives of the people that made-up Hillside Community Church. The Reverend Edward Mayus had little to offer on this subject and admired the way I interacted with the people. Dad did more listening as our relationship changed. My Father reconnected with the Larkins family, and he asked for forgiveness from Jenny for the way he allowed the church to handle her heart. Many mornings, when we were at the restaurant, Jenny would bring young Joshua around.

Young Josh screamed, "There's Uncle Wookey."

"Uncle Wookey?" I asked in surprise.

"One day I joined Abe and his family to ride some horses. Well, it's been many a year since this old guy had ridden. When I mounted the horse, it started a little quick gallop, and I was screaming Woo! Woo! So, Josh nicknamed me Uncle Wookey. I kind of like it; it suits the new me," he explained.

He was slowly regaining his strength at the same time discovering himself as a man, as a human being. My Dad was shedding his professional leader mask. He called this time, his overdue Sabbath. He shared that this period of observance had caused him to rethink his life. He and Martha had taken a recent vacation together as a couple to St Lucia. My father was surprised at how much he enjoyed this time. His past personal holidays were merely treks across the world attending or speaking at conferences or some mission trip. They may have squeezed in some sightseeing opportunities in between doing the Church's work, but it was never a real vacation as man and wife. It was always two human beings in relationship with an organization.

Martha came back and told Hayleigh that though she loved my father with all her heart, this was the first time she started to know him. She knew about him, what he did, what he said, where he was going, but she never knew him as a man. Martha was falling in love again as if it was the first time. She remarked that one night, overlooking Rodney Bay toward Gros Islet, my father broke down and cried uncontrollably, asking for forgiveness.

Martha as she remembered, he confessed, "My loving helpmate Martha, I am so sorry, will you forgive me." She started to interrupt him when he continued, "No, Dear, you have to hear me out. You have been by my side through thick and thin, you have made my life comfortable, allowing me to do my work. But I never once reached to you, a beautiful person who deserves so much. I never touched you." She told Hayleigh how he sobbed in shame for his weakness and Martha could not stand seeing him hurt, but he needed to confess. She recounted this last portion, "I am not talking about physically, I'm speaking emotionally, and spiritually. I have discovered you this time in paradise, and my joy has sobered me. I see you now Martha; you are beautiful." Martha was rescued that night by my Dad. When he returned home, he visited the Mary Tree out back with Martha. He said his last goodbye to his first wife and my mom, turning the page to a new life ahead. He was valiant, and I was proud.

Last week Dad and I had breakfast. I asked him, "Dad, you know my time is coming to an end at Hillside. What are your plans?"

"I guess I can't get you to stay on any longer?" he inquired. "I'm proud of the work you have done.

"Dad, I know in my heart that my time is up. The people are seeing. Their hearts are coming alive in their new-found freedom. Love is now spreading like yeast in the dough. If I were to stay any longer, they would learn to only rely on me. They are made for the human journey; it is where the glory will be revealed. If I am to model leadership, I must let them go like an eagle which drops her hatched young in mid-air."

"That's just it Edward, who is going to be this leader? You have not started one single new program. Our people are giving of themselves naturally. They are living life together as if they are one body. There is no oversight, it just happens, and you equipped them for this. I have not seen anyone display your leadership. I was praying the other day for God to reveal your secret to me. I am fearful of coming back to take over."

"Dad, I did not equip them; I just gave them eyes to see what was already inside them. Every person desires to love and wants to love someone. No one teaches a caterpillar to become a butterfly. It's already there. The people are just beginning to live in this relational freedom of God. The burden is not heavy; it is as light as breathing."

"Where did you learn this, son? I have attended so many conferences on leadership and what I have seen you accomplish in a short time is miraculous. These conferences on growth are about servant leadership, but in the end, the leader is still pulling strings. The only servant-hood is that we work long hours for the sake of the church under the hyper-critical eye of performance. Yes, we serve by sacrificing; the problem is that our offerings are our family and loved ones. Those are the people placed on the altar. Edward, I've spent my life walking the thin line of leading out front and servant leadership, which is leading from behind. They are both the same Edward; just the other side of the same coin. Either way, I'm the one pulling from out front or pushing from behind. Then the leader decides that the only way he can control the people is by creating a heavy yoke around them to keep them on one path."

"Dad, there are many paths; as many trails as there are stars. I'm not leading out front or from behind. Within, is where I lead. I have placed myself in the lives of humans. That is a servant leader. It's always been that way; people are blinded to this truth." The words flowed from my mouth like breath from eternity, and the authority in which it was said did not escape my father.

"Edward, who are you? Something has happened. Tell me, son," he pleaded.

This was the relationship I've always yearned for with my father. Authentic openness between two human beings that love one another was my life's longing. I just smiled and said, "I am," hesitating a little, "Becoming a new creation."

I could tell my father was not buying my response and that he knew there was something more. Shaking his head, he said, "You're not telling me everything. I have a lot of decisions to make in the next few months. What you have created, cannot exist without you. This is a new wine. It can't be poured into an old wineskin."

***

Weeks later. Only forty days left till I move on from Hillside. I had just finished my last elder's meeting, and it was late at night. The others had left. I ventured into the dark sanctuary to be alone with my thoughts and to pray. I stood beneath the dimly backlit shadow of the cross. My concerns drifted to Hayleigh who had been bravely fighting through the cancer treatments for the last several months. She still held faith that I would eventually heal her. I wish I could have the same sense of hope that she had. While I desired her healing; I had a greater trust in her purpose being revealed. Purpose is what brings about wholeness. Purpose is what connects the dots between love and suffering. It brings life into context. Purpose is the arc of our story. I had not yet reached the end of my arc.

"Hayleigh told me I'd find you here," came a loud recognizable voice interrupting my meditation.

"Giles, what are you doing here?" I asked as he walked and gave me a big hug and a repeated slap on the back.

"Julie and I are leaving for a romantic getaway tomorrow; I have you to thank for that. Your words have given me a consciousness that I have never experienced before. I see things in a different light," Giles complimented me.

"Thanks, Giles, I am blessed to call you friend. Surely you did not come all the way over here this late to chit-chat. Is it about Hayleigh?" I cautiously inquired fearing that he may have some news about Hayleigh's lab results from her test last week.

Giles shot back an expression grinning, "Edward, are you implying that we don't meet late at night?" he questioned. I smiled back a nod. Continuing, he said, "It concerns Hayleigh's results." My chest tightened, and I rested back on the Eucharist table under the lit cross bracing for the news. "It's good Edward; I thought that you might want to be the one to tell her."

"How good? Is she healed?" I asked. Hayleigh's cancer was the single issue that conflicted me about my journey. If I was becoming Jesus how can I endure watching her suffer? The pain would be too great. She is putting all her trust in me. This would be too much to bear.

Giles answered in his doctor-speak, "I clinically cannot say that she is healed, but she is in remission." My soul joyfully leaped inside of me as tears rolled down my eyes as if a heavy stone had rolled off my shoulders. "Remember Edward, the tumors can start to grow again, she is only in remission, but I am hopeful; ah what the hell am I saying, I'm speaking to . . . You."

I peacefully replied, "Today she is free, she is living."

"There is another subject. Did you hear that Ayazz is resigning as Director of Research? He wants you to consider the spot as Interim Director," Giles stated. "He is apprehensive about approaching you based on the last encounter. We skyped the other day; he is a frail, broken man."

I had been avoiding this matter since that day. The haunting memory of me pounding his car in anger and the word that I heard from Stephen to forgive, was pressing from inside my heart to be set free. I knew what I had to do. I had known it for a long time. Every time I spotted Ayazz's prayer beads that I placed in the broken bottle, it reminded me. Something deep inside of me as a man, as Jesus, spoke to my heart that the next path of my journey would only be revealed after this act of love was completed. I need to love my friend Ayazz and help him heal his broken heart and set him free. But more importantly, I needed to forgive his son, the murderer of my brother. This was my journey as it unfolded, this was my reality. I could hide no longer.

"Where is he?" I asked.

"He is still in Rome; he has never been back since the encounter in front of your house. He visits his son in prison every day. The trial starts in a few weeks. His son is facing life incarcerated. Ayazz and his wife are devastated."

"Can you get a message to him that I am coming. I'll leave this week," I requested to Giles.

"Sure, I will let him know. One more thing Edward; before I go, I have something to give you," Giles said as he dropped a small glass vial with a lavender cap into the large chalice on the communion table.

"What is this?" I questioned.

Giles answered, "Remember when I told you I kept a sample of your stem cell DNA so that later we could study to see if your DNA had changed. Were you transforming into Jesus? The scientist in me needed to have this knowledge. I needed to understand the reason. I remember that night when we implanted the DNA of Jesus into your body. I had every intention of crushing this crazy idea of yours when I held that paperweight in my hand. You never flinched when my hand descended. My slight three inch move to the right missing the crushing of the blood sample was the first act of faith in my entire life. I can't explain it; I don't have a reason. I don't need one Edward. I believe in you."

"Your trust in me makes your belief in me the same as the belief in yourself," dropped from my tongue as naturally as breathing. "Go rescue that beautiful bride before she worries that another late-night escapade is happening." We smiled, hugged and Giles raced out the door.

I picked up the DNA blood sample from the cup remembering my thoughts months before concerning the death of Stephen. I wrestled with God and myself. One more coffee for Stephen to drink; one more traffic light to alter time enough so that my brother could spend another night in this life. But then I would not be standing here in the story I am living. Purpose is how God controls the randomness of life. Without it, you're just silver ball in the arcade game of life.

A voice I recognized startled me from behind the cross, "How long were you going to keep the secret, Edward?" Out from the darkness, Caine Banks slithered toward me. "Your secrets safe with me Edward. We can both do good work and build the Kingdom. Think of the things we could do," Caine pleaded his case to me as his eyes glistened with a vulnerable craving that was hard to discern.

I just gazed at him as he slowly approached like a lion stalking his prey, staring at the vessel of blood in my hand. "Are you tempting me, Cain?" I wondered out loud. "What is this truly about?"

Cain lunged and grabbed my hand holding tightly with both his hands; his cold fingers were trying to pry my iron clad grip away from the vessel. "Edward, please share it with me, I need this, I need to be sure!" he begged.

I twisted my arm away from his weak grasp. "Need to be sure about what?" I asked.

Caine dropped to his knees pleading to me, "I need to know for certain, that my life, my miserable, horrible existence is for some reason. Now I know why you are different, why people follow you. Why they love you. I want to be loved; I want to love someone."

"Caine, you are loved, God loves you . . . all the years in the church, and you don't know this?" I questioned.

Caine sobbed then screamed, "All the years in the church got me this!" Banks rolled back the sleeves of his suit revealing tiny round scars, too many to count. I stood there in shock at the distorted skin scarred beyond imagination. "Every time I disappointed God my father burned me with a cigarette at night; sometimes two or three times. I wanted to please God and my father. But I never could," continuing to weep. "I hated him, my Dad, but I wanted to love him so bad." Caine cried softly. "When he died," pausing to breathe, "I remember standing in front of his coffin. I finally got to love him, and I did. And it didn't hurt."

Peering into the soul of Caine Banks was the hardest thing I've ever done. This was hell. Caine could only love the dead, and his love for the dead returned a quiet, silent peace where hurt, did not exist.

Caine continued his confession, "That is why I control everything, I don't want people to disappoint God, I don't want them to hurt. My beliefs, my doctrine is all I have. It's all they have. Please, Edward, share the beautiful precious secret with me. I'm begging."

"Caine, you already have it, you only need to open your eyes and see. I will walk with you on your journey, you will find it."

"No! You are lying!" he screamed as he lunged toward me picking up the brass cross off the table and moving toward me with it raised.

"Stop!" I commanded. Banks froze. "Caine, your salvation is not here," opening my hand with the vial. "It is here," pointing to my chest; I gripped the glass tube tightly until a pop is heard and the blood liquid dripped down my fingers to the floor.

The countenance on his face immediately changed to anger as his eyes pierced the squinted glare. Now was not the time, for Caine's redemption, not even for Jesus. I turned my back and walked away toward the door.

Leaving, I heard him say, "You are a fake, and a phony. I'm going to let everyone know about your secret that you will not share. You are like the kid that stole the answers to the exam. It's not fair! I'm going to call a meeting and reveal everything."

I was saddened as I left. Opening the door, I looked back and said, "You are loved, Caine." After a pause, I said, "Caine, there is no cosmic pop-quiz at the end of life."

"Who are you, Edward? You can't even heal your own wife," Caine asked with menace.

***

A few days later I was boarding a plane for Italy when I felt the vibration of my phone as I flashed the boarding pass under the scanner. It was Hayleigh. Walking down the jet bridge, I answered, "Hayleigh, what's up?

"Timothy Sludge just called and seemed worried," she said. "Caine Banks has called an emergency meeting in three days, and you are to be there."

"Tell, him I will be in Rome for a few days, and I will be back this weekend for my last talk on Sunday," I replied.

"Edward, this meeting sounds important; your father has been calling all morning since you left," she questioned.

"Hayleigh, my time is ending," I blurted before the jet door is closed.

***

The night had darkened Rome when I arrived at the Columbus Hotel outside the Vatican and near the Regina Coeli, the prison where Abisali Imwas, the murderer, and son of my friend Ayazz. I was meeting Ayazz in the morning, and we would go over to the prison together. The proprietor of the hotel remembered the name.

"Are you related to Stephen Mayus, he always stayed here when he came to visit; he was a fine young man. It's a shame his life was cut short. He was going back home to stay; he told me," the old man recalled.

I said nothing. It was quite sobering to be there that night. The old man, Giuseppe, took me upstairs to my room.

"This is the room your brother stayed that night. I remember because it was a quick visit. He loved it because he could open the window and hear the jazz coming from the alley. It's the best view of St Peters. I remember the morning he left; the last time I saw him. I made him wait a few minutes because my wife had some cookies she made for his trip home. She cried that night because if she had not delayed him, he would still be alive," he reminisced. "Five minutes, five stinking minutes . . . Ohhhhhh!"

"Life is precious my friend. It is like a pearl buried in the field. The joy is in the purpose of finding it; the reason it is buried in the field is the mystery we cannot know. You will spend a lifetime searching for reason, but purpose is the gift of grace along the journey. It's a mystery from the one who hid the pearl. Goodnight my friend," I blessed him as we hugged.

I was also anxiously looking forward to meeting Father Paulo Martelli. I had decided to reach out to him since I would be in Rome.

The call was strange; when I called him, he was in Switzerland vacationing and indicated remorse that he could not meet me. I then started to tell him about the events that had taken place because of Stephen's gift which Paulo had sent through the Vatican post office. His attitude immediately shifted after the recounting of the many changes and events that had taken place. He indicated that he would take a train and can meet me on my last day in Rome. I was incredibly grateful.

***

I could walk to the prison Regina Coeli where I stood outside the gate waiting. Soon after, a cab pulled up. Out stepped a little old man wearing sunglasses; he was frail and weak. I walked over to hold the door and was shocked when I discovered that it was my friend Ayazz. I held his hand helping him out of the small cab. He grabbed my hand and said he was so happy that I was here. He motioned to follow him as he shuffled toward the main gate. Once inside we registered and made our way to the cafeteria to wait for the prison officer to escort us to Abisali.

"I live on this stuff," Ayazz said as he handed me my small cup of espresso. "It is good to see you my friend; I never thought this day would come. I spent many nights in agony thinking about the suffering you must feel. My wife and I, we are so sorry."

"Ayazz, friend, I forgive you and Abisali; I need to ask forgiveness for my anger toward you on that day you came over to my house. It took a lot of courage; I was not ready to respond. A lot has happened since Ayazz; one day we may have time to talk." I pulled out of my pocket the prayer beads he dropped that day in front of the house. "I kept these since that day hoping to bring them to you one day."

Ayazz reached out with his old trembling hand and smiled a heartfelt-thanks. "How are you and your wife Beenish holding up?" I asked.

"We both cry and suffer through this with no end in sight; I cannot see any reason for this to happen. Can you see any reason for this to happen to two good families?" he pleaded.

"Will the reason make any difference Ayazz?" I countered. "The suffering will still be piercing your heart; reason will not ease your pain."

Peering through his sunglasses, "Edward, do you know the origin of my name?"

"No."

"It is the Muslim name for the town my family came from, Emmaus. There is a story in your tradition. Doesn't it say something about your Lord's disciples walking with him and not recognizing him until he was gone? Your believers did not see the very God they worship. Do I have the story right Edward?"

"It is what you say," I replied.

"I don't see Allah; I can't see God in this Edward?" he started to cry. "How do I see God in this situation?"

I reached across the table and removed the sunglasses, "You open your eyes Ayazz. You are forgiven, you have always been forgiven. You are loved. Sometimes our religions hide this gift of grace. Man, was created to see God; not just beliefs. God is among us Ayazz; he has always been here," as I touched his chest.

"This way Mr. Imwas," the guard interrupted. We followed him through the dark, musty halls of prison cells housing men in small caged rooms that once housed men and women of God. Regina Coeli was once a monastery and convent.

We are ushered into a visiting room with a window. Abisali was gazing out the window holding tightly onto the bars.

"What are looking at son?" asked Ayazz.

"Freedom." He replied, vacant and without hope. "Who are you?" he turned toward me and asked.

"I am," with hesitation, "Edward."

"Edward is the brother of Stephen," Ayazz added. "He has something to say to you."

Abisali turned away looking back out at freedom. "There was no reason for him to die. I did not intend for him to die. It was not Allah's will. He was not the one. He interfered with God's will. It should have been the priest. I did not even know it was Stephen until my father told me."

"If it were God's will, then you would not be here, and Stephen would be living," I quietly then continued, "But you are still forgiven, I forgive you."

He then turned and looked at me.

"I forgive you Abisali," I said emphatically looking directly into his eyes till he had to turn away.

"His eyes were like yours. His head was just lying on the stones across from me, and he mouthed the same words. No sound. Now I hear it every day. I hear him from the dead. I beg Allah to make me deaf."

"He is not dead Abisali, Stephen is still living. Nothing can stop the love of God," I quietly spoke. "He gave his life to save his friends life; there is no greater love that a man lay down his life for his brother. Today Stephen is free, and you sit behind the bars of your soul yearning for the freedom you thought you would find in hate."

Abisali continued, "Allah has forsaken me. My name means 'Fighting Warrior.' Your brother slew me with those words of forgiveness. Now I sit in a cell; doubt pours over my soul. God has caused me to kill my own family. Look at him. I've reduced him to a frail, weak, unhappy old man. For what?"

"God did not do this Abisali, the leaders of your religion did this. You followed them, not God," I responded to Abisali's lost soul. "The leaders of religions never pay the price. They are always honored and given their place, but the families and followers always pay the price."

"Time to go Mr. Imwas," the guard interrupted.

Abisali, looked at me as he was walked away and said, "I ended the life of your brother with a sword, he killed my beliefs with a word." Ayazz and I left. Walking outside the prison, Ayazz stopped, and we spoke once more.

"Edward, where does your wisdom come from?" Ayazz asked. "All our problems in the world come from our leaders. You are right." When I was growing up in Syria, I never hated Christians. We are taught hate by our leaders. Someone taught my son to hate, and now he hates himself."

"Ayazz, you speak the truth, a man cannot hate unless he hates himself. Likewise, one can only love another if they love themselves."

It was the last time I saw Ayazz. A month later Abisali hung himself in his prison cell. The note he left, was a goodbye to his family. He knew he was forgiven, and he loved them so much that he could only show it by laying down his life, thus ending their suffering death.

***

The ten-minute pre-dawn walk to the Vatican the next day was full of reflection. I was to leave that morning on a flight home. I was anxious to meet Father Paulo to discuss the situation. He seemed intently interested when I told him the story.

I arrived at the main entrance and was greeted by a young man whom Paulo Martelli had sent. He ushered me through the empty square where the Pope gives his Wednesday and Sunday blessings. After a long walk, near a portico, I could see a tall figure that I was positive had to be Father Paulo.

"Edward, it is a blessing to meet you finally, I feel that I know you through your brother Stephen. I hope you have not eaten yet. I have breakfast prepared for us."

We both are ushered to a small elegantly decorated room with gold-leaf chairs and a marble table. It was a little too much for my taste. I was wondering if I was being treated this way because of my recounting of the events since the arrival of Stephen's gift. However, Father Paulo seemed reserved, polite, and guarded which gave me a sense of uneasiness. It felt as if he was holding something back. As we were finishing the light breakfast, I opened the discussion with a question.

"Father Paulo," I started.

"Please, call me Paulo; it took your brother over ten years to start calling me Paulo. I'm afraid we don't have ten years to accomplish this task," he laughed.

"Fa . . . Paulo, now that this miracle is going public, what are your thoughts?" I asked. I mused to myself that this is the first time I am beginning to think that I just may be changing into Jesus.

Paulo looking down at his watch discovered it was time for us to move on, "Edward, indeed this is quite a miracle. I have arranged for you to meet someone with whom I think you should speak."

We immediately left and walked what seemed like a mile through long ornate corridors through histories of man's search for God. My mind could not help but wonder if I was going to meet the Pope. Then a door opened to my left where we are greeted by another long candle-lit hallway. At the end, a door opened into an empty ornate room. Paulo welcomed me into the Pope's Room of Mysteries. There were only two window seats where I could see that the sun had risen as the rays illuminated the fresco paintings that ordained the walls of this room. I sat on the seat as my eyes journeyed the path of God's mysteries from the Incarnation to the Resurrection. There was something about this chamber that felt natural. To be amongst all these mysteries was spiritually invigorating. My mind continued through these artistic representations of a soulful timelessness that brought assurance of the relationship I had known. Then the sound of the large door opening startled me from my contemplative interlude.

Paulo entered and said, "Edward, I'd like you to meet someone."

I rose and was ready to greet the Vicar of Christ.

"John, meet Edward. Edward, I am glad to introduce Father John D'Amellio, the lead scientist of the Vatican and a good friend of Stephen," Paulo proclaimed as he sat on a chair that was brought into the room. I shook Father John's hand, and he seemed greatly appreciative to meet as he took the other window seat. I was disappointed and confused.

"I am excited to hear more about this miracle you have experienced," he said. "First, I need to tell you something. I first met your brother about two years ago, in Afghanistan on a medical mission trip. He was an excellent physician with a heart bigger than life. It was there that he met Caterina and they fell in love. I have never seen anyone love greater than your brother. At the same time, I have never seen anyone suffer greater than your brother. When the diagnosis came back for Caterina, everyone was shattered at her terminal diagnosis. Caterina returned to Italy to live out the remainder of her life, and Stephen followed. One night, your brother and I were drinking a bottle of wine consoling each other about Caterina's condition and the suffering your brother would endure losing his lover. That night we talked about miracles. I mentioned my work on the Miracle of Lanciano and your brother's eyes brightened. He looked at this as a possible hope for one last miracle. He called her for her blood-type, and she told him that it was a match. Edward, your brother, had come alive with hope. He wanted me to extract a sample from the specimens that are housed at the Vatican. I told him I would think about it. He spent the next several months talking with me and trying to convince me to do this. I eventually and reluctantly agreed. He was beyond joy. I grew to love Stephen as a brother. His analysis of my study of Lanciano was insightful for spending such a short time with the data. He sometimes worked twenty hours a day looking for the clues that would save his Caterina.

"I read his journals; I am familiar with this story. Shouldn't we be talking about this miracle that has taken place? I took the DNA stem cells. I am the match. The miracle is happening to me," I exclaimed.

Paulo interjected, "There is more to the story Edward."

John continued, "Edward, the night I stayed working late so that I could extract some of the specimens, a weight came upon me, and I was conflicted. I held in my hand the very blood DNA of the Son of God. To hand this over to Stephen would be a violation of my allegiance to the Holy Catholic Church and the Holy See himself, the Vicar of Christ. I did not know what to do; so, in my weakness, I extracted a blood sample and placed it in the tube."

"I can only imagine the courage it took, John," I sympathized.

"It was my blood Edward," he said. John then paused to gather himself, "I'm so sorry, I was conflicted. I could not bear to extinguish Stephen's hope. When Stephen found out that Caterina's blood type was not a match, I thought the matter was closed. You can only imagine how shocked I was when Father Paulo Martelli knocked on my door yesterday and told me the story. He told me I needed to meet with you today. Please accept my apology."

I just stared at Father John, balancing between disbelief and anger. Turning to Father Paulo, for understanding and reason I asked, "Is this true? There is no miracle?" He gazed motionless into my eyes. A few more long moments passed, and my thoughts drifted back home. What do I say to Hayleigh? Her faith is buoyed by me being Jesus. This is going to crush her spirit. I don't know what to make of my journey. Am I back where I started? God has forsaken me. Again.

I stood up and looked around The Room of Mysteries. "If there is no miracle, then who am I?"

"You are Edward Mayus, beloved son of God, in whom He is well pleased. Open your eyes; the miracle will be revealed," Paulo stated confidently. "It's time to go. You have a plane to catch."

It was a silent walk through the halls and into the vast Vatican Plaza. My mind is twisted in thoughts that left my reality vacant. Paulo was gracious enough to arrange a car to take me to the airport. As we pass the Vatican gate, I notice the sign, *Largo deli Alicorni*. A chill came upon me.

I turned to shake Paulo's hand, and he embraced me as I whispered, "Is this where...?" He only nodded yes. I continued as the overhead sign clicked out the last five seconds signaling that it would be safe to cross. **BEEP BEEP!** The alerting sound blasted.

Paulo interrupted my crossing, causing me to stop "Edward, your journey continues my friend."

I smiled and thanked him again as a loud horn sounded as small delivery truck ran through the light. I felt the wind brush across my face from the speeding vehicle. I looked back, and Father Paulo smiled and gave me the sign of the cross.

Final Dream

Trust in dreams, for in them is hidden the gate to eternity.

-Khalil Gibran

The car ride through the streets of Rome was a foggy blur. I can hardly remember moving through security. I am looking forward to decompressing on the flight home before I enter the lion's den awaiting me. I needed to hear from God to wash this forsaken feeling that had washed over me. This was the feeling I had lived with my entire life until this journey started. I could not bear going back to that life. The flight was only half full, and I had the whole row of seats to stretch out. I opened my iPad and placed my headphones on, looking forward to relaxing music. Then came the ding signaling a text. It was from Hayleigh. Instantly I remembered that Caine held his meeting last night to expose me as the fraud. I chuckled at the irony of the meeting after the revelation at the Vatican.

The text read this way.

The meeting was miraculous. I wish you could have been there. The people all supported you, Edward. So, did your father. There is a meeting next week to dismiss Caine Banks and decide the future of Hillside. Below is the video of the last few minutes of the meeting. I was shocked.

As I watched the video, I am reduced to tears of joy. Caine laid out his case against me in his typical accusatory manner. My father sat in the front row not knowing what was transpiring. Caine told of his suspicion from the beginning. He recounted in detail Giles and my conversation that night he hid behind the cross. There was much murmuring in the crowd.

Finally, Caine asked the people who remained silent and confused, "Hillside has always stood on the side of truth, and that must always be our foundation. I don't know what scientific transformation took place in Edward Mayus; I'm not a scientist. What I do know is that Edward lied to us all along. Christ would not have hidden this truth. Denied you and you," as he pointed to the crowd, "And you, the truth on how he changed. He kept it from you and held onto this secret for himself. How can we trust a man who is misrepresenting himself? I am proposing that we go back to where we were as a church before this false prophet took over."

Then you could hear a loud opening of a door in the back. Walking down the aisle was Abe Larkins and to my surprise, Johanna and Emilee. My sister took the microphone and asked if she could address the people. Caine obliged as if he had a choice. Johanna walked back and forth gathering her thoughts as she addressed the crowd.

"Some of you know me; for those that do not, I'm Edwards sister, Johanna. I must confess, when Edward told us last year at Thanksgiving that he would be the interim pastor for Hillside, my soul was crushed. It was devastating news. I left that night in tears. Why? Most of you old-timers know, I'm the black sheep of the family, the abomination, the invisible non-existent member of the Mayus family. You will not see me in the family portrait on the Church's website. I don't exist in the world of the church. My only connection to a family was with my two brothers who loved me unconditionally. We lost Stephen; a week later I was losing my last brother to the church where I did not exist; never seen as a person. It was one final betrayal I could not take. But Edward, whoever he has become, changed things. I can see it, I experienced it, and so did you. I enjoyed coming back, and you treated me well, you saw me, I was no longer invisible. Edward and I talked one night. I thanked him for all he had done; for bringing me back home again after so many years. He informed me that my journey was not complete. This troubled me. Then one day Edward said that I am selling my heart out to a movement, to political leaders both secular and religious, who want me to be seen, as gay. Edward said, I see you as human and only human. It is the only place where love can exist. Edward set me free that night. I became more than gay; I became more human with the unending ability to love other humans. Here you see me as human, a creation in the image of God. This love has set me free. Edward, whoever he is, helped us all get here. Love is here. Wherever there is love, there is God."

The murmur went through the crowd about stories of encounters with Edward. Caine tried to regain control of the meeting. He tapped on the mic, as if it was his gavel, interrupting the stories of the people by saying, "While I appreciate the courage it must have taken to rise and defend your brother given the sinful lifestyle you lead, And, your lack of being a witness to the faith. I have to still stand on the truth of our Lord."

Dad stood immediately chastising Caine Banks, "Well, Caine; now I'm going to stand on the truth of the Lord. That woman you have failed to see; that stood before you; that's my beautiful little girl." He started to break down and cry until he contained himself and continued, "Who has grown into a woman, a wonderful human being, whom I have failed to see over these many years. I see you now my little Johanna, my precious daughter. I was blind, and now I see. Forgive me."

"I see you too Daddy," she softly spoke.

"Honey, I was lost, but now am found. Will you have me back?" he pleaded.

She ran over to my father, and they embraced and cried together. Dad then motioned with his hand for Emilee to come over and they all three just cried. I could hear Hayleigh whimpering in the background as the video went dark.

My father officially announced his resignation that night. He told everyone that he was going to spend time with his daughter and family and learn how to be a better human being. This was now his calling. This was his work. For the first time since hearing about the blood, I was at peace. Somehow, I knew my journey would continue. I am not forsaken.

***

I awoke inside the train car. I was wondering where I was. The train was empty. No people, no more sunglasses. I could tell we were stopped. The steam was drifting up the windows from below. I made my way to the back, opening the last door where the Brakeman was sitting just like the first time I saw him. I looked to my left where I last saw Mom. She was not there; it made me a little sad.

I looked over at the Brakeman; his cigarette was nearly burned down to his lips. He said, "Well you did it."

"Did what?" I asked.

"Journeyed well," he answered as he threw away the butt.

"But it's not what I expected; it did not turn out the way I thought," I replied.

The Brakeman motioned with his hand to the Engineer that it was time to roll again. "A good journey is never what we think it's going to be. That is called reason. A well-done journey reveals purpose and requires trust."

The train started to roll.

"Where are we going now?" I asked.

"We; ain't going nowhere. Your time on this train is over unless you want to do what most people do and keep repeating the same journey over and over. Go ahead, and get your ass off my train," he said with a smile.

I leaped off the side of the last car and tumbled down a small ravine. I finally stopped rolling and stood up brushing the dust off. I looked back, and the train was gone, so were the tracks. There was not a hint of the past journey. I walked a little more and there up on a hill was a silhouette I'd recognize anywhere.

"Stephen!" I shouted. He waved to me, beaconing me to come. I ran up that hill as fast as I could. As I cleared the last elevation, I lost my breath and limped toward him unable to speak. We embraced one another and tears were rolling down my cheek, but Stephen just keeps smiling with a radiance I cannot explain.

"Dude you look horrible," he said, "You are out of shape man."

I looked up at him playfully slapping him across his face, "You haven't changed."

"You don't have much time Edward," he said.

"What do you mean, I just got here," I asked. "You don't have the time to talk with your brother?"

"I don't have time Edward; I'm free of time, that's what eternity is. The next time we talk you will be free of time."

"Stephen, I have to ask you about the gift you had sent me before you died."

"I don't know what you're talking about Edward. We don't have the past any longer. We only have the present, where we were created to live. We know each other, but only in the present. I have no desire to look back; it's gone."

"Stephen, are you in heaven?"

Stephen started to laugh answering, "Edward, heaven is not defined by space or time. Eternity is without a beginning or end. There are no words to describe it. I cannot give you an answer that you will understand, but whatever you may hope it is; it is so much more."

"I can't wait to finish my journey," I said to Stephen.

"Edward, you never complete your journey, it just gets better and better. It's never what you expect it to be. The path reveals the trust and love for God. Just when you think it could not possibly get any better, another path presents itself."

His next words went silent, but his eyes spoke an unfathomable illuminated joy that I had never seen as I heard a gentle voice, "Mr. Mayus you need to bring your seat back up to its upright position, we are making our final approach."

Hayleigh's Miracle

Miracles are a retelling in small letters of the very same story which is written across the whole world in letters too large for some of us to see.
- C.S. Lewis

There is never a better feeling than coming home. In some way, our journeys are always pointing home. The drive revealed a crisp blue Autumn sky that met the changing colors of burnt orange and golden yellow leaves that still dressed the half-naked trees. The seasons were changing. The Fall brought on the feeling that this leg of my journey was ending, but I had an anxious anticipation of the next turn of the narrow path. My dream with Stephen was bittersweet because I knew that would be the last time I see him for a while. I was still amazed that the clarity of focus and sight had not left me. Each color of each leaf seemed to leap off nature's canvas as if the paint had yet to dry. The brilliant green hillsides along the Appalachian foothills lining the country roads still danced in unison with the swaying trees that were directed by a hidden symphonic conductor. I could hear in my mind Copland's *Appalachian Spring,* beaconing me to a stream that I will drink from one day.

Approaching Eden, my heart sank at the thought of crushing the burning hope of Hayleigh's faith in me becoming Jesus was about to be extinguished. Turning onto the long driveway my soul is lifted to new heights as the arched cathedral entrance of autumn trees rained down their leaves like snowflakes in a glass globe blanketing the path before me in a 'hosanna-like carpet.' The warm feeling inside blessed me as if the heavens were shouting that peace and glory are about to be revealed. For the first time since the Vatican, I knew I was not forsaken. I was not alone.

Hayleigh and Grandma Abba had emerged to greet me on the front porch. Hayleigh had jumped into my arms before I had a chance to drop my duffel. Grandma Abba stood by observing with a smile on her face as I reached my hand toward her. She held it with both her small thin hands and kissed the tip of my finger.

"It's so good to see you, Baby," Hayleigh blurted out after our kiss had ended. "Did you get my text about the meeting?"

"Yes, I did; thank you, it made the long flight tolerable," I told her as she ushered me into the house. Walking in, I noticed a small cigarette butt crushed near the door. I thought strange since no one smoked cigarettes. The table had a nice bottle of wine already breathing with warm bread steaming under a cloth covered basket in front of the crackling fireplace. "I have a lot to talk about; with both of you. It was quite a revealing trip. The trip did not turn out as I thought."

Hayleigh injected quickly, "I bet it was an exciting trip, how did your meeting with Ayazz go?"

Hayleigh's rapid quick conversation was balanced out by Grandma Abba's silent observation as if she knew something had happened. Hayleigh continued her exuberant chattering of hopefulness which was making it more difficult inside my soul to reveal the truth she needed to hear. After pouring the wine, she finally rested back and asked, "Now Edward, who goes first? Do you want to hear about the meeting? Or do you want to tell us about Rome?"

"I think I should go, first honey, because it will affect what happened at the meeting," I replied. Grandma Abba's countenance changed to serious as she intently listened from the chair across from the love seat Hayleigh and I shared.

Hayleigh eagerly turned sideways and brought her legs up so that she could face me.

I started, "The meeting with Ayazz went well. We reconnected, and I asked him for his forgiveness for the way I treated him." Then I noticed prayer beads lying on the table. I picked them up and recognized them as belonging to Ayazz. I also noticed that a tiny cross was added. "Where did these come from?" I inquired.

Hayleigh answered, "I do not know. A small black man delivered them right before you came. No note no nothing. All I know is that it was an overnight express delivery from Rome. I thought you bought something and had it shipped."

"What did he look like?"

"He was an older wrinkled gentleman with a funny hat with stripes."

"Hmmm."

Hayleigh then started to recall the meeting when I interrupted her by placing my hand on her knee.

"Honey, there's more," I sternly calmed her excitement. "Before I left for Rome, I called Father Paulo Martelli, Stephen's friend at the Vatican. We met this morning before I boarded my flight home. I explained what had transpired up to that point. I wanted to get his guidance since the news was going to get out soon."

"It already has Edward; I got a call this morning from USA News. I did not say much but did describe how grateful I was since battling cancer. I felt it was happening for a reason. I let him know that I had faith in my healing," she said with assurance.

"Hayleigh, I'm not becoming Jesus," I said crushing her heart.

Hayleigh's eyes began to tear up, as she rocked back, placing her hand over her mouth. The grandfather clock ticked off many pendulum swings before Hayleigh asked, "I don't understand Edward, you and Giles, that night. It happened, Edward!"

"It was not the blood from Lanciano, Baby. I'm sorry, so sorry." She just sat there in silence staring at me with her beautiful eyes filled with tears as I explained the encounter with Father John D'Amellio. Grandma Abba stood up and walked away. She turned and looked at me telling me she was going to pray. Glancing back at Hayleigh, my heart was aching. I too was crying. I leaned over placing my head in her lap. Time just anxiously drifted through the pendulum swings of emotion until the silence is broken.

"Hayleigh, I am sorry I took this journey. I caused you so much pain; please forgive me," I sobbed into her breast. We stayed in that moment, she never said a word, but her touch on my temples eased my mind as she stroked my hair. That touch I had learned to love was the same as a touch from God. "Hayleigh, I should never have taken that DNA, what was I thinking?"

I sat up and grabbed her shoulders with my hands, "Can you forgive me?"

Her eyes were still wet with tears, but her look had changed from fear to peace. She smiled and cupped her hands on my face saying, "Don't be silly Edward." Then she started to giggle lightly moving to a slow, gentle, joyous laugh.

"Hayleigh, are you alright?" I inquired. I was concerned that she was losing it. I had just told her that her anchor of hope was gone and she is laughing with joy. Her eyes sparkled. "Hayleigh, what are you thinking, tell me."

"Edward, Baby, it's a miracle, it really is. It happened!" she softly stated as her hands slid down to my chest. She pointed at my heart with her finger. "It happened right here Edward, and I would not change one thing."

"Hayleigh, I don't understand."

"It was you! All this time it was you. Edward, I'm not sure how long this remission will last, or if I will ever be healed, but I would not change one thing. If I died tonight, I would be the happiest woman in the world. You have loved me as perfect as any man could this last year. You gave me what I needed. And it was you, my darling Edward. All along I thought you were Jesus, but it was you. I married and loved you; I needed your touch, your caress, your hearing of my heart. I always felt that God loved me, but now I know. He does. You became my Jesus in the flesh, and all this last year it was you, my knight in shining armor. God lived in you."

I slid back on the sofa, "I never thought of it that way. It is real, isn't it?" Wiping my face with a sigh, "He does live in us, doesn't He? We just never see Him. I have been looking for Him my whole life, and all along God was right here," holding my fist tightly to my chest.

***

Hayleigh and I just lounged on the sofa holding each other in the holiest most sacred time of our lives. It was merely now. There were no choirs, songs, nor words needed. As Stephen said, there are no words to describe God's presence, it just is. The only sounds are an intermittent crackle of a log and the light, soft, breath-like wind noise you hear from a burning flame dancing in the air above the dying wood. The moment eventually ended as the embers crumbled and the flame flickered signaling the present is passing, and a new present is being born. It is the rhythm of a journey well lived.

"What will I say to the people tomorrow?" I asked out loud to Hayleigh.

Just then Grandma Abba reappeared. "You'll tell them the good news. It's all true. God does live inside us. We are His image. Jesus showed us what incarnation looks like; what it looks like when God lives inside of a man. He was the perfect image because He was one with God.

Edward, you got a glimpse for one year what it looks like to be Jesus. You stopped resisting Him because you accepted that he was placed inside you by DNA. Now you know you always had His DNA. Every human has the image of God in them. That's how we were created. That is the message of grace, not religion."

Religion searches for reason, and never finds purpose. They think the purpose is to have better reasons. The people are blind, and their religion does not want them to see. Religion gives them reasons based on principles instead of eyes to see."

"You will tell them the story of your journey. How you discovered God is never found outside. God is not out there. God is in here," pointing to her heart. "Life's journey is a narrow path that reveals a God to trust. Few take it. Trust only occurs in relationship. Our relationship is the pearl of great price that is already buried in the field of our hearts. The journey is the life-long excavation of our heart."

Hayleigh and I were stunned at Grandma Abba's discernment.

"Do you want to tell them tomorrow Grandma Abba?" I asked with a smile.

"Who wants a piece of pie and coffee?" she asked ignoring my question heading to the kitchen.

It is indeed a thin line between the ordinary and sacred.

ACKNOWLEDGEMENTS

I am indebted to Angie Cramer, Carol Gardner, Gary Newsome, and Debra Mikell, for tirelessly reading my writings over the last eighteen months. Not only did they give me valuable insights but also the encouragement and confidence to plow through this work when doubt started to creep into my mind.

I also want to thank Wayne Jacobsen, who visited me for two days. His influence about humbleness and humility helped shape the final work. His recommendation to add *Chapter One: Stephen* proved to be difficult writing, but set the arc for the rest of the story.

I also want to thank Forrest Stiltner who designed the front cover with a keen insight for creating interest in a timeless way.

ABOUT THE AUTHOR

RJ Blizzard is an author and writer of the thin space between the sacred and the ordinary. "It's a narrow space, and few choose it. The Tree of Life grows here. Outside this thin space, people eat of the Tree of Knowledge of Good and Evil. Outside this thin space, there is no truth, and nothing is what it appears to be."

He is a master storyteller who once spoke of these fables at retreat centers and conferences. Now he writes of people and their journeys to find the thin path where they become more human. When two or three people find it together, it is incredible. RJ Blizzard once spoke, "There is nothing more sacred than a man, or a woman becoming more human. The thin line they walk is the watershed."

His novels are authentic life portrayals of human beings, existentially surviving to find transcendence and purpose.

Transcendence can be found in the grace of both love and suffering.

He enjoyed a successful business career as an ex-seminarian, in which he made millions. He is quick to recall, "And lost a little more."

"When it comes to life, I would have to say that my greatest spiritual influence has been the music of Bob Dylan. I can still remember that day when the words cut my heart, "...He that is not busy being born, ...is busy dying." First time I started to understand what being born again actually meant."

He loves life, music, theater, poetry, philosophy, good wine, Padron cigars, and every waking present conscious moment with God's beautiful creation, especially his friends.

You can Contact RJ Blizzard at

www.rjblizzard.com

Printed in Great Britain
by Amazon